Danaville's Rainbow

Danaville's Rainbow

DON BOWLIN

To order additional copies of this book, contact:
Xlibris Corporation
1-888-795-4274
www.Xlibris.com
Orders@Xlibris.com
27738

To Susan

My wife, my love, my friend

The Lord will bless you with good crops and healthy cattle and prosper everything you do when you arrive in the land the Lord, your God, is giving you. He will change you into a holy people dedicated to himself; this he will do if you will only obey him and walk in his ways. All the nations in the world shall see that you belong to the Lord, and they will stand in awe.

—Deut. 28:8-10

AUTHOR'S NOTE

DANAVILLE'S RAINBOW IS a work of fiction. The story is taken from my observation of and interface with farm people, small town officials, businessmen, various clergy, and other personalities. Historical reference to and the use of much-researched information about the Dead Sea Scrolls, with emphasis on the copper scroll number two, play an important part in the story.

Danaville is the fictional name of a town in northwest Florida. Some events occur in actual cities such as Panama City, Tallahassee, Tampa, Pensacola, and Dothan, Alabama. Other towns were given fictitious names to better serve the purpose of the story.

The Kelly farm is a composite of many farms—their function and spirit having existed for 250 years and, hopefully, will do so for 250 more. The Kellys represent the many thousands of farm families who have perpetually nourished this nation and others through good and bad times. These hardworking, dedicated, God-loving people have always been the backbone of our country. Perhaps that was why God picked the Kelly farm and family to carry out his plan, and to remind this nation and the world of his power and love.

PROLOGUE

THE KELLY FARM was well-known in Mason County, Florida, and in several adjacent counties as an example of successful farming. The Kellys had operated their highly productive three-hundred-acre produce business, three and a half miles north of Danaville, the county seat, for three generations. They worked hard like many other farmers but were close-knit, active, caring, and loving Christians who quietly expressed their faith by their everyday life.

All who knew the Kellys had a deep respect for them. "They seem to have a far-different bloodline than other people," said Marvin Gardner of Gardner's Drugstore. He smiled slightly when he said that to a customer one day as they were discussing farming in general. The Kellys and their farm seemed to always be mentioned during such a conversation. Actually, Marvin was a people watcher, politician, rumor spreader, and expert on most any subject. His character and demeanor had been magnified by his position as a pharmacist—he filled prescriptions for and talked to almost all of the community. Gardner knew a lot about his customers and would say just enough to any one of them about someone else—to enhance his standing in the community.

The farm was started in 1926 by Frank Kelly. He had saved $2,400 over a five-year period of hard, physical work. That was a good amount of money in those days. Frank had built a reputation for his skill and determination; and local farms were glad to hire him for planting, maintenance, harvesting, and many other needs. He was a smart, hard worker. He had had his eye on an old run-down three-hundred-acre farm with a large house, two barns, and other smaller buildings—all needing an immense amount of repair. At the age of twenty-three, young Kelly—six feet two inches tall, well muscled, with dark brown hair, dark blue eyes, and a ready grin—said, "When things get tough, you just try harder." Everyone liked his disposition.

Frank quietly worked a deal to buy the property from old man Cannon. Josh Cannon, who was eighty and lost his wife two years before, had been retired nine years. He couldn't tend the place anymore, and it depressed him to watch it deteriorate. His granddaughter had convinced him to move in with her family. Josh agreed to sell the antique farm acreage for $500; the house and other structures, which needed much repair, for an additional $600. That left Frank with only $1,300. It seemed impossible he could prepare at least a small portion of the fields as soon as practical to start providing income—although very little in the beginning—and fix the major items on the house at the same time. An old Ford tractor and a run-down one-ton truck were included, adding more expense.

With all the negatives staring Kelly in the face, he was determined to have his farm and make a go of it. He had prayed for guidance while working and saving his money, and he knew God was instrumental in the negotiations with Josh Cannon. Frank felt confident and happy about what his future offered. He mused that he and God would run the farm. He was going to need some human labor. Surely, he could find one or two good men that would be interested in a share arrangement from crop income.

It wasn't but a short while before Frank took on two men who had good farming experience. They lived within two miles of the farm—one north and the other south. Jimmy Lee was Frank's age, and Chuck Webber was ten years older. Young Kelly had made good choices. They seemed compatible with him and his work ethic. He had a very positive outlook for the future.

After two years, with one hundred acres producing, the farm had been shaped into a good-looking business. With two hundred acres remaining to be developed, thirty of them for pasture and a retaining pond, there was still much hard work ahead, but the fundamental steps had been made. In the meantime, Frank met a very pretty young lady at Danaville's First Methodist Church, by the name of Christine Belton. They fell in love and were married eight months later.

Not only was Chris happy as Mrs. Frank Kelly, she was also thrilled to help upgrade the house interior and work in the yard. When they could afford it, she would purchase a chair or linoleum for the kitchen floor or make curtains for the windows. She had a knack for cooking and quickly won the hearts and stomachs of the men. Chris stayed busy and happy—pleasantly surprising Frank with her homemaking talents. After a year, the farm began to reflect the work that was going into it. A quiet pride was developing as the four of them labored hard, long days in the fields and on the house and barns.

In 1929, Christine gave birth to a son, which made Frank ecstatically happy. He teased Chris, saying they had another farmhand. They named him Seth—not knowing he would eventually take over the farm operation and continue its development. Seth, in turn, would marry Alice Conners in 1956. He and his wife would have two children, John and Patricia, starting the third generation of Kellys. The farm was increased another one hundred acres during the next twenty years—pasture was improved for the dozen dairy cows. The holding pond was retrofitted with heavier pumps to supply the larger sprinkler system. The farm acreage was now at maximum use.

John was twenty-two years old in 1978 when Seth had a serious heart attack. He was confined to bed at first by Dr. McNally, with instructions to rest and adhere to the prescribed diet and medication he had given Alice to administer. She was a dedicated nurse for her husband. Pat, John's sister, one and a half years younger, was a good cook and a big help to her mother during these times. Both John and his mother had a feeling Seth wouldn't be around long, even as Dr. McNally told them he wanted to get Seth into the hospital within two or three days to run tests.

It was now up to John to keep the farm going. It was a big responsibility, and he constantly prayed about it. Tom Huggins, the fifteen-year full-time farmhand, who had given notice a month before, was moving his family back to his boyhood farm home near Crestview. His father had recently passed away and left a small dairy to him. He was going to be missed. The timing of these recent events was staggering to John. The new Kelly farm boss would rely on God's guidance, just as his father and grandfather had. He and God would run things. His first order of business was to find at least two farmhands to not only tend to the current day-to-day work but also to develop the remaining seventy acres and continue upgrading every facet of the farm. This would add to expenses, but he was confident it could be worked out.

John was much like his father, Seth, and his grandfather, Frank. In fact, stand them side-by-side at age twenty-two, and they would look almost like triplets. The genes were strong. John was six feet tall, weighed 195 pounds, had a farmer's tanned face, brown hair, and a solid, strong body. He could look directly into a person's eyes while talking or listening, and react with a genuine smile or laugh, if so moved, or be serious and concerned.

The attractive farmhouse was large and comfortable. The surrounding yard and other grounds were meticulously maintained. No one would ever know how much work had been done to it since Grandpa Frank started in 1926—all family members, and even the hired help, had contributed through the years. With the large shading oak trees standing guard on the smooth lawn surrounding the home, anyone passing by would readily agree it was indeed a beautiful sight. Even the various crops reflected careful planning and care. Some people were outright envious.

Alice was a loving, energetic mother to John and Patricia, and a doting wife to their ill father. Not only did she watch over Seth, but she was instrumental in running the house. She was not only an excellent cook, as Patricia was learning to be, but also made sure everything was kept clean and orderly. She was only forty-five and would prove to be a pillar of strength in the years to come. Later, when John married and had a son, Alice would be called Granny, at first by her grandson, then by all the family. She would proudly accept her new name and respond to it with love. Seth, who would have been called Grandpa, would not live long enough to hear it from his grandson.

The past year's crop production and sales had been good. John now had a little breathing room and started immediately looking for a couple of good farmhands. He wanted to start developing the last seventy acres as soon as possible and have them producing the next year. He prayed about that and many other things.

In the year 2000, when John's son Lyle reached age eighteen, the Kellys would experience and deal with events that would lead to a miraculous discovery affecting people worldwide.

CHAPTER ONE

JOHN KELLY WAS sitting in his small office, adjacent to his bedroom. It was the beginning of another beautiful summer morning. Granny would have breakfast ready in twenty or thirty minutes, so he had to hurry. He was listing the names and telephone numbers of a few farmers in the county that he knew well and could count on. Perhaps one of them would know of one or two good farmhands who were available. He felt a tinge of desperation, but he knew it was fruitless to worry about not finding help. The Lord would provide.

"Breakfast, John," Pat, his younger sister, had called out from the head of the stairs. He pushed his roller chair back and stood up. He thought about his workday and all the things that had to be done. As he descended the stairs, he made a mental note to make some of his calls right after feeding the livestock and turning the cows out to pasture. Pat would feed the chickens and gather the eggs.

Granny was pouring coffee when John walked into the kitchen. "Your dad had a bad night," she said. "I think I should call Dr. McNally. I'm sure he'll arrange to see him right away."

"Mama, I'll call him to come out. He doesn't want us moving Papa around too much," John replied. "Doc told us several months ago not to allow him to do anything strenuous."

Alice was a strong, practical woman. She deeply loved her family and the farm. Her faith and positive outlook set an example for everyone. However, there was a slight sign of concern on her face.

Doc had told John, after his dad's last examination three weeks ago, that he probably wouldn't last a year. John and the others would take it one day at a time and make life as comfortable as possible for beloved Papa.

John finished his breakfast sooner than usual and headed for the barn. After tending the livestock, he returned to the house and made several calls as planned. Most of his farmer friends were already busy with their daily regimens, but he did talk to Bob Proctor and Clarence Tillman. Both men told John they would talk to others and see if they could come up with a name or two. Proctor said he might know of a young black fellow who had some hands-on farming experience. He asked John if it would be okay to contact him. John was put out with Bob Proctor. He had known him for a number of years and respected him, but he didn't like the slight inference that Proctor put into his question. "Any man that is honorable and believes in working for a fair wage can work for me. If this gentleman is interested, have him call me."

The next evening, after dinner, Proctor called. "John, the man I mentioned to you yesterday is available and will talk to you. His name is Carew Hinson. He wanted me to call you because he's never worked for anyone but his dad, and he's a little nervous."

"Bob, you tell Carew to come see me late Saturday afternoon. Tell him I look forward to meeting him. Let me know if that's a good time for him to come."

Perhaps, John thought, this Hinson fellow would turn out to be the kind of person and worker that would fit his requirements and, just as important, blend in with the family.

LATE SATURDAY AFTERNOON, John was hosing down the cow-barn floor when Pat walked in and told him Carew Hinson had arrived and was standing on the back porch talking to Alice. "Tell him I'll be right there," he said as he turned off the water and coiled the hose near the faucet. He wiped his hands on an old rag and headed for the house.

"WELL, CAREW, IT'S good to meet you," John said as he held out his hand. Carew had a firm grip, with large biceps showing under his short-sleeved shirt. He smiled and said softly, "I'm happy to meet you too, Mr. Kelly. Mr. Proctor said some nice things 'bout you, and I wanted to meet the man who runs this farm. It's a sight to behold." John saw right away that Carew wasn't bashful, but was quiet-spoken and had a gentle manner. "I'm only two years older than you—not old enough to be a 'mister.' I'm John to everyone," he said, smiling.

They liked each other immediately.

"We'll have something to eat after a while. In the meantime, I'll show you around."

Later, as they all were sitting at the dining table enjoying the conversation along with roast beef and all the other good things, Carew was still thinking about what he had seen on the "short" tour of the farm. He was deeply impressed with the property and the Kellys. If John offered him a job, he would accept it without hesitation.

John looked across the table at Carew and knew, regardless of not having seen him work or heard him talk about farming, that God had brought them together. He felt very good—and relieved. After dinner, John took Carew out to the fields and showed him the areas where various crops were soon to be planted. The majority of the fields were already showing growth of corn, green beans, tomatoes, and other plants. The two contract workers for planting had been doing a good job but John was strapped for time in having to oversee them and simultaneously take care of the milking, feeding stock, conducting maintenance on the equipment, and a dozen other things. He would breathe a little easier if Carew accepted the offer that was about to be made to him.

"Yes, John, I accept your offer," Carew said ten minutes after hearing John's proposal. "It would be an honor to work here for you and be a part of this farm." It was a pleasant moment for both of them, neither one knowing they would have a good working relationship for many years. In fact, Carew would be accepted as one of the family almost immediately.

John knew that Carew was looking for a place to stay since his folks had sold their old place. "Carew, would you accept my invitation to live here on the farm? I would like for us to build a nice apartment for you on the upper level of the main barn. We'd insulate it, put a carpet on the floor, and add a small kitchen—though you'll eat all your meals with us—add a bath and put in air-conditioning and heat. I've got an extra TV, in good shape; that's yours. What do you say?"

Carew was speechless for a moment, caught his breath, and said, "I don't know what to say, John. There's so much that's happened to me in the past several hours; it's hard for me to take this all in at once. You bet I'll accept the apartment, and I'm ready to start work on it right now."

"We've got an extra bedroom that you are welcome to until we get the apartment finished," John said. "I know a man south of Danaville who is a good carpenter, and I'm sure he'll accept one of our hogs for the work we need done. Besides, there's enough farmwork to keep us both plenty busy without spending our time building a mansion," he added laughingly. Carew smiled and thanked John for the accommodation. Carew had been brought up in a religious family and believed in the power of God. He, like John, knew his power had brought them together—his prayers were being answered.

John made the deal with Mr. Rustin, the carpenter, and work was started several days later. Though Carew liked staying in the house, he was ready to have his own place. After two weeks, he moved into his apartment.

Alice gave him a few items for his small kitchen, with instructions that he eat all his meals with them. "You need a full nutritious diet to be a farmer, and you'll get it from my kitchen," she said with a smile. Carew was pleased with his quarters, and when John dropped by with a telephone and a small used TV, it thrilled him beyond words. After John had left, Carew brushed a tear from his cheek. *He could not know that in twenty-one years, he would be involved, along with his extended family, in a world-shaking miracle, right on this farm.*

JOHN HAD KNOWN Sara Kessel since high school days. They would always say hi to each other. She would smile, but he wasn't quite sure how to react. He was shy, and anyway, he didn't have much time for girls. He played football and basketball, and at all other times, he was involved with the farm. So, other than being distant friends, John never let himself get too close to Sara—or any other girl. One day John was in Kessel's Farm Supply Store buying cow feed and, not really knowing why, asked Mr. Kessel how Sara was doing. With a hint of a smile, Dick Kessel said she was fine, that she was attending Jackson Junior College and would complete her first year soon. John told Mr. Kessel to tell her hello for him and walked out to the loading dock to check on his order.

Kessel had always respected the Kellys. He had visited their farm several times over the years. He had watched John grow up and thought highly of him. What John didn't know was that Sara had mentioned to her dad on two or three occasions that she had liked him since the tenth grade. He just didn't seem interested in her. Dick mused that perhaps he could be a go-between without either one knowing. He knew his daughter would not like to feel manipulated. Neither would John. It had to be their idea.

Sara was pretty, with large dark eyes and dark hair that reached her shoulders. She had a "get it done" disposition that belied her five-foot-three-inch height and trim figure. There was no doubt that when she walked by more than one set of eyes glanced her way. This did not deter her thoughts of John Kelly, however. Her mission was to capture his heart. She knew it might not be easy, but she was determined.

Two weeks later, on a bright, sunny Sunday morning, John, Alice, his mother, and Pat were coming out of church. As they shook Rev. David Lawrence's hand, Sara and her parents were standing off to one side talking to several people. Something made

John walk over and speak to the Kessels. At the same time, he looked directly at Sara, and she was looking at him with a warm expression. John knew right away that a silent language was being spoken, and it made him feel good.

Sara knew that John felt touched as she had. She was thrilled to know that the possibility of them becoming closer was at hand. She also knew the first move would be up to her. Sara was confident she could win John Kelly's heart.

John, Carew, and a part-time helper, Red Reddington, were in the fields on Monday morning, plowing and planting. Even though it was early spring, John already discovered it was going to be a warm day. The two tractors were doing their job, although the old Ford would wheeze now and then. The Deere felt and sounded good to John, as he made his usual sharp turn at the field boundary to perfectly parallel the rows he had just plowed. The outer property fence was one more run to his right. When he finished, he intended to shut down, have some cold water from his large thermos, and rest for fifteen minutes or so. The simple act of taking a break, having some water, sitting in the shade of the tractor, and looking out over his land was indeed a satisfying feeling. He silently thanked God for his blessings.

Later, as he sat there and thought about the season's crops— most in the ground stretching upward and the others in process of being planted today—he thought of Sara and the way she had looked at him yesterday at church. John had been touched by that look. Maybe she had been planting seeds in his heart. Maybe she had succeeded. He got up, waved at the other two, and mounted his tractor. There were a lot of hours left in the day.

Carew was a gem. His work ethic and common sense were a joy for John to witness. Of course, nothing was said to him about being pleased with his performance. John knew that would embarrass him. Carew didn't want or need acclamation. He was totally satisfied just to work and see his own accomplishments.

JOHN HAD BEEN slowly working up the courage to call Sara. Four days had gone by since seeing her at church, and something told him to talk to her. After dinner, he went into the empty living room, not wanting his mother or Pat to hear his conversation. With no idea of what he was going to say. He dialed her number.

"Hello, Mr. Kessel, how're you? This is John Kelly."

"Hi John. I'm fine. This is a pleasant surprise. What can I do for you?" Dick Kessel was pleased, having told Ann, his wife, several days ago that he thought John would call Sara before the week passed.

"Can I speak with Sara?"

"You sure can. She's in the kitchen. Give me a moment, and I'll get her to the phone."

'John, old boy,' he thought, 'your forehead is a little moist, and there are a couple of butterflies in your stomach.'

"Hi, John." Sara's voice sounded so very nice on the phone—soft-spoken, yet self-assured. "It's great to hear from you. How's planting going?"

He suddenly felt more relaxed. She had asked the question that would make conversation easier.

"I was wondering if you'd like to come to the farm on Sunday after church and eat dinner with us. I'd bring you home late in the afternoon after showing you around. Besides, the Kellys have spent a lot of money at Kessel's Farm Supply. Your visit would be a partial payback."

Sara laughed and said, "You mean my coming to dinner is only a partial payback?"

"Well, I hope there would be other visits so I could collect the full amount," John said, cautiously, realizing how quick and smart she was; however, that even made him more attracted to her.

"I'd love to, John. I've been wanting to see your farm for a long time."

"Good, I look forward to Sunday. By the way, several weeks ago, I hired a full-time hand who you'll enjoy meeting. He's special, and a new family member. Got to go. Enjoyed our talk."

"Me too," she said.

After the Sunday trip to the Kellys', Sara had determined John was going to be her husband. She was well aware he didn't know that, but she also knew he was very interested in her. It was only a matter of time—the sooner the better. She would soon be twenty and had just completed her first year at Jackson Junior College. Her original plan upon graduating from high school was to attend junior college, then work full-time in the store. Her dad had agreed because for the past four years, Sara had worked weekends and summers, showing a lot of interest and knowledge about the business. With her personality, looks, and general business skills, Dick Kessel didn't regret not having a son to inherit his farm-supply business. When Sara told him she wanted to forego her second year of college and start full-time at the store, he was surprised but not shocked. He sensed she had special plans that she didn't want to discuss at the present, but he was patient. Sara discussed everything with him. He could wait.

It was midsummer 1979. Sara and John had seen each other every weekend for two months, and sometimes in between, when John came to the store to pick up items. Once they went for a hotdog lunch at Gardner's Drugstore. It was a busy time at the farm, and John had to double his routine efforts some days in order to save time for Sara. She was fully aware of his shyness, but also of his feelings for her. They had moments alone and would hold hands, lightly embrace or even kiss. Both of them felt those moments were too short and much too rare. Sara was very happy, and her father and mother were well aware of their daughter's intentions. They had already discussed the possibility of having John Kelly as a son-in-law. It pleased them, but her mother didn't want Sara to get hurt. Dick Kessel knew that John would never mislead his daughter. In fact, Dick knew for sure that young Kelly was in love with her.

John continually thought about Sara. There was hardly an hour that went by that something they had done together or said went unremembered—perhaps her trying to milk a cow and his laughing at her or her putting a handful of chicken feed down the neck of his shirt. He had fallen in love with her, and he was certain she loved him. His love for the Lord, for the farm, Sara, and his family was a dissection of his strongest feelings that he would learn to balance.

John and Sara were married eight months later, on January 20, 1980, at three in the afternoon. The Danaville First Methodist was full. It seemed the entire county had turned out. It took Sara, Granny, and Pat a few hours to address the invitations—it was evident all the recipients showed up and brought a friend or two. Though it was not a "formal" wedding, it was a beautiful ceremony conducted by Reverend Lawrence.

Afterward, people were crowded elbow to elbow in the church fellowship hall. With all the friends and acquaintances wishing them well—and the closest friends and family shaking John's hand, kissing Sara on the cheek, and hugging them both— the two of them were getting anxious to get started on their honeymoon.

John had hired a young man, who was the photographer at the *Mason County News*, to record the wedding, various guests, family of the bride and groom, and, with John's whispered instructions, shoot a series of snapshots of Sara.

The cake was cut, toasts were made, and soon after, the new couple departed through a gauntlet of rice-throwers and well-wishers, bound for the farm to change clothes, and start their drive to Tallahassee. They would spend the night there and drive on to St. Petersburg the next day. After three days, they would return to the farm and settle into a loving, sharing relationship. Sara thought her heart would burst with love for John. He, in turn, felt God's hand in bringing them together as husband and wife, and gave thanks.

Granny, Seth, Pat, Carew, and Red were all happily excited. The family had been expanded by one and, who knows, perhaps even more in the future. All of them smiled at that thought.

Patricia had been dating Paul Daniels for almost a year. Paul was the son of Lawrence Daniels, president of the Danaville Bank and Trust. His father and the board of trustees had recently appointed young Paul as assistant bank manager, a move that didn't go unnoticed by the Kellys, Danaville, and most of Mason County. Pat was very proud of Paul. John, Sara, and Alice noticed her increased happiness, and looked at each other as if to say, "Well, it's just a matter of time."

Everyone had been very prophetic. Within two months, Pat had invited Paul to dinner at the farm. As the meal was ending, Pat told everyone that she and Paul were engaged. As she said that, she lifted her left hand out of her lap, where she had slipped on the ring, and held it up for all to see. Paul grinned and put his arm around her shoulders. Everyone at the table was delighted. Alice got up, walked around the table, and hugged her daughter and then Paul. The others gathered around Pat and Paul and showed their happiness and congratulated them. John eyed Pat's ring and discreetly sucked in his breath. It was beautiful—and expensive. "The Kellys can relax now; we've got a banker in the family," he said. Everyone laughed.

Pat felt close to Sarah and would miss the everyday conversations with her when she and Paul got married and lived in Danaville. However, she would see her as much as possible—she liked being around Sara.

Pat became Mrs. Paul Daniels six months later, in March 1981. It was a beautiful wedding with all the trimmings. The church was filled with many friends of both families. It was noteworthy that the Kelly friends outnumbered those of the Danielses, although all of them liked both.

After their reception, the newlyweds drove to Panama City for an overnight stay at a nice beach hotel. On Saturday morning they would depart by plane to Atlanta, and then on to Cancun for five days. The Kelly household would miss Pat's daily presence, her ready laughter, and her contribution to managing a large house. However, Alice thought, Sara had already shown her dedication to making John happy, and she also added a positive, humor-filled relationship to the household.

CHAPTER TWO

THE DAYS FLOWED into months, and sooner than expected, John and Sara celebrated their first wedding anniversary. Rather than go out to dinner to one of the very few restaurants within ten miles, the two of them chose to celebrate the day by sitting down with their family to an extraordinary dinner prepared by Alice. Sara's parents the Kessels, Pat and Paul Daniels, Carew and Red—all were there to wish the best to a loving and caring husband and wife. Of course, Alice was beaming because of the occasion and the accolades she received for her food.

Two months later, Sara became pregnant. She and John were overjoyed. Sara, however, failed to mention to John that after Doc McNally examined her, he talked at length about pacing her daily activities, not doing any heavy lifting or even standing for long periods, to get plenty of rest. He also gave her a diet regimen. She had listened to Doc, knowing he was right, but also knowing she had responsibilities at the farm. She could be careful and still cook, vacuum, do laundry, and work in her beautiful yard—she would be careful.

Dr. Kenneth McNally was a "good friend of the Kellys". He had treated the family for a number of years. Doc was also the Kessels' doctor and had known Sara since she was a baby. Doctors in small towns know just about everyone, having treated them or

members of their family at one time or another. The county hospital
was more a twenty-bed clinic with several doctors than anything
else. It had a small surgical section for minor emergencies, x-ray,
and child delivery. All major cases were referred to Panama City
or Dothan, Alabama, each being less than fifty miles away.

When he had examined her and confirmed her pregnancy, he
found a slight iron-deficiency anemia as well as elevated blood
pressure. Her mother had aborted twice before Sara's birth. Doc
made a note to monitor Sara more often than he would those
patients who had good first-exam results, especially during the
first trimester of her pregnancy. He prescribed an iron supplement
and told her to restrict intake of salt and saturated fat, and then
advised her to follow the daily minimum physical routine as noted
on the typewritten instructions, which he gave to her.

A few days later, as she and John were eating breakfast with
Alice—Carew having eaten and gone out to the barn—he said,
"Sara, honey, aren't you doing too much around the house? You
said last night that you didn't lie down and rest yesterday. Shouldn't
you start doing that? I want you to get off to a good start for you
and the baby."

Alice added good-naturedly, "Remember, sweetie, you've got
to take care of two now, instead of one."

"Oh, John, Alice, I'll be fine. It's early in my pregnancy, and I
can still do a lot of things." She laughed. "Remember, dear, we're
farmers, and chores must be done."

John took a last swallow of coffee, arose from his chair, and
stepped around the table to her. He looked down into her beautiful
brown eyes, smiled, and said, "You and that baby are my life.
Please take care of both." After giving her a kiss on top of the
head, he went out the back door to work.

Sara sipped her coffee, reflecting on what John had said. She
thought, "I'll be careful and not do too much. I'll rest at the first
feeling of tiredness." She remembered the washing machine had
been started before helping Alice with breakfast. She hurriedly
got out of her chair and went to the utility room.

Later, as she was folding clothes, the phone rang. It was her mother wanting to drop by later in the morning. "That'll be great, Mom. Make it about twelve, and you can have lunch with all of us." Sara wanted to straighten up the living room and, if time permitted, trim the roses near the front porch steps. She'd have to hurry along to get things done before her mother arrived.

Alice had always liked Sara's spunk, but she had an ominous feeling about her daughter-in-law disregarding her and John's advice and concern.

Two months later, Sara had a miscarriage at the Mason County Community Hospital in Danaville. John was feeling pretty despondent when he met Doc McNally coming out of the delivery room. "Sara's going to be all right. I'm sorry, John, but she lost the baby because, I suspect, of too much physical activity and not adhering to her diet."

John stared at Doc and said, "Had you given her a lot of instructions, like to rest and not do heavy house work and eat only certain foods?"

"I certainly did, John. I also gave her iron supplements to take. Didn't she tell you?"

"No," John said in almost a whisper.

Doc continued, "I think Sara was so eager to please you and your mother and show that she was able to carry the baby and also manage the house without slowing down, especially in her early pregnancy, that she felt it a sign of weakness if she told you."

"Most of this is my fault," said John. "For the past several months, I've had 'farm on the brain.' She probably told me the things you wanted her to do, but it evidently went in one ear and out the other. I really feel bad about this."

Doc McNally put his hand on John's shoulder and said, "You can't hold yourself responsible. Look, you two can and will have a baby. Right now, we've got to bolster Sara's spirits, letting her know this is not the end of her potential motherhood, but the beginning. I feel strongly she still wants a baby, and all of us working together can make that happen. Go in and comfort her. Tell her that I want to see both of you in my office one month from today, okay?" Doc smiled and walked down the hall.

John stood there for a moment and thought, "Doc's right." He turned and went into Sara's room. She was lying on her side, facing the window. John knew she wasn't asleep, but said in a low voice, "Sara, are you awake?" She turned onto her back and looked at him, trying to smile. It was evident she had been crying.

"Oh, John, I'm so very sorry."

He sat down on the edge of the bed and bent over and kissed her. "Honey, there's nothing to be sorry about." He took her hand in his and lightly squeezed it. He smiled at her and continued speaking, "Doc told me that there were some complications. Mix those with you working a little too much around the house and the situation developed."

"I failed you and God. I should have told you about what Doc McNally had instructed me to do, to better ensure my pregnancy." She was crying again, but continued, wanting to flush the hurt out of her heart, "I've prayed so hard for forgiveness."

Sara was lethargic for several days after returning home from the hospital, but soon began to feel better. With all the support she was receiving from John, the family, and Reverend Lawrence, she realized the loss of her baby was over and done with. She relegated the terrible experience to the recesses of her mind and directed herself to a positive direction. She thanked God for his blessings, knowing that was where her strength really came from.

John and his mother had talked about the change they saw in Sara, and how thankful they were. His spirits rose dramatically.

After a number of weeks, John and Sara returned to Doc McNally as he had requested. Doc told Sara there was no reason at all to doubt her safely having a baby. He explained again the importance of following his plan. With doing that and keeping her positive attitude—and he smiled when he said that—she would do fine. He advised them to wait six months before she became pregnant again. "The second time will be the charm. We'll do things with a different approach." The meeting finally ended with Sara leading the way out of Doc's office with a new feeling of hope. As John passed Doc, who had opened the door for them, Doc whispered, "I'll keep in touch with her." Those few words, coming from their well-trusted doctor, bolstered his feeling that they could have a son—or, he thought with a hint of a smile, a daughter.

"JOHN! JOHN!" RED was running toward the holding pond where John was checking the master water pump that supplied the field sprinkler system.

"What's wrong, Red?" He turned away from the pump and hurried to meet him.

"Carew fell off a ladder in the barn an' hit his head on the concrete floor. He's out; he's unconscious."

John said, "Let's go!" As he sprinted up the slight incline from the pond, Red was surprised at how fast his boss could move and ran hard to catch up.

As the two of them turned into the front of the large barn, Red pointed toward the back. "He's behind that big stack of feed."

When they found Carew, he was on his back and trying to move. He was making a low moaning sound and bleeding from the right side of his head. John's thoughts were racing. Was it only Carew's head? *Check his head first, then his body . . . try to communicate with him . . . he must have a concussion . . . don't know how he hit the floor . . . is his back broken? Must handle him very carefully.* "Red, run to the house and call the Danaville Fire Department. Tell them we have a man who can't be moved . . . at least, for now. He has to have immediate attention. Also, call the hospital and get word to Doc McNally. Tell Sara to bring a couple of blankets and a clean bedsheet . . . and some water. Hurry!" Red was gone.

When John looked back at Carew's face, he was squinting at John and slowly moving his lips. John got onto his knees, leaned over, and put an ear close to Carew's mouth.

"What happened, John?" he whispered. "Where am I?" He tried to move, but John put his hand on Carew's chest and told him to lie still. *At least he recognized me . . . that's a positive sign.* His breathing seemed okay, and his pulse was steady.

"Dear God, this is a good man. Please use your limitless loving power and heal him," John prayed. "Carew, can you hear me?"

"Yes," he said weakly.

"Where all do you hurt?"

Carew was silent for a few moments, then spoke, "My right shoulder and my head. Especially my shoulder." John heard Sara and his mother coming. Sara was calling out to him.

"Over here, behind the feed stack," he said. When they arrived, Sara wasted no time spreading two blankets over Carew. She and John began tearing the sheet into strips about a foot wide. As they folded one strip into a pad and raised Carew's head just enough to slide the pad under, Red appeared. "EMS is on the way, an' I called Doc McNally's nurse." He put down a plastic one-gallon bottle of distilled water that he had spotted in the utility room.

"Good deal, Red. Let's see how much the blood flow has slowed. We'll gently wash the wound and take a look." After a few moments, John could see that Carew's head was swollen at the point of an approximate two-inch cut. The blood, however, had begun to coagulate—that was a good sign.

Carew had slowly come around and was speaking a little more coherently. He tried to move again, but John told him to lie still, as he gently felt his right shoulder. It was evident the shoulder was dislocated. He had seen several during his high school football days. Carew must have landed on that shoulder first, and then his head. Maybe, he thought, he won't have a debilitating injury.

"I hear a siren," said Red. "It won't be but several minutes before they're here."

"Good. It seems like hours since you called them," said Sara. Actually, it had been approximately fifteen minutes.

Red went outside to guide the EMS ambulance around to the rear of the barn. Soon, the vehicle backed up near the wide door, and two men got out, one with a medium-sized medical bag, and hurriedly walked to where Carew was lying. One looked at his eyes and examined his ears, then his head wound; the other put a blood pressure cuff on his left arm and pumped it up.

Cliff Martin, the senior specialist of the two, knew John and spoke to him, "We need to get your man to the hospital the sooner the better. I don't think his head injury is real serious, but one never knows until it's examined closely. He definitely has a dislocated shoulder. It's hard to tell how bad. The hospital will x-ray it before resetting it."

Cliff's assistant brought in a gurney and a stretcher board. He placed the board on the floor beside Carew. The board would be used to support Carew's entire body, not allowing any motion in the limbs, back, or head. John kneeled beside him. "I know you hurt, but these men are going to move you onto a stretcher, here beside you. You'll be at the hospital soon."

Carew tried to apologize for being so much trouble, and John cut him off. "Just settle down, ol' buddy. Anyone of us could have fallen. Just think how lucky you were. You'll be at the hospital soon." The two EMS men carefully placed Carew on the board and strapped him down. They lifted the board up onto the gurney and rolled him out to the ambulance. The assistant climbed into the back with Carew. Cliff closed the rear doors and got into the cab. With lights flashing, the ambulance slowly pulled away and followed the drive around the house to the road, where it accelerated toward Highway 77 and Danaville.

"Red, you stay with mama. Sara and I are going to the hospital and find out about Carew's injuries," John said as they walked toward the garage to get his car.

Alice called out to him, "John, you or Sara call me as soon as you find out anything." He backed the car out and departed in a hurry.

By the time they arrived at the hospital, the EMS crew had unloaded Carew, and he was now in the emergency room. John parked the car, and he and Sara walked hurriedly through the doors. A nurse came toward them. John recognized her from church. "Hello, Mr. Kelly, Mrs. Kelly. Your man is in there." She nodded toward the ER.

"Go on in. Dr. McNally and Dr. Cox, one of our surgeons, are examining him." He thanked her, and they entered.

"Hi, John, Sara," McNally said. "Carew said he was doing some barn flying, and he crashed." There was a thin smile on his face. John looked down at Carew as Dr. Cox was cleaning the head wound. A nurse stood by with scissors and razor to remove the hair around the wound. When Carew spoke, John immediately knew he was going to be okay.

"Well, John, you now know how far I'll go to take the day off." Everyone smiled. Doc McNally even chuckled.

Dr. Cox rose up from examining Carew's head wound, looked over at Doc McNally and the nurse, and said, "I'm going to send him to x-ray for head and shoulder. He shows no outward sign of concussion, but further examination will tell us if there is and to what extent. He needs stitches for the cut and cold packs for the swelling. His shoulder is separated, and the pictures should tell us if there is ligament damage. I think, after resetting his shoulder, it should be okay in two or three days." He looked at Carew. "After we know a little more, I recommend you stay with us overnight for observation, then you can go home if everything checks out—and I expect it will."

After Carew had had his x-rays and his shoulder reset, the staff moved him to a room. The Kellys stayed a while to bolster his spirits.

"Other than being a little sore, I feel like I could go home right now," he said as he looked at John and Sara. "There's a lot to do. Red could finish that wiring job in the barn." He added with a slight, painful grin, "I wouldn't want him to miss a chance of doing some 'barn flying.'"

John and Sara laughed heartily. "Like the doc said, an overnight observation of you would be a wise thing to do. You get some rest, and I'll come for you when they check you out." Sara called Alice and Red and told them all the details. They were relieved and happy. "Like us," she told Carew. "Alice said, 'The Lord answers prayers.'"

John shook Carew's left hand, and Sara kissed him on the forehead. With that, Carew accepted the inevitable and said, "You two go on home, and I'll look forward to tomorrow." After John said a short prayer of thanks, he and Sara left for the farm.

JOHN BROUGHT CAREW home the next afternoon, with a big welcome from everyone. Although his shoulder and head were sore, he was extremely happy to be home. The doctor told him he should heal within days but, in the meantime, not to use his arm to do any lifting, pushing, etc. Doc would remove the twenty stitches from his head wound in a week.

John had made it clear to Carew that he was to take it easy for a few days. He would know when his shoulder was ready for normal use. In three days, Carew was doing light work—feeding the chickens, hogs, and cows. He did no heavy lifting. It was obvious John and Red were keeping their eyes on him.

Within two weeks, after seeing Dr. Ross for a follow-up, he was back doing his regular work. His shoulder was still a little sore, but Carew was back—and happy.

CHAPTER THREE

THE MONTHS HURRIED by. All of a sudden, it was late February, a busy time of the year. John, Carew, and Red began checking and preparing their equipment for the planting season: the two tractors, trucks, harrows, plows, fertilizer spreaders, seeders, and many other items. It often amazed John how much farm equipment had changed during the past fifteen to twenty years. Some of the tools and equipment on the Kelly farm had been in use for over twenty years, but now most of it was newer and much more efficient.

Sara had taken good care of herself since having the miscarriage. When she told John she thought she was pregnant again and needed to see Doc McNally, the news sent goose bumps down John's spine; it thrilled him. However, he knew it would be best to keep his enthusiasm in check—to show a little, but let her set the tone of the event. He watched her closely as she talked about carrying another baby. She seemed positive and happy about it, but he wanted her to feel God's presence and know she could count on his help for her to have a successful term and birth this time.

John told Carew and Red that he'd be taking Sara to the doctor. Both of the men knew how important it was for their boss to be with Sara at this time. They had the mountain of work in hand. They assured him with slight smiles that somehow they'd make out without him. He knew them well, that they were trying to reassure him and relax him at the same time. John grinned at them and went to get Sara and leave for their appointment with Doc McNally.

WHEN DOC RETURNED to the examining room, after Sara had dressed, he gently tapped a large manila envelope and said with a smile, "I've worked up a slightly different overall plan with instructions for your next nine months. If you adhere to 'our plan,' you'll deliver a healthy baby. I don't want you to hesitate one moment if you wish to talk to me about anything—morning, noon, or night." He put his arm around her shoulders and looked into her eyes. "You're going to have your baby. Let's go out and talk to John."

Alice was all smiles as she put dinner on the table that night. She knew Sara would carry the baby full term this time and have a successful delivery. Alice would be a grandmother this time because of her conviction that God had deemed it so. Pat and Paul were present, having been invited several days before Sara's examination. When Sara and John told them the news, they were very happy. Pat proclaimed herself "Aunt Pat" and pointed at her husband, saying, "Uncle Paul." Carew also felt like an expectant uncle. Skin color or lack of bloodline made no difference to the Kellys; he was one of them; he was thrilled. Red couldn't stay for dinner, and Carew could hardly wait 'til morning to tell him the good news.

The baby was due October 8. It was a cool, sunny mid-September morning as Sara and Alice sat on the back porch. "You've done real well the past eight months, Sara. I'm convinced Doc McNally is a real wise man, and you are a determined mother-to-be," Alice said.

"There have been a few times, Alice, when I became a little nervous and unsure, but John and prayer gave me courage and determination. Now with him kicking"—she had determined from the start that it would be a boy—"it's a sign of a baby preparing to greet the world, and I'm ready."

Lyle Matthew Kelly was born October 7, 1982, at 7:00 a.m. He weighed eight pounds seven ounces. Although Sara was weak and tired, she was ecstatic. John was fit to be tied. Doc McNally tried to cover his elation with his professional demeanor, but it didn't work—a very happy pair of Kellys saw through it at once. All of the family, except Carew and Red, were at the hospital— the new grandparents, Alice (without Seth, who was at the farm under the watchful eye of Carew) and Dick and Annie Kessel; Pat and Paul; John, the "floating on air" new father; and Sara, the new, exhausted mother.

A nurse came in and asked that only two people at a time visit in the small room. Finally, everyone except John went down to the nursery to look again at little Lyle. John gently took the sleeping Sara's hand. He looked at her beautiful, serene face and felt so in love with her. He gave thanks for her and their new son—that God give him the wisdom and love to always put them first for the rest of his life. John got up, looked at his wife one more time, and walked down the hall to the lobby to call the farm. Hopefully, Carew would be close to a phone.

"An eight-pound boy! That's terrific!" Carew could barely control himself. John gave him all the details, assuring him that Sara and Lyle were doing well. "When will they be coming home, John?"

"Hopefully, in two days. Doc McNally still wants to watch things for a while. Sara and others asked about you and Red. They know, however, that someone needs to keep an eye on papa and the farm. I'll be home with Alice in early afternoon, and then you and Red can come see the new Kelly and his mama. I'll come back again tonight."

This was such a special time for the family, but many friends wanted to wish their best to John, Sara, and their new son—Karl and Tisha Pasternak, their closest neighbors; Rev. James Lawrence and wife; Carlton Laney, Danaville High School principal, and wife; Lawrence Daniels, president of Danaville Bank and Trust, and wife; and many others. Most of these folks would visit the farm, starting two days later.

When John checked Sara and his new son out of the hospital, Doc McNally told her she must rest a few days before becoming very active. He wanted her to build up her strength. Annie, Sara's mother, happily volunteered to drive out each day for at least a week to help Alice keep an eye on Lyle and his mother. Alice, now "Granny," as John so aptly named her, was glad to have some extra help. Annie would be tabbed as "Nana." That seemed to have solved the grandmother identity.

Though John was extremely proud of Sara and Lyle, he was also happy to have plenty of work. He could keep out of the way of the various women visitors who wanted to see Sara and their son. When someone like Reverend Lawrence was to come by, John would come to the house in his work clothes if he was nearby. He'd visit for a few minutes and then rejoin Carew and Red in their daily duties.

Things began to settle down after two weeks had passed. Sara was feeling almost like her old self, and Lyle seemed healthy in every way. Doc McNally was very pleased by how Sara had followed his instructions and how Lyle was progressing. Sara felt very close to Doc, and she thanked God for guiding Doc's skills in taking care of her and Lyle.

Doc, in turn, admired Sara's courage.

EIGHT MONTHS LATER, on a Saturday morning, Alice got up to start her day, glanced over at Seth's twin bed, and knew instantly that he had passed away. A pang shot through her body as tears rolled down her cheeks. She bent over and kissed his forehead, stood for a long moment, and prayed for his soul. Alice put on her robe and went down the hall toward John and Sara's room. About that time, John came out of the room, buttoning his shirt. "Good morning, mama," he whispered. "You need something?"

Suddenly, John knew when he saw her tears. His heart sank. He put his arms around her and held her tight. "Mama, we knew he didn't have much time left."

"I know," she said, "but I'll miss him so, and I know you will too."

John paused for a moment, and then said through his own tears, "More than anyone will ever know. He was also my best friend."

Sara came out, tying her robe. "What's the matter? Is it Seth?" Then she realized it was.

The three went in to see Seth. They stood beside the bed looking at a body that had freed its soul to the Lord. John said a long prayer that gave them all comfort.

The funeral brought people from Danaville and across Mason County and beyond. Seth was loved by many people and remembered for caring about his church, his family, the community, and his beloved Kelly farm.

When all the family returned to the farm after the funeral, they sat in the living room. Some were having coffee and snacks that had been prepared by friends; others, just sitting and talking. Sara was holding Lyle in her lap. John came over, picked him up, and said to him, to be heard by all, "Son, your granddad loved you for the short time he knew you. I'll tell you all about him one day."

"I will too," Granny said with a slight smile.

DURING THE NEXT several years, the farm was very productive. John was able to pay off the Danaville Bank and Trust loan that had been hanging around his neck for three years. Now he could afford a complete overhaul of the smaller tractor's engine, new tires for one of the trucks, and offer Carew and Red a small raise in pay. Sara had convinced him they should consider some type of savings or insurance program for their son's college education.

Lyle had now grown into a fine-looking lad of six years. Sara was apprehensive when she took him to school on his first day. She knew he would thereafter be boarding the school bus out by the mailbox each morning. Like many mothers, this caused Sara anxiety. Lyle, however, wasn't fazed and thought of all this as an adventure. As he grew older, John and Sara remained lovingly consistent in parenting, and he did very well in his studies and with the other students. He was bright, liked school, and loved helping out around the farm.

It had been rumored by some church members that Reverend Lawrence was going to retire. John phoned him one evening and found the rumor to be true. He told David, as John referred to him when they were conversing one-on-one, that he was sorry to see him leave the church—he would be missed. The reverend told John that it was time, and he was ready after forty years in the ministry. He and his wife were moving to Port St. Joe, on the coast, approximately eighty miles from Danaville. David drew a big laugh from John when he said, "My time will be filled with praying, playing golf, fishing—and graying."

John wished him well and thanked him again for his church leadership. "Do you have any idea who our minister will be?"

"There have been several names mentioned to our Staff Parish Committee, but the Conference—as you know, the ruling body of our church—seems to favor Dr. Wade Butler. He is a very capable minister and extremely knowledgeable in biblical history. Wade's current church is First Church in Quincy, Florida. I've known him for a few years. He'd be good for this community. He wants to come here, and I believe he will."

They talked for a few minutes more and said good night. John reflected for a moment about how things were always changing— he felt sure they were almost always for the better. Lawrence wants to move on, and Butler wants to come to Danaville. God was at work again.

Two months later, when Reverend Butler preached his first sermon, John and Sara liked him immediately. They made an effort to get to know him well. He was a very open person and exuded his Christianity. It wasn't very long before he and his wife, Barbara, came to the farm for dinner, and the two families became good friends.

CHAPTER FOUR

SARA WAS AMAZED when Lyle celebrated his fourteenth year. Time flew around their busy farm life. He was tall for his age, and by all physical appearances, he would be almost a duplicate of his dad. Lyle was always eager to take on more responsibility around the farm, and that pleased John. Almost from the day Lyle was born, John had had a deep-rooted feeling that there was something extraordinary about his son. He felt he was being reminded—sometimes in his dreams—he, Lyle, and the family would face a spiritual happening that would challenge them all. John would push the feeling to the back of his mind, but from time to time, it would float to the surface. When he had discussed the feeling with Sara several years previously, she exclaimed she had a similar situation, but was reluctant to tell him—thinking it was a motherly thing. Because of their faith, they decided everyone was in good hands and leave it at that.

High school was easy for Lyle. He had good study habits, due to his mother's influence early on, and respect and love for his family. Being highly intelligent also helped.

When Lyle turned seventeen, John felt it was time to review the amount of saved funding for his son's college education. He sat down in his office and opened a small lockbox and removed a bank savings book and an insurance-policy folder. Upon looking at the balance numbers in each, he breathed a sigh of relief. He and Sara had started the fund when Lyle was one year old. Knowing college costs were rising year by year, they had allowed for inflation as best they could. John now felt there was enough money for Lyle's four years at Florida State University. He shook his head in disbelief that his son would be leaving for college in less than two years.

"Dad, why do I need a college degree just to come back to the farm and do what I already love to do?" asked Lyle several times during his junior year in high school.

As usual, John answered patiently, "Because you'll need the knowledge and skills you develop at FSU to face the increasing difficulty of the business end of farming, especially for midsized farms such as ours." John explained the competition between buyers of produce and how negotiating for the best prices took an understanding of the marketplace. He emphasized the deluge of paperwork and/or payment that was involved: reports to state and federal agricultural entities, the IRS; county and state taxes; salaries; and insurance on employees, family, property, equipment; and many other details.

"When you plant a seed in the ground, it needs nurturing until it's harvested—then farming begins to get complicated," said John.

Lyle stood at the dais on high school graduation day as the class president and valedictorian. His family—consisting of his father, his grandparents, his Aunt Pat and Uncle Paul, and Carew and Red—were there, looking happy and proud. Lyle also considered Carew and Red family in his heart and mind. They, in turn, were honored to be there.

When he started speaking, his classmates and the entire audience sat attentively. Lyle spoke well, and his message was positively received. His subject was the importance of the family in the student's education and the respect the student owes them. Lyle ended his speech with a reference to his family.

He added, "My father and mother are my council and guides. They are here with my three grandparents, my aunt Pat and uncle Paul, and two dear friends, Carew Hinson and Red Reddington."

After the last diploma was given, and a loud cheer by the graduates, the ceremonies were over. Later, the Kelly family and friends gathered at the farm for a reception honoring their almost-grown graduate.

Three months later, Lyle stood on the walk leading to his dorm at Florida State University, looking around at all the other large buildings and the endless number of students walking by. He was overwhelmed, especially in contrast to the farm and Danaville. However, he had been to Tallahassee with his dad several times over the years and, most recently, when he played in the high school state basketball finals. He knew that as much as he would miss the farm and family, he would make the best of the next four years.

TERESA CARTER WAS a pretty young woman of eighteen. She was slightly petite, being five feet four inches tall, and weighing 110 pounds. She lived in Tampa, Florida, with her mother and stepfather, Arlene and Enrique Cruz. Teresa's older sister, Clara, lived in Naples with her husband. She was far enough away that Teresa did not see her but two or three times a year. They respected each other, but there was no real sisterly love. Teresa was not exactly lonely, but she tended to be a loner. She had confidence in herself. She had done well in high school, and she was now packed and ready to leave for her first year at Florida State University.

Enrique was a Cuban escapee from Fidel's "paradise." The details were never discussed by Enrique with anyone. He was employed by the Gelb Corporation, a large food-supply company in Tampa. He married Arlene Carter when Teresa was ten years old. At that time, Teresa's older sister seemed to be vying for her mother's attention most of the time, especially when Enrique was around. Teresa could see by his manner that he didn't like it, but he was still decently nice to both girls and, at the same time, kept his distance. Arlene, on the other hand, was very close and loving to her daughters.

Arlene was an accountant. She had her own successful business and enjoyed her work. She had saved a lot of money over the years for the purpose of putting her daughters through college. Clara had told her mother she did not want to go to college. Arlene tried to convince her it was necessary these days to have a degree, especially for women. Clara was not moved by her mother's pleas. To the surprise of everyone except Teresa, Clara announced to her mother, one week after her high school graduation, that she was pregnant. Within two months, Clara had married the boy, and they moved to Naples.

Teresa's mother never discussed Enrique with her, except to say he was nice to her and he had a good job. He treated Arlene nice, but showed little affection for her in front of the girls. There was something about him that Teresa couldn't fathom. He acted as if he was always preoccupied with other matters. In her mind, he was a strange man.

On the morning Teresa was to depart for Tallahassee, she was up early to have breakfast with her mother and Enrique. He usually left very early because of his cross-town drive; thus, Teresa seldom saw him until in the evenings. She felt she owed her mother the courtesy of saying goodbye to him in her presence. He responded in the manner Teresa thought he would. A few words such as "have a pleasant trip" and "stay well." Then he took a last sip of coffee, arose, and walked out of the room. Daughter and mother talked for a few minutes, her mother wiping her eyes and blowing her nose. Teresa and her mother would miss each other terribly, but this time in their lives had been coming for years. They both understood its necessity and hugged each other.

Through prearrangement, Teresa was riding to Tallahassee with her best girlfriend, Jenny, and her mother, Mrs. Lowell. The Lowells had been friends of Arlene for many years. Their daughters had grown up together. Arlene had wanted to drive Teresa to school, especially since it was going to be such a big change in the life of her daughter, but her most important client had called two days before and wanted a complete tax audit in three days. This canceled Arlene's plans for her trip. Teresa understood her mother's predicament, told her not to worry, and called Jenny Lowell. Jenny's mother was happy to take Teresa along.

Within a half hour, the doorbell rang. Teresa and Arlene greeted the Lowells, and they all helped Teresa carry her luggage and several boxes to the car. The expedition had started, and everyone was in fine spirits. Arlene knew that her daughter was making her first big step in adult life and was joyously happy for her, as she cried.

LYLE HAD BEEN at FSU for two years. He came home as often as possible, which averaged twice a month. At the end of his sophomore year, John had surprised Lyle with a very nice six-year-old Chevrolet Impala sedan. One of John's good friends, who worked at the Mason County Agriculture Center, offered the car to John for a very special price. John could see that it was an outstanding offer. As tight as things were financially, it would solve a big problem for Lyle.

John knew that Lyle would be home the next day to start his summer break. He parked the car in the barn. Carew and Red, after walking around it, with admiring comments, decided to wash and wax the Chevy. When they finished, it looked new.

John met Lyle at the bus station at noon the next day in Danaville. On the way to the farm, Lyle related how glad he was that he was home for three months, and he didn't have to think about classes and uninteresting professors droning on and on. "Dad, it's hard to realize that I've finished two years of college. Only two more, and I can come home and really be of use to you and the farm."

John smiled broadly, anticipating the surprise for Lyle. "Son, all of us uneducated hick farmers are tickled pink to have a 'joe college' to work with us this summer."

"I know that you, Carew, and Red are gonna sock it to me while I'm home. That's okay. I'm ready and willing," Lyle laughingly said.

After a few more minutes, John turned the car into the farm drive and drove past the house and up to the barn. Carew and Red were sitting on a long wooden bench under one of the large oaks. They waved as John stopped the car. Lyle was happy to be home for a long while, and it showed.

"Lyle, why don't you come over here and stand in front of the barn doors while Carew opens them up. There's something I want you to see." Lyle, with a questioning look at his dad, walked to within six or eight feet of the barn and stopped. Carew and Red pushed the sliding doors open as Lyle was still looking at his dad. Then, he turned and immediately saw the front of an older Chevrolet. "Son, catch this," said John. Lyle's reflexes were quick as he reached and caught a set of car keys. All of a sudden, he knew what was happening. He walked slowly to the car, taking it all in. "This is great, Dad. It's a beautiful car." John walked over and put his hand on Lyle's shoulder and said, "I figured you could save bus fare or not have to depend on a couple of your Danaville buddies for transportation."

Carew added, "Now you'll have to fight off those cute college girls, Lyle. You'd better weld up the passenger doors, or the girls will jump in when you stop at a light."

"I don't have time for girls," Lyle said with a big smile.

That particular trip home for Lyle was memorable: his first car. His father always managed to surprise Lyle with great timing.

Lyle's mom and Granny were grocery shopping when Lyle arrived and were not there when John gave him the car. They later drove up, waving at Lyle as they got out. They were happy to have him home for the summer. Lyle hurried over and hugged them. "Come and talk with me while I take care of some things in the kitchen," Granny said. He had his arm around his mom as they walked across the back porch toward the door. "Granny, I'll always follow you into any kitchen." They all laughed.

Lunch, like every meal at the farm, was outstanding. Granny was a superb cook, and she really enjoyed pleasing her men.

Afterward, John, Carew, and Red walked out onto the back porch while his mom, Granny, and Lyle were deep into a conversation. John started to sit down in one of the rocking chairs when he glanced to the south and was startled as he looked at the sky. It was a deep blue black. "Look at that sky," John said.

Carew and Red turned around and walked over to John. They too expressed wonder on their faces. Red spoke first, "I always catch the morning weather report on both the Weather Channel and WDLP in Panama City. Neither one showed anything but a clear, warm day, an' the same tomorrow." Carew nodded in agreement.

John watched the sky intently for a few seconds and said, "It's moving this way pretty fast, fellas. We'd better make sure all the outbuildings are closed up and all loose items moved into the barn. That thing could have heavy wind and rain in it, or a tornado with hail." Carew went to the kitchen screen door and called to Lyle, "We need a little fast help, college boy. Looks like a thunderstorm is sneaking up on us."

It didn't take long before the men had secured all moveable items in the yard and closed all the outbuildings. They stood together and watched the approaching storm. "Lyle, go turn on the TV to WPCF. Maybe they have some data on this thing," said John.

As Lyle hurried across the yard toward the house, he thought, "Well, I can drive my car later. First things first."

There was a distant sound of thunder.

While they kept their eyes on the oncoming storm and waited for Lyle and the latest on the weather, John moved Sara's car into the garage alongside his pickup truck. Carew and Red repositioned their cars away from the large oaks to the lee side of the garage. This offered little protection in case of a tornado or violent winds, but it was all that could be done.

Lyle reappeared from the house and walked hurriedly over to where they were standing and said, "The weather guy reported a heavy thunderstorm moving north, having mostly cleared the Panama City area. Their Doppler radar showed no tornado cloud formation. He thinks there will be only moderate to strong surface winds in our area. In fact, he mentioned that Danaville was directly in the path of the heaviest rain and wind."

It was turning quite dark as the four of them mounted the back porch steps. It was now raining, and the wind was picking up. John's mind was focused on the crops. They had already gathered and transported about half of the vegetables during the past ten days, but the remainder of the farm's yearly income was still in the ground.

John asked Lyle if the weather report had mentioned anything else. "Well, yes. I forgot to include that the way this storm developed was quite unusual. Something about the lack of low barometric pressure. I was on the way out of the room and didn't hear the rest of it."

"Let's all go into the house, out of this wind and rain," said John. The four of them went into the large kitchen, joining Sara and Granny. They had put mugs on the table and were brewing coffee.

"YOU BOYS SIT down and relax. We've seen worse than this, John. Remember when you were about eleven years old and we had the big storm with hail the size of golf balls? Other than shingle damage on the roof, we made it just fine." Granny crossed the kitchen to a side table and picked up a plate of fresh cookies. "Though we had lunch a little over an hour ago, these will go well with the coffee." They munched the cookies and drank the coffee as the lightning and thunder increased its tempo.

Even though the rain had increased, along with the thunder and lightning, everyone sat at the kitchen table, sipping coffee and making small talk. After thirty minutes or so, the rain slackened; and the lightning began to lessen; and the thunder boomed distantly. The storm was letting up. Lyle walked to a window and scanned the porch and backyard. "Looks like the worst is over—in fact, it's much brighter now," he said. John mentally breathed a sigh of relief and followed the others out onto the back porch. His concern, for the crops especially, had been the possibility of high wind and hail; neither had occurred. "Thank you, God," he thought.

As they stood on the back porch, each of them thought how different the storm had seemed, how it was reported on TV to have formed so quickly and unusually. It certainly had looked menacing, but turned out to be much less than it appeared. John and Lyle were still wondering what the weatherman on the TV meant when he reported how unusual the storm was in its suddenness and makeup.

The four men began to look at the trees and the buildings to check for damage. Except for some medium-sized branches lying across the yard, the trees were in good shape. All the outbuildings and the house appeared undamaged. Carew and Red checked their cars and found them safe. John was greatly relieved. He knew the crops would be found undamaged. He and Lyle were walking toward the chicken house to let out the chickens, which had been shut in prior to the storm, when Sara exclaimed, "Oh, boys, look at that!" They turned to see her pointing toward the barn. John first thought she was pointing out some damage, but he immediately saw a fantastic sight as he looked between the roofline of the barn and the large branches of two oak trees. Carew and Red trotted up, and they too saw the same thing—a huge bright rainbow, its vivid prismatic colors almost touching the ground in the center of the vegetable fields, approximately one-half mile distant.

Granny exclaimed, "It's huge and so bright. I've never seen one so close." Everyone was awestruck.

They hurriedly walked to the other side of the barn, away from the larger trees, to get a better view. The lower arc of the rainbow became dimmer, the colors dissolving forty or fifty feet above the ground. Carew said, "I estimate that it stops right in the middle of all the fields."

"I think you're right, Carew—and it's much larger than any rainbow I've ever seen," John said. They all just stood there quietly, taking it all in.

"Dad, have you noticed that as it goes skyward, it begins its arc, except this one gradually fades just before it turns downward?" John nodded in agreement.

WHEN THE STORM PASSED OVER DANAVILLE, prior to hitting the Kelly farm, most people just accepted it as a "pop up" summer thunderstorm. They went about their business as usual, except for the lightning, which put on quite a display especially north of downtown. Some people, however, watched the storm with a certain curiosity. Marvin Gardner, the owner and pharmacist of Gardner's RX Drugstore, stood inside the front entrance of his store, looking out at the rain and wind with several customers, and thought how fast it had appeared.

Marvin had another thought—that the Kellys and others along Highway 77 would be getting heavy rain, lightning, and wind. In fact, the wind was blowing pretty hard as it pushed the rain north along Main Street.

He mentioned to the three customers standing beside him not to go to their cars just yet because of the heavy lightning. They quickly agreed. Marvin turned and walked back to his work in the pharmacy. After thirty minutes or so, he glanced toward the store entrance and saw the rain had stopped and the darkness had evaporated. It struck him odd that as threatening as the storm looked while it was approaching, it now was practically gone.

He reached over to a shelf near the counter and turned on a small radio. He only used it for weather reports prior to heading to the golf course or to do a little bass fishing. A commercial was just ending. As luck would have it, the weather report was next.

Marvin listened closely as the report talked about the intense thunderstorm now over Danaville, heading north. The weatherman said how curious it was that the cell formed very quickly, without normal weather signs, and its relatively fast movement directly north.

Carla, one of Gardner's clerks, walked out in front of the store and looked northward, up Main Street. Marvin happened to be looking toward the front entrance when he saw her pointing. Two other people who were walking by, stopped, and also were intently looking north. Marvin walked out and joined them. "Oh, Mr. Gardner," Carla said excitedly, "look at that!"

Marvin was almost speechless when he saw the beautiful rainbow with its unusual position in the sky. Several other people joined them on the sidewalk, staring speechless at the spectacle. He said to no one in particular, "I've never seen anything like that. It's got to be several miles away, yet against the backdrop of those dark, receding clouds, the colors and the shape are very definable."

At least two dozen people were looking at the rainbow. Several had parked their cars and joined others along the sidewalks. Some people in the A&P, Miller's Clothing, and other stores heard about the beautiful colors in the sky and hurried out to see what was going on.

For some inexplicable reason, Marvin knew the rainbow was near, or at, the Kelly farm. He decided to telephone John Kelly and walked quickly into his store and called the farm. After many rings, Granny answered, sounding a little out of breath. "Hi, Granny Kelly, this is Marvin Gardner. How are you?"

"Hello, Mr. Gardner. Did downtown Danaville get much of the storm?" said Granny. He quickly told her about the rain and lightning, and then questioned her, "Are all of you looking at a rainbow now?"

Granny answered with a lilting rise to her voice, "We sure are. It's beautiful, an' it's coming down in the center of our farm fields. I'd tell you to come see it, but I think it's beginning to fade and won't last much longer."

He asked her about its shape, saying that from his viewpoint in Danaville, it looked as if the arc was incomplete—that it came to earth on one side and continued only a little past midpoint on the other side. She confirmed his observation and said all of them had been discussing the same thing, when she heard the phone. Marvin told her that the rainbow looked larger than any he had ever seen. Granny replied that even though it was literally in their fields, John, Sara, Lyle—all of them—could follow the upward sweep of the arc, extremely high in the sky, and then, just as it started downward, far away, it disappeared.

Marvin thanked Granny, asked her to give John his regards, and hung up the phone. He sat at his desk for a few moments, wondering about the event, then started sorting through new prescriptions to fill.

Talk about the rainbow persisted for a few days in Danaville. The *Mason County News* even mentioned it in a short paragraph on page 2, under editor Jim Summers's column, "Talk about Danaville." After that, interest faded away.

CHAPTER FIVE

JOHN AND LYLE leaned against the fence, looking out toward the location where the rainbow had almost touched the ground. It had faded away thirty minutes earlier, but they lingered on, discussing the uniqueness of the event. Finally, Lyle slapped his dad on the back and said, "Hey! I haven't driven my car yet." He pulled out the keys and walked toward the barn. John smiled and walked over to the house.

The remaining summer passed uneventfully, and time had come for Lyle to return to college. He was now twenty and would be entering his junior year. The farm was doing well, and he had enjoyed his time at home. In fact, it was always difficult to leave the farm and head for Tallahassee. Things were looking up, however, because only two years remained until his graduation and a degree in business administration. His minor would be American history. His dad was responsible for Lyle's interest in his country and its people, and he planned to pursue the subject, as time allowed, in the future. First and foremost, however, was the farm. His degree in business administration would be a great help when his dad retired.

Two nights before he was to depart for FSU, Lyle and Carew were sitting on the front porch, reminiscing about past times: the farm, fishing and swimming at Crystal Lake, Lyle's stardom on the Danaville High School basketball team. On and on it went between the two of them. Lyle respected Carew. As Lyle was growing up, Carew always had time to answer a work-related question. To show him how to do a certain job regarding "working the soil" or changing the generator on the tractor. They had spent a lot of time, after the work of the day, talking about farming, people, even the so-called power brokers in Danaville and the county courthouse. Carew was an observer of people. Even Lyle's dad had remarked several times how Carew seemed to have a sixth sense about people he had met or had done business with. John Kelly looked upon Carew's talent as important and extremely useful, especially when there was business at the bank, or negotiating a purchase of fertilizer, plant sprays, fencing, or other farm supplies. Carew possessed an innate talent of judgment about people and situations, which John considered an integral part of the farm's operation and success.

"I sure hope school goes well this year, Lyle. Just two more years and you'll be home full-time," Carew said. Lyle started to respond, but saw Carew was pausing only to think through his next comment. "Your dad works way too hard. I've told him several times to slow down, but he has a stubborn streak in him. He always says he feels good, and I worry too much. When I went to see Doc Ken about a bad sore throat a few months ago, he said it would be a good thing if your dad worked a little less and relaxed a little more."

Lyle was quiet for a moment, and then he said, "Is there anything seriously wrong with him, Carew?" He had a concerned look on his face.

"No, I don't think so. Doc McNally knows that running a farm is hard work, even on good days. He said your dad was in his midyears, and it just makes good sense to practice a little preventative maintenance. I'll continue trying to put a halter on him, but you know you can't press him too much." Lyle felt a little better, but still, a small red flag went up in the deeper regions of his mind. He would try to keep an eye on his dad without its being obvious.

THE NEXT MORNING, after breakfast, Lyle washed his car and told his mom he was going to Danaville and wouldn't be back for lunch. It was his last day at home for a while, and he wanted to see a couple of his old high school buddies before they all went their separate ways back to college. Charles Huggins had called Lyle the afternoon before and suggested they get together, perhaps with one or two others. Even though Lyle was not the partying type—like Charles, Randy Gardner, and Martin Hardcastle—he had always stayed in touch as much as possible. He had agreed with Charles to meet at Gardner's Drugstore around ten o'clock. The three or four of them could sit in a booth and shoot the breeze and let Randy Gardner pick up the tab. He had excellent connections with the owner. It was Lyle's plan to visit with the guys, have lunch, pick up a set of wiper blades for his car, and return to the farm. He wanted to talk to his dad, as well as Carew and Red.

When Lyle arrived at the drugstore, Charles was already there. He told Lyle that Randy was on his way, and there would be just the three of them. Marvin Gardner walked over to their booth, shook their hands, and said, "Well, well, well, I have the honor of having two of Danaville's finest in my emporium, and I understand that one more is expected shortly." The boys laughed. Lyle had always thought Mr. Gardner had the makings of a politician. Marvin turned and pulled up a chair from a nearby aisle table and said, "Don't worry, when that son of mine arrives, I shall retreat and leave you to your devices. By the way, Lyle, it's been sometime since I've seen you. I hope all is well with you and your family. I've seen your dad once in the past month, and Carew was in the other day to pick up a few items for your granny. Other than that, the Kellys have been sparse."

"Well, Mr. Gardner, you know my dad loves that farm. He stays busy, and he makes sure the rest of us do the same," Lyle said with a smile.

Randy came in and waved. He stopped at the soda fountain and said something to Carla, the waitress, and then he walked over and joined them. "Hi, guys, and you too, Pop. Sorry I'm late, but I had to get a jump-start from Mom's car. Pop, I've got to get a new battery."

Randy's dad arched his eyebrows and said, "Somehow, that does not surprise me, especially on the eve of your return to school." They all laughed.

Marvin looked over at Lyle and said, "Before I go back to work and leave you men to your serious conversation, there's something that's been on my mind since last June, Lyle. It's about that unusual thunderstorm and, especially, the rainbow afterward.

"After the storm had passed over Danaville—and I guess, by that time, it had also passed your farm—I went outside and looked north. I saw a beautiful big rainbow, but it was very different. It was two-thirds of a 180-degree arc, with the lower part turning downward in the vicinity of the farm. The upper end just faded away after passing the midpoint of the arch. I quickly came back inside and telephoned, knowing that all of you were probably outside, but your granny finally answered. She confirmed the rainbow was pointing down to the center of your fields. I found this to be very odd, but very interesting. It didn't seem possible such a rainbow could occur, yet I saw it with my own eyes."

All three of the young men were listening intently, especially Charles and Randy. Lyle was more reflective because he was the only one that had witnessed the phenomenon. "Yes, Mr. Gardner, what you saw is essentially what my family saw. What you didn't see was the broad band of colors stopping what appeared to be forty or fifty feet above the ground. It was beautiful. I guess I would call it a once-in-a-lifetime experience of nature at its best."

Marvin arose from his chair and said, "Well, I've got a drugstore to run so that I can keep my son in college." He shook hands with Lyle and Charles, wished them good luck at school, and walked toward the pharmacy.

About an hour later, after the three had finished lunch, Charles told Lyle he was impressed with the "rainbow" conversation. "You know, Lyle, based on how the event occurred, I feel there's more to it than meets the eye, but I guess we'll never know what it is."

"Well, that's history. I've got to concentrate on my seventeen hours this coming semester. I'd better head for home, guys. Keep in touch. Don't forget to study when you get back to school," Lyle said.

Charles and Randy looked at each other, made a clownish face, and winked. Lyle shook hands with each of them, and left them standing at the booth as he walked out of Gardner's Drugstore.

While going to his car, Lyle briefly thought about his conversation with Mr. Gardner. Then he started a mental list of all the things he had to do before leaving for Tallahassee the following morning.

TERESA CARTER'S FIRST two years at Florida State were greatly satisfying. She had made a pledge upon graduating from high school that she would absorb the college academic atmosphere and excel in her studies. Teresa's mother was her motivation. Arlene had, consciously or unconsciously, provided an example of success by the way she had developed her accounting business. Teresa had made the dean's list all four semesters, with a 3.7 grade point average. Her mother was ecstatic. Enrique mumbled a "congratulations" and walked away.

Teresa had become good friends with several girls in her dorm. She realized, as time passed, that she had chosen them carefully. They, like her, were studious and conservative in their college life. This appealed to Teresa. All five of them respected each other and understood when anyone of them wanted some "alone" time, mostly to study, write, or call their family, or do some reading. They liked to be around boys, and there was occasional dating but no steady boyfriends.

Teresa was also preparing to leave the next day for Tallahassee and her junior year at FSU. This time, her mother, Arlene, and her stepfather, Enrique Cruz, were taking her. She didn't look forward to the trip with Enrique in the car, but she was determined to make the best of the two-hundred-plus miles. Arlene was going to miss her daughter during the three months until Thanksgiving.

She was already starting to miss Teresa, and they had not even packed the car. Enrique had made reservations for him and Arlene at a La Quinta for one night. They were to return to Tampa the next day. The sooner she was out of the presence of Enrique, the better she would feel.

Teresa could not have dreamed how significant this school year would become.

THAT NIGHT AFTER dinner, Lyle sat on the porch with his dad, mother, Carew, and Granny, reminiscing about the summer and his upcoming junior year at FSU. The past three months had been great. It was going to be hard to leave again. "Well, at least I see a light at the end of the tunnel—I think it will turn out to be a shining opening to opportunity."

"It seems to me, you've made most of your opportunities, just by working hard. All of us here really appreciate your attitude," John said.

Carew had had no college, but was looked upon by everyone as very smart and shrewd; he was always methodical and analytical in everything he did. Lyle respected Carew's mind as much or more than he did that of some of the professors at FSU. He loved his dad immensely, but Carew was like a close brother, even though he was only two years younger than his dad.

Lyle was sleepy. He looked at his watch, saw it was past ten thirty, and told everyone he had to hit the hay. He wanted to leave for Tallahassee around 9:00 a.m., putting him on campus before eleven. His new roommate was to arrive that afternoon, and he wanted to get settled in before he met him—he was Bill Kraven from Ft. Lauderdale. Lyle thought that unlike his previous roommate, who had hailed from Blountstown, another small panhandle town, Kraven was a "gold coast" Yankee and would probably be hard-pressed to talk slow and sensible. Lyle mentally reprimanded himself and thought it best to give his new roommate every consideration.

The next morning, Lyle loaded the last of his things into his car and said laughingly, "It's time to hit the road and switch from 'physical' to 'mental.'" He hugged his mom and Granny, and shook hands with Carew and Red, then his dad. He and his dad held their handshake longer. John looked at his son and felt a pride unlike any before. Lyle felt an indescribable bond.

With a "See you soon," Lyle got into his car, drove around the looping driveway, and out onto the county road to State Highway 77 to Danaville and 1-10 East.

CLASSES STARTED SEVERAL days later. It appeared that Bill Kraven was going to be an acceptable roommate. The two of them probably wouldn't be bosom buddies, but Lyle thought their coexistence would last. The daily routine soon settled down, and it was college life as usual. Bill was a rabid fan of football—FSU Seminole football. The season started with half of thirty thousand students going stark crazy before, during, and after the first game, and continuing on for at least eleven weeks. Lyle liked football and occasionally attended a game, but every two weeks or so, he drove home westward on a Friday afternoon and pushed football to the back of his mind.

During the third week of school, Lyle needed to purchase an additional book for one of his business classes. His dorm was not very far from Bill's Bookstore, so he decided to walk. Bill's "Lookstore," as it was called by freshmen and sophomores, was a prime location to look at girls. The bookstore, however, had been on campus for more than fifty years and had an outstanding inventory of books and many other student supplies.

As usual, there was a crowd in the store, and Lyle worked his way through and around students until he got to the section he needed. He stopped behind a girl waiting for the aisle ahead to open up. For some odd reason, he had an urge to sneeze. He went for his handkerchief, but not in time. He did manage to cover his mouth and nose, as he turned his head and let go. Lyle murmured, "Excuse me," and applied the handkerchief to his nose and blew.

"Bless you," said a nice, lyrical voice emanating from the girl in front of him, as she turned and looked at him pleasantly.

Lyle looked at her over his handkerchief and was totally stunned. She was a very pretty girl. He usually was in command of himself and difficult to startle, but not this time. Though he had dated occasionally in high school and several times in his first two years at FSU, he never became interested in any particular girl. There was a unique difference this time. It was almost like his feet didn't touch the floor. He couldn't remember feeling like he did now. Lyle stood there for what seemed to be minutes, but was only two or three seconds. He was so smitten with the girl's pretty face and manner that he was tongue-tied, but finally said, "Thank you. I'm very sorry."

"If I had had any idea that I would cause an allergic reaction in someone, I would have stayed in the dorm," Teresa Carter said in a soft, very articulate voice.

Lyle was quick to reply, "It wasn't you. I don't have any allergies that I know of. The only thing I can come up with is my eyes commanded my nose to sneeze to get your attention." She laughed and Lyle smiled. "My name is Lyle Kelly, and I do apologize for sneezing so close to you."

Teresa had an uncanny feeling as she looked at Lyle. He was not only handsome, but was also the first boy that had affected her in such a way. "Nice to meet you, Lyle, in spite of your technique. I'm Teresa Carter, the allergy girl." They both laughed.

After a few moments, the crowd began to dissipate, allowing them to move toward their respective book section of interest. Lyle touched her arm lightly as she started to move away and said, "It was very nice meeting you. Good luck this semester."

"It was nice meeting you too, Lyle. I must say, your method of getting my attention was unique," Teresa said with a beautiful smile. She then moved off through a small group of students in front of her.

Lyle stood there a moment and watched her go. He had wanted to get her address and phone number, but was uncertain if he should. "She might have a boyfriend or had a dislike of my sneezing or I just don't appeal to her or whatever other negative she might have about me," Lyle thought, his mind racing. He felt as if a great treasure had slipped through his fingers. When he turned to go to the business-administration section, he saw Teresa far across the store, standing and looking at him. His heart did a flip-flop as she quickly went out the door.

CHAPTER SIX

L YLE DROVE HOME Friday afternoon to spend the weekend. It had been three weeks since he saw the family and the farm. He called his dad or mom occasionally, but seeing them and talking in person was much preferred. The same feelings applied to Granny, "Carew," and Red. Lyle felt as if his ordered world was on the verge of changing. Even now, his drive home, which he always enjoyed and looked forward to, was fraught with a longing to see Teresa. Come Monday morning, he would go to the registrar's office and hopefully find which dorm she was in.

When Lyle arrived at the farm around five, Grandpa and Grandma Kessel were there. It was good to see them. He loved them both, but especially Grandma Kessel—she reminded him of his mother. She had the same expressive facial features when talking or smiling, and she carried herself like his mother. He gave her a long hug and then shook hands with his grandpa. "You look great, Lyle. College seems to agree with you," Grandpa said.

Lyle thanked him and immediately thought of Teresa. "I've been home fifteen minutes and I start thinking of her. I met her just yesterday and we talked for a whopping ten minutes. She astounded me. I was so taken I couldn't even ask her for her phone number or anything. She must think I'm a real clown."

By that time, Granny, who seemed to always to be in the kitchen, came into the living room, followed by his mom. They hugged him and he kissed them both on the cheek. After all of them had talked for ten or fifteen minutes, Lyle asked his mom about his dad. She said he and Red were working on a new door for the chicken coop.

"I'd better go and see if they're doing it right," Lyle said with a grin.

Granny told him, "We're going to have dinner about six, so don't wander off.

Lyle went out to the barn and saw his dad and Red working at the large carpentry table in the rear of the building. "Hey, son," John said as Lyle walked up. Red smiled and nodded.

"Hi, Dad, Red. What's up," Lyle said, as he shook hands with both of them.

"Oh, this door to the chicken house was in pretty bad shape. Thought I'd get Red to help me before he headed home. Was the traffic bad on 1-10? It's Friday, and that means everyone hits the road for the weekend, you know," John said.

"No big problem," He could hardly remember the trip because of his preoccupation with thoughts about Teresa and how he had torpedoed his chances of getting to know her.

John looked at Lyle for a moment and said, "Son, you seem lost in space. I asked you how your car was running. Is all well at school?"

"I'm sorry, Dad. I was thinking of something else. Yep, everything is fine at good old FSU. The car is doing great. I had the oil changed last week, and the fellow at Zippy Lube said he'd never seen a cleaner car."

His dad smiled and finished screwing the last hinge to the door.

"Well, Red, it looks as if we door experts have done our job. We're all caught up for the day. Lyle will help me hang the door later." Red was rather pleased to hear John proclaim the week over and done. After many years, he had fallen for a nice woman, Jenny Cooper, whose husband was killed three years previously in a sawmill accident. She and her two teenage daughters lived in Benton, ten miles west of Danaville. John later told Lyle that Red brought her by the farm one day. He always seemed to seek John's approval on personal matters. John had told Red later that Jenny seemed perfect for him.

Lyle stood there, hearing his dad, but distantly thinking of Monday, when he would try to contact Teresa. Suddenly, he felt a strong hand grasp his shoulder. Lyle spun around and saw Carew standing there with a big grin on his face. "It seems every time it gets nice and peaceful around the farm, you show up," Carew said.

They shook hands and talked for a moment. Red wished them all a good weekend and, without trying to show it, walked happily toward his car. John, Lyle, and Carew looked at each other, smiled, and headed for the house and Granny's great cooking.

After dinner, they sat and visited for a while. Grandma and Grandpa Kessel finally gave in to the clock and said it was getting late. After goodbyes and hugs, John, Sara, and Lyle walked them to their car. Carew helped Granny load the dishwasher and cleaned the kitchen. Granny and Carew always got along famously.

TERESA HAD BEEN in a quandary all weekend since her encounter with Lyle on Thursday. She had never been affected by a young man as she had been by Lyle. She couldn't pinpoint exactly what it was about him, but he appealed to her. He was very good-looking and had an easy-going, self-assured personality with a dash of humor. "Gosh," she thought, "what am I going to do? I couldn't just volunteer my phone number or which dorm I'm in." Teresa fretted about her situation. She wanted to see him again, but she had played it too smooth. When she phoned her mother, which she did almost every Sunday night, her mood was evident. Arlene knew something was bothering her daughter. "Hon, you sound like you have the world on your shoulders."

"Oh, mom, I met a very nice boy in Bill's Bookstore," Teresa said. She told Arlene the details of her encounter and then added, "I'm sure he felt I didn't care to get into a conversation with him. He didn't ask for my phone number or what dorm I lived in, or anything. I walked away, and I should've stayed."

Arlene paused a moment, then laughingly said, "Perhaps he was tongue-tied, honey. Your good looks scared him. I have a mother's intuition that he will find a way to reach you."

"You think so?" Teresa said. "You know me, I'm not a boy-chaser, and I wouldn't have these initial feelings about just anyone."

They talked for a few minutes more, then Teresa thanked her mom and told her goodbye. She felt much better. Later, when she turned off her bedside lamp, she said a prayer asking for a little help.

Lyle's return trip to Tallahassee on Sunday afternoon was uneventful. He parked his car two blocks from his dorm and grabbed his overnight bag and the small box Granny thrust into his hands just before he drove away. Granny always surprised him with a delicious cake, pie, or cookies. He trudged up the hill, past the science building, to the dorm.

Bill Kraven was sitting at the small window desk, when Lyle walked in. "Well, the farm boy made it back again," Bill said.

"As I remember, you were sitting at that desk when I left on Friday," Lyle said. "Don't tell me you've been there all this time. If so, I'll call the *Guinness Book of World Records* and give them a scoop."

"Funny, funny, funny. My, you're sharp today," Bill said.

Lyle was reluctant to ask Bill if there had been any phone calls over the weekend. He decided that Bill would have mentioned it if there had been. Bill returned to his reading as Lyle grabbed a towel and trudged down the hall for a shower. His first class was at ten on Mondays. That would give him time to go by the registrar's office and try to get some information on Teresa.

Lyle arose at six thirty the next morning, and after shaving, he dressed and went to the cafeteria for breakfast—Lyle was a breakfast person. He returned to his room and reviewed some study notes in preparation for his philosophy class at ten. Bill left for an eight o'clock class and, as usual, was running late. A few minutes before nine, Lyle departed for the registrar's office. He had a growing anticipation as he crossed the campus for Westcott Hall.

When he told the young clerk at the registrar's service counter that he'd like to locate a Ms. Teresa Carter, she asked for his FSU ID. On showing her his card, the clerk smiled and said it would take a moment. Lyle began to feel good and was humming to himself when she returned. She handed him a student directory that had Teresa's name, dorm name, and phone number. Lyle was elated and thanked her graciously.

He found it easy to concentrate on his three classes that day. Having the information about Teresa actually put his emotions in a calm state. He had already made the decision to call her that night after dinner. All she could do would be to show disinterest or agree to see him.

Lyle picked up the phone and dialed McNee Hall, Teresa's dorm. He was nervous, but hoped for the best. A girl's pleasant voice answered, "McNee Hall, may I help you?"

"Ms. Teresa Carter, please," Lyle said, with slightly sweaty palms. The receptionist told him to please wait a moment.

He waited for what seemed an hour, although it was only about three minutes. He had begun to think she wasn't in, when her soft voice said, "Hello."

"Hi, Teresa, this is Lyle Kelly." There was a very quiet moment when Teresa heard his voice. Her heartbeat picked up markedly. "It's him," she thought. "I knew he'd call. I've got to be real calm."

"Hello, Lyle. How did you find me? I was going to give you my number last Thursday, but you didn't ask," Teresa said.

He shifted the phone to his other ear and sat down. "I found your number and address at the registrar's office. The reason I didn't ask you was my knees were knocking, and I couldn't think."

She laughed. "Well, I must admit I was afraid if I gave you my phone number, you wouldn't call, and I didn't want to disappoint myself." They continued to chat for several minutes. Lyle was feeling much better by then and felt a surge of happiness wash over him.

"I'd like to come over and see you sometime soon," Lyle said.

After a pause, Teresa said, "The only thing is, I have a history test Wednesday morning, and I've got to study for that tomorrow night. Would you like to come over Wednesday evening about seven?"

Lyle thought for a moment about his own study schedule, then said, "Sure, I'd like that."

"I'll see you then, Lyle. Good night," Teresa said.

Lyle put the phone down and sat there thinking. His life was changing rapidly. One week ago, his routine was his classes, a little social life, and going home to the farm every two weeks or so. Now, he had met a great-looking girl with a fine personality that appealed to him. She seemed to be attracted to him also. He was caught up in the moment, however, and he knew his priority was his studies.

TERESA WAS SMILING when she entered her room. Dianne Coffer, her roommate, was sitting at her desk, writing. She looked up and said, "You look like you just won the lottery. Was that the Lyle you told me about?"

"Yes, it was him. He went to the registrar's office and got my phone number. It's apparent I misjudged his tenacity. He's coming over Wednesday evening. We're going to visit in the parlor and get acquainted. I hope I can concentrate on my classes 'til then."

Dianne arose from her chair and walked over to Teresa, put her hand on her shoulder, looked into her eyes, and said, "Teresa, it's about time you allowed a good man to come into your life. From what you've told me this past weekend, he seems to be the unique type you need. I'll say a little prayer for you." She hugged Teresa briefly and added, "Look at it this way—you two were evidently meant to meet each other, so relax and enjoy your meeting."

"That's one reason I'm happy we became roommates. You have an understanding of people. I truly appreciate your encouragement," Teresa said.

Dianne smiled and went to her desk. As she sat down, she said, "I'm very lucky to have you as a friend."

Tuesday and Wednesday were an eternity for Lyle. After an early dinner at the cafeteria, he and Bill Kraven, his roommate, walked back to the dorm. They were silent for a while; then Bill laughed and said, "Well, the farm boy goes to meet the city girl tonight. You'd better put on a fresh pair of overalls and slick back your hair." Lyle smiled and gave Bill a little push off the sidewalk.

"I must admit this meeting has been on my mind since last Thursday, the day I first saw her at Bill's Bookstore. I wonder what her reaction will be when she finds I come from a farming family," Lyle said.

Bill thought for a moment, then said, "I'll be serious for just a nanosecond, Lyle. From what little you've told your old roommate about it, it appears she is highly interested in you and probably wouldn't care if you were an undertaker."

After a shower and shave, Lyle stood in front of his open closet and pondered what to wear. He didn't like to wear a coat and tie unless it was a very formal affair, and even then he felt like a mummy. Teresa would have to accept him as one who preferred to be casual.

Dressed in chinos, a blue denim sports shirt, and wearing casual tan walkers, he headed toward McNee Hall. As he neared the large four-story brick building, he felt slightly nervous.

Teresa had been ready for a half hour, but she would never admit that to Lyle. Dianne had watched and smiled as "calm" Teresa changed her mind three times on what to wear. After putting on two different outfits, she finally settled on a simple summer casual dress and donned a pair of sandals. As she opened the door to go down to the parlor, it was as planned, 7:05.

Lyle had told the receptionist that he was expected by Teresa Carter at seven. The pleasant-looking, freckle-faced girl told him to please have a chair. He had arrived at ten 'til seven. Approximately fifteen minutes had passed, when a soft-voiced female said hello. He quickly pulled his eyes off the magazine he had been scanning and looked up and saw Teresa smiling down at him. "She's beautiful," Lyle thought. He grinned, arose from his chair, and said, "Hi, Teresa, you look great." As he spoke, he reached out, and they shook hands.

"Let's sit on the far side of the room, Lyle, where those large couches are. We'll be away from this traffic area and it will be quieter," Teresa said. Lyle agreed and followed her across the lobby. Teresa sat at the end of a large overstuffed couch. Lyle sat across from her in a single lounge chair. They talked for about an hour, each telling the other about their families and themselves. Teresa was almost hypnotized by Lyle's voice as he told about his dad, mom, Granny, Carew, and Red, and a few details about the farm and his attachment to it.

In turn, Teresa related her closeness to her mother and even a little about Enrique. She wanted Lyle to know she was leery of her stepfather, although her mother seemed to be happy with him. Teresa also mentioned her sister in Naples, Florida. Lyle was entranced with her expressive, soft voice. However, the few details she gave about Enrique made him wonder about the man.

At a pause in the conversation, Lyle asked her if she wanted to walk over to the Student Union building for a Coke. She happily agreed and, with Lyle following, went over to the receptionist to sign out.

They walked across the campus, talking and laughing, each closely attentive to the other. After about an hour of listening to some soft rock music, sipping their Cokes, and more conversation, they agreed it was time to leave. The walk back to Teresa's dorm did not take enough time, Lyle thought. He had no idea that she felt the same way. Soon, they arrived at McNee Hall and stood off to one side of the entranceway.

"Lyle, it was a very nice evening. You are an interesting person, and the Kelly farm sounds great," Teresa said.

He stood there, feeling very relaxed and thankful he had met her. "Well, Teresa, it wasn't a fancy evening, but it sure was enjoyable." He reached for her hand, and she was quick to respond. As he held her hand, he continued, "I sure would like to see you again soon."

"And I would like that very much," She said. All during this time, they continued holding hands. Lyle finally, slowly and reluctantly, withdrew his hand and asked her if Friday night would be okay. She said that would be great. They agreed upon a time and then told each other good night. Teresa's eyes were sparkling, and she had a beautiful smile on her face as she walked to the door. She stopped and gave him a slight, almost imperceptible wave, then walked inside. All the way back to his dorm, he was ecstatic. He knew he was "hooked" and he liked the feeling.

CHAPTER SEVEN

SEVERAL MONTHS PASSED; and early spring was painting the grass, trees, and shrubs with fresh green and flowers with an array of colors. Another planting and growing time of the year had begun. Carew was in the pickup truck returning from the outer fields after examining the young green beans, peas, and turnips. Winter had been a dry one, and he, John, and Red had run the sprinkler system quite often. He glanced out the passenger side window as he drove east to turn onto the main north-south road to the barn and saw an ominous blue-black sky to the south. Carew immediately stopped the truck and got out to look closely at the approaching clouds. He could hear the rumbling of thunder. He saw several quick flashes of lightning embedded deep in the larger mass of clouds. "I hope we get a good soaking rain out of this," Carew thought. He got back into the pickup and drove to the barn. A cool, light breeze began to blow as he walked to the house to find John and Red.

John had finished running the milkers, and Red was stowing the milk in the ice house, as they called it. When he walked out the door, he heard a rumble of thunder. He looked to the south and saw the dark clouds. Carew saw him and called out, "Looks good, doesn't it?"

"It sure does," John said. He walked over to the pickup and opened the door. "Let's see if we can pick up a weather report."

Even though the truck had been through some rough years, the radio still worked. John tuned to a station in Panama City as Carew climbed into the seat beside him. They waited while two commercials played. After a public service announcement reminding listeners to obey school-zone speed limits, the announcer gave the local and Panhandle weather. He described a large thunderstorm twenty miles north of Panama City, moving directly north into Mason County. In its path were the communities of Crystal Lake, Wausen, Red Hill, and Danaville, the county seat. The storm had appeared within a short time, without the normal buildup, which usually required an hour or so. The announcer stated their Doppler radar had only recently picked up the system and was showing tops of forty thousand feet. Wind gusts of thirty to forty knots with heavy rain and hail expected. He went on to say that the storm is very much like the one last June, a very unusual system. It is well-formed and moving at approximately twenty-five to thirty knots. He emphasized the possibility of a tornado, but the Doppler did not show any sign of a tornado "hook" signature at this time.

John looked at Carew and said, "You know, this storm looks a lot like the one we had last year."

"It sure does. According to that weather report, its track is the same. The suddenness of it is eerie."

"Well, we better check things and batten the hatches. Red's in town at Kessel's, picking up a load of fertilizer and chicken feed. I hope they don't load him 'til this storm blows over," John said.

Carew got out of the pickup and went over to one of the tractors, climbed up, and started the engine. John parked the pickup in the large barn. Carew followed. Soon they had most everything done. Making sure the chickens were safe, they trotted to the back porch just as it began to rain. As they stood there watching the daylight disappear, the rain turned to small hail. Granny called to them from the kitchen door, "You two get yourself in here and keep Sara and me company." John and Carew entered the kitchen just as the hail intensified. It was hitting the roof of the house and porch with a loud intensity. Granny spoke again, with excitement in her voice, "Those hailstones are now as large as golf balls!"

SARA HAD BEEN monitoring the kitchen radio—static and all—during the storm. She had kept a running commentary to John and Carew of the various weather comments from the radio announcer. "It's just like last time," she said. "They can't explain the sudden appearance of this storm. The weatherman told how he remembered the unique storm last year and how this one was almost a duplicate of that one." Sara didn't like thunderstorms, and it was noticeable.

"I'll agree to that," John said.

"Yeah, this one has more lightning, and it has hail," Carew said.

THE HAIL ABATED after about fifteen minutes, and within an additional twenty minutes, the lightning, thunder, and wind waned considerably. The storm was moving on north. They all walked out on the back porch to survey the grounds and buildings. The ground was covered with hailstones—a white blanket that looked like snow. There were leaves and smaller limbs mixed with the ice. John kissed Sara on the cheek and told her to relax.

"Carew, we'd better get moving and inspect all roofs and windows, then drive out to the fields and see how much damage we have to our young crops," John said.

Carew put on his cap and said, "Yeah, I got uptight when the hail began to fall, especially as the hailstones got larger."

After checking all the buildings, looking in on the pigs and chickens, and finding most all the cows were in the cow barn, with a few that had ventured outside when the hail let up, the two men got into the pickup. They drove around the main barn, through the yard gate, and started down the center road to the fields.

In a few moments, Carew spoke excitedly, "John, stop the truck! Look at that!" John's eyes followed Carew's pointing finger. "The hailstones haven't fallen on these fields. They seemed to have stopped at the row headers."

"Yeah, I don't see any hail down any of the rows on either side of this road." He put the truck in gear and drove slowly. They both were gaping. After passing several fields, John stopped the pickup again. "Let's take time and drive the perimeter of all the fields. I don't know what to say. I've never seen or heard of anything happening like this, and I'll bet no one has. It's not a fluke. Look how the road is covered, but the hail stopped in almost a straight line at the edges. This really gives me the willies."

Carew was quiet for a moment, then he said, "John, it's as if some directed force protected our fields." Both men became quiet, each involved in their own thoughts, each trying to understand what they were seeing. Over the next few moments, the central part of the fields became brighter. They got out of the truck, looked into the sky, and immediately saw the lower end of a rainbow pointing downward, almost on top of them. The angle of perspective was foreshortened because of their being so close to the center of the fields, but both of them could make out the band of colors which faded twenty or thirty feet above the ground.

"THIS IS SOMETHING," Carew said. "John, we're witnessing something other than just a weather phenomenon. Except for the hail, this storm was just like the one last June. An' the rainbow seems to be in the same location. It's huge!"

John was dumbfounded. He stood there looking at both the rainbow and the hail. "Come on, Carew, let's ride to the far west end of the fields and look at the rainbow from a better perspective." In a few minutes, they arrived at the west property fence line and parked. As they stood by the truck, they looked at the magnificent rainbow with its one-half arc—just like a year ago. The two men didn't speak; they just tried to absorb it. After fifteen minutes or so, the rainbow began to slowly fade. John faced Carew and said, "There's some kind of message here, and I can't begin to understand it."

"I was thinking the same, John," Carew said. "In fact, I never quite forgot last year—it has been in the back of my mind all these months. Now that I've seen this storm, and especially the same kind of rainbow again, it's uncanny. The only difference is the hail. It seems to emphasize our fields by how the hailstones stopped at the beginning of all the rows. John, that alone has got to have great significance."

John shook his head and, with a serious look on his face, got back into the pickup with Carew and drove slowly to the house. "Except for family, Carew, don't mention anything about the hail in these fields. Until we can understand why and how this happened, it's best to keep it quiet. I'm sure the rainbow was seen by many people, and it alone is gonna raise enough questions."

"You're right John. I hope the gossip chain in Mason County doesn't get out of hand. We ought to get in touch with Lyle and let him know what's happened.

John was quiet for a moment, then said, "That's a good idea."

"Hey, guys," Red said and waved as John and Carew drove up and stopped beside the main barn. The hail had just about melted. Sara and Granny were standing beside Red with expectant looks on their faces. They walked over to where John and Carew were leaning against the truck. Red continued speaking, "What's up with you two? You look like you're thinking too hard. Me and about half of downtown saw the rainbow."

Granny spoke up, "John, we saw the rainbow too and noticed its location, but what else did you see?" She knew him like the back of her hand. She knew he and Carew had seen something significant. Sara was all ears.

John looked toward the fields and said, "It was strange, mama. The hail didn't fall on our fields. It fell along the main road and all the access drives and around the perimeter fence, but it didn't fall on our fields." As he said this, he turned back and faced all of them and slowly shook his head. Sara had a little flutter in her throat. Granny stood there dumbfounded. Red looked over at Carew, who was nodding his head in agreement with John's comment. All of them stood there talking, almost in hushed tones, for a few minutes, then walked toward the back porch. As they approached the house, Red looked toward the front drive and quietly told them that Sheriff Bernam had just turned in off the county road. There were two other cars farther behind. John stopped, as did the other three, and waited for the sheriff to drive around to the side driveway and stop. John and Carew walked over to the blue-and-white patrol car and greeted him as he opened the door and pushed his six-foot-five-inch body to a standing position.

"Hi, John, Carew, everyone." He nodded at Sara, Granny and Red as he shook John's hand. "Looks like you folks had a little weather," Bernam said. John and Claude Bernam had known each other for fifteen years. Before becoming sheriff eight years ago, he had been a state game warden, working out of Mason County.

John shook Claude's hand and replied, "Yes, it was moderately rough for a short time. Luckily, everything is okay." He was still edgy, and he didn't want to show it. John didn't want the sheriff to know about the hail in the fields.

The other two cars had pulled up and parked off to one side, beneath a large oak tree. Grandpa and Grandma Kessel got out of the first car. Granny, Sara, and John went to meet them while Carew and the sheriff continued to talk. Marvin Gardner stepped out of the last car and hurriedly walked over to say hello to the Kellys and the Kessels.

After everyone had greeted each other, John said he had discovered that the way to have company was to build a little ol' thunderstorm, throw in a pretty rainbow, and they would come. Everyone laughed and headed for the large back porch. Granny had told them she was going to put coffee on. Sara stayed behind with John.

All of them, except Granny and Grandma Kessel, who were in the kitchen preparing the coffee, stood around on the back porch, talking about the day's event. Everyone kept looking out toward the fields. John was relieved that other than wet grounds, small limbs, and leaves, the yard showed no signs of hail.

MARVIN GARDNER WALKED over to John and Carew, who had been quietly discussing the importance of informing Lyle of the events and asking him to come home for the weekend—Friday was two days away. As Marvin got near, John asked him how business was at the drugstore, thinking he could perhaps steer the conversation that was about to take place, away from the storm and get him to talk about himself, which Marvin liked to do. John knew Marvin well enough to know that he was an inquisitive man and liked to gossip. "You Kellys are the luckiest people in the world. To be so close to the end of that rainbow—that must have been something," Marvin said. "I saw the one last year as I stood in front of my store. I saw the one today from almost the same spot. The rainbow today was an exact duplicate of last year's, just like the storm was. John, from the viewpoint of all of you that were here, it must have been spectacular."

John explained the events of the storm, from the time Carew spotted the approaching dark clouds, the lightning, the rain, and the wind. He omitted any mention about the hail. Marvin was quick to comment, however, that he had noticed small amounts of melting hail just before he turned off the county road. John quickly said the hail was a minor problem and had evidently fallen in a small area.

"I feel like Marvin," Sheriff Bernam said. He had edged up to the three men as Marvin had been talking. "Last year, I saw only the fading remnants of that rainbow. This time, I came out of Kessel's Farm Supply and noticed several people who had stopped and were looking north. I almost dropped my cigar when I saw it. I knew it was in your vicinity, so, being as curious as I am, I decided to come out here and see how all of you took this event. It must have been something to have been so close to it." John assured him that it was a beautiful sight, and he and the others would never forget it.

After cake and coffee, Sheriff Bernam and Marvin Gardner returned to town. The Kessels stayed for another hour or so. In the meantime, while Grandpa Kessel was talking to Red, John made a discreet motion for Carew to follow him out to the barn. Both grandmas were in the kitchen. "You know, Carew," John said as they stopped at the side barnyard fence. He put a foot up on the lower cross-plank and leaned on the fence as he looked toward the fields. "I've always respected your viewpoint and even your advice on matters around here. You and I have come a long way together. What happened last year was sort of a fluke, we thought. This time we had the same kind of storm. Identical, you might say, except with more impressive results. The rainbow in itself is mind-boggling, but the hail and its pattern in the fields is beyond comprehension. What's your opinion about all this?"

Carew was also looking at the fields and John could tell he was reaching way down inside of himself for meaning to what he had witnessed. Carew didn't speak for a few long moments, then he said, "John, what you and I witnessed with the hail, and the four of us witnessed with the rainbow, in my heart I know it has to be spiritual. I think I became convinced of that, when I saw that the hail didn't fall on our young plants—the corn, beans, tomatoes—all of it. The rainbow, after each of the two storms, had the same odd shape, seemed to be the same size, and pointed downward at the same place in the middle of our fields. What are the odds on that? It seemed as if each one was sending us a message of some kind."

To this point, there had not been time for the five of them to sit and discuss the event. John planned to broach the subject when they all had dinner. At the present time, however, he felt as if he and Carew were sharing something unique—something that was in the process of changing them, the farm, the family, perhaps even Danaville, and the entire county. He nodded in agreement with what Carew had said, and added, "Let's call Lyle tonight and see if he can come this weekend. The family needs to determine how to go about finding an explanation. I'd like to invite Reverend Butler to join us. I think we need his input."

At that time, Red joined them, saying the Kessels had departed to return to the store. John then told Red what he and Carew had discussed. "Now, I think the three of us should go out to where the rainbow was pointing downward and look around. I don't know what I expect us to find, if anything at all, but it won't hurt to look."

They got into the pickup and rode to the center of the fields.

CHAPTER EIGHT

ENRIQUE LUIS CRUZ was born in Cuba in 1957. When he was eleven years old, he escaped to the United States with his father and mother, in 1968. He grew up in Miami, Florida, and ultimately attended the University of Miami, graduating with a degree in marketing. After two years with a medium-sized grocery-supply company, he applied for an advertised position as assistant marketing manager of canned goods with a large food wholesale supply company, the Gelb Corporation. Though he was only twenty-four, his self-confidence and evident drive got him the job. The food-supply business was tough, competitive, and full of "deals," especially when it came to shelf position of the products, in-store advertising, and newspaper ad incentives. Enrique quickly learned his job, plus the art of manipulating people. After six years, he asked for and received a transfer to the company's Tampa branch. In the beginning, he held the same position as he had in Miami, but the company did increase his salary, with the understanding he would become marketing manager for central and north Florida within one year. Enrique was very pleased with the company and his job. As time passed, he kept his eyes and ears open and made a point of becoming acquainted with key people in the company. One of those people was Frank Bovitz, vice president of finance. Bovitz was a mover and shaker, and he knew a lot of powerful and influential people in the state. Enrique had his compass set for a course beyond where he was now, and Frank Bovitz could be very useful. Three months after meeting and becoming friends with Frank, the company made Enrique their marketing manager.

Enrique had an appetite for money, over and beyond friends. Through Frank, he became acquainted with Alejo Gomez, a wealthy Cuban who lived in Ft. Lauderdale and operated a network of loan companies and pawnshops, used-car lots, and bail-bond offices from Jacksonville to Miami. Enrique had a strong feeling that Gomez had other business activities that were not discussed, even by Frank Bovitz.

After a year and a half of success in marketing management, Enrique decided it would improve his position in corporate life if he were to marry. He had thought about this before but kept putting off, trying to find someone who would put him first. As independent as women appeared to him, Enrique thought that was impossible. He wanted a woman who would easily be accepted by his company management and would not question his long hours and frequent trips throughout the state. In turn, he would show her affection and respect. Enrique felt he could never love anyone. The word "love" made him uncomfortable. He realized he must give a portion of his feelings to a woman, but he could never give all of himself to a wife or to anyone. It was important to him to have a marriage that looked good and felt comfortable, especially around his cronies.

His company always threw a huge Christmas party, and other than the employees, select customers and other guests were invited. The company president would always fly up from Miami with several board members and officers and their wives. The Tampa Racquet Club was a favorite for the yearly bash.

Enrique had met several women over a six-month period, but to no avail. In his mind, each was a washout. Then it happened. Janet Kaplan, his secretary, introduced him to her close friend, Arlene Carter. Arlene wasn't enthused about dating because she had a comfortable life, running a very successful accounting business and raising an eight-year-old daughter. She didn't want to disappoint Janet, her long-time best friend, so she accepted.

Arlene went to the party with Janet and her husband, David. It wasn't long before Enrique appeared at the table. Janet was relieved because she knew how unpredictable he was, especially around women. She introduced Arlene to him and hoped for the best. Enrique was very impressed with Arlene. He thought she was extremely attractive and had a magnetic personality, but being his usual egotistical self, he remained slightly distant. Arlene thought him to be a good-looking man, although reserved. Before the evening had passed, their conversation had warmed and they even danced several times.

As the party was breaking up, Enrique asked Arlene if he could call her later. She was inwardly pleased and gave him her business card. He liked the idea of her owning her own business and being independent. He also had no negative feelings about her having a daughter. He would judge the eight-year-old later.

On the way home, Janet and David remarked to Arlene how well she seemed to enjoy the party. Arlene admitted to herself the she had had a good time and that Enrique was interesting and a smooth dancer. Janet smiled. She knew by Arlene's silence that for starters, the evening was a success.

"NO, MR. KELLY, Lyle isn't here. He should be in about ten o'clock," Bill said. John asked him how his classes were going and got the expected "everything is movin' along," or some such answer. John asked him to have Lyle call him whenever he got in. He assured Bill there was no emergency. Wishing him a good night, John hung up.

Lyle walked in the door about 10:20. Bill told him of his dad's call. Lyle felt a twinge of apprehension because his dad never called at night. Bill sensed Lyle's concern and explained there was no emergency. With his mind more at ease, he picked up the phone and dialed home. He and his dad conversed for about ten minutes. The first thing John told his son was not to let Bill know the gist of their conversation. His dad went on to briefly explain why Lyle should come home for the weekend so the family could discuss the matter. Lyle could readily tell that his dad had been affected by the events of that afternoon and wanted to hear all the details and help any way he could. He told his dad he would see him early Friday afternoon. On putting the phone down, Bill asked if everything at home was okay. Lyle, for effect, gave him a slight smile and said it was just a farm matter that needed collective attention by the family. Bill returned to his reading, seeming satisfied that all was well with his roommate.

Teresa was very understanding when Lyle told her that he had to go home for the weekend to help his dad with a family matter. He assured her that everyone in his family was well, that this was a farm-related matter only, and he would give her the details when he returned on Sunday.

Lyle arrived home around two thirty on Friday. It was good to see the family again, even though it had been only two weeks since he had last seen them, and he could never get enough of the farm. He was anxious to hear the details about the storm and whatever it was about it that bothered his dad and, evidently, Carew also. Even Lyle, having experienced the unusual storm of a year ago, had a strange feeling that this one was guided by some force that meant to get their attention.

The presence of Rev. Wade Butler was noteworthy and further convinced Lyle that one thing his dad was considering was a spiritual element.

After everyone shook hands, Lyle hugged Granny. They gathered in the living room where it was quiet and comfortable. Lyle had assumed earlier, the discussion about the storm would be held the next day, but it was evident that his dad was intent on understanding what was happening. John told the group that Red was running a bit late, due to an uncooperative hog that had escaped his pen. Almost on cue, Red came into the room and apologized for holding up the meeting as he shook hands with Lyle and Reverend Butler.

Granny had prepared a platter of fresh baked cookies and a large pot of coffee. The group sat down with their refreshments and became quiet—an unstated signal to John that it was time to start.

John cleared his throat and said, "Lyle, we all have discussed our unique experience at great length for the past two days. We now need your and Reverend Butler's input after Carew and I relate what we saw last Wednesday. Before we get into the details, however, I think we should agree to not discuss this with anyone outside of the family. Sheriff Bernam and Marvin Gardener drove out here just as the storm was moving on. They stayed a short while, and after seeing the farm was still standing, they went back to town. Be wary around Bernam and Gardner, they both tend to talk a lot. Also, Lyle, your grandma and grandpa Kessel came and would be here today, except they had to be in Panama City on business. We must brief them as soon as possible, perhaps tomorrow night. If approached by Jim Summers or any representative of the *Mason County News* or, for that matter, any county or state official—and it could come to that—refer them to me, Lyle, or Carew. The same goes for TV and newspaper people at large. I have no idea what we in this room are going to find out in our investigation, but we sure don't need a bunch of people tramping around on our farm." Everyone nodded in agreement.

Although everyone in the room, except Lyle and Reverend Butler, knew all the details about the storm, they sat with rapt attention as John continued speaking. "The storm was like the one we had a year ago; in fact, it was almost an exact replica. It was uncanny. The only difference was that this one produced hail." Then John told Lyle and the reverend how he and Carew observed the pattern of the hail on the ground in the fields, how astounded they were that not one hailstone fell among any of the crops, how the hail covered the ground on the main access road and completely around the perimeter of the farm, right up to where the crop rows started, but none of the crops were touched. When the storm moved north and started breaking up, a large rainbow with an odd shape appeared, just like it had last year. It was brighter and was pointing downward in the center of the fields, just like the first one. It faded within ten minutes or so.

Lyle looked from his dad over to Reverend Butler. The reverend was sitting with his head slightly down, looking at the floor in front of him as if to find a neutral space in which to concentrate his thinking. Everyone else was quiet also. Lyle's mind was racing, trying to comprehend the event, especially his dad's description of the hail. Carew was standing at a window with his hands in his pockets, looking out at the front yard. Lyle broke the silence, "Carew, what's your impression of what has happened?"

Carew turned back toward the room and looked first at Lyle, then at John and Reverend Butler. "At first, I thought it was some kind of weather phenomenon—I even thought that of last year's storm also—but when I saw the hail and the same kind of rainbow, I knew it was somethin' else. Somethin' that was beyond nature itself." John nodded his head almost imperceptibly.

Reverend Butler spoke up, "When we all came into this room and sat down, I wasn't aware of all the details of the storm and the amount of impact it has had on all of you. But now, I think it incumbent upon all of us to ask God for his guidance in understanding these happenings." The reverend stood, and the others also rose from their chairs. His prayer was delivered with a passion that reflected the enormity of what had occurred. Reverend Butler was fully aware that a message of great magnitude from God had been delivered, or was in the process of being delivered to the Kellys.

DURING ANOTHER HOUR of discussion, it was agreed that John, Lyle, Carew, and Red would closely examine the ground area where the rainbow had pointed. Carew suggested some soil samples be taken for testing to see if anything unusual turned up. John asked Lyle if he could have the samples examined by FSU's geology department—without divulging too many details. Lyle understood his dad's meaning and said he'd give it his best shot.

Red suggested that perhaps some of the young green beans, which occupy ten acres located in the center of the fields, ought to be collected and examined by the Florida Agriculture Department. John thought that was a good idea. It was important to have these things done without divulging what they had witnessed.

Reverend Butler declined John's dinner invitation because of two hospital patients he had to visit. Red also departed soon afterward. He was on his way to see Jenny, his fiancée. Within an hour, Granny called Sara and the three men to dinner.

Lyle awoke the next morning faintly hearing his dad and mom talking in the hall. Soon there was a light rap on the door as John Kelly opened it only enough to accommodate his body. "Good mornin', son. I thought we'd get an early start after breakfast. You, Carew, and me will see what we can find in those fields, if anything. We'll collect some plant and soil samples, as we discussed last night, for you to take back to Tallahassee tomorrow. Granny said she'd like to pack everything so that it stays moist. I hate it that you will have to cut your Monday classes in order to get our samples into the hands of the experts. I'll give you a signed check to cover any lab fees, labor charges, or materials they might want compensation for. Hopefully, there won't be a big expense involved in this or any future tests we may need. If there is, we'll find a way to cover them. I think the important thing is to keep others from sticking their noses into what has happened and what we are doing."

"Okay, Dad. I can handle things in Tallahassee. In fact, having one of the finest university libraries in the south at our disposal, as well as the Internet, gives us access to endless information. Tell Mom and Granny I'm starving. I'll grab a shower and shave and be right down."

As the door closed, Lyle sensed his dad was more uneasy than he showed. The enormity of what confronted the Kelly family was felt by all of them. It would not be an easy task finding a meaning to what had happened. Lyle headed for the shower with his thoughts racing. His mind turned to Teresa—he yearned to see her. There was much to tell her, and he needed input from her

regarding the strange events at the farm. She possessed an
outstanding ability to analyze situations and problems. Like him,
she relied on a spiritual dimension in her psyche from which to
draw insights and make value judgments. Lyle knew that God had
brought them together, and he felt strongly that she believed the
same thing.

An hour later, Lyle, his dad, and Carew got out of the pickup
after parking at a prearranged spot on the access path adjacent to
the three-acre bean field—as close as possible to the dead-center
of the crop fields.

They stood looking at the bean field. After several moments
of silence, John spoke, "Fellas, I have no idea whatsoever what
we are looking for. I suggest we spread out and walk abreast,
maybe forty or fifty feet apart, and see what we find. Keep your
mind and your eyes open." The three of them walked slowly, not
knowing what to expect, if anything. After about thirty minutes,
Carew held up his hand and called a halt. He dropped down on
one knee, looked closely at the ground in front of him, then raised
his eyes, and looked farther down the rows of young bean plants.

"What've you found?" asked Lyle.

"Come take a look," Carew answered. John and Lyle, readily
noticing the excitement in Carew's voice, walked quickly over
to him.

"Get behind me and look over my shoulder, and I'll point out
what I see. See how the soil is slightly darker with a definite edge
curving through the rows and away to our left? It's like an arc.
Now look closer—it comes toward us, but curving and passing in
front of and away from us."

John and Lyle finally saw the edge of the darker soil as it
curved toward them and then away. The curve of the consistent
arc was slight—meaning the arc or circle was rather large.

"Let's walk along the edge of it and see where we end up.
Carew, you go to the left. Lyle and I will go to the right and see if
it is a circle."

They slowly walked along the edge of the darker soil, which
obliquely crossed under the rows of beans. After approximately

forty minutes, the three of them met with the realization they had traced what seemed a perfect circle. Spreading out farther apart, the men walked up and down the rows to determine if the soil was consistent in its darkness and found that it was.

All three were standing motionless, looking at the area they had defined. A shiver ran down Carew's back. He had a deep indescribable feeling that the circle was caused by the storm, and the rainbow pointed it out to them. This was no freak of nature. It had to be God's work. He looked over at John and Lyle; he guessed they were feeling the same.

John slowly looked left and right, surveying the bean field. He turned, facing Carew and Red, shaking his head in disbelief at what they had just discovered, and yet knowing that God was giving them further instructions. "We have to ask him for more help," he thought. "I think we ought to take soil and plant samples from the outside and inside of the circle. Lyle will take them to the state agriculture department for testing. We'll work out a way to hopefully get some information without giving any hint as to what's going on. I pray. Come on, guys, there're some burlap bags in the back of the truck. Let's get those samples, then go back to work. Feed is needed in the milking barn, and I want to replace the generator on the small tractor."

They squeezed into the pickup and silently drove back to the main barn, each of them thinking about what they had seen.

CHAPTER NINE

LYLE ARRIVED BACK on campus around 4:00 p.m. on Sunday. It took two trips from his car to carry his clothes, overnight bag, and the cardboard box with the bean-field samples to his room. It was a warm, sunny afternoon, and he was perspiring when he closed the door the second time. He placed the sample box containing the bean plants and a small bag of soil on the floor against the wall under the window. It would be safe there, out of the small room's traffic pattern. He knew Bill would be curious about the box when he returned from his weekend trip visiting his family in Jacksonville. Lyle had decided to tell him that the samples were for routine examination to determine the quality level of the soil and bean plants. That was true, but he did not want to disclose any details about the occurrence at the farm to anyone except Teresa.

He picked up the phone and dialed her number, thinking of all there was to tell her and wondering how she would react. He was anxious to hear her voice.

Teresa answered the phone, "Oh, Lyle, I'm so glad you're back. It seems you've been away for weeks. Can you come over this evening?"

"I had hoped I could. I've got a lot to tell you. There's so much that has happened at the farm, things I need your input on. I don't mean to sound mysterious, but the story I tell you will truly get your attention. I'll be over in thirty minutes. We'll get something to eat later."

"He does sound mysterious," Teresa thought. She would have to be cautious when talking to or around Dianne, her roommate, about Lyle's family and the farm. She had a strong feeling that something very unusual had occurred, and Lyle had truly been affected by it. As Teresa sat there thinking, she felt butterflies in her stomach. It's a good thing Dianne is down the hall, she thought, as she got up to change clothes.

There were a few girls with and without dates in the parlor when Teresa stepped from the elevator. She saw Lyle walking toward her, and as they met, they clasped hands and smiled. "Lyle, I've missed you so much. Let's get out of here. There're too many people around."

"I was going to suggest the same," Lyle said. "It's a nice late afternoon. We can find a bench under the trees and have a little privacy." Teresa squeezed his hand and agreed.

The first thing Lyle did, after they found a bench and sat down, was to kiss Teresa. She returned his kiss with fervor. "I love you very much, Teresa, and I need you." "And I love you, Lyle. You mean everything to me." Lyle turned slightly so that he could look into her eyes. He wanted her to grasp the magnitude of what he was going to say about the happenings at the farm. She looked at him expectantly. He then started to relate the events of the two storms. The first one, he explained, seemed not to be unusual, except for the quickness of its buildup and the strange shape of the rainbow afterward. Teresa was totally locked on to his every word. The second storm, he explained, was almost a duplicate of the first one. Its track was the same and its level of ferocity was about the same, except it hailed. He told her that the sheriff and Marvin Gardner, the owner of Gardner's Drugstore, had shown up right after the rainbow had dissipated. All of the family answered the two men's questions, or reacted to their comments, without revealing any details about the hail or the rainbow. There was a long pause; then Lyle, as if searching for the best way to explain what he, his dad, and Carew found in the bean field, stood up and started slowly pacing back and forth in front of Teresa. His voice was softer as he continued to speak—as if someone would overhear him, although there was no one within two hundred feet. When he told her about the hail stopping at the edge of the fields, and the slightly darker soil and its circular pattern in the center of the bean field where the rainbow had appeared to point down, she stood up and touched his arm. Lyle turned and pulled her to him. She was so affected by what he had told her, so full of awe, until she had to tell him.

"There is no doubt in my mind that what you and your family experienced is spiritual and holds some yet to be explained powerful meaning. It's as if something is being pointed out to you."

He held her close and spoke softly, "I felt exactly that way when I saw what had happened in the fields, especially the darker soil area in the bean field—its circular shape. I had goose bumps then, and I've got 'em now. The other night during our family discussion, Reverend Butler said it is evident that God is sending a message to us, a message of great magnitude. We all agreed with the reverend that we not discuss details of the two storms with anyone outside the family. Teresa, Dad readily agreed when I told him you were to be included as part of the family." She tightened her arms around him, but said nothing—she was deep in thought about all that Lyle had told her. She too now had goose bumps.

As they walked across the campus to his car, he told her about the samples he had brought from the farm and what he planned to do. He explained that his dad and Carew held a straw of hope that the results of tests on the beans and the soil might offer some kind of clue as to the "why" of the event.

Later, they faced each other in a booth, eating grilled chicken salads at Munchies, a favorite with students. They were rather quiet, but talked about family and school. Each of them would do a lot of thinking on their own, along with praying, later in the evening.

His roommate was sitting at his desk when Lyle entered the room. They greeted each other, both commenting on a good visit home. Lyle thought, "If Bill only knew what kind of weekend I had, he'd never believe it."

"I noticed the boxes under the window. Did your granny send some of her famous cookies or a cake?' Bill said with a smiling anticipation.

"No, not this time. Those are plant and soil samples that my dad wanted examined by the state agriculture department. It's routine for farmers to have this done periodically to check for early onset of infestation to plants and acid buildup in the soil. Just being cautious," Lyle said. Bill shrugged and commented he was disappointed. He thought Granny's baking was the best. He turned back to his studies, and Lyle got ready for bed. Tomorrow was going to be a long day.

Lyle lay there trying to slow down his racing mind and relax. His thoughts were on his family and Teresa. How difficult it was going to be for all of them to deal with the phenomenon that had occurred. He prayed silently for a long time and then drifted off to sleep.

ON MONDAY MORNING, after Friday's storm, Marvin Gardner was sitting on a high stool behind the pharmacy counter in his drugstore, closely scanning Saturday's edition of the *Mason County News*. It didn't take very long to go through the eight pages of county politics, two fender benders, the Danaville and Varnum society page, high school sports, and a few other items. On page 8, at the bottom of the last column, there was mention of the storm, but with little detail. It did relate how it was almost a duplicate of the one that happened about the same time last year, but no mention was made of the oddly shaped rainbow. The storm of last Friday, and especially the rainbow, had been on Marvin's mind constantly since it happened. His trip out to the Kelly farm and the noticeable reluctance of the Kellys to say much about what happened only heated up his nosey mind. He put the paper aside and picked up his phone and dialed Jim Summers, the owner and publisher of the paper.

"Hello, Jim. This is Marv at the drugstore. What's new in the news business?" Marvin listened patiently while Summers ran through his worn-out litany of greeting.

"How you doing, Marv? Still pushing pills to all those blue-haired ladies? Gonna run a new ad in next Wednesday's paper? Just kidding, Marv, just kidding. You're one of my best advertisers. What can I do for you?"

Marvin smiled to himself, knowing that Jim was only half kidding. It was evident that the editor, or whichever staff member wrote the small article about the storm, didn't give it much thought. "All's well with me and the pill-pushing, Jim. I just wanted to know if there was more information on the storm last Friday than you printed in your paper. You, or the reporter who wrote the piece, didn't happen to talk to the weather service in Panama City, did you?"

There was a moment of silence before Jim answered. "It was just a summer storm, Marv. You talk like it was something extraordinary—something that merited a team of reporters and the story run on page 1." Marvin caught the sarcastic tone in Jim's voice. He knew that Jim Summers was dedicated to his newspaper and its responsibility to the community. He wished he had phrased his question a little differently, perhaps starting with an inquiry about Jim's health or the status of his family.

"Aw, Jim, I'm sorry I riled you up. There's no one in this county that has more respect for the *Mason County News* than I do. I guess my interest about that storm and its twin last summer has me excited and curious. I was hoping that someone at the paper had seen what I, Sheriff Bernam, and a handful of others saw. I've got a hunch we didn't see it all, but the Kelly family did—and they're being mum about it. Now, when wouldn't someone talk your head off about the weather? Bernam and I even went out to their farm, checking up to see if they needed any help and also to find out more about that odd rainbow. The Kellys were nice and friendly, like they always are, but still, there was something they chose not to talk about . . . I could read it in John Kelly's eyes."

Jim Summers, like many in Danaville, knew how Marvin Gardner liked to talk. He also knew that being the owner and pharmacist of a drugstore, Marv was overly inquisitive and an open conduit to gossip—local politicians and the other merchants watched what they said around Marv. Jim's newspaperman's curiosity had been tweaked. He would quietly run an inquiry about the storm, but he would say nothing to Marv about it.

Remembering that Gardner's Drugstore was a steady advertiser, Jim accepted Marv's attempt at an apology. After they both talked a moment longer, Jim put down the phone and started making some notes.

IT WAS THURSDAY, six days after the storm, and Sara had called John and Carew to dinner. As they were walking up the back porch steps on their way to wash up, Sara met them at the kitchen door. She told John that Lyle was on the phone. Carew and Sara started a conversation while John went into the living room. He sat down in his comfortable wingback chair, propped his feet on the ottoman, and picked up the phone. John and Lyle were very close, and it was always a pleasure to talk to him.

"Hello, Lyle. How's my favorite son?"

"Hi, Dad, I'm doing okay. This has been an interesting week, and I'm still wound pretty tightly about the event and how it's affecting the family. I had a long talk with Teresa. She feels God has sent a sign—that it's not a fluke of nature. And it can't be explained away by meteorological mumbo jumbo. She's really affected by what we experienced and wants to be a part of the revelation, whenever it happens. Teresa is a wonderful person, Dad. I want you to meet her as soon as possible."

"I've wanted to meet Teresa since you first told me about her and now more than ever. Perhaps she can come with you next weekend. I'm sure her folks would agree to her spending the weekend with us. Check it out and let me know so that Granny can spiffy up the guest room."

John asked Lyle if he had heard from the state ag. lab. Lyle told his dad that was the primary reason he called. He explained that the lab called while he was in class and Bill, his roommate, happened to be in and took the message. He explained that Bill had no idea what was going on and was not inquisitive. The soil and the bean plants showed no negative results. He added, with a slight clearing of his throat, that they were healthy.

His dad paused before commenting on his son's report. John's mind had been prepared to accept that the samples had been affected by a strange radiation or a chemical change of some kind.

"Well, I suppose we have to go in another direction, son. At least we've learned something. Come home next weekend and we'll get everyone together and discuss how we should proceed. I plan to talk further with Reverend Butler. He is highly focused on this matter, and we need him."

Lyle totally agreed with his dad and told him he would call Teresa right away.

John, Carew, and Red were in the next day, one week after the storm, inspecting the sprinkler system, looking for sprinkler heads that were malfunctioning or needed alignment. This was done twice each year and took several days. Red had been working the center section of the crops and started walking into the bean field. He had spotted the six-foot high two-by-four posts they had installed about fifty feet apart four days before, along the edge of the mysterious circle of darker soil. He walked down a row to the nearest post and looked at the ground. His heart felt as if it had skipped a beat because it was easy to see that the soil inside the boundary line had turned darker.

John was approximately two hundred yards away when he heard Red yell and saw him waving his arms.

About five minutes later, John walked up to Red, who pointed down. He didn't say anything—and probably couldn't if he had tried. John immediately saw what Red had discovered and sucked in his breath and swallowed hard.

Both of them walked slowly along the edge of the circle, seeing the now darker soil didn't vary—it was even in tone everywhere they looked. When Carew walked up, he started to ask what was going on, but immediately saw what had happened and stood there in wonder.

Later, the three of them returned to the house and were sitting on the back steps, discussing their latest finding. "It's as if that soil was made darker to make sure we see it," said Carew.

John looked down at his clasped hands and mumbled, "I think there's much more to come." He got up and looked at Carew and Red. "Perhaps our family meeting Saturday evening will help us begin to understand the 'what' and 'why' of all this." Carew and Red slowly nodded in agreement.

Wade Butler had been a Methodist minister for thirty-six years. Though he was only five feet eight inches tall, balding and rotund, he was thought of by the community as a dedicated and excellent preacher, a Bible scholar, and strong leader. His sermons were always moving and thought-provoking. The church was packed every Sunday. Wade had just completed his tenth year at Danaville First Methodist Church. He loved the town and its people and wanted to continue to live there after his retirement.

For the first time since graduating seminary, he was faced with the biggest challenge he could ever expect as a minister and servant of God. In fact, he had a strong feeling that the occurrence at the Kelly farm was just the beginning of an act of God that would parallel any of his powerful miraculous acts as recorded in the Old and New Testaments of the Bible. However, he knew well the magnitude of his responsibility. He had to pray for guidance in protecting the Kellys from outsiders while the Lord's purpose was served—whatever that may turn out to be. Reverend Butler was totally aware there had to be contingencies made to counteract attempts by citizens, the news media, the U.S. government, other governments, or other groups to take control of the events. Wade's number one priority for the Saturday-night meeting with the Kellys was to point out the importance, no matter the situation, to not say anything or do anything that would give away their mission.

"In a very intriguing way, all of us have been assigned to protect the grace of God," the reverend thought.

Jim Summers didn't waste any time after talking with Marv Gardner. He was on the phone immediately to the U.S. Weather

Service at Panama City. He talked to meteorologist Calvin Bolter.
Jim was surprised at the helpful attitude Bolter showed. After a
few moments, the meteorologist had informed the newspaper
editor that all U.S. Weather Service stations keep daily digitized
video radar logs on all significant weather on file for posterity. The
data is used to compare one storm with another—to gain various
extreme-weather profiles, such as thunderstorms, hurricanes,
rainfall, tornadoes, lightning, hail, and sustained heavy winds.

Summers explained to the weather expert that he needed
comparative data on two thunderstorms—one the past week and
the other one year ago. Bolter chuckled and said that the station
staff had dubbed those two storms as Oddball One and Oddball
Two. He confirmed they did indeed have data on the storms. Jim
asked Bolter if he could visit the station and review the tapes—
that he needed details for a story he wanted to write. Calvin told
him they would be happy to set up a review, just give them a one-
day notice. Jim said he would be calling within a day or two.

SHERIFF BERNAM AND Chief Deputy Beck were sitting in
Bernam's office talking after lunch on Friday, one week after the
storm. "Dan, you know I don't go 'round makin' mountains out
of molehills, but that doggone storm, and especially the Kellys,
has me buffaloed. I was talking to Marv Gardner over at the
drugstore and he, like me, is mystified that this last storm was just
like the first one, except this one had somethin' else to it that the
Kellys aren't talking about—they act like it was just a run-of-the-
mill thunderstorm."

Dan Beck had been in the law enforcement business for a
dozen years and knew his way around. Although he had worked
for Claude for four and a half years, he was a deputy sheriff for
Mason County before that. He knew everyone of any importance
in the county, and he knew who he could and could not trust.
Beck had his contacts and knew how to use the various county
offices as leverage to put pressure on a particular problem. He
was a good officer, but he was prone to overstep his jurisdiction

at times. Deputy Beck was six foot four and carried his 240 pounds authoritatively, but he was courteous and soft-spoken to people, except those who caused problems.

"Well, I could just 'happen' to be going by the Kelly farm and make a courtesy call on John—ask how things are goin'—see if I can determine if they are truly sittin' on something," said Dan.

The sheriff swiveled around in his chair and stood up. "It wouldn't hurt anything if you paid a friendly visit to John Kelly, I s'pose. Make sure you ask no direct questions about the storm. Just test your vibes and see if you learn anything. In the meantime, I think I'll drive by Gardner's Drugstore and chat some more with Marv."

"HEY, LYLE," DIANNE Coffer said, answering Lyle's call. She liked Lyle because of his friendly, but serious, manner and his evident feelings for her roommate. "Teresa is in the shower. I'll have her return your call posthaste, okay? Bye now." When Dianne put down the phone, the thought returned to her that something important was on Teresa's mind. She wondered what was going on.

It wasn't long before Teresa returned Lyle's call. She told him how the miracle was on her mind and how she needed to discuss more of her feelings about it with him. She had had time to analyze and pray about what he had told her. He quickly agreed and said his dad wanted to hold a family meeting including her this coming weekend. Many things had to be discussed, not least of which was a plan to deal with the press and the public if and when the time arose. He said his family was looking forward to meeting her. Teresa happily said yes—that she would call her mother to let her know she would be spending the weekend at the Kelly farm.

Lyle asked if her mother would have a problem with that. He was pleased when she replied that she and her mother were very close, and would want her to do so. Teresa was thrilled about the trip to meet Lyle's family and the farm. Now, however, they both needed to give at least half their mind and energy to their books and classes.

Teresa called home Friday evening. Her mom, Arlene, was happy to hear from her younger daughter again. Though she loved both of her daughters, Teresa was special. "Hi, Mom, how are things going? I thought I'd call early because I know you and Enrique usually eat out on Friday evenings."

"Oh, Teresa, I'm happy you called. I was going to call you tomorrow because it's been too long since we've talked. I miss your voice and our conversations. How's Lyle? Are you two still floating on air?" she laughingly said.

"Lyle's fine, and yes, we're still floating on air. Mom, as I told you before, he is truly special. His dad, mother, grandmother, and the others want to meet me. I'm finally going to see the farm I've heard so much about and get to know all the people who work it and take care of it."

Teresa thought about the coming meeting at the farm. Goose bumps appeared on her arms. She knew she could not mention one word to her mom about what was going on. Perhaps one day.

"Well, it sounds as if you and Kyle are building quite a relationship. I wouldn't be a good mother if I didn't tell you to go slow and be careful of each step you take. I love you very much, honey, and I want you to be happy."

"I love you too, Mom. We'll be leaving Tallahassee next Friday afternoon and return late Sunday afternoon. I'll call you again next Wednesday or Thursday evening."

After putting the phone down, Teresa looked over at Dianne, who had lowered her book and was smiling from ear to ear. Teresa began to smile also and told her roommate she was looking forward to her trip to Danaville and the farm. Dianne said it would be a great weekend, and she was happy for her. Teresa thought, "If you only knew what Lyle, his family, and I will be discussing, there would be a look of wonderment on your face, and you too would have goose bumps."

Enrique lowered the Tampa Tribune he was reading and said, "Well, how're the two love bugs making out? Are they married yet?" He was smiling slightly, but the remark wasn't lost on Arlene.

"Rick, I wish you wouldn't make remarks like that."

Arlene had noticed a growing sarcasm toward Teresa from him since she had been attending FSU. In fact, Arlene had been the recipient of a few verbal barbs from Enrique lately, and she couldn't understand why. She hated to entertain the thought, but he was growing distant. He laid the *Tribune* down and walked out of the room.

Though Enrique had been a quiet man since the day Arlene had met him, she had noticed a change toward her during the past year. Even his Latin politeness had diminished, but more than that, his longer hours at the office and more frequent business trips did not go unnoticed by her. Enrique never discussed the details of his work, and Arlene didn't ask—she knew that was not a subject for discussion. Their relationship was changing.

Teresa told Lyle she had told her mom about the upcoming trip to Danaville and the Kelly farm and that her mom was pleased for her and wished her a good time. Lyle knew that Teresa did not tell her mom the "why" or "what" of the trip. She was looking forward to meeting the Kellys and the others. She felt her trip with Lyle was going to be the beginning of a new and unusual direction for her future. She was in awe of what she suspected lay before her. Lyle had said the same thing.

CHAPTER TEN

EARLY MONDAY MORNING, Jim Summers called meteorologist Calvin Bolter in Panama City and set up a meeting for the next day at 10:00 a.m. The editor of the *Mason County News* was doing what any newspaper reporter would do—following a lead. He didn't anticipate any unusual story—he was just doing his job.

The drive to Panama City, south on State Highway 77, took approximately one hour. The weather station was located at the Bay County Regional Airport. Summers parked his car in the station parking lot at 9:55. He was always punctual, and was soon standing in front of the reception desk, admiring the very pretty young lady smiling at him. "You must be Mr. Summers," she said. "Please have a seat, and I'll tell Mr. Bolter you're here."

Jim glanced around the room, looking at the many framed photos—a sunset breaking through storm clouds, two waterspouts (one in the gulf and the other in West Bay near the ship channel), and a great shot of several lightning bolts simultaneously zapping the ground.

"Mr. Summers? This is Mr. Bolter." Jim turned to see the receptionist and a man in his midthirties with a pleasant look on his face walk through the door. Calvin Bolter stuck out his hand and said, "I'm very happy to meet you. We don't get many news people in here. Glad you came."

The editor quickly sized up the meteorologist as an "all business" type, whose handshake and demeanor indicated friendliness. Summers felt that Bolter was looking forward to providing him with as much weather data as the station had. "I've been looking forward to seeing how you fellows roll the dice and predict the weather. I'm glad to be here," Jim said with a smile.

"I'd like for you to meet the station chief, Ron Saltano," said Bolter as a man of Jim's age walked into the reception room. The editor and Bolter's boss greeted each other warmly. "It's not every day we get to 'show and tell' to a newspaper," continued Bolter. "As Calvin said, we don't get many chances to show off, so we're happy you're here. We think you'll be interested in the graphic and verbal information we have on the two 'mysterious' storms. I smile when I say that, but on the other hand, both of them are in the records as uncanny, to say the least."

Saltano took Summers by the arm and gently steered him through a doorway and down a hall. "Before we review the computer disks, I thought you'd like to see how we observe and track the weather on a twenty-four-hour basis," Saltano said.

The three of them entered a large windowless room full of electronic equipment in various-sized cabinets, and a few tables with weather charts spread on them. The most dramatic to Jim were several large computer-monitor screens to one side of the tables. He had always been infatuated with the sweep of a radar and how it displayed cloud formations and movement. At home, Summers would flip on his TV to the Weather Channel to see what was happening or going to happen around Mason County, before watching the news or a movie.

As Saltano noticed the editor watching the weather station's most important piece of equipment, he said, "Jim, that's our bread and butter. It's the Doppler, called NEXRAD, Next Generation Radar, which painted the two storms as they formed just south of us over the gulf, and tracked them until they dissipated a few miles north of Danaville. It gives us extraordinary color-coded visual information—as you will see in a few moments from archival recordings."

Calvin added, "The NEXRAD is state of the art. It's used by the National Weather Service throughout the country to detect and record the buildup of frontal systems, instantly identifying and tracking the forcing mechanisms that produce storms, along with damaging winds, lightning, hail, and tornados. In fact, it can detect a tornado by spotting the hook-shaped cloud which spawns the twister before it drops to the ground. NEXRAD is able to depict weather phenomenon in great detail, up to 125 miles from this station—some detail is noticeable up to 250 miles. So, to sum up the NEXRAD's capability, we see the daily weather—color-coded for temperature, precipitation, wind velocity and direction, cloud density and heights, lightning—all as it forms and moves over water and land. The larger TV stations have Doppler, and they offer local weather reporting, but the National Weather Service is integrated nationally as well as worldwide.

"Our NEXRAD unit is mounted and enclosed in a special weatherproof dome atop a one-hundred-foot tower located out back of the station," Saltano said. "If you feel like climbing some stairs, we'll take a close-up view of it later. Move your chair around to the left and face the center console, and we'll take a look at two digital videos of storm one and two. Afterward, we'll be happy to answer your questions as best we can, but please understand, there are a number of questions we can't answer ourselves about these storms—and neither can our people in Maryland."

Jim was fascinated by what he saw on the screen and heard from his hosts. Though he was a weather layman first-class, he could now understand that the two storms were, for lack of a better explanation, very odd, very unexplainable.

Jim looked at Saltano and Bolton with respect. He had not anticipated such a briefing or thought there would be much information he could use. Now his mind was really cranked up.

Afterward, the three men sat and talked for about ten minutes. Jim had several questions, mostly about the investigative review by the National Weather Service headquarters and what may come from that. Saltano said it may be weeks or several months before any information would be forthcoming, but it was his feeling that no one could solve the "why" and "how" of the two storms.

As promised, they walked out back of the building so Jim could see the tower and the Doppler perched on top. He thought about this "tree" of technology, standing tall and silent, seeing things that were unexplainable. "Whew," he said to himself as he turned and faced Ron and Calvin. "I truly want to thank you for your time and effort. It's been extremely interesting and helpful. I've got to head back to Danaville. The newspaper business demands a tight working schedule, and as usual, I'm squeezed for time." He shook their hands, and they all walked back inside so Jim could exit out the front door with a smile to the receptionist. As he later drove across North Bay Bridge on the way back to the *Mason County News*, his life and love, he wondered if the window he was in the process of opening was one of opportunity or would just be a huge headache. Something very strange had taken place, and Jim felt, based on what he had seen at the weather station and what Saltano and Bolter had told him, that it could be extremely time-consuming, with he would have to venture into the unknown.

LYLE AND TERESA were nearing Danaville. He had kept up a running commentary about northwest Florida—towns such as Quincy, Chattahoochee, Marianna, and Cottondale, none of which could be seen from 1-10 West because it bypassed all towns and cities. They were passing through low rolling hills of trees, a few farms, and over many overpasses. Teresa responded with comments of her own, but Lyle knew her mind was really on the events and the coming weekend—as was his. She had had a case of stomach butterflies since awakening that morning. She was thrilled about meeting his family and seeing the farm, but she knew as important to her as that was the meeting on Saturday night with the Kelly family and Reverend Butler was foremost on her mind; Lyle felt the same way. He had his own case of butterflies. His thoughts were on Teresa, and how all this would affect her, especially a very unusual family meeting with people she had never met.

He looked over at Teresa and found her eyes on him. She smiled slightly and reached for his hand. "Other than our love for each other, I have a strong feeling this is going to be the biggest thing in our lives," Lyle said.

Teresa added in a soft voice, "Yes, and many other lives also." After a few moments of silence, she added, "I'm so looking forward to meeting everyone, including Reverend Butler."

"All of them are very special. You'll love them and they'll love you," Lyle said.

It wasn't long before they exited 1-10 and turned north on State Highway 77 and Main Street of Danaville. Lyle had driven through town many times, but now Teresa was with him. The circumstances as to why she was here were extraordinary. As they drove north out of town and neared the farm, they both were occupied with thoughts about the important weekend ahead.

John Kelly sat on the large back porch in his favorite rocker, looking out at the fields. It was Friday, and except for the livestock and chickens, work slowed during the weekends, other than for an emergency—a new litter of pigs, a cow deciding to have her calf, or one or more of the milking machines stopping at an inopportune time, and other things. Carew and Red were changing the oil in the two trucks. John knew that both men were busy being busy, thinking their work would speed up the clock, making Lyle and Teresa arrive sooner. Carew and Red were really attached to Lyle, and wanted to see him as well as Teresa. They knew he would only settle for the best, and they were anxious to meet her and make her feel at home. Another part of their anxiety was the meeting the next night.

John's thoughts returned to what had been foremost on his mind since the storm. He thought about his dad, Seth Kelly, and how he had sat on this very same back porch on a warm summer night and quietly told him, approximately twenty years ago, how God had helped him build the farm into a success. The several times, during the early years, that the crop-yield failed due to lack of rain or some kind of blight, the bank loans became like a large boulder strapped to his back, but he continued to work and pray.

He had always believed in God and felt he had a partnership with him. Seth Kelly was a determined, good man and treated everyone with the same warmth and respect. Growing up, John had been very impressed with his father and prayerfully thanked him now for lighting his way. He knew his own success was due to his father, Granny, and, most of all, to God. Sara was his heartbeat; Carew and Red were his brothers. Now, it was evident God had sent a message to the family. The Kellys, along with help from Reverend Butler, would not only ask for divine guidance, but form a plan that would, as long as possible, prevent the news media and people in general from knowing what was taking place on the farm.

Sara opened the screen door and excitedly said, "John, Lyle and Teresa just drove up."

John arose from the rocking chair, cupped his mouth with his hands, and made a shrill whistle toward the main barn. Red came to the large doorway, wiping his hands and looking toward the house. John then motioned for him and Carew to come to the house. With a smile, he went through the kitchen, the dining room, down the hall, to the huge front door, knowing Lyle had parked in the circular driveway to give Teresa a good view of the house and to make sure she was ushered into the correct entrance.

Granny was already on the porch, waiting at the top of the steps, when John and Sara passed and went down to greet Lyle and Teresa. John knew—the moment he saw her dark auburn hair, pretty face and sparkling brown eyes, and the way she smiled—that Lyle had found a treasure. After John had greeted them, she put out her hand, and he took it. "I've really been looking forward to meeting you, Mr. Kelly, Mrs. Kelly."

John pulled her a little closer, smiled into her beautiful eyes, and said, "Teresa, always call me John. We've waited a long time to meet you, and I'm glad we did. I know Lyle has told you about the Kellys—I hope we measure up. A warm welcome to our farm." Sara took Teresa's hand in both of hers with a warm smile.

Lyle noticed Teresa seemed pleased, and it was evident she liked his dad and mom. John and Lyle bear-hugged; then the four of them climbed the steps to see Granny. Carew and Red had appeared and stood behind and to one side of Granny, waiting their turn to meet the special guest. After hugging Lyle, Granny, showing happiness, turned to Teresa and hugged her also. Teresa was not surprised. "Welcome to this family, young lady. I hope you stay!" Teresa smiled, her eyes twinkling, and stole a glance at Lyle.

John gently took Teresa's arm and steered her over to Carew and Red, who were standing expectantly with big smiles. "These two make this place run. Even though they aren't Kellys by name, they're Kellys by their love and devotion. We love them too."

Both men shook her hand. It was quite evident they were thrilled to meet her. "Red and I helped keep Lyle on the straight and narrow," said Carew. "Anything he does good at is because we taught him." He looked at Red and overdramatized a big wink with a big grin.

"That's right," said Red. Lyle had edged up beside Red and Carew. Red put his arm around Lyle's shoulders and continued the teasing. "He went off to college to get away from farmwork and, lo an' behold, brings home a real treasure. So, thanks to Carew and me, he's turned out okay." Red was looking at Teresa during his teasing, and she was thoroughly enjoying the banter.

Lyle took Teresa by the hand and said to everyone, "Let's go inside and start showing our guest around." Everyone started moving across the porch toward the front door, but halted when a Mason County sheriff's patrol car drove up and parked behind Lyle's Chevy.

JOHN RECOGNIZED DAN Beck, the number-one deputy sheriff, when he got out of the car. As the deputy started walking toward the house, he waved slightly. John responded, and at the same time told his family to wait a moment. He then went down the steps to meet the deputy. "Hi, John. I hope I'm not interrupting anything. I was on my way back to town from some business in Graceville, and thought I'd stop in an' say howdy." John thought, "Yeah, Dan, and I'm sure you and the sheriff cooked up your visit to see if you could get more information on last week's storm."

"Glad you dropped by, Dan. However, Lyle just got home from Tallahassee, and he brought a guest. We were just going into the house. Everyone's kinda waiting for me to join them."

"Aw, John, I'm sorry. I'll come by at another time. It's been a long while since you and I chatted about your family and the farm. I've always thought you had an outstanding farm, and enjoy hearing about how things are going with you. Take care and tell the family I said hello."

As the deputy turned and walked toward his car, John thought, "I have a feeling you'll be back, or the sheriff will. Claude Bernam also has a big nose." "So long, Dan," said John. He quickened his steps back to the porch and his waiting family.

"What was that all about?" asked Lyle when his dad joined them. All the others were also expectantly waiting.

John half smiled. "Deputy Beck was doing exactly what I told Carew and Red he and the sheriff would be doing—snooping around, trying to get a line on the storm, etc. There'll be others too. That's one of the reasons, among several others, we are meeting tomorrow night. By the way, Lyle, your grandma and grandpa Kessel will be joining us."

Lyle looked at Teresa and said, "I wasn't sure if they would be here or not. As I had mentioned to you several days ago, Grandpa Kessel is up and around after a siege of gout. All the family will be here now. That's great!" Sara smiled. She was happy.

Teresa felt the love and warmth around her. There were no strangers here. She felt perfectly at home.

Sara and Granny led them all into the cool confines of the large house.

CHAPTER ELEVEN

FRANK BOVITZ PUT down the phone and swiveled his chair around to look out the large window at the great view of Tampa Bay. He really wasn't seeing the water; he was deep in thought about the conversation he had just had with Alejo Gomez. After a few moments, he dialed Enrique's extension. When Enrique came on the line, Bovitz asked if he had any plans for dinner. Enrique was a little surprised at the short notice because he would have to tell Arlene, which could be a little sticky at this time of day. However, Frank must have an important reason for such a late invite, so Enrique accepted without hesitation. They were to meet at Parham's at six. The popular upscale restaurant was only several blocks from the office.

Arlene had just walked into the kitchen to plan dinner when the phone rang. She was surprised that it was Enrique. He hardly ever called home during working hours. "Arlene, Frank Bovitz wants me to have dinner with him. It's a business thing, and I shouldn't be too late. However, don't wait up."

Before she could respond, Enrique hung up. It wasn't the first time he had been so abrupt. In fact, it had been happening more frequently the past few months. There was a slight feeling of despondency, but she quickly put it aside and decided to vacuum and dust the living room. She would make herself a salad later. Arlene had an independent nature brought on by her years of raising two daughters and running her own business. She would not allow Enrique and his growing cold attitude to upset her.

Enrique's mind had been spinning with various possibilities as to the reason Frank wanted to have dinner. He knew Bovitz and Gomez had ties, but to what extent was unknown. Other than initially meeting Gomez through Bovitz at dinner one night soon after his promotion, he couldn't measure the man. Although that evening happened almost two years ago, Enrique could recall how reserved Alejo Gomez was. He remembered Frank had remarked to him several times during the past six months that life could change for the better if one was loyal and kept his eyes and ears open. Frank always locked eyes with Enrique, and said that with a serious tone.

When Enrique stopped his car in front of the restaurant, he had come to the conclusion that this meeting with Frank involved Gomez. He smiled slightly as he got out of the car, took the parking ticket stub from the attendant and walked into Parham's.

Perhaps this was the time his life was going to change—for the better.

ONE OF THE hostesses led Enrique through the main dining room to a quiet alcove. He saw Frank and Alejo before they spotted him. They were seated at an isolated table, leaning toward each other, deeply engrossed in conversation. Enrique thanked the young lady and said, as he walked up to the two men, "Good evening, gentlemen."

"Well, Enrique, we didn't see you come in," said Frank. "Please sit down. You remember Alejo Gomez?"

"Oh, I've not forgotten meeting Enrique," broke in Alejo. "I would never forget such a man. You impressed me very much." It was evident to Enrique that this dinner meeting was going to be about him, and he was beginning to feel uncomfortable. He knew this could be the start of an important association for himself, however, and he would make the most of it.

"Thank you, Alejo. I remember you very well, a man that successfully manages a number of diverse businesses—that's impressive."

Alejo looked pleased as he picked up the bottle of wine sitting on the corner of the table and filled Enrique's glass.

After the three ordered dinner, Frank lightly cleared his throat to signal it was time to discuss the reason for their meeting. "Enrique, your work has been exemplary for Gelb Foods since coming up from Miami. Your marketing expertise has had a positive impact on our sales growth for the past year. You are an asset to the company, and I think you can be an asset to Alejo."

Enrique didn't show it, but he was awestruck by Frank's statement. There was no doubt he was being "stroked" by his boss to make him feel obligated to them and to offer him something. It was the "something" that had his red curiosity flag waving in his mind. It was true Enrique wanted to improve his station in life— to have more money and recognition—and he wasn't selective as to how he got it as long as it appeared legitimate. His thoughts were rushing, and he knew he needed to respond to Frank's comments, but before he did, he wondered just how tied-in Frank was with Alejo.

"I appreciate your kind words, Frank. I hope I can continue to make a contribution to Gelb Foods," Enrique said.

The waiter appeared with their salads, and the three men were silent as they were served. When the waiter left, Alejo looked at Enrique and said, "Frank has told me much about how you handle your job at Gelb—how well you deal with the buyers and even top management of the various stores you sell to. Your style appeals to me, and evidently to Frank also. He thinks you can be a big help in several of our operations."

The cat was now out of the bag. It was clear to Enrique that Alejo and Frank were working together. He was now part of whatever was going on. Enrique Cruz had been charmed and drafted into an organization without an opportunity to walk away from it. Frank was his boss at Gelb and would cover for him in his association with Alejo, and Enrique would be forced to cover for Frank. He was well aware that Alejo—and Frank, for that matter— would do whatever was necessary to prevent him talking to anyone about their relationship. "Well," he thought, "I wanted to move up in money and prestige, and this is it. There's no turning back."

"I'll be happy to help in any way I can," answered Enrique. "I'm honored you have considered me."

Alejo and Frank glanced at each other and smiled. One after the other, they shook Enrique's hand and welcomed him into the fold.

As they finished dinner, Frank changed the conversation from fishing and golf to what Enrique had been waiting to hear about—what they were going to ask him to do. "As you know, Enrique, Alejo has a variety of businesses he controls, but one of those is real estate and very hush-hush. The land business in Florida is booming more than ever. Competition between those who are buying and selling is fierce. Real estate investors, lawyers, and buyers and sellers—all fighting like a feeding frenzy of sharks, especially those who are chasing large land developments, commercial or residential. That's why we must keep our transactions secret, never letting anyone connect us, and especially Alejo, to the land investment company we have set up. Since you are a marketing guru for Gelb—even though that is food—you would be a natural to scout out real estate leads we come up with from customer contacts." Frank paused, locked his eyes on Enrique's, and continued, "Gelb is going to expand its business to include northwest Florida—meaning, you'll be in that part of the state from time to time. Staying an extra day or so in Pensacola, Tallahassee, or Panama City would provide time to wear your other hat and root out information from Alejo's leads."

Enrique's mind was spinning, but he kept a calm, businesslike face as he accepted the meaning of this startling information and offer. And he knew he would accept their proposition—he really had no choice—and it greatly appealed to him. This offered the kind of life he had often thought about.

TERESA FELT VERY comfortable as she sat beside Lyle in the Kellys' large living room, and joined in the relaxed conversation with all the family members. It was evident they liked her, and it was as if she had known all of them for a long time. Granny finally stood up and announced they would have dinner around six—in about an hour. Sara suggested Lyle show Teresa around. She was eager to see the farm, and as she and Lyle departed, John and Red headed to the cow barn to milk the cows. Carew stayed to help Granny.

As she and Lyle walked through the house, she was impressed by how tastefully furnished and orderly it was. One wall of the large hallway that continued from the foyer was decorated with family photographs. Teresa touched Lyle's arm, stopping in front of the display, and asked him to identify who was who. Many of the photos were yellow with age. Those were of the early Kellys— Granny and Grandpa as newlyweds, John at about five, and a number of cousins, uncles, and aunts. One large oval-framed portrait was of Lyle's great-grandfather, Bertram Kelly, Frank's father. The latest photo was John and Sara's wedding.

Teresa was fascinated as she learned more about the family. She was also impressed with Lyle's evident love and respect for his Kelly roots. He showed her the upstairs rooms, pointing out her bedroom and private bath. She was fascinated by how everything was so comfortable looking. The house exuded a loving warmth and care.

They passed through the large dining room and walked into the kitchen. Granny was in the process of checking the roast in the oven. She smiled at Teresa. "You'll soon find out that this kitchen is the heartbeat of the house. All my men are always poking their nose in here, hoping to get a sample of what's cooking."

Teresa was impressed with the large back porch that overlooked the stately oak trees and the shaded back and side yards. Lyle pointed to the left, and she discovered a body of water through the trees. "Oh, Lyle, you have a lake!"

He laughed. "Well, it's not a real lake. It's a four-acre holding pond for watering the fields on an as-needed basis. We also pump water to the livestock from there. There is fishing to provide a little relaxation from time to time. Even though rains supply most of its capacity, dad installed a large deep well about ten years ago to supply extra water during drought conditions. Let's go see Lake Kelly," he said with a big smile. "I think you'll like the way we've fixed it up."

She was almost running down the back steps, pulling him along. "The farm is magnificent. I can hardly wait to see the barns, and of course, the mysterious bean field," she said with a sudden, serious tone to her voice.

"We've got a busy day tomorrow, but we'll fit it all in. The meeting will start around seven," Lyle said as they followed the wide path toward the pond.

REVEREND BUTLER SAT IN HIS STUDY, looking out of the window at a mocking bird, which was perched on a limb of a small tree nearby. The bird would cock its head one way and then another, scanning the ground for lunch or perhaps to take a small bug or worm to its little ones in a nest somewhere.

Wade was always amazed at the great eyesight birds possessed. Their lives depended on it. God controlled every aspect of nature. He looked down at his old, worn Bible, spread open on his desk before him, and thought about the many references to man's dependence on nature for his existence that were found throughout this book. Prior to seeing the bird, Butler had been praying. As he looked at the Bible, he tried to envision again why God employed nature with two very unusual thunderstorms, one year apart. The significance of each storm ending with an unusual rainbow, the last one leaving an indelible, precise circular pattern on the ground, was not comprehensible. The reverend knew, deep within him, that God was sending a message to the Kellys, which could have all kinds of ramifications for the world.

As he sat there full of awe, he fully understood it would be up to him, with his deep faith, Bible study, and dedication to God, and the Kelly's Christian values to find the spiritual meaning to this extraordinary event. Because of all its implications, he could not share it with any Christian scholars who could be of help to him. He was sure that later, this would drastically change.

Betty, Wade's wife of thirty-two years, lightly rapped on his door and opened it. "We'll be eating a little early, dear. I've got a special Methodist Women's meeting at seven." Wade turned in his old leather swivel chair, looked at his best friend with a forced, slight smile.

"As you know, the Kelly phenomenon has consumed every fiber of my body. Its significance is beyond my ability to understand why it happened. I know it's the work of God—but why?"

Betty walked over to his chair and put her hand on his shoulder. "You and I have been discussing this event for the past several days. We've not been sleeping well. Even with your strong spiritual energy, it's easy to see and to understand that you are carrying a huge weight on your mind. I want to help you so very much, but all I can do is listen to you, constantly pray, and give my feelings and advice to you as the Lord moves me to do so." Wade put his hand over his wife's.

"I know deep down that God will guide all of us through this, but it's still very difficult to know that it's up to me to provide a direction for the Kellys, and even for you and me. We cannot allow any of this, and what's to come—and I feel there will be more—to be known by anyone else. At least until God gives us direction, and I know he will. Tomorrow night I'm going to stress to everyone at the meeting how important it is to keep this event totally to ourselves as long as we can. Already there are a few key Danaville citizens who are curious about the storms and their rainbows, having noticed from town where the rainbows occurred. Sheriff Bernam, Deputy Beck, and Marvin Gardner have already been to the farm, sniffin' around. I heard yesterday in the barbershop that newshound Jim Summers is all of a sudden interested in thunderstorms. So, my dear wife, we have to pray that the Lord will show us the way."

IT BEING LATE spring, the sun was just beginning to make long shadows in the yard. It was a little after seven, and dinner being finished, everyone had gathered on the back porch, relaxing and talking. After a short lull in the conversation, Teresa, sitting between John and his mother in one of the high-back rocking chairs, looked first at Granny, then at John, and spoke, "I've never been near a place like this farm. The atmosphere feels unique—very heartwarming and secure." She felt she could relate her feelings, and felt a need to do so. It was obvious the family completely accepted her as one of their own. Teresa knew that tomorrow was to be very special for her—she was going to see the bean field.

John nodded and smiled. "We know what you mean."

The conversation finally evolved into the next night's meeting. Carew said he had so many feelings pent up inside of him that he prayed he'd be able to put them into some kind of order, and contribute to the group. Red agreed. Sara, Granny, and Lyle commented that all of them, especially with Reverend Butler leading the way, could better understand what had happened and why. However, it seemed extremely important that a plan be devised to ensure that the local citizens and the news media not learn what has or is happening. John added that the family and the farm had to be protected from the onslaught of the entire world if details of this event leaked out. Everyone quickly agreed.

Red excused himself and headed home. His parting words were, "I'll pray the best I can tonight." All nodded with a few audible amens.

Farm families tend to go to bed early because of their early start each day. It wasn't long before the back porch was vacant except for Lyle and Teresa. They sat close together in the large swing, conversing little, each thinking about the events and certainly about tomorrow night. "You know, Teresa, you and I care for each other so much and we're setting out together on an awesome journey that's going to test us. I love you beyond dimension, and we must support the family with all of our strength."

"Lyle, you are my heart and you know that I'll love you forever. I'm ready and anticipating whatever God asks of us." They kissed and held each other.

"Let's go watch some TV," Lyle said. "Relax our minds a little before hitting the sack. We're going to be busy tomorrow."

"I'm for that. It's been an eventful, fulfilling day," Teresa replied. The two walked inside.

It was more than likely that everyone didn't sleep very well, anticipating the next day. Each had their own perspective on how they were affected by what had happened and what it meant, but they all knew it was God's work.

CHAPTER TWELVE

J IM SUMMERS WAS sitting at his PC keyboard, but he wasn't typing. His editorial for next Wednesday's *Mason County News*, was staring at him, only half finished. Jim's mind was on the meeting he'd had with the meteorologists in Panama City, and what he had learned about the two unusual storms. The editor decided he would call John Kelly and try to meet with him. Perhaps Summers could at least get a clue as to what the family had experienced—if anything.

He looked at the clock on his desk and realized it was too late—it was a little after 9:00 p.m. Tomorrow being Saturday, the editor concluded it would be better to try to talk to Kelly then. Jim knew that John, and probably his entire family, was already showing a little evasiveness. Sheriff Bernam had mentioned to him that when deputy Beck had gone by the farm and talked to Kelly, it was evident he wasn't in any mood to talk about anything. In fact, John showed a little impatience and kept the conversation short. That in itself stirred Summers's curiosity.

Saturday morning promised a clear, warm spring day. At six thirty, John was sitting at the desk in his small office, making a list of items needed for the livestock and replacement parts for the irrigation system. Carew, Lyle, and he had finished the normal morning chores early because it was going to be a busy day. He wanted the family to visit the bean field, especially for the benefit of Teresa, and there was preparation for the meeting that evening. Teresa had quickly volunteered to help Sara and Granny with refreshments and other things. Red arrived in time for breakfast and explained that Jenny, his wife, would come in the afternoon, due to taking her daughters to spend the night with their grandmother.

Teresa had slept soundly in the different but very comfortable bedroom. She and Lyle had parted the evening before with a warm, lingering kiss, each heading for their rooms, not only tired but also having mixed expectations for the next day. It seemed she had just put her head on the pillow and closed her eyes when she heard stirrings in the house. The light coming through the two windows told her it was morning. She turned on the bedside lamp and glanced at the clock. Teresa was amazed. It was 6:40— almost eight hours of sleep. The day she had been anticipating had arrived. She felt rested and ready to get up, shower, dress, and join anyone that was downstairs. Later, she walked into the kitchen where Granny, busy putting a tray of biscuits into the oven, smiled and said, "Good morning, dear. Did you manage to sleep well?"

"It's been ages since I've slept so soundly," Teresa answered. "Oh, Granny, Sara, this is such a wonderful house and family. All of you have made me feel so at ease. Even with what is ahead of us all, there is certain calmness that I feel, which gives me an unafraid feeling."

"Yes, Teresa, all of us know that God is in charge, and we are his tools; we just don't know now what for. We'll know in due time. He's speaking to you also. That's what you're feeling." Granny, with her twinkling eyes, looked at Teresa and read her face. "Do you want to help me and Sara feed four ever-hungry men?"

Teresa looked very pleased and said, "I'd love to!"

It wasn't too long before Lyle, Red, and Carew came in the back door, and almost simultaneously, John joined them from the hallway. He said, "It's amazing how the aroma of Granny's cooking attracts so many people at one time." Everyone was looking at each other and laughing. Granny felt the warmth of the family members as they gathered around the large breakfast table. Lyle looked at Teresa as she was bringing a large platter of biscuits from the kitchen. He tried to be sly as he winked at her when she gave him a wide smile. John caught the exchange out of the corner of his eye, but pretended not to have noticed. He and Sara were extremely pleased with Teresa, and they had a definite feeling that she was to be their daughter-in-law. It was a comfort to them in spite of the unknown events that lay ahead of the family.

As they were finishing breakfast, John announced they would take Teresa out to the bean field in about an hour, as soon as he finished his paperwork. John always worked in his office on Saturday mornings. It had always seemed he could think more clearly about the income and bills at that time. Teresa wanted to help Sara and Granny clean up the kitchen. Granny had been telling her about the family history, and she wanted to hear more. Lyle, Carew, and Red walked out to the barn. Teresa said she'd meet them there in a short while.

"AIN'T THAT CALF a beaut?" exclaimed Red. The three had walked into the cow barn, and a week-old light tan jersey calf was busy getting breakfast from its mama.

"She came at a good time," said Carew. "One of our older milkers has been treated twice by the vet, and he didn't give her more than another year." Lyle had always been intrigued about the farm animals, observing their habits and watching them grow up. They contributed much to the success of the farm, and it was always a little sad to lose a pig or a cow through sickness or just old age. Sometimes, one would have to be done away with—a procedure that was not easy to watch.

As they turned to walk over to the milking machines, Teresa peeked around the open door, waved, and came over to them. "Well, I did pretty well for a city girl. I found the cow barn all by myself," she said.

"You did good," said Lyle. "Usually, all the girls get lost when they walk around this farm." Everyone began to laugh, even Teresa. Lyle reached over and took her hand and gently squeezed it. She was a good-natured young woman, and she knew he liked to tease her but he never went too far. She knew it was just another way of his showing that he loved her.

They all exited the barn in time to see John walking toward them. "Well, let's head out to the bean field," he said. With Teresa sitting in the front with him and Lyle, Carew and Red in the back, John headed the pickup down the narrow road toward their destination.

Teresa was contemplating what she was going to see. Even though Lyle had described the bean field phenomenon to her a week ago, her heart was beating a little faster now that the vehicle was slowing down. Lyle was sitting next to the door. He pointed to the left, over the steering wheel, and said, "That's the field over there. We should be seeing the marker posts any time now."

John slowed the truck to a crawl. Everyone had their eyes fixed on that special place. "There're the posts. The far ones are kinda hard to see from here—it's a pretty large circle."

He stopped the truck and everyone got out and walked along the row headers until turning across the bean rows toward the nearest post, about fifty yards away. Teresa began to see more posts as they marched off in a far-reaching arc. When they arrived at the edge of the circle, Teresa looked down and immediately saw the edge of the darker soil as it spread away from her. She was awed, knowing this was undoubtedly the work of God.

"It's amazing!" Teresa said.

"Yeah, if not more than that," answered Lyle.

Carew walked over several rows, squatted, and looked at the plants in front of him. "John, these plants are even darker green than last week."

"You're right," John said. "At first glance it's hardly noticeable, but the color is darker. It looks as if the entire circle has been further emphasized—to make sure we don't miss it."

Everyone was quiet for a few moments; then Lyle spoke up, "It's obvious to me we're being directed to concentrate on the center of the circle—to do something. Like Red said earlier, I think we are to dig there. There's something we must find."

"We've got to find the exact center of the circle first. I think we should box the circle, mark the corners of the box, then run a heavy cord from opposite corners. Where the cords cross will be the center-point," John said.

Everyone agreed. "Dad, I didn't know you knew geometry," Lyle said, trying to inject a little humor into the conversation.

John gave his son a grin and said, "It's just plain ol' common sense, son." Carew, Red, and Teresa relaxed.

"Maybe tonight we can discuss how we're going to dig the hole and when," said Carew.

"I think we ought to head back to the house," John said. "It's not too long 'til lunch. Sara and Granny like for their diners to be on time."

They all piled into the truck and drove slowly away from the bean field. It was uncanny, Teresa thought, how reverent everyone seemed to be, but it was highly understandable.

AFTER A LIGHT lunch, Granny and Teresa hurriedly cleaned the kitchen while John and Sara led the others out to the back porch. "Everyone get comfortable," John said. "I'd like for us to discuss our upcoming meeting tonight with Reverend Butler." It was only a few moments until the two other women joined them. All of them looked expectantly at the number-one Kelly as he continued, "We need to come to some conclusion as to how we feel about what's happened and how it's affected us, and how it may affect Lyle's maternal grandparents, Richard and Ann Kessel, along with his aunt and uncle, Pat and Paul. They'll be here too. I have said nothing to them about what is happening, so they are going to experience the same awe and acceptance that we all did, and they need to know. When the meeting with Reverend Butler is over, everyone present will understand what we must do. All who may yet join us, we'll greet with open arms and tell them they are part of our family—to help spread God's message that is buried below the bean field."

Everyone on the porch readily agreed with John. There was an upbeat tone as they discussed how they were affected by the events—what it meant for each of them. Some wanted the reverend to address particular questions dealing with what the long-range future might hold for them; the others wanted his insight for the immediate future—during the drilling and right after. None seemed afraid, but everyone was highly expectant—looking forward to what was about to occur. John took heart at the family's Christian resolve.

Teresa added, "I know I've been dramatically changed. When I first met Lyle in Bill's Bookstore at school, an unusual feeling filled me with serenity—as if he was sent to me. Now I know that he was. God brought us together to do his work. My heart is full of love for all of you. In fact, I think all of us were chosen long ago to help him deliver his message that is buried beneath the bean field." She looked into the faces around her, and they were all smiling.

"Amen," Lyle said as he reached for her hand.

"You know," said Carew, "speaking about the bean field, why did he pick that location for the circle? It's dead center in the middle of all our fields."

Granny quickly spoke up, "Because that's where he wanted it to be."

Everyone smiled.

John had been thinking the same as Carew, but didn't say anything. He had spent the past several nights lately reading entire chapters in his Bible rather than his normal several selected verses. His prayers were much longer too because of a need he had. Unable to readily go to sleep, his mind trying to comprehend what lay beneath the center of the "circle," he would get out of bed quietly and go into his office. After carefully closing the door, not wanting to wake Sara, he sat for an hour or so, putting his thoughts on paper. He would then return to bed, wondering why God would want his family to dig in the center of the bean field—how wide a hole, how deep, and when to start digging. Finally, after praying for a long time, John would finally drop off to sleep, laden with one or more unusual dreams that included people he didn't recognize, walking around him and pointing at him. After breakfast each morning, details of the dreams were vague and soon became nonexistent.

The family had an early dinner and, by six thirty, was sitting in the living room. The men were making small talk about farmwork to be done the coming week, while Sara was showing Teresa some needlepoint she had been working on. "Someone just drove up," Lyle said. His chair was facing the front windows, and he had a good view of the front drive. As he arose and started walking toward the front door, everyone else got up, ready to greet their visitors. When Lyle opened the door, he saw Reverend Butler and his wife emerging from their car. A small quiver ran through Lyle's body as his expectations began to grow. He greeted the Butlers with a handshake and invited them in. As they walked up the front steps, the rest of the family came out onto the porch.

"This is a royal greeting," the reverend said. He and Betty smiled and shook hands with everyone.

"Well, it's not every day our preacher and his wife come to see us," John said. "I apologize for not having a red carpet rolled out." They all laughed, even though there was a slight feeling of apprehension in each of them. "There's a new one among us, Reverend, that you should meet." John held out his hand to Teresa, who was standing nearby. As she stepped over to John, he gently took her by the arm and introduced her to the Butlers. It was evident they were immediately impressed. Betty and her reverend husband took Teresa's hands and smiling, welcomed her to their hearts. Teresa responded in turn, and commented that she felt very close to everyone standing around her. Lyle took this all in with a happy heart. They entered the house and gathered in the living room, standing and talking. A little later, the door chimes sounded. John opened the front door and greeted his in-laws, the Kessels. They knew everyone except Teresa, and were eager to meet her. After Lyle's introduction, his grandparents were immediately impressed with the beautiful, vibrant young woman. Dick and Ann Kessel knew they were looking at their future granddaughter.

John was rather anxious to start the meeting, so he asked everyone to please be seated. "Get yourselves some coffee, tea, or a soda. We'll have a break later on and enjoy some of Granny's cake and cookies." He directed Reverend Butler to a prominent chair, facing the group.

BUTLER PLACED SEVERAL books and a yellow writing pad on the table beside him. Betty sat next to him. He had a pleasant look on his face as he surveyed the faces of the group. All of them were looking at him expectantly. He cleared his throat and said, "Let's all relax and pray for guidance and understanding of what the Lord wants us to do. As long as we open our hearts and minds and trust him, he'll let us know."

Everyone stood, and without a word, moved close together, forming a circle and held hands. As they bowed their heads, there was an eerie silence—none of them could even hear the other breathing. Reverend Butler's voice was soft but well heard when he started praying. All of them were intensely tuned to his words, knowing he was relaying their deepest feelings. Wade's prayer lasted approximately two minutes, but was eloquent and eased the "fear of the unknown" in everyone's heart. He knew it would take time for everyone in the room to reset his thinking—to allow God to work through them.

This was a profound new time for the Kelly family, and as events unfolded, it would affect Mason County, the state of Florida, and the entire world. The reverend knew this, and so did John. Careful plans had to be made as soon as possible to keep what had happened so far, and what may follow, away from the public— especially starting with the news media. Both men wanted to initiate an overall plan with contingencies during this meeting, and set another within four days. Lyle and Teresa wouldn't be present for the second one, but John and Lyle had already discussed how they would use quick communications when needed—any hour, day or night—while Lyle was at school. John spoke to his family about the importance of retaining their demeanor as it had been prior to the last storm, but in no way answer questions posed by others, except in general, nondetailed terms. Otherwise, he continued, do not lie, but rather, think ahead and not let the questioner get too far. Reverend Butler agreed, and a general discussion followed.

Lyle, holding two cups of coffee, walked over to his chair, handing Teresa her cup, and sat down. "If we dig an exploratory hole, wouldn't that possibly be seen by some passerby as odd? Especially if we find we need to set up a water-well drilling rig or even a mobile oil-well rig just in case a deep hole is needed."

"Well, for one thing, the bean field is almost exactly in the center of the crops, a good distance from the three roads bordering our fence line. Unless someone is suspicious enough to use binoculars or fly over and around in a small plane, I think they'd assume we were drilling for water, although they may think it's an odd location," John said. There were several heads nodding in agreement.

Dick Kessel was leaning against the doorway leading to the dining room. "I have a feeling from what John has said about Sheriff Bernam, his deputy Beck, Marvin Gardner, and last but not least, Jim Summers, that their antenna is already raised. Elsa Reese, bookkeeper for the *Mason County News*, mentioned to Ann here the other day that editor Summers visited the U.S. Weather Service in Panama City recently. He told Elsa he wanted to learn more about thunderstorms, especially the one last week. I think we can expect him to want to ask a few questions, if not many."

"That's almost guaranteed," John said. "He represents the news media and has a lot of contacts, especially across the state. We must be extremely careful when he starts asking questions, and I think that will be sooner than later." Everyone agreed.

Pat reminded everyone about the snacks on the side table, laughingly saying how she, Sara, and Granny had slaved over a hot oven all afternoon. All of the group got up and went over to survey the goodies and refill their coffee cups. Lyle saw the reverend making some notes on his yellow pad, and asked if he wanted any cookies or a refill of his coffee cup. Wade looked up, smiled, and said no, he had some thoughts he wanted to note while they were fresh on his mind.

Butler looked around the room and tried to assess the mood of the close-knit family. He knew all of them felt the heavy weight of anxiety, based on the unknown, and awe of what they had observed. He too was deeply affected by the event. Being a minister for many years had never challenged him like it was doing now. History had been void of "signs" and "miracles" that were observed and experienced by men for many centuries. There were many accounts of individuals having been involved in one way or another with God's power, but with all of his studied knowledge and experience with people, Reverend Butler could compare the "storm event" only to the kind recorded in the Old Testament. In terms of getting the attention of one or many, God had power that could never be measured. The reverend felt a powerful love for the Father, yet felt weak in dealing with and finding meaning for his message left in the bean field.

It was obvious that God had chosen the Kelly family to convey a powerful message to them and to the world. The event and its implication would eventually be known everywhere, but first, he and the Kellys had to pray constantly for the Lord's revelation and to be vigilant against others' learning about this holy occurrence until its meaning was evident. The reverend was confident they all would know when that time arrived. Wade's thoughts were interrupted when Teresa stood before him, offering him cookies from a large plate. He smiled and told her he wasn't hungry, that he'd like to talk to the group for a few minutes and then call it a night. Teresa turned around and asked everyone to sit down, that Reverend Butler wanted to say something.

After coffee cups and glasses were put aside and all were seated, Wade put the yellow legal pad on his lap and made eye contact with his dear friends. He cleared his throat, looked down at the few notes he had made on the pad. He again told them his thoughts about God's power and how he communicates with people—many of whom do not hear him or feel his presence. "All of us in this room, however, positively know he has given us a direct, unmistakable message of great magnitude. Our duty in understanding this message is to pray for his divine guidance with open minds and hearts. Whatever it is he wants us to do will be revealed through our faith in him." All of them discussed their feelings about what the message could be.

Finally, Reverend Butler said, "I've got to go home and get some rest. I've been up for the last two nights, and all of a sudden I've discovered I'm real tired. I'll bet you're all tired too. This is just the start of a huge change in our lives, one I hope we can control with God's help. In time, it could change the lives of millions of people. I have no doubt I'll see you all in church tomorrow. Our next meeting will be on Tuesday night, if that's agreeable." They all nodded yes. He smiled as he and Betty headed for the door. John and all the rest followed them out onto the front porch, wishing them a good night.

THE STORM DATA Jim Summers had reviewed at the Panama City National Weather Service had taken his mind hostage. Although he and his small staff continued to meet the paper's twice-weekly deadline for area news, social items, and his editorials, he felt his daily time and effort was about to be challenged; something very unusual was happening in Danaville, and for the first time in his career, he was uncomfortable with how to initiate an investigation about, of all things, two storms—or something greater.

His office door was closed and he sat in his large old swivel chair, his feet propped on the cluttered desk. He had to talk to John Kelly about what was seen and experienced at the farm, if anything. Summers knew that if the Kelly family had witnessed any oddity during the recent storm or the so-called strange rainbow afterward, they wouldn't tell him anything.

As good as the Kellys were—Christian, warm, friendly, involved in the community—they never discussed their family or their farm business with anyone. Jim suddenly got out of his chair, walked out of his office, and headed for the coffee pot, located in the layout department. Maybe a hot cup of his staff's infamous printing-ink coffee would clear his mind. He had to call John and set up a visit to the farm. The editor would disguise his real purpose as gathering information about local farmers and their economic and other contributions to Mason County. "That's it," he thought. "I'll convince him of the importance of the article for the community. He should cooperate on a story like that—and while John talks, perhaps he will show me around the property, giving me a chance to look around." Summers felt a slight chance it might work.

He would actually publish such a piece for the paper, gaining Kelly's confidence and keeping the door open for the editor to make other visits to the farm. Feeling confident his plan would work, Jim returned to his office and started outlining the "community" story. He'd call John Monday evening.

CHAPTER THIRTEEN

AS LYLE AND Teresa drove back to Tallahassee on Sunday afternoon, both were more relaxed than last Friday on the way to the farm. They had discussed how their lives had recently changed and that the Kellys had bonded even more than ever. Teresa knew Lyle loved her, and she was wholly accepted by his family. Lyle was thinking how much she meant to him, and it was uncanny how close his dad, mother, Granny, and the others felt to her. Weaving through his mind simultaneously was the enormity of God's presence in all this.

"I wish we could attend the Tuesday night meeting," Teresa said. "They're going to discuss how to start digging the hole in the bean field."

"I'd like for us to be there, but Dad said he'd keep us informed of all that's happening. Meanwhile, it's back to the books. Only a few weeks 'til we get our pardons for the summer."

AFTER LYLE AND TERESA had departed, John and Carew were sitting on the back porch, discussing the meeting the night before. Carew noticed John didn't look well and sounded tired when he talked. "You feelin' all right, John? You're not comin' down with somethin' are you?"

John looked Carew straight in the eyes. "Oh, I don't know. I haven't slept too well for the past several nights, and I'm a little tired. This experience we all are involved in is quite a load. How about yourself?"

There were several moments of silence, then Carew replied, "It's a load all right. I'm not sleeping well either, and Red says the same thing. Even when I'm working, my mind constantly reminds me what has settled over all of us. It's obvious we're getting all the work done, but only minimally. God has put something on us and he expects us to figure it all out, John. We've got to trust him with no conditions. That's what my load is."

"I agree to that, but it's difficult. Reverend Butler said we have to open our hearts and minds and not to worry or be afraid. I'm trying, Carew, I'm trying," John said quietly.

Just talking about it helped both men feel better. They sat there in silence, gazing toward the pond. Several ducks were fussing about something—it was always enjoyable to observe wildlife around the farm. It was an integral part of a farmer's life, but now, neither man paid much attention to that.

"Let's ride out to the bean field and see if we can come up with an idea of just what would be the best way to start digging; that, if needed, could be very deep." Carew readily agreed to the suggestion, stood up, and retrieved his hat off an adjacent rocker. John saw his eagerness, and it made him appreciate his dear friend.

Within fifteen minutes they were standing at the perimeter of the faint circle of slightly darker soil. Even the bean plants within the circle were still a little darker green than those outside the circle. There had been no visible changes. John had thought several days ago, the darker circle and plants within might change back to their original visible state, but wasn't surprised they had not.

"As you said before, John, we'll plot the center of the circle. I'll find a couple of spools of heavy cord, and we can run the two spans tomorrow morning."

John put his head on Carew's shoulder. "You really come in handy around this farm from time to time, Brother Hinson." They both laughed. Each of them knew it would be important to keep some sense of humor. It was a needed relief valve.

The next morning, John, Carew, and Red cut the stakes from a batch of two-by-fours approximately six feet long found in the barn attic. After driving them into the rich soil along the edge of the circle, approximately thirty or forty feet apart, the men backed off one hundred feet. The stakes were easily seen and outlined what appeared to be a perfect circle. They were all amazed. How could a rainbow leave a circular pattern such as that? It was further proof that the entire event had been (and would continue to be) under God's control.

They soon left the area and headed back to finish the late-afternoon farm routine. John wanted to check the livestock-feed supply. Carew went to the pump house to make sure the timer was set for the fields' sprinkler system to start at sunrise the next morning. It was near five o'clock, and the sun was still hanging well above the horizon, when Red bid them a good evening and headed home. He'd be back at his usual 7:00 a.m. the next day—it being Tuesday. He, like John and Carew, was anticipating the second meeting with Reverend Butler. Red knew they were going to start planning a way to deal with the events—whatever they turned out to be.

ON THAT MONDAY NIGHT, Lyle and Teresa went to the main FSU cafeteria for an early dinner. Lyle had suggested that it would be a secure place to discuss further plans on telling Teresa's mother about the "event" at the farm. They had to convince her to return with them to join the Kelly family for an unknown length of time to ensure her safety. Both of them knew it would be extremely difficult for Arlene to leave her home and business. Teresa knew, however, that her mother was very practical and would listen to reason and weigh her options.

The other matters they had to tell her about, were about their engagement and leaving Florida State. As Teresa has said earlier to Lyle in a quite voice, "Mother is going to be stunned. But all of this must be done."

Lyle nodded. "Yes, it must be done."

"When I talked to her this afternoon, she was ecstatic that we wanted to come down on Friday. In fact, she sounded as if she was going to cry with joy. I know my mother extremely well. she tried to sound happy, but as we talked on, it was noticeable she was depressed. I have strong feeling it's Enrique.

Lyle reached across the table and took her hand. "Well, it looks like we have one more reason to see her. By the time we all talk this out, I think she'll be more inclined to come back with us."

They discussed their plans to give up school, after returning to the farm with Arlene. Time was quickly passing, and they needed to be with the family during and after the exploration drilling—and beyond.

"The key thing to be discussed at the meeting on Saturday night will be the exploration, along with working on a plan that will keep the public out of the family's hair when the drilling starts within a week or so. Dad said he'd call and fill us in. I gave him your mother's number.

"We'll leave Friday afternoon around two o'clock. That'll put us in Tampa around six or so. Isn't that a good plan?" Lyle said with a wink and smile.

"That's a great plan" she replied as she squeezed his hand and smiled back. "I'll call her tomorrow and let her know our approximate arrival time, so she can have one of her outstanding meals ready for us."

Teresa was worried about her mother, but knew there was a much more important issue at hand—God was in the process of revealing what he expected of the Kelly family. That preceded everything else.

DEPUTY DAN BECK was sitting in his patrol car pointed north on the shoulder of State Highway 77 when an old Chevrolet pickup passed, also headed north. Beck recognized the vehicle and the driver. It was obvious old man Pasternak had been fishing. Several cane poles stuck over the tailgate. The deputy's radar gun indicated the truck was only three miles per hour over the limit, which was acceptable. However, he decided to pull it over. Dan would just say hi to Karl, ask about his fishing day, and just be neighborly; it would give him a chance to perhaps bring up last week's thunderstorm. Maybe the old man would know something of significance since he lived within a mile of the Kellys.

Karl saw the blinking red-and-blue lights in his rearview mirror, and his heart sank. He knew he hadn't been speeding, and he recently had his taillights checked during the car's state inspection. He was already late in getting home, and Tish was bound to be worried. The fish had been biting, and he'd lost track of time. The drive from Crystal Lake to home usually took about fifty minutes. Now he wouldn't get home 'til after dark. Karl slowed and pulled over on the wide grassy shoulder. He felt pretty sure that the deputy just wanted to say hello and talk awhile, but time had run out and he would let Beck know he had to get home. Karl rolled down his window and waited.

"How ya doing, Karl?" the deputy said good-naturedly as he walked up.

"Doing fine, Deputy. I hope I haven't done somethin' wrong."

"Oh no, Karl. I was patrolling earlier, down toward the Bay County line, keeping an eye on some of the young beach bucks coming this way, heading home after a hard day's surfing. I'd pulled over to have a little coffee out of my thermos and watch my radar, when I recognized your fishin' buggy. I just wanted to say howdy and find out if you'd had a good day on one of the lakes."

Pasternak was uncomfortable, knowing he must have at least a short conversation with the deputy, perhaps massage his ego a little. "Yeah, I really roped 'em in. Must be the phase of the moon or whatever. My icebox is blessed. Deputy Beck, I'm runnin' real late getting home. I know my wife is already worried."

"Why sure, Karl. I'm sorry I'm holding you up." Beck knew he'd have to ask his questions hurriedly without raising questions. "By the way, me and others in Danaville were sure mystified by that storm last week. Especially the odd rainbow that showed up afterward, just like last year. Since it was in the general vicinity of the Kelly farm, I wondered if you'd had a good view of it. I mean, you live only a mile from there."

Pasternak suddenly knew the deputy was on a fishing trip of his own, and his mind quickly went on defense. He told Dan Beck that he had been inside his house during and for a time after the storm; he had not seen the rainbow.

The deputy kept the friendly look on his face and leaned down closer to Karl. "I know you are a good friend to the Kelly family, and have lived close to them for a number of years. I would think he would have mentioned something to you about the storm, and especially that rainbow."

Karl cleared his throat and looked into the deputy's face, although he could not see his eyes because of the growing darkness. "Well, it's true we've been friends many years, but we don't talk a whole lot. He's said nothing to me about the storm."

Beck was quiet a moment, then continued, "Well, I was just curious. I hope I didn't make you too late in getting home. Sittin' out here at night watching cars go by gets a little lonely. Recognized your car an' just wanted to say howdy."

As the deputy backed away a step or two from the car, Karl put it in gear. He told Beck good night and pulled up on the highway and headed home. As he looked into his rearview mirror, he saw the deputy walking back to his car. Pasternak wondered what was so interesting about that rainbow.

CHAPTER FOURTEEN

ON MONDAY MORNING, after tending the livestock and eating breakfast, John and Carew drove out to the bean field to locate and mark the center of the "unique" circle. It took them about an hour and a half to sight and box the circle, drive four corner stakes, and run the cord. Afterward, they walked out to where the cords crossed and the official center of the circle was now located.

"Well, that's the spot," Carew said. "It just makes me more nervous and full of wonder as to what's down there."

John stood there, looking at the spot under the crossed cords. He knew exactly how Carew felt. "Whatever is down there is not for us to question. Remember what Reverend Butler said? We've been chosen to carry out God's will without question. He'll reveal all to us when it is time." John inwardly wondered where some of his thoughts were coming from lately. It felt as if he were just a conduit, and had no control—just keep his mind open, trust all that's happening. "Oh boy," he thought, "that's a tall order."

"I know, John. I will. But I feel in my heart that not many people since the beginning of time have directly experienced God's awesome power. We've witnessed a little of it, and I know, like you know, that there's a lot more to come. It's hard to understand."

THAT EVENING, JUST as the family had finished dinner, Sara answered the phone in the kitchen, "Hello, Mr. Summers. No, we've finished dinner. Yes, he's nearby. Let me get him to the phone. No, it's no trouble at all." Sara laid the phone down and went into the dining room, where he and Carew were still sitting at the table and talking. "John, Mr. Summers wants to talk to you."

As he rose from his chair, he smiled at Sara. "Thanks, dear, I'll talk to him from the living room." John looked at Carew and rolled his eyes as he left the room. Carew knew what he meant.

"Hi, Jim, what can I do for you?" John listened patiently as the newspaper editor apologized for calling at this time of day, that he knew it was difficult to reach him during normal working hours. John thought, "When did I ever have normal working hours?"

"That's okay, Jim, the best time to reach me is in the evening."

Summers continued, "I've been working on an idea for a lead article I'd like to run in the paper within several weeks. It would tell how important farming is to our county, plus the surrounding counties, and the state. I want to feature several Mason County farms and their owners, you being the primary one. It would be a great piece for Danaville and the county—and for your family." The last phrase was added to play to John's pride.

"With all that's confronting the family, and the inevitable discovery that will be made and whatever follows that, sure makes bad timing for Jim's idea," John thought. "However, if I refuse to participate, that could add emphasis to questions already being asked about the latest storm and rainbow."

"What would this entail, Jim? You know how busy farm life is."

The editor smiled to himself. He had Kelly's attention.

"Really not much. I'd come out there the next few days, and we'd sit and talk—me making notes. I'd make some pictures of you and your wife, perhaps of the house. In fact, one that shows those beautiful oaks."

John's mind raised a red flag—he'd make sure there would be no photos of the fields—not even in the background of any photo. He would manage that, however he had to at the time. "Jim, let me see what I can arrange, and I'll be in touch tomorrow."

"That's great John. I sure do appreciate your cooperation. It'll be a good story. I'll look forward to your call tomorrow. Good night."

After John hung up the phone, he sat there contemplating what just took place. He did the only thing he could have done—agreed to let Summers do his story. John suspected the editor's motive was part legit and part to ferret out information about the storm. Later that night as he was getting ready for bed, he told Sara about Summers's request. She was sitting at her dressing table, putting lotion on her face. "Do you think it's a good idea to have him traipsing around the property?"

"There's really no way I could refuse him. I'm sure his story will be a good one for the community; for that reason, I can't turn him down. As you can guess, he also wants to get a bead on 'the storm.' Don't worry, dear, I plan to discuss this with the family at tomorrow night's meeting. I'll also call Lyle and let him know. We'll gently prevent the editor from wandering off course. I told him I'd let him know tomorrow. I'm sure he'll want to come out within two or three days."

Sara turned and faced him as she brushed her hair. "We'll handle this situation in good fashion, and any others that will undoubtedly crop up." She came over and kissed him, and lay down, nestling her head in the crook of his arm. With her beside him, even the great cloud of unknown seemed manageable.

John was wide awake when the alarm buzzed at five thirty. It wasn't unusual for him to beat the clock, but this particular morning he felt rested and ready to start a busy day. For the past week, he had not slept very well. As he went into the bathroom to start his morning ritual, Sara stirred, hearing Granny walk by their door, heading for the kitchen. Another great day at the Kelly farm, she thought.

IT WAS TUESDAY night and the meeting was about to begin. All members of the family, except Lyle and Teresa, were present.

They would be missed. Reverend Butler and his wife Betty brought the total count to twelve, but the living room was accommodating and comfortable. Sara, Pat, and Granny had prepared a side table again, but this time there was a large cake and a pie, plus the standard Kelly coffee and soft drinks.

"Reverend, I think we're ready to start," John said.

The reverend stood and asked everyone to rise and hold hands. He pretty much gave the same prayer as the one in the first meeting; this time, putting emphasis on each family member's praying often, asking for guidance.

After the group sat down, Butler opened a spiral notebook. "There is a gentleman in our congregation who is a retired geologist, and a dedicated Christian. He's served on several of our committees during the past seven or eight years, and has been a great help in the work of our church. In fact, John, you may know him. His name is Brandon Cook."

John nodded his head. "Yes, I've talked with him on one or two occasions, but I didn't know he was a geologist. He seemed like a good man."

"He definitely is," said Butler, "and I want to suggest to all of you that you allow me to talk to him about joining our group here. If he's willing, and I believe he will be, he can be of help to us in planning the dig in the bean field. I personally think it would be advantageous to us if we had an idea of what kind of soil and/or rock strata lie beneath the surface so we know what kind of tools we need and how best to use them."

Everyone seemed to like the idea. However, John had a slight concern about an outsider joining the family to help find an answer to the "mystery." Not for a moment did he doubt the reverend's judgment—what he had said made good sense, and the family would welcome Mr. Cook if he decided to join them. John would let Wade handle the arrangement. It was agreed the digging would be delayed until the reverend had gotten an answer from Cook and John had met him.

Further discussion included how best to protect the beans. Carew mentioned he thought they could save 80 percent of the crop if they carefully planned entry and exit from the field service road, and keep the working area around the "hole" to a minimum—dependent upon the equipment that was to be used.

After a ten-minute break for refreshments, the group reconvened, and the remainder of the evening was spent discussing the great importance of thoughtfully and carefully reacting to questions by outsiders regarding the storm and rainbow. John said it was very likely the digging would be observed because he was convinced the snooping would be increasing.

He told the group about Jim Summers's upcoming visit to the farm to do an interview and take a few photos. "Summers wants to run a feature about farms in Mason County and what they mean to the local economy. He said we would be the lead in the story. Even though he's going to print the piece, it's an attempt by him to also snoop around concerning the storm. I couldn't say no, or even put him off for a while—it would be too obvious. I'll closely steer him around while he's on the premises." Everyone thought John was on top of the situation.

The meeting came to a close around nine thirty with a prayer. The Butlers were the first to go, soon followed by Red and his wife, the Kessels, and a little later, Pat and Paul Daniels. Sara, John, Granny, and Carew, all helped to straighten up the living room and put away leftovers before going to bed. They were all tired.

Summers phoned John Wednesday evening. After listening to the editor explain he would need only a couple of hours to interview him and perhaps one or two other family members, and take several photos, John said he was available the next afternoon around two o'clock. It had rained a little earlier, but according to TV weather news, Thursday was to be a better day. Jim sat back in his chair and made a few notes regarding his upcoming interview with John. He had decided not to take his young photographer with him. Summers wanted to do this alone, to perhaps make it easier on the Kellys and hopefully easier for him to move around and make more observations.

John told the family about the next-day visit by the editor. He repeated what he had said at Tuesday night's meeting—that everyone carry on as usual. "If Summers asks a question, give him a straight answer. I'm sure he's going to bring up the storm, and certainly the rainbow. If he does, just tell it like it is. I'm fairly certain he knows nothing about the hail—and that's key. As they say in the military, 'that's classified.'" John had a thin smile on his face, but everyone knew what he meant. All they had to say was: yes, it hailed some; no, it didn't damage our crops—end of comment. They also knew John would be with Summers the entire time.

Jim parked his car in the Kellys' front driveway at 2:10. It was Thursday and a sunny, clear day, just right for sharp photos. Other than shooting for the feature story he was here for, changing to a telephoto lens might not go unnoticed. He took a moment to slowly scan the property. He was still impressed at the scene—it gave off a magical aura; it was beautiful. Summers got out, then reached back in and picked up his camera and briefcase, and headed for the wide front steps.

Sara had been in the den across the hall from the dining room. Having heard the faint sound of a car door slamming, she walked toward the large leaded-glass front door. She thought, "That's the heartbeat of the *Mason County News*, here to interview John and whomever else, and try to pick up all the clues he can about the storm." She exhaled, opening the door just as he stepped onto the porch. "Hello, Mr. Summers. Welcome to the Kelly farm."

"Why, hello, Mrs. Kelly. It's a distinct honor to be greeted by the real boss of this magnificent place." They both laughed and shook hands.

"Please come in. We'll walk through to the back porch, and I'll find John. He's somewhere in the vicinity."

Pat, who was spending the day with her family, came out of the kitchen with Granny to greet the editor. They stood near the steps and talked, while Sara walked over to the end of the porch where a clapper bell, approximately eight inches in diameter, was suspended from a perpendicular arm bolted to a roof-support column. She clanged the bell two times. It was loud enough to make the editor jump slightly at the first sound. "John's somewhere in the recesses of the barn—he should be here shortly," she said as she walked back over to the other three.

"That used to be called the dinner or emergency bell, wasn't it?" asked Summers.

Granny answered quickly, "It still is. That type of bell has been used by farms for many, many years. Sure comes in handy."

John had emerged from the barn and was walking toward them. Jim told the ladies to not wander off because he wanted to make pictures of everyone before the interview started. He then walked down the steps to meet John.

Summers left the farm about two and a half hours later, disappointed. The interview had gone well; so had the photo session. But the editor felt Kelly, other than the interview, had filled the remaining time with a detailed tour of the barns, milking house, cooler, chicken house, and yard, plus the hogs and cows— even walking down to the pond to see the two large pumps for the sprinkler system. Jim had wanted to visit the fields, but when he asked, John looked at his watch and replied that it would take too long. Perhaps they could do it at another time. To put it mildly, Jim felt he had been manipulated.

The feeling that the Kellys were hiding something was gnawing at him, and he was determined to find out what it was. In the meantime, the editor had several other farmers to visit within three days. That wouldn't give him the time he preferred to meet his deadline. But he'd have to do it. Jim had told John the story would be printed in one week.

That night after dinner, Sara and Granny were watching TV in the den when the phone rang. Sara told Granny she'd get it, walked over to a small table near the bay window, and picked up the receiver. "Kelly farm. Oh, hello, Reverend Butler. It's good to hear from you." After a few seconds, she continued, "He's in the shower . . . no, no, no, I don't mind. Okay, here's a notepad, now for a pen or pencil." Sara soon found a pencil in the table drawer. "I'm ready." There was a pause while she took some notes. "Tell John that Mr. Cook would be very happy to help us anyway he can. Meeting at your house, or here at the farm, tomorrow night around seven or seven thirty . . . yes, John will call you back within the hour. Thanks, Reverend, good night."

Sara and Granny were discussing having Mr. Cook working with them when John came in. Sara filled him in on the phone call from Reverend Butler. "I'd better return his call sooner than later. I'll use the kitchen phone. I'm looking forward to meeting Brandon Cook."

Later, John told Sara he had suggested to Butler that he bring Cook to the farm so he could meet the Kelly ladies along with Carew and Red. The reverend said that would be fine. They all wanted to meet the geologist.

Sara told John that Lyle called around noon and said he and Teresa were leaving for Tampa Friday afternoon. They will explain to Teresa's mother what's happening, and the importance of her returning with them to the farm.

"Our son's gonna be sizing up his future mother-in-law, huh?" John said with a smile. Sara and Granny laughed. "I need to bring him up-to-date with the latest details here. I'll give him a call," he said as he picked up the phone.

Lyle was glad to hear from his dad. He listened carefully to the happenings of the past two days, including Jim Summers's interview—how the editor was given minimum information about the storm and a lot of facts and figures about the farm. Lyle smiled, knowing his dad was in charge; and it was a good feeling. After voicing his love for everyone at the farm, he hung up.

CHIEF DEPUTY DAN BECK AND HIS ASSISTANT, Deputy L. D. Woods, walking into Sheriff Bernam's outer office at 11:45 a.m., stopped in front of the secretary Mildred Hughes's desk. "Good morning, Mildred. Hope the best-lookin' secretary in Mason County is having a good day." Beck looked down at the slightly overweight fifty-year-old graying woman and thought how much she evidently disliked him—she was very protective of Sheriff Bernam and made sure no one except the county judge or the county attorney had direct access to him. This didn't sit well with

Dan. He was the chief deputy and should be able to go and come as the sheriff allowed without clearing it through his secretary. But he knew it was the way the game had to be played.

"I'm having a very good day, thank you, Chief Deputy Beck. I suppose you want to see the sheriff. He can give you only ten minutes or so. He has to leave at twelve for a luncheon appointment." She picked up her phone and punched Bernam's extension. "Sheriff, deputies Beck and Woods are here to see you." A moment later she looked up at Beck and told him they could go in. Dan looked over at Carlton, rolled his eyes, and led the way to the sheriff's closed door.

When the two deputies entered the spartan office, Bernam put down his coffee mug, got out of his high-back leather chair, and while moving over to his coat tree, said, "Good morning, men. What's up?"

"Just wanted to let you know that I talked to Karl Pasternak last night. He was on his way home from fishing. Said he didn't see the rainbow; he was in his house the whole time. Karl was fidgety about gettin' home, so I didn't press him. He drove on."

The sheriff retrieved his gun belt, and while strapping it on, looked at his number-one deputy and said, with slight irritation to his voice, "Dan, I told you the other day that I wanted you, Carlton, and the other two deputies to casually talk to anyone who observed that storm and determine if they saw anything unusual. Other than a few comments about the rainbow, I don't think you're gonna find out much. Remember, the word is 'casual.' Now, if you gentlemen don't mind, I have an appointment to keep."

It was obvious to Beck that the sheriff didn't want to pursue the subject, for whatever reason. Well, he was going to stay the course and see what he could turn up. There was more to this thing than met the eye. Only when he'd gathered some solid, irrefutable facts would he confront Bernam again, dumping it all in his lap in one fell swoop. Maybe that would get the attention of his boss, and a little more of his respect. The three of them walked out of the sheriff's office, past Mildred Hughes's desk, and into the hallway. With Bernam in the lead, they descended the stairs to the lobby, not a word being said.

CHAPTER FIFTEEN

JOHN AND SARA met Reverend Butler and the geologist, Brandon Cook, at the front door. They welcomed each to the farm and showed them into the den. It was less formal than the large living room and a little smaller—more comfortable for the three men to discuss the unknown tasks at hand. After Sara had chatted with Cook for a few moments, she excused herself and left the men to their discussion. John had looked forward to meeting the geologist. The reverend had had many good things to say about him, and that was good enough for John. He was anticipating what the geologist would say once he had given him all the details of the happening—especially those about the soil coloration and the circle.

After relating the events to Cook, he paused, looking at him. "Brandon, I know the reverend has told you that he and my family know this is the work of God. It has the potential to reveal a message that will rock the world. We need your help in finding out what's below the center of the circle in the bean field and how best to get to it. We have to do it safely and quietly. But before that, I assume we must determine what kind of soil, rock, or whatever is below the surface."

"John, when Wade told me the situation, my heart jumped into my throat. I also felt this is the beginning of a message from the Lord. We can determine what's below the surface by core sampling. That part will be relatively simple. What comes after that depends on what we find."

Brandon Cook was seventy years old. He was five feet nine inches tall, with a fringe of silver gray hair around his bald head. His wiry body was slightly stooped at the shoulders, but he was energetic and had a quick, intelligent mind. John was impressed with him.

Cook continued, "As you know, John, this farm is sitting on soil made up of sand, loam, and clay. But there are a lot of limestone formations throughout northwest Florida, from within twenty-five feet of the surface to depths of fifty to seventy-five feet. I'll contact the Florida Geological Survey tomorrow and have them send charts of this area. That'll tell us a lot, but my guess is we'll hit limestone within forty feet, if not something else before then." John and the reverend looked at Cook, knowing exactly what he meant.

The geologist went on to explain there were many crevices, voids, and caverns in the limestone—some with water, some without. He said he felt that water-well drilling equipment would do the job, and if need be, it was relatively simple to expand a test core drill-bit hole of four to six inches, to one of at least thirty-six inches in diameter. Thirty-inch-plus steel casing could be installed to make working down-hole accessible by man, if needed.

"One thing we don't know is what lies in wait for us; we had better be ready for anything," John said. The other two nodded in agreement.

Brandon Cook was laid back and methodical. He was eager to help plan the drilling exploration, and as soon as John settled on a drilling company, the geologist would work closely with the driller to ensure a safe step-by-step operation. Cook would first conduct a series of studies that would profile the local subsoil and strata, providing a picture of what to expect during the drilling.

The geologist looked at John, and said, "It'll take me a couple of days to get those charts from the FGS, and another day or two of examining the surrounding area in and around the bean field. I think we could start drilling in a week or less. The first objective would be to drill a small diameter hole for studying core samples, seeing what's down there so we can plan a larger working hole of up to thirty-six inches or so in diameter to accommodate a man and perhaps some tools. That could take a day or so—according to what we find."

John replied, "It's important we get started as soon as we can, but I really can't see us doing so for at least a week or ten days. Wade, I want you to help me talk to a water-well man once I find one I think we can take into our confidence. I know of several, one in Mason County and two in Jackson County. The more outsiders we bring in, the trickier it gets to maintain security. There's no doubt people are going to see us bringing in a driller and we can explain that we are drilling a well, but they'll notice you two coming and going. And who knows how many others may have to join us before we discover what it is we are supposed to find." Wade nodded his head in agreement. Cook was looking out of the window, seemingly lost in thought, but nodded his head also. "Lyle and Teresa have to be here when we drill; in fact, I want all of my family to be here," John added.

"I'd like to see the site tomorrow, John, if that fits in. I'd like to see the soil within the circle. Otherwise, get a feeling for where we'll be centering our efforts," Cook said.

"Come around 1:00 p.m. I'll take you out there for a short visit. Then you can go and come as you wish. My farmwork is calling and I have to answer."

As John walked his two guests to the front door, he was already thinking which of the three well-drilling experts he'd call first. He decided on Clayton Parker's company in Jackson County. Clayton was an old friend of his whom he hadn't seen in over two years, but was remembered as a Christian and a successful businessman.

"Good night, gentlemen. Brandon, I'm sorry I didn't meet you sooner. It's my loss. I look forward to a friendship far into the future—whatever that future turns out to be."

While taking John's extended hand, Cook broke into a warm smile. "I feel the same way, John. It's a pleasure to work with you, Reverend Butler, and the Kelly family, on this great spiritual event. I'm sure we and the world are going to stand in awe at what finally transpires."

"I'll be waiting for your call when you set a meeting with a drilling company," the reverend said to John. "God bless us all with fortitude."

"Amen," said John. With that, his two visitors went to their car, and John went in to see Sara and Granny, who were sitting in the living room having iced tea and talking.

LYLE AND TERESA had deferred taking I-10 to I-75 on their trip to Tampa. Teresa had suggested they take US 27, more along the west coast, missing heavier traffic, and cut across north of St. Petersburg to Tampa.

As they drove into the city limits of Tampa, Lyle thought how this was the largest city he had ever visited. The traffic was terrible. Nothing like downtown Danaville on a Saturday night—or even Tallahassee. He laughed. "What are you laughing at?" Teresa said in a giggly voice. She was in such a good mood until his sudden burst of laughter had released her good feelings about bringing him to meet her mother.

"Oh, I was just thinking about this ol' country boy driving this beautiful city girl through this metropolis to meet her mom. Boy, have I come up in this world!" They started laughing, and he found it difficult to follow her directions. Soon they quieted down enough for her to tell him to "turn left here, go straight ahead, turn right at the next corner." They turned onto a quiet street, driving slowly past very nice but moderate-sized homes.

Teresa pointed ahead, and excitedly said, "This is it—the one with the porch light. I'm so happy you're going to finally meet my mom." Lyle noted she had not mentioned Enrique. He turned the car into the driveway, which ran to a detached garage behind the house. Lyle stopped adjacent to a walk that led to the front porch. Teresa reached over and pulled at him. He responded by leaning over, and they kissed. "Welcome to my home, Lyle." He squeezed her hand.

"What we discussed on the way down will be pretty heavy stuff for your mom. She's got a big decision to make," Lyle said. "Let's not tell her until tomorrow night." Teresa squeezed his hand back. "I agree wholeheartedly. Give her a chance to enjoy our company. I know she's looked forward to our arrival."

As they exited the car and started to unload the backseat, Arlene Carter came out onto the porch. She waved, came down the steps, and hurriedly walked to meet them. "You're finally here," she said as she and Teresa hugged each other.

"It's great to be home, Mom, even for two days." She turned to Lyle, who was standing a little behind and to one side of her. "This is Lyle. I've told you a lot about him, now here he is in person." Teresa was laughing as she took his hand.

Arlene stepped over in front of him, and held out her hand. Lyle took it. The three of them now formed a triangle. "I'm very happy to meet the mother of this wonderful young lady." He looked intently at Arlene. "Even in this weak light, I can see where your daughter's beauty comes from."

"Welcome, Lyle. I'm so very happy you're here." Arlene was pleased.

Teresa squeezed his hand firmly.

Upon gathering their luggage, the three of them went into the house. Lyle didn't want to appear obvious to Teresa's mom, but his eyes were absorbing as many details as possible—chairs, tables, pictures—anything, everything. He wanted to feel and remember the place where Teresa grew up.

It was a very comfortable-looking and well-kept home. When they put down their bags, Lyle and Arlene locked eyes for a short moment—both were very respectful of each other. He had seen she was a very calm and graceful woman. Lyle was impressed by her manner. He liked her.

"Teresa, as soon as you show Lyle the guest room, we'll have one of my 'thrown together' dinners." Arlene chuckled as she went toward the kitchen. Teresa winked at Lyle.

After a great dinner, Teresa and her mother quickly cleared the table. "Lyle, please make yourself at home. You can watch television in the den if you wish, or today's paper is on the coffee table. Teresa and I are going to clean the kitchen and have a little mother-daughter conversation." Arlene was smiling as she disappeared through the door. Lyle walked into the comfortable-looking den and sat down in a winged-back chair, picked up the *Tampa Tribune*, allowing himself to semirelax and enjoy his surroundings.

BRANDON COOK CAME TO THE FARM on Friday afternoon. John liked the geologist and was anticipating his joining the family in helping to discover whatever was beneath the ground. Cook was highly impressed when Reverend Butler introduced him to John. It was very evident to him, that the farmer and his family had been chosen by God to be his messengers for a powerful revelation to the world. Brandon was thrilled to be involved in this spine-tingling event.

When they reached the circle in the bean field, Cook was awed by what he saw, and again by what John told him about the initial darker soil and how it became darker. An hour later, the two of them returned to the house and further discussed the how and when of the forthcoming drilling.

John reiterated to Brandon that he should feel free to visit the bean field any time, and yes, perhaps testing the soil again would be a good idea.

Kelly walked the geologist to his car and thanked him for coming out. Cook quickly let the farmer know the thanks were all his. This was a privilege.

Sara and Granny were sitting on the back porch, enjoying their Sunday afternoon. It was a pleasant day, temperaturewise, but it was the first day of May and the broiling summer was on its way. John walked out the kitchen door and went over and sat down in the swing beside Sara.

"Did you and Mr. Cook have a good meeting?" asked Sara as she reached and put her hand over his.

"Yes, we did. He's a good man, and I'm happy we have him with us. I think he'll be a big help, and I told him to visit the field any time. He wants to run a few in-depth soil tests, more from a geological standpoint than an agricultural one."

"What does he expect to find?" Granny said.

"I'm really not sure, Mama. I think he wants to find why the soil turned darker, and I don't think any of us will ever know, except that God did it to show us a location for something. But Brandon is a scientific man, and he has to try."

John kissed Sara on the cheek, got up from the swing, stretched his arms, and stood for a moment, looking toward the far reaches of the fields. "Well, I've got Clayton Parker's home phone number. I'm gonna call him and see if he's interested in meeting me here Monday or Tuesday. I want to get things moving, and I think the Lord does too. Lyle and Teresa are due back at school from Tampa Sunday evening. We need to get in touch with them as soon as they return.

John went to his office and dialed Clayton Parker, who ran his business out of his home. Clayton's wife answered and was very friendly and said she'd get her husband. It was only a minute before the well driller came to the phone.

"Hello, John, been a long time since you and I've talked. How're you and your family?" John was pleased that Clayton asked about his family and also indicated regret for not having had contact with him for more than a year.

"We're doing fine, Clayton. Thanks for asking. Yes, it's been too long, and I'd like to rectify that. Is it possible, on such short notice, for you to drive over to the farm Monday or Tuesday? I'd like to discuss an important project with you. I prefer not to discuss details on the phone as to what it is. When we talk, you'll understand why."

There was a slight pause. "Why, sure, I'll be glad to come. It'll be good to see you again. But it'll have to be Monday. I have to meet a potential new customer on Tuesday."

"That's great, Clayton. I truly appreciate you coming. Let's make it around 9:00 a.m."

The well driller agreed, and with a warm goodbye, hung up the phone. He turned to his wife and said, "John Kelly sounded strange. It sure got my attention."

"How's that?" his wife replied.

Clayton thought for a moment. "He said he had a project to discuss but not on the phone. I'm going over to see him tomorrow. John is a good man, and I trust him. The word he used was 'project.' That got my attention."

LYLE SAID GRACE while the three of them held hands. It was an uplifting blessing. During Arlene's great dinner of tossed salad, homemade oil, and vinegar dressing with bits of feta cheese, beef tips, small roasted potatoes, and asparagus, a lot of talking went on. First, Lyle was totally impressed with Teresa's mom and the meal. She was very intelligent and had a good sense of humor, but underneath that he knew she was very observant and could read people well. Lyle himself was never uneasy around people; he had a lot of self-confidence. But he was aware Arlene had already sized him up. He knew the next evening when he and Teresa told her of their intentions she was going to be surprised, possibly confused, and certainly hurt. He and Teresa knew they had to be patient and make Arlene a part of their mission—to convince her there were no other choices, and that in a short time she would also be part of the Kelly family.

After the meal, they were sipping coffee and eating cheesecake, also engineered by Arlene, when the outlet door to the garage in the utility room opened and closed. Arlene looked at her daughter and quietly said, "Enrique is home."

Teresa glanced at Lyle and slightly rolled her eyes. Lyle wanted to meet him. He had always had a curiosity about people. This was going to be an important one—to meet the man that had given Teresa a cold shoulder much of her growing-up days, and who was now giving her mother a more intense version of the same.

While Lyle was quickly thinking these things, Arlene got up from her chair, walked into the kitchen, and said in a pleasant voice, "Enrique, come into the dining room and meet our guests." There were some other words, which Lyle and Teresa couldn't make out but guessed were Enrique's unhappy response to Arlene.

Arlene returned to the dining room, Enrique lagging behind. As she entered the door, she stood aside to allow her husband to come into the room, but he stopped in the doorway. "Enrique, this is Lyle Kelly, whom you've heard so much about, and I think you know that beautiful young lady with him."

"Good evening, Lyle. Welcome to Tampa." Enrique then nodded toward Teresa. "Hello, Teresa."

Lyle had walked the few steps around the dining table to formerly present himself to Enrique and shake his hand, but the Cuban was beginning to slightly move back through the doorway. "I've had a long day. Good night." Though Lyle didn't show it, he was astounded as to how ill-mannered and cold Teresa's stepfather was. Arlene told Enrique good night and everyone would see him at breakfast.

"Either of you care for more coffee or my wonderful cheesecake?" Arlene said with a smile. Lyle declined the offer as did Teresa.

"Mom, if I eat any more or have more coffee, I'll never sleep, even as tired as I am."

Lyle agreed. He was impressed that Arlene acted as if all was well—that Enrique had not spoiled the evening.

He thought about what Teresa had told him two weeks ago regarding her stepfather—how he was indifferent and rude to her and more so lately to her mother. Lyle felt sorry for both of them, especially Arlene—she had to put up with the Cuban's growing bad behavior daily, except when he was away on business. It was evident she was too smart and independent to allow her home to be tainted with his growing hostility.

Teresa showed Lyle into the den. "It's all yours for a while. I'm going to give Mom a hand—she wants some 'mother-daughter' time." Lyle smiled a fraction, but he still had Enrique on his mind, plus dreading the next night when they would reveal their irreversible plan to Arlene.

"I'll see if I can find a dull movie on TV and try to unwind a bit. If you find me asleep when you finish, just pick me up and take me to my room and tuck me in."

Teresa gently patted him on the head as he sat down in a recliner chair. "Don't hold your breath, dear." She chuckled as she left the room.

He awoke when Teresa and her mom came into the den. "Let's get you to your room—you need to turn in," Teresa said. He looked at his watch and readily agreed. It was almost eleven o'clock.

CHAPTER SIXTEEN

D RUGGIST MARVIN GARDNER had been very busy for three days, filling prescriptions for a number of Danaville citizens who had come down with a touch of stomach virus. He hadn't been able to keep his nose on the trail of the 'storm' rumors, or at least those people who, like him, thought the Kellys were hiding what occurred at their farm. He picked up his ringing phone, anticipating another prescription call-in from a doctor's office. He was surprised to hear Sheriff Bernam's voice. "Hi, Marvin. This is Claude Bernam."

"Well, Sheriff, glad you called." Gardner's mind was going one hundred miles per hour. He had wanted to talk to Bernam for the past several days, but the drugstore had kept him busy lately, and he had been unable to visit with his regular drop-in customers, or phone his business buddies as he usually did.

"I'd like to talk with you and Jim Summers about the Kellys— for your help in trying to find out about that rainbow and whatever else happened out there," the sheriff said.

Marvin was surprised at Bernam's directness. It wasn't that often the sheriff would share his investigation of an event of any magnitude, and this one surpassed them all. "Uh, sure, Claude. When and where?"

Bernam was silent for a moment. "How about early tomorrow night, about seven at Grogan's Cafe in Varnum?"

"That's fine. It being a Saturday night, my assistant Dorothy will work 'til nine and close up for me. I'll call Summers. I feel certain he'll want to come. If there's a hitch, I'll let you know."

The sheriff grunted an okay and hung up. Marvin wondered how in the world Claude ever had the savvy to re-win his badge in the last election.

Gardner immediately called the editor. At first, he seemed to hedge when told what Sheriff Bernam wanted, but finally agreed to join them on Sunday. Jim Summers, being a true newspaperman, was reluctant to share his own "rainbow" investigation with anyone, especially the unlikely pair of Marvin Gardner and Sheriff Bernam. He would not reveal the detailed official information about the storms he had gotten from the NWS in Panama City.

The druggist put down the phone and stood there, wondering just what Claude had on his mind.

JOHN AND SARA were deeply concerned about the unfolding of the "divine event" and its effect on the family. The two had agreed, in several private talks between themselves and with Reverend Butler, that once the event and its ramifications were known, all the divergent human elements in the county, state, nation, and the world, each with their own agenda, would be pounding at their door. The family's safety and that of others could be at risk.

Lyle and Teresa had come to the same conclusion. Even in the midst of God's growing event, they wanted to get married as soon as possible so the coming revelation could be better served by them as man and wife. But first, they knew it was important they cease their studies at FSU and move to the farm and face the coming days with the family. The two of them knew their future was totally changed forever. It would be served only by following God's will.

On Sunday, after Friday night's meeting and before returning to school, Lyle had asked his parents to walk down to the pond for a private meeting with him and Teresa. When the four sat down at a large oaken picnic table made by Lyle several years ago, each of his parents had a curious look on his or her face. Lyle explained he and Teresa wanted to immediately leave school, move to the farm, and get married—that they deeply loved each other. He described the strong feeling they had that their future was through the family and the farm. Lyle finished by saying that he and Teresa were convinced that during and after the event's revelation the farm and family would be threatened in many ways. The entire family must be together to meet whatever threat arises.

Lyle added that when he and Teresa went to Tampa on Friday they would tell her mom of their plans and what had occurred at the farm. He looked at his future wife as she nodded in agreement. "We must urge her to come to the farm. She can't stay in Tampa.

There was a long moment of silence. John and Sara looked at each other searchingly. Finally, John spoke, "I think your mother and I have known something like this was to be expected. We've known almost from the time Carew and I saw the hail pattern around the fields and then the circle. Something big was at work, much bigger than mankind." He reached across the table and turned his right hand palm up in front of Teresa. She put her left hand in his with a faint smile. He then took Sara's right hand with his left. Sara then reached and took Lyle's open hand, and he in turn took Teresa's right hand—the circle was complete. Sara squeezed her son's hand, and he passed it on. As Teresa squeezed John's hand, he prayed aloud for the Lord to give them light and show them through the unknown as it unfolded ahead of them.

"Teresa, Sara and I are thrilled you are joining the family. Everyone loves you." As John was talking, he and Sara got up and walked around the table, their arms held out to her and Lyle. It was a very tender moment for all of them.

"Welcome to the farm, dearest," Sara said. "Your mother will be very welcome—if she comes—and we hope she does. She must. After you two talk to her, Lyle can call me, and I'll be happy to tell her our feelings and let her know our home would be her home for as long as she wishes. Or as long as it takes for God's will to be carried out."

The four of them returned to the house, having agreed not to say anything to anyone about their conversation.

LYLE HAD JUST opened his eyes to his strange surroundings when there was a light knock on his door. Teresa opened it and took a couple of steps into the room. "Okay, you lazy bedbug, it's late, and the day is rushing by. We've got places to go and things to do." He smiled at his wife-to-be. She was beautiful, standing in the doorway dressed in sandals, white shorts, and an old FSU Seminole T-shirt. Her hair was pulled back and tied in a short ponytail.

"Well, I'm sure glad the owner of this establishment sent their best waker-upper. I think I'll go back to sleep so you can do it all over again." She laughed, blew him a kiss, and walked out of the room, closing the door while saying, "Up! Up!"

Lyle lay there thinking about the talk they had the past weekend with his parents—how they were so happy that Teresa was going to become their daughter-in-law. They also accepted their son and his wife-to-be's leaving school and moving to the farm. Their lives had been changed by the recent rainbow. However, all of them knew that was only the beginning. He and Teresa looked forward to their marriage, though it was to be in the midst of a new direction for the Kellys and their beloved farm. They were to serve God's purpose and nothing else.

He got up and headed for the shower while thinking about what kind of reaction Teresa's mother would have when they told her about leaving school, their coming marriage, and the impact of God's act on the family and what they would find beneath the bean field. Lyle and Teresa had concluded they must convince Arlene that her life would be changed forever by the looming events and that she would have to return with them to the farm. It was not going to be easy.

After showering and shaving, Lyle put on chinos, a short-sleeved pullover, and comfortable Trailblazer walkers. He would be on his feet most of the day. Teresa and her mother had mentioned they wanted to visit Busch Gardens. After they had described the popular open zoo and amusement park, he wanted to see it.

He walked out into the hall and followed his eyes, ears, and nose toward the kitchen. The smell of bacon, coffee, and the sound of female voices told him he was on course. With the weight of the coming evening's talk with Arlene pushed to the back of his mind, he felt good.

"Good morning," he said as he entered the kitchen. Before he could say anything else, Teresa quickly came over and kissed him on the cheek.

"It's about time," she said. He smiled and took her hand.

"I hope you slept well in our luxurious guest bedroom," Arlene quipped. "You two go sit at the breakfast table, and I'll serve you. Nothing but the best for my house guests."

Lyle really liked Arlene. She had a natural, quick humor.

It was almost eight thirty when the three of them finished their leisurely breakfast. They had planned their day, most of it to be spent at Busch Gardens. Lyle pitched in with helping to clear the table and volunteered to clean the kitchen, whereas Arlene said an emphatic, yet loving, "No way."

Teresa walked out of the kitchen, saying she had to change clothes, while Lyle stayed behind. "Where is Enrique this morning?"

Arlene quickly replied, "He had to go to his office. Said he had to finish a report for a Monday-morning meeting."

Lyle thought, "Yeah, I'll bet he couldn't wait to get away from us."

Arlene asked about his family. She knew their watermelon production had been very good the past year, along with corn, tomatoes, and several other crops. She smiled at Lyle and said Teresa kept her informed. Lyle was pleased that Arlene showed interest in his family and the farm.

He, in turn, inquired about her accounting business and asked a few questions relative to its application to farming. She gladly responded to his questions, and they talked until Teresa walked in.

"Hey, you two, let's go and enjoy this beautiful day. I'm rarin' to go see some African animals and have lunch at the Swiss Chalet." She smiled and winked at Lyle. He stepped over beside her and lightly bumped his shoulder against hers. She bumped his in return. He looked into her clear, beautiful eyes, and thought again how fortunate he was. "Thank you, Lord," he said silently.

Arlene folded the dish towel she had been using and hung it on a wall rack next to the stove. "Give me a chance to go check this and that, and we'll be ready to go." When she walked into the den toward the hall, Lyle pulled Teresa around and they kissed, taking their time. It wasn't long before Arlene was back.

"Okay, I just set a new mother's record for a pretrip facial touch-up. Head for the garage while I set the alarm." Teresa smiled at Lyle and rolled her eyes.

Lyle was ready for a little relaxation. He knew Teresa was also. It would be a good day.

THE THREE OF them had a good day, indeed. Arlene drove, providing a running commentary as she pointed out various sites. The city's skyline was impressive to Lyle, but he liked the scenic views of Hillsborough Bay, and the quick tour of Ybor City—the Cuban district with its outstanding old restaurants. They soon were approaching Busch Gardens.

Teresa quipped, "Our chauffeur finally found her way. I guess we'll keep her." All three laughed as they were directed to a parking space.

After several hours of fun, including an early light lunch, it was almost 5:00 p.m. Arlene said earlier she had made reservations for six o'clock at Cibilo's Steak House. It was one of Tampa's best, yet casual dress was acceptable. As they departed Busch Gardens, Lyle thought how appropriate that Arlene chose a steak house—he and Teresa would need a good intake of protein to give them strength for their after-dinner mission.

Cibilo's was already busy when they arrived. Arlene found a parking space on the far side of the lot, saying she preferred parking herself rather than use valet service. "Too many foreign attendants, too many dents and scrapes," she said.

Lyle chuckled. Teresa took his hand when they emerged from the car and as the three of them walked toward the restaurant,

Teresa squeezed his hand. When he looked into her face, he saw a thin smile and serious eyes. He nodded slightly, smiled, and squeezed back, trying to assure her all would turn out okay. The door was opened for them and they entered. Lyle thought, "When we emerge, Arlene's world will be different."

They were seated in a quieter area located in the back. It was exactly what Teresa had requested from her mom—slightly isolated. Arlene didn't comment when asked by her daughter to request a quiet spot; she had already surmised Teresa was going to announce her engagement and talk about plans for the wedding. Her daughter was home with an outstanding future son-in-law. The problems with Enrique paled in contrast to her current happiness.

Lyle was very impressed with the restaurant—red leather, dark wood, and medium sienna brick. Even the muted blue and dark ochre carpet was nice. Teresa touched his arm and turned her head toward a far wall. When he followed her movement, he saw a long brick wall where a wide open area exposed a portion of the large kitchen. Several chefs were grilling steaks and other food. The scent of the cooking meat was fantastic. If his grandpa Josh had been there, he would have said, "Folks, we're in high cotton."

The three of them enjoyed the food and atmosphere. Teresa had eaten there twice before, but being with Lyle made it a special occasion. She was anxious to tell her mother about her engagement to Lyle and their coming marriage. However, Teresa felt the heavy burden of what she and Lyle had to do right after that. Lyle was sitting there thinking the same thing—tell Arlene about the event and their leaving school. He felt the hardest thing for her would be to join them, give up her business (at least for a while), and become a family member at the farm. Enrique would never join them. It was evident to Lyle and Teresa the relationship between Arlene and Enrique was all but over. Arlene had been unhappy with him for a long time.

The dinner talk had slowed, dessert refused, but coffee ordered. Teresa could see through her mother's attempt to hide her anticipation of hearing about her daughter's engagement.

Lyle looked over at Arlene and silently prayed, "Dear God, please help Teresa and me at this difficult time. Open Arlene's heart and mind to receive our words and fully understand the reality of your holy event at my family's farm and why we have to leave school and move to the farm . . . why she must come with us. Amen."

"ARLENE, YOUR DAUGHTER and I are deeply in love. I'm sure you've known that for some time." Lyle reached and took Teresa's hand. "We want you to know we are engaged and plan to get married soon."

Arlene broke into a wide smile. Teresa got out of her chair, stepped over beside her mother, bent down, and kissed her forehead. Arlene rose, and they hugged. Because of being in a restaurant, both of them tried to keep their tears of happiness discreet. It was impossible. Several guests turned in their chairs and smiled in comprehension. Arlene looked at Lyle, who was standing. She reached out; and he moved to her; and they grasped hands.

"Oh, Lyle, I'm so happy for you both."

Lyle was happy also, and he showed his joy by hugging Arlene and then Teresa. The three sat down and enjoyed the moment.

Lyle told Arlene that Teresa's engagement ring would be forthcoming—that they had had no time to shop for one. A large occurrence at the farm had occupied all available time, and final exams for the semester would start at the end of the following week. Teresa could see a big question mark on her mother's face when Lyle mentioned the "large occurrence at the farm."

"A ring is not the most important thing." Arlene said as she looked at Lyle. "I know one will be forthcoming. But what happened at the farm?" Teresa caught Lyle's eye and nodded slightly.

Lyle looked at Arlene and knew what he was about to tell her would confuse her and scare her. And even though she was a very intelligent, strong businesswoman and loving mother, she, like most anyone, might become upset and show disbelief and denial. "Time will tell," he thought. "Here goes."

"Arlene, the occurrence I referred to was called a miracle by our minister, Rev. Wade Butler. The family shortened that to 'event' for the reason of security. It all started with a thunderstorm and rainbow a year ago. The very same kind of thunderstorm occurred over two weeks ago with an identical rainbow, but this time, there was much more."

Teresa was watching her mother closely. Arlene's face changed as she hung on to Lyle's every word.

He gave all details of the recent storm: how it formed, how the hail fell in such a precise pattern, the rainbow pointing downward over the bean field, the center of the farm. He emphasized the perfect circle of very slightly darker soil. How it darkened more over a few days, as if to make sure it was seen and to emphasize its importance.

He noticed Arlene sat dumbfounded. There was a perceptible look of disbelief.

The remaining details of what was going on at the farm were given to Arlene—the general plan of action and how the family would carry it out were included. Nothing was omitted. Lyle was careful to make sure she knew all that he and Teresa knew. It was important for the decision she would ultimately have to make.

Arlene finally spoke, "How does your family feel about what is happening? What does your Minister Butler think this means?" She was obviously feeling the magnitude of this information.

"Mom, we are all totally in awe, yet we know there's much more to come."

Lyle continued, "What has transpired, if known by anyone at this time outside of the family other than several highly trusted outsiders, would be a threat to us, the farm, the nation, and the world. Arlene, Teresa and I feel the family must protect God's plan—whatever that may be. Given the state of our country and that of the world, our family has a gigantic and difficult task to accomplish. We must be secretive about what has happened so far, and everything that transpires in the future, 'til it's taken out of our hands.

"There'll be many people who would go to most any means to find out about the event, and when we find whatever is beneath the surface of the bean field, there'll be many more who would do anything to get control of the finding. When I say anything, I mean people would destroy the farm, even hurt or possibly kill anyone trying to protect God's work. This is truly the biggest thing to happen to this world since his miracles, as told in the Old and New Testament.

"I'm astounded," whispered Arlene. She looked searchingly at Lyle, then Teresa. "I don't know what to say. It's so powerful, so overwhelming. Everything else by comparison seems unimportant." She held Teresa's hand as if she would never let go.

"Now comes the difficult part, Mom. What we are about to say will disappoint you, but it has to be done for the family, and more importantly, for God."

Arlene's facial expression did not change. She did not move. It was as if she had not heard Teresa's words.

Lyle cleared his throat, took a swallow of water, and put the glass down slowly on the table. "Teresa and I are leaving FSU immediately and moving to the farm. We'll get married as soon as possible. We've discussed this thoroughly and prayed a lot about it. There's not much time before all of the family are going to be very busy. We'll just have to forfeit this semester and possibly our degrees. Believe us, Arlene, we really don't have a choice in this matter. God's plan, whatever it turns out to be, has to be carried out, and we are an undeniable part of that plan." Lyle let out a breath and sat back a little from the table. Teresa had reached over and covered his hand with hers while he had been talking. The three of them sat quietly, thinking.

The waiter appeared and offered more coffee. Teresa declined, but Lyle and Arlene accepted. They had been in the restaurant for almost two hours and realized they soon had to leave. However, Teresa and Lyle knew they had given Arlene a lot to digest. She needed as much time as it took to let her emotional side settle down and her intellectual side to take over.

"Mom, all of the Kellys think you should come to the farm with us and stay during the dig. Whatever it is we find, we'll then know more about what we should do and how we should do it. As we've said before, this is big. The public doesn't know yet what's going on—but they will; it's just a matter of time." Teresa looked lovingly at her mother.

Lyle added, "No one can say for sure how people will react when they find out what's happened. As I said before, I feel, and so does my dad, that when they discover there has been a divine event and we have found something powerful of God's making, people throughout the world will want to see, touch, steal, or even destroy it. There will be chaos throughout the United States, and even here in Tampa. People will divide into various factions, some good, many not good—the religious order around the world could change. Reverend Butler believes this also. Arlene, it's not as if we have a choice. We don't. Your safety could be at stake. Teresa and I don't want you to stay in Tampa during this time, and neither does the rest of the family. And we know this makes some large problems for you.

Arlene was quiet as she slowly looked at Lyle and Teresa. The restaurant was crowded now at the height of its dinner hour. Their table was isolated, but the noise was building and it wasn't easy to talk. She leaned in closer to the two, "You've given me a lot to think about and I need some time to digest it. As you can see, I'm a little numb." Her attempt to smile was weak.

"I think we should head home. We've been here a long time, and Cibilo's probably wants this table," Teresa said. "Come on, Mom, we can continue in the car."

When they got to Arlene's car, Lyle asked if he could drive them home. He didn't want her driving while her mind was processing the staggering information she had just received. Teresa agreed with a nod.

With Teresa sitting in back, talking with her mom and giving directions to Lyle, the drive home was uneventful.

CHAPTER SEVENTEEN

MARVIN GARDNER PARKED in front of Grogan's Café, three spaces away from the front entrance. He noticed the sheriff's car parked nearby. Marvin was amused. Claude was always early to everything. The druggist didn't see Summers's car—that wasn't surprising. For a newspaper editor, he was a tad slow, always arriving at the last minute.

The Café wasn't very busy—only one couple and a lone diner, sitting near the front. Marvin walked to the back of the room, where Bernam was sitting, sipping coffee. "How's it going, Sheriff? It's 6:50. You must have been hungry." Gardner was smiling as he sat down. The sheriff gave him a nondescript look and put his coffee mug down and took a bite of the cheese-toast appetizer he had ordered.

"Where's the editor? He seems to always be runnin' behind. If this place was on fire, he'd miss most of the story."

"Well, we said seven, and he's not late yet."

"The sheriff is his same, impatient self," Marvin thought. He turned and looked toward the front door when he heard Summers's voice as he spoke to Charlie Grogan when he passed the cashier's counter.

Before the editor sat down, there were greetings and handshakes. As he took a chair, the sheriff asked him what was new and chuckled. Summers mumbled something about smart-alecky lawmen, while picking up a menu.

Marvin was in his element. "Here I am, getting ready to discuss the Kelly farm storm and its unique rainbow. I'm going to be an insider with the two men who will be key in learning what happened." His thoughts were interrupted when the sheriff thanked them both for coming.

"It's important the sheriff's department finds out what occurred at the Kellys'. From my own contact with the family right after the recent storm's rainbow had disappeared, I had a feeling in my gut that the family was sitting on an experience they did not want to share.

"Chief Deputy Beck got the same impression when he talked to John Kelly later. We don't have just a whole lot of people who compared this storm with the one last year, or observed the same odd rainbow. What about you, Marvin? You were out there that day."

"Yeah, I got the same feeling. I remember after the first storm, I tried to discuss the rainbow with Lyle, who was in the store with my son just prior to the boys' returning to school, and he couldn't or wouldn't give too many details. I soon pushed it to the back of my mind, and the months went by. When this second storm happened, I saw that it appeared to be an exact copy of the first one. I was dumbfounded when several others and I, standing in front of my store, saw the exact same rainbow as the first one. That's when I drove north on 77 and decided it was over the Kelly farm. I was convinced then this was no fluke of nature. I saw Claude ahead of me and followed him to the Kellys. When we got there, the rainbow had faded, but there were hailstones on the ground."

Bernam looked at the editor and added, "After we visited for a while, trading small talk with John and other family members, I asked a few questions about the storm, but got no revealing answers. John commented he and his two farmhands had to go inspect the crops for hail damage. It was evident we weren't invited to go along, so we left. That's pretty much where it stands as of now."

Summers knew much of this. Gardner had been almost relentless in recounting the day of the storm to him. The editor wasn't about to give up any detailed information regarding his own investigation. He had already considered what had happened—or was happening at the Kelly farm—could be a tremendous jolt to people everywhere.

The editor knew he had to be very careful in how he did his job as a newspaperman, and a member of the community. "I think we should keep a close eye on the farm without being obvious," he said. "It could be helpful to know who visits the farm."

"I thought the same thing," Bernam said. "I'm steppin' up patrolling 77 north. I can assign one man to check that farm area twice a day, say, around midday and early evening. I don't think that'll draw much attention, plus my man can still cover his regular assignment."

"How about Reverend Butler? Would it do any good to casually talk to him?" Gardner looked at the other two, expecting plaudits for his question.

Summers thought for a moment, and said, "That might be a good idea. Let me handle that." Bernam and Gardner nodded in agreement.

They ate their dinner and continued talk about the odd weather mystery, and weather in general. The editor said nothing about his visit to the NWS in Panama City or what he had learned about the two storms. Finally, he said he had to leave. The other two agreed it was time to end their meeting. They all went dutch on the not-too-good food and coffee.

ENRIQUE CRUZ WASN'T comfortable with Teresa and her boyfriend being there. It was an imposition on him. Arlene had easily noticed his additional aggravation, and he didn't care how it affected her or Teresa. Nowadays, his entire world revolved around the Gelb Food Company and his new, and more important, affiliation with Frank Bovitz and Alejo Gomez. That was his aim— not living his life as a family man with only an eight-to-five job. His life was changing, and all he could see was money and self.

He had come home to an empty house around six thirty. The quiet was enjoyable, but was interrupted around eight forty-five when he heard the garage door open. They were home. He picked up a book and headed for his bedroom.

Enrique had been wanting to leave Arlene for several months now, but he didn't want to pay alimony. He owed her nothing. She had a successful business and was capable of taking care of herself. They had no shared credit cards or other contractual debts. He contributed one half the expenses for food, utilities, yard upkeep, or any house repairs that were needed. These were the things he was in question about. Frank Bovitz had said when he was ready, he'd point him toward a good divorce attorney. He added that Alejo Gomez would cover all legal fees if needed. Enrique was pleased.

Arlene, Teresa, and Lyle were tired from their all-day outing plus an emotional dinner. Arlene tried to be upbeat, but her mind was overflowing with the awesome information Lyle and Teresa had given her. Her world had been turned upside down. But there were going to be many others that would have to face the same, or more.

They sat in the living room, sipping cold fresh orange juice Teresa had served. "Mom, I love you so very much, as I do Lyle. It's been very difficult for us to tell you what is happening and what the family must do. You are accepted as a family member also. We all have to stick together. Our bond is our strength to see us through the completion of the divine event."

Teresa was talking softly because she and the others had seen Enrique's car in the garage. She knew he was in his room with the door closed. For the past four months, he had been sleeping alone in a bedroom located in the rear of the house.

Lyle got out of his chair, went over to Arlene, and sat down on the couch beside her and Teresa. "It seems time is compressing hour by hour. I'll be talking to my dad tomorrow night and will get an update on what's happening at home. He's supposed to talk to a well driller within a day or two. I think the drilling will start very soon. This is strong stuff, Arlene. It's the most important thing that will happen in our lives. It's bigger than anything we can imagine. You must join us."

Arlene was quiet for a few moments. Her daughter and future son-in-law sat patiently. "I think I can turn my clients over to a close accountant friend of mine, Marilyn Nobles. She'll do it. She has two other people in her company and can handle the extra work, especially since she lost a large account last month. We could work out an equitable split of fees. I'll have to hurriedly contact my accounts and tell them I have to go away for a while . . . or something like that. That's going to be tough to do. Of course, we don't know what the future holds, do we?"

She dabbed at her eyes with a tissue. "For the time being, I will leave the house in the hands of another friend who can be counted on to watch over it. My neighbors will be told I was called away on a family matter. That sure fits, doesn't it?" She showed a faint smile. "Other than my checking account, I'll leave my savings and stocks where they are, hoping they're protected but understanding that's very contingent.

"As far as Enrique is concerned, our relationship has been over for quite a while. I should have faced that reality long ago. I've prayed about it constantly. Evidently, God is acting. I'll tell Enrique it's all over—that he'll have to leave immediately. I truly don't want anything else to do with him." Teresa and Lyle looked at each other, knowing Arlene had just let the long pent-up pain out of her heart. It was a giant step for her.

"Oh, Mom, you can't handle all these details without help. You mustn't confront Enrique alone. He may grab his things and walk right out, or he may not; that's what worries Lyle and me."

Lyle got up from the couch and slowly walked around the room. Teresa knew he was deep in thought. Arlene admired Lyle's maturity and, after only one day, highly respected him. Her eyes followed his every move. Finally, he stopped in front of her and spoke softly, "Perhaps you can talk to Enrique in the morning— the sooner the better. I want to be here when you do. After leaving with his personal items, I'm sure he'll want to return later next week for any other things that belong to him. If it's after we leave, your friend who will be keeping an eye on the house could handle that. I'll bet he could bring someone with him for insurance."

Arlene looked at Lyle for a long moment. "It's going to be a tight fit, timewise, but with God's help, we'll get it done. Teresa, you need to call your sister in the morning. I'll talk to her too, to fill her in on my being away for a while. I'm worried about Carla and her family." She assured Lyle she understood the reason for secrecy.

"Teresa and I have talked it over, and we feel it important that we don't return to school unless you're with us. We will spend the night there, load our things, and head for Danaville. If we leave here late Thursday morning, we can be in Tallahassee by midafternoon and at the farm by midday Friday. How does that work for you, Arlene?"

"I can be ready by then. It's more time than I first calculated."

"Arlene, I need to call Dad and let him know what's going on, that Teresa and I are staying here for a few days 'til you're ready to travel with us. He'll let us know what's happening at the farm." Arlene gave him a slight smile and told him to talk as long as he liked. He sat down on one of the two matching chairs beside a table with a phone. He picked it up and dialed the farm. Arlene patted Teresa's hand and told them she was going to her room and hopefully get some sleep. She rose from the couch with her mom and gave her a quick hug and said she'd follow her soon. Teresa moved over to the other chair beside Lyle and sat down. While Lyle dialed the farm, she looked at his tired face and thought how very much she loved him.

SARA ANSWERED THE phone. It was 9:40 p.m. in Danaville and rather late for the Kellys, but she was happy to hear her son's voice. After they chatted several minutes, he told his mother that Arlene had gone to bed. She was very tired after a traumatic evening. Sara said to tell Arlene she would call her tomorrow. She then asked Lyle to wait while she got his dad to the phone.

"Hi, son, hope everything's going okay, given the circumstances."

"It is, Dad, although we all are emotionally drained. We've talked at length to Arlene about what's going on. As you can guess, she's was shocked. Teresa and I emphasized the importance of her coming to the farm as soon as possible, and I think she fully understands why. We'll all leave late Thursday morning for Tallahassee, spend the night, pick up our things, and drive to the farm on Friday afternoon. She'll tell Enrique in the morning that it's all over and he will have to leave immediately.

They talked on for several minutes. John related all that was taking place—his meeting with Cook, the geologist, and setting up Monday's meeting with Clayton Parker, the water-well man. They would hopefully start exploratory drilling as soon as possible. His dad said he wanted Parker to do the drilling, and hopefully he could start within a week or so. He assured Lyle that all of the family were doing well and waiting with high expectations.

Lyle put down the phone, stretched out his legs, and told Teresa the details of the conversation with his dad. She stood up and reached for his hand and pulled. He stood and they embraced and held each other tightly for a moment, then kissed. Their passion was fleeting, being compressed between the various demands left on their hearts and minds from the day's events, and what tomorrow would bring.

"Sweetheart, tomorrow's going to be a full, emotional day, starting with Enrique."

"I know," Teresa said as she looked into his eyes and hugged him again.

Except for a night light, they went down the hallway in near darkness, hand in hand until reaching Lyle's room. They stopped, kissed quickly, wishing each other a good night. Teresa continued on to her mother's room. Lyle looked forward to his bed. It had been a traumatic day.

CHAPTER EIGHTEEN

JOHN, SARA, GRANNY, and Carew were in church as usual on Sunday morning. The meaning of the service to the family was totally different now than it was two weeks ago. They had a feeling of God's presence that they had not experienced before. Reverend Butler's sermon, "The Unlimited Power of God," was like a personal message to each of them. They drew strength from the service for the task ahead.

The congregation was unaware of that unlimited power at work only several miles away. They were attentive to the reverend's eloquent sermon—he was an excellent preacher—and most of them would readily agree that the Lord's power was constant and immeasurable, and felt it in their hearts, but none of them could know his power was at work so close to them as they sang the closing hymn. The three-hundred-plus souls in attendance would be witnesses to a great event in the very near future.

After church, the Kellys chatted with friends, greeted a few people they had not known before, and talked to Reverend Butler for a moment. John discreetly told the minister that he had a meeting set up with a well driller on Monday at 9:00 a.m. Could he come? Butler nodded his head with a slight smile and turned to greet others.

The Kellys arrived home about twelve thirty. Sara and Granny headed for the kitchen to get things ready for lunch. Granny had left a small roast with potatoes and carrots simmering on top of the large gas range. Sara had prepared French green beans and yeast rolls the night before. She put the rolls in the oven and would warm the beans in the microwave just before everyone sat down. John became amused watching the two women do their Sunday noon kitchen ritual. Not a wasted movement. It was almost a dance.

As they were enjoying the meal, the conversation turned to the morning's church service and Reverend Butler's sermon—how it filled them with courage and determination to do God's will. John commented that the rest of the congregation would only understand when the divine event was revealed in the near future.

He then turned the conversation to Lyle, Teresa, and her mother. "I hope by this time Enrique has left or is leaving, and there's been no trouble out of him. Teresa and Lyle's presence has been and will be helpful to Arlene.

"When Lyle called last night, he told me Arlene was convinced, as we are, that the unknown reaction of people everywhere when the Lord's power and might is revealed to them will likely be threatening and cause havoc. It's hard on her. She has another daughter in Naples, Florida, who is married and has a three-year-old girl. Arlene is concerned about them, but knows she can't reveal what's happening because of the importance of security for at least ten days or so. Like the rest of us, she will ask God to protect them against all harm—to bring them into the larger family circle as soon as possible."

The four of them were concerned about Arlene and the transition she was making. They understood it was extremely difficult for her.

AROUND 2:00 P.M., JOHN got a call from Clayton Parker. "John, I know we set up a meeting for tomorrow, but a problem has come up. My Tuesday appointment said he had to change our meeting to Monday—the only time he has for the entire week."

"Well, it's very important that we talk. Can you possibly come over today?

The well driller seemed relieved at John's question. "I'll be happy to come. I appreciate your understanding,"

"No problem, Clayton, glad to oblige. Can you be here by four or four thirty?"

"Sure can. See you about four."

John put the phone down and told Sara of Clayton's coming visit. She and Granny hoped he would be willing to pledge his secrecy and take on the job.

Carew told everyone he was off to his apartment for a short nap. Sunday afternoon was his time to have a rest. He always looked forward to it. John told him he wanted him to be present when Parker arrived. Carew said he wouldn't miss it for the world.

John called Reverend Butler and was going to explain the circumstances of the meeting change with Parker and ask if he could make it to the farm by 4:00 p.m., but his wife answered the phone. She told him Wade was visiting a couple of sick church members and wouldn't be available until after five o'clock. John asked her to tell the minister that he would later fill him in on the details about the meeting with the well driller.

ABOUT TEN MINUTES until four, a red dust-covered, mud-splattered pickup truck with a large Parker Well-Drilling Company logo on its doors pulled up to the house. Clayton Parker pried himself from the cab and headed up the front steps to reacquaint himself with John Kelly. Like many others, he was very impressed with the farm. He had seen it over a year ago, and it now looked even better.

John greeted Parker with a firm handshake at the front door. "Welcome, Clayton, glad you could come over today. Things work out for the best 90 percent of the time. This is one of those times."

"Howdy, John, it's a pleasure to be here and see you again." John showed the well driller into the living room where he met Sara, Granny, and Carew. Granny hurried into the kitchen to get coffee as the rest of them were sitting down. After a few minutes of friendly small talk about farming and well-drilling, and everyone sipping their coffee, John cleared his throat slightly to signal it was time to start discussing the important business at hand. He looked at Clayton and told him it was extremely important that everything discussed for the rest of the meeting be held as secret. Parker nodded in agreement. John said they needed to drill a hole in the very middle of the most central field on the farm. It was important to all of them that they work closely together and say nothing about it to anyone. "If asked what's going on, stretch the truth and say 'farmwork,' or some such thing."

Clayton knew this was big. He had an inexplicable feeling of a power working in the room—a power that put goose bumps on his arms. The urge to be part of whatever was happening here on the farm was strong. He trusted and respected the Kellys, and agreed to John's conditions of secrecy.

John and Carew revealed all that had happened to date, and what had to be done in the bean field as soon as feasible. Their story was staggering to Clayton. He realized his life and that of his wife were drastically being changed.

The three of them talked about different aspects of the drilling. John told Clayton that retired geologist Brandon Cook, another recent family member, had studied several west Florida geological survey maps and felt there was a shallow limestone strata in the immediate area. "He thinks, through a combination of geological assessment and, to the recent event, that whatever we find will be in an accessible location—more than likely, a cavern."

"Cook means we will likely drill into a dry cavern?"

John nodded, "That's right."

"I've hit a number of those in my day. Some had water and the others didn't. Our best bet is to drill a 3-7/8 inch hole first, taking two or three core samples as we go along, to ascertain the various strata and measure the depth to the top of the limestone— if there is any. Then we'll switch to a thirty-six-inch bit and redrill the small hole all the way down to the limestone. After that, a change to a twenty-eight-inch bit will be made to bore through the 'stone.' This size hole will accommodate a medium-sized man. A thirty-inch steel casing will then be inserted down to the limestone to safeguard the wall of the hole, making sure it doesn't collapse. John, all of this is dependent on my guesswork as to how the various strata are made up. I've got a hunch that I'm right."

John looked at the well driller with a hint of a smile. "Clayton, whatever you think needs doing is what we'll do. You're totally in charge."

It was a few minutes after five when the three men headed to the bean field to show Parker the darkened circle and plants, and also plan how to bring in his large mobile drilling rig. John knew there would be significant damage to the beans. At least 25 percent, if not more—but that was unimportant now.

Parker was in awe when he saw the circle and its perfection.

DEPUTY BECK WAS cruising south on State Highway 77 and was approaching County Road 26, which led to the Kelly farm. He noticed a dirty old red pickup truck waiting at the stop sign to let the deputy pass. Beck saw the Parker Water Well Drilling sign on the truck door. He knew the Pasternaks had a windmill water pump and likely didn't need another well. The well driller had to be coming from the Kellys. But they had a large retainer pond and a widespread sprinkler system, plus a deep well and pump for the house. Why would a well driller be visiting them?

The deputy made a mental note of what he saw and continued driving to Danaville. He glanced in his mirror and saw the pickup, about fifty yards behind, keeping pace with him. Beck pulled onto the apron of Minor's Exxon, and waited until the truck passed. After a few seconds, he fell in behind the pickup. When he did, the vehicle's license plate was barely readable at fifty to sixty feet. He finally made the plate out as Jackson County. The deputy wondered why John Kelly wouldn't use or talk to one of the two well drillers located here in Mason County?

When Beck saw the truck take the left turn lane under 1-10, he wheeled his patrol car around and drove back to Burger Castle. He would see the sheriff in the morning. First a big, fat cheeseburger, then home to watch television. He was now off duty.

AS CLAYTON DROVE home, he was totally hyped. His mind had trouble absorbing what he had heard and seen an hour and a half ago at the Kellys. He was totally convinced God was at work through the Kellys and had nudged him to be part of his plan. He decided it would be best to wait a couple of days before telling Rachael, his wife, about the phenomenal change that was going to take place soon. She was the nervous, worrisome type, and even though she was a Christian, it would be better for her if he revealed details slowly.

JOHN AND CAREW had milked the cows and were sitting on the back porch after a light supper with Sara and Granny. There was a strip of orange-red lying on the horizon as darkness advanced across the sky and the crickets tuned up for their nightly concert.

"Be sure we fill Red in on all of today's details," John said. "I don't want any family members to not know what we're doing. I'll call Reverend Butler a little later and tell him about our meeting with the well driller, that he starts drilling a week from tomorrow. Sara will call her parents, along with Pat and Paul, bringing them up-to-date. Though we talked to Lyle last night, he and Teresa need to know we now have a firm date for drilling. I'll call them right after I talk to the reverend."

Carew asked about living space for everyone. "We have six bedrooms, including Granny's and mine and Sara's. We can make two or more temporary rooms out of the den."

"If push comes to shove," Carew said, "there's the hay storage area in the barn that can be rearranged for several temporary sleeping quarters."

John stood up and stretched. He suddenly felt the tiredness as it slowly enveloped his body from his toes to the top of his head. "You, Red, and me are going to be real busy tomorrow morning. After early chores, we need to put our heads together and make up a plan for those extra sleeping spaces. We need to also lay in a supply of extra food. It's hard to say just how much. I'm thinking enough to feed a maximum of fifteen or twenty people for maybe four to six weeks, perhaps longer. I just don't know. When we purchase supplies, we should go up to Dothan, Alabama. It's a fair-sized town and only thirty-two miles away. No one there would recognize us. We don't want people around here to notice when we start stocking up."

Carew quickly added, "You know, there's one big thing in our favor. We have plenty of milk, eggs, and vegetables."

John smiled broadly. "I love you, Brother Carew. Only you would think of the most obvious. All of this is going to be expensive, but I'm sure everyone will donate to the cause. I'll go start my telephoning, and you can begin drawing up our contingency plans for all our visitors. We'll have a list of things on paper and can share the information with Red and the ladies in the morning— they'll have some good ideas. Sara and Mama can figure the food supplies."

"We've got that extra freezer stored in the large tool shed," Carew said. "We'll need it." John had forgotten they had saved it when they bought a replacement two years ago. "Check it out, Carew, and see if it still works." John went inside and told Sara he was going to call Reverend Butler regarding his meeting with Clayton Parker. Then, he would call Lyle. Sara put her arms around John and told him she was concerned about her son, Teresa, and her mother. John hugged her and said he was sure Lyle and Teresa could handle things.

CHAPTER NINETEEN

LYLE AND TERESA were having a light breakfast of cereal, orange juice, and coffee. It was 6:40, and a sunny Sunday morning. Neither one had slept well during the night. Teresa said her thinking machine was working overtime, and her mother was restless also. Lyle agreed it had been a tough night.

"Good morning, you two. You're early birds." Arlene had walked into the kitchen without a sound, startling them. She was wearing a robe and soft, fleecy slippers. Her attempt to be upbeat fell way short. "I heard the other shower running," Arlene said in a soft voice. "Enrique will probably make an appearance in a short while. It wouldn't be surprising if he wants to leave the house right away to eat breakfast at a Denny's eight blocks from here. He does that every once in a while, and this morning he'll want to get away from you two. He doesn't relate to even me most of the time."

"Mom, as soon as he comes in, you or Lyle and I will tell him there's an important matter that must be discussed." Teresa looked at her mother for a moment, then glanced at Lyle. Arlene was slightly nodding her head.

"The quicker the better," Lyle said. "It'll be better for you and for everyone." Arlene sat down with them, and they discussed the matter. She said she wanted to initiate the conversation, but added, if she seemed to be faltering, for Lyle to step in. Arlene went on to say that an objective voice would be helpful against Enrique's brusque personality.

Enrique suddenly appeared and walked through the kitchen, heading for the door to the garage. As he passed, he spoke to Arlene in a low voice, almost a whisper, "I'm going out for a while."

He had almost reached the door when she said to him in a confident, almost hard tone, "I think it best you stay here for the time being. I have something very important to say to you." He stopped, turned around, and faced Arlene with a quizzical look. He also glanced at Teresa and Lyle. It was evident he was surprised.

"Let's all go into the den where we'll be more comfortable," Arlene said as she led the way. Enrique walked several steps behind the other three.

As they entered the den, Enrique spoke, "What's this about, Arlene? I need to go."

She answered softly, "You'll be able to do that in a little while."

Lyle thought how appropriate the Cuban's last statement was. "He does need to go. I'm impressed with Arlene's businesslike demeanor. But if she appears to falter, I won't hesitate to step in." He shut off his inner voice and sat down beside Teresa. Arlene sat down in a wingback chair across the room, facing Enrique, who remained standing.

"It's all over, Enrique. I gave our marriage all that I could during the first years. At the very best, you were indifferent to my daughters and kept a slight distance from me. For more than eight years, I let this go on with you getting more distant and less communicative. Now, your increasingly secretive going and coming is the last page in a long and boring book."

Silence engulfed the room. Enrique did not dare show his relief. He had no desire to let her know this was exactly what he had wanted. Now there was no alimony or other monetary problems involved. It was a clean break. His voice had a serious tone when he responded, "I'm really surprised at this. I don't know what to say."

Arlene broke in, "You never did know. The many times that my two daughters and I tried to reach you in the early years to have some kind of family relationship, you shunted us aside—especially Carla and Teresa. Later, when Carla married and Teresa went off to college, you concentrated solely on Gelb Foods." She made sure her emotions were in control. It wasn't her nature to be rude or tough to anyone, not even to a man who showed most every day that he didn't love her or even care for her or anyone else—only himself. Arlene also had been convinced by a strong feeling of God's presence, through Teresa and Lyle, that she was to go to the farm with them.

"Enrique, you will have to pack as much as you can during the next several hours and leave by noon today. You will be able to pick up any remaining items on Tuesday between noon and 5:00 p.m. If we are not here at that time, I will have appointed a person or persons to let you into the house and to stand by while you gather the balance of your things. Now please hand over your house keys and the extra set of keys to my car."

Though he was relieved, Enrique didn't like Arlene giving him orders, especially in front of Teresa and her farmer boyfriend. "I am above this," he thought. "Just wait. One day they'll see me sitting on top of the world." Prying Arlene's keys off his key ring took an extended moment in the quiet room. "Here are the keys," he said as he put them on a lamp table. "I'll be out of here soon." As he turned and walked out of the den, he had a slight smile on his face. The Cuban would tell Frank Bovitz that he had decided to call it quits with Arlene.

Arlene felt as if a boulder had been lifted off her back. Teresa had no idea how long her mother had been miserable while living with Enrique, at least during the past two years. Arlene's only regret was her procrastination—that she failed herself and her daughters. Now she was going to be free, and a big change was about to happen in her life. She stood up and proclaimed it was time to get started contacting the several people needed to secure her property and finances and take over her business, all on a temporary basis. Teresa went over to her mother and hugged her.

Lyle was behind and slightly to one side of Teresa. Arlene looked at him, smiled, and held out an arm for him. He took it and made a three-way embrace. "I'm very proud of you, Arlene," Lyle said. "You handled a very difficult problem very well. Let's say a prayer of thanks before tackling a mountain of details."

Just as they finished, Enrique emerged from the hall, carrying a suitcase and a folding bag. He headed for the kitchen and garage. As he passed, he said he had about five or six more loads to take to his car. He caught Lyle's eye and gave him an ominous look. Lyle wondered if their paths would ever cross in the future.

Arlene said she was going into her office, a large three-room addition to the back of the garage—connected to the house by a short hallway from the sunroom. "Since my rolodex and files are there, I'll use that phone to call all the principals."

Teresa and Lyle went into the kitchen, picked up the dirty plates and coffee cups, put them in the dishwasher, and turned it on. After wiping the counters and the breakfast table, Teresa told Lyle there were some small family heirlooms in the house that needed to be packed. Her mother would want to take them with her to Danaville.

"What kind of heirlooms?" Lyle said. "A French eighteenth-century bedroom suite or an early American settee with side chairs?" He stood there with hands on hips, grinning at her.

"Lyle Kelly!" she said, while bursting out with laughter. "You know better than that. I'm talking about a few pieces of jewelry, several small framed photographs, and some needlepoint—all of these from my grandparents. Though mother has some very nice jewelry in her lock box, the things I mentioned are more priceless to her."

He walked over and put his arms around her. "You're a priceless jewel to me, and you'll never be an heirloom." She giggled and hugged him.

She told Lyle they needed to find several small boxes and bags to pack some of her favorite collected items. They would be a reminder of where she, her sister, and her mother lived together in her younger years. Enrique would never be a part of that memory.

Lyle followed her as she went into several rooms, looking at various objects, such as photos, plaques, or other things. She stopped in the dining room and unhooked a twelve-by-sixteen-inch framed painting from over the side table. Teresa explained that her mother bought it in Amsterdam on a trip to Europe after graduating from college. It was a very well-done landscape of a canal and windmill. Arlene loved it. They continued to move from room to room, bypassing Enrique's previous quarters, and ended up in the master bedroom. Teresa said they'd let her mother choose whatever she thought important to take. Lyle reminded Teresa that space in the cars was limited, and necessary clothing, shoes, and toiletries should have priority. She smiled at him and said it was easy to get carried away. He understood.

IT WAS DIFFICULT for Arlene to ask Marilyn Nobles, to take over her three major accounts. Marilyn, like herself, was a CPA with her company of three employees and several large accounts. The two of them had been close friends for years. They trusted each other and shared discussions of their failures and successes. Arlene felt the three clients she wanted to retain in case things settled down after the event, would be willing to go along with her request. She would try to meet with all three the next day or by Tuesday and inform them that major personal business would require her leaving town for several weeks. Arlene would resign the several smaller accounts, counting on Marilyn to return all of their records. Her attorney would issue an affidavit stating their validity.

She knew there were going to be many questions from her clients about the suddenness of her actions, but she would do the best she could and pray they would understand, and that when she returned it would be possible to restart her business. The phone conversation with Marilyn was lengthy but productive. Arlene promised she'd see her before leaving town.

It was 1:00 p.m. She would have a sandwich, check with Teresa and Lyle, then continue her calls. Next, would be Mark Zimmerman, her attorney and confidant; then her banker and financial consultant, George Wilson. She didn't like to call them at their homes on a Sunday afternoon, but she had no choice. Only Zimmerman was in, and readily agreed to meet her the next day in his office. Wilson was playing golf. She'd have to call him Monday morning.

Arlene had a close friend whom she trusted implicitly, Frank Booth, a retired Tampa police detective. He and his wife were almost like family. Though they didn't care for Enrique, they would all get together for dinner from time to time. She would call Frank later in the day and ask him to watch over her property for a while, letting him know about her edict to Enrique, and to keep an eye on him as he moved the rest of his belongings out of the house. Booth assured her he would. She said his house key and garage door opener were in her possession, and she would bring them to him the next day or on Tuesday.

There was less weight on Arlene's shoulders now that she had begun to make a little order out of her chaotic mind. It was a good feeling to have a no-questions-asked reaction from her business and personal friends.

She pushed back the high-back roller-chair from her desk, and let her eyes wander around her large office—her nest as she often referred to it. Many hours had been spent there, most of them pleasant—but always under some pressure. That was the nature of her profession, no room for error. But she had always loved her work and was good at it. Now, she had to lay it aside for something much more important. God would understand that her sudden adjustment to a new environment would not be easy.

Arlene came out of her office and went to the kitchen. Teresa was adding sliced cold chicken to a Caesar salad she'd made, and Lyle was pouring iced tea. "It's about time you showed up," Teresa said with a big smile. "Lyle and I were going to come and drag you in here. It's past lunchtime."

"I've accomplished more than I expected, it being Sunday. I've worked up an appetite, and your salad looks great." Within minutes, they sat down to eat. Lyle gave thanks, with emphasis on God's blessings to them and the family, as they prepared to help carry out his plan.

CHAPTER TWENTY

JIM SUMMERS REALLY didn't want to get hooked up with Sheriff Bernam or Marvin Gardner in their quest to find out what had occurred at the Kelly farm, during or after the storm two weeks ago. He felt it was a delicate situation, and those two will end up alienating a lot of people and complicating his investigation of what happened at the Kelly farm and why. The editor knew what they didn't know—that the storm last year and the latest one were duplicates, as proven by the NWS. The meteorologists proved to him the storms were not of natural origin. That fact, along with their dissipating their energy over the Kelly farm, encouraged a growing feeling in the editor, that this was the beginning of something huge; he had to be very careful. He'd keep a distant association with Bernam and Gardner, only to divert their attention away from his own investigation.

"Hello, Reverend Butler. This is Jim Summers. Hope all is well with you and your wife."

"Why, hello yourself, editor. We're fine, thank you. It's been too long since we've talked. What can I do for you?"

Summers knew that the reverend and the Kellys were close, and he had to be very careful the way he posed his questions or even his conversation. He didn't expect much in detailed information from Butler, but being a newspaperman, it would be unacceptable to not try.

"Well, Reverend, I have a few questions to ask, and wondered if you would feel predisposed to answer them."

There was a moment of silence. Jim knew the reverend was arranging his mind to meet the unexpected in his query.

"Fire away, Jim. I don't have a lot of time, but I'll do my best for you."

"Many thanks, Reverend. I'm trying to get a fix on the thunderstorm that came through a couple of weeks ago, and like the one about a year ago, spent itself over the Kelly farm, leaving a unique rainbow. I want to do a story about it, but John Kelly won't give me much information. Has John talked to you about it? Is there anything you can tell me?"

After a slight hesitation, Butler spoke, "Not really. I have to treat all private information given to me by anyone, especially one of my members, as privileged. Just like a doctor-patient or an attorney-client relationship. I can tell you we had a conversation about the storm, but that's all."

"Sounds as if there are elements to the storm that he would not share with me," said the editor. Jim felt sure Kelly had given the reverend details of the storm, and they must have been unique.

"Jim, I know your job is to get the facts when working on a story. You've already talked to John, but all I can say is, you'll have to ask him again. It's up to him."

"I understand, Reverend Butler. Thanks for your time, especially on a Sunday afternoon."

"It was good to hear from you, Jim. I sure would like to see you in church next Sunday."

"I'm Presbyterian, Reverend. If I left Minister McDuffie's flock, they'd come after me with a warrant."

Both laughed as they hung up.

The editor was a little perplexed after the short conversation with Butler. Summers didn't expect much when he decided to call him, but he was looking for any word or phrase that would provide a clue. The only worthwhile comment by the reverend was his admittance that Kelly did talk to him about the storm. It could have been a general conversation, or specific details about "that" storm. Jim Summers had a feeling Kelly and the reverend must have had more than one in-depth conversation about what happened on that stormy day at the farm. He would have to figure a way to find out what was said.

In the meantime, Jim would arrange a meeting as soon as possible with Ralph Tobias, the county attorney, and find out if there's a legal procedure of some kind that would allow him to inspect the farm's premises on foot or fly over the property in a helicopter or an airplane. That could be a good way to collect physical evidence, if there is any. "Aerial photography has proven to be very effective for many federal and civil uses," he thought.

AFTER PUTTING THE phone down, the reverend stood there, thinking about all the ramifications the storm could stir up among key citizens in Danaville. Though the *Mason County News* was only a biweekly paper, it could easily be a springboard for quickly dispersing information statewide and nationwide. As a whole, Mason County citizens relied on the paper to keep up with what was going on and trusted its editor.

It was 6:20 p.m. when he and his wife Ruth sat down to eat a light supper. Just as Wade finished giving thanks, the telephone rang. He rose and retrieved it from the kitchen counter. After saying hello to John Kelly, he listened for a few moments as John told him about his meeting that afternoon with Clayton Parker. He explained that due to Clayton's change of schedule they had moved it up a day. Drilling would start in eight days. The reverend understood and said he was going to get in touch with a trusted minister friend of his who would contact the proper Catholic, Protestant, and Jewish officials.

He told John that God's work so far was a continuing happening without parallel, and as he had said several days ago, when they complete their task of recovering and the details get out about whatever the Lord has placed under the bean field, there's going to be pandemonium—everywhere. John agreed.

Butler said, with a chuckle, his supper was getting cold and that Ruth was giving him that loving "Hang up" look. John laughed and replied that he well understood.

Both men bade each other good night and hung up.

John next called Tampa. It was 7:45 p.m. there. Teresa answered after the third ring. "Hi, Teresa, this is John. Hope all's well with you three."

She was very fond of her father-in-law-to-be and was happy to hear his voice. He was a very positive man, and his attitude was infectious to everyone around him. "Hello, John. It's so good to hear your voice. It's been a long day, but we've made a good start on all the details Mom wants to accomplish. We should be ready to leave here Thursday morning. I'm looking forward to seeing the family again. Just a moment and I'll get Lyle."

He told her the family was praying for them.

John updated his son with the latest details around the farm and about the meeting with Clayton Parker and that the drilling would start in one week.

Lyle asked about housing for everyone that was gathering at the farm. His dad explained how that was being handled. After another few moments, he hung up the phone, turned to Teresa, and they embraced. "Oh, Lyle, even though I'm scared about the unknown we're facing, I'm so blessed to have you and your family."

PAUL DANIELS INFORMED John that he and his father wanted to make a donation of $5,000 to help defray expenses at the farm. It was evident the money would be needed for what was to come, especially as the extended family gathered there for however long it would take to understand and deal with the full implication of whatever was yet to happen.

Given the circumstances, John accepted. There was a time when he would have graciously turned down the offer, but things were different now. The family had to share everything because the unknown could keep the family restricted to the farm for a long time. All of them had quickly agreed to donate to the "cause."

Pat and Paul were due to have dinner at the farm and would arrive about six. Sara had talked to her sister-in-law around midmorning, but did not divulge any details regarding what was currently going on. John had cautioned the family about what they said on the phone. He wasn't being paranoid, but wanted everyone to practice being very careful; he felt that at some point, especially after the discovery, the telephone lines would more than likely be tapped. All conversations dealing with their plans and activities would be held only during face-to-face meetings.

DEPUTY BECK WALKED across the lobby of the Mason County Courthouse, his leather boot heels clicking on the expansive marble floor and echoing off the walls that climbed to the high rotunda. He hurriedly went up the broad stairs, two at a time, passing others who looked at him with questioning faces.

When he entered the sheriff's outer office, Mildred Hughes wasn't there, so he knocked on Bernam's door, opened it, and walked in. "Mornin', Sheriff."

"Good morning, Dan. Mildred had to run an errand, but she told me you were on your way. What's up?"

The deputy went into detail about seeing Clayton Parker's pickup waiting at the intersection of 77 and County Road 26. "I can't figure what a water-well man was doin' coming from either the Kellys or the Pasternaks. Those are the only two families living on that road for several miles. And from what I know about the water supply at the two places, and their ability to pump even larger quantities, neither one needs another well."

"What do you think is going on?" Bernam said as he looked directly into his deputy's eyes.

Beck sat down in one of the chairs facing the desk. "I think Parker and Kelly probably had a meeting about some forthcoming drilling. As you know, Parker's company is in Jackson County. He didn't drive twenty miles on a Sunday afternoon just for a social visit."

The sheriff sat quietly looking out the window. Dan got up and was slowly pacing around with his thumbs hooked into his broad leather belt, waiting for Claude to say something. The deputy had a strong feeling he was on to something, and he was getting impatient with his boss's too-slow reaction.

"You know, Dan, we've got to be a little cautious. Right now, there's almost nowhere we can go with this thing until we get a real lead, or someone we aren't aware of now comes forward with something substantial."

"But why can't we get a little more direct or aggressive with Kelly? Not overbearing or anything like that, but more official?"

Claude's eyes narrowed to almost slits. "Because when you hunt rabbits, you don't make a lot of noise. If you do, they'll jump in a hole and be hard to find."

Dan was frustrated when he left the courthouse. It was clear the sheriff wasn't going to push very hard to investigate what had happened at the Kellys. Why? The deputy asked himself. Is Bernam afraid of antagonizing them or their friends, or maybe afraid of what he may discover? Even Beck had an inexplicable feeling there was something of great magnitude taking place.

The deputy had two traits that fed his drive to get his job done: he could manipulate people while performing his duties, and felt he was a better lawman than the sheriff. Dan was careful to keep the latter under his broad-brimmed hat.

He had made up his mind to do his own investigating without Bernam's knowledge. It would be risky and could easily cost him his job, but he also felt the sheriff would kind of look the other way as long as the deputy was careful. The first thing Beck was going to do was plan a way to slip onto the farm property and see what was going on.

Ralph Tobias picked up his buzzing phone and punched the intercom button. "Yes, Mrs. Birch?"

"Jim Summers is on hold. Wants to see you."

"Do I have anything on schedule late this afternoon?"

"No, you're all clear."

"Tell him to be here at four.

The editor was disappointed, but he had to take what he could get. It was almost 11:00 a.m., and he would soon finish a story he was writing about the Danaville school board. Another fifteen minutes of reviewing photos of the Mason County bass fishing tourney, and he'd have several hours free before visiting the county legal beagle. Jim hadn't seen Tobias since a Lion's Club meeting four or five weeks ago. He didn't agree with the attorney's politics, but that was of little consequence to the editor. His interests were dedicated first to the facts of a story and then the source.

Summers decided to look in on several business acquaintances along Main Street, something he did frequently because it was good for his advertising sales—and many times turned up a story or two. He'd drop by Gardner's Drugstore first. Twenty minutes later he walked up to Gardner's pharmacy counter.

"Hey, editor," Marvin said in his usual loud voice.

Two customers waiting nearby for their prescriptions eyed Jim quizzically. "I'll be with you in a few minutes," the druggist said. "Coffee's on me."

Jim really had nothing specific in mind to discuss with Gardner, but thought it would bolster the druggist's ego to feel he was one of three key people in the community to be working on the Kelly "mystery." Jim wanted to ask if any of his customers during the morning had mentioned anything about the Kellys.

"Good to see you, editor. Enjoyed dinner and the conversation at Grogan's Saturday night. What brings you to my emporium?" Marvin always seemed to be in a good mood.

"Oh, just in the neighborhood. Thought I'd drop in and find out if you'd had your ear to the ground lately."

Gardner smiled as he sat down. "Well, it's only been a day and a half since we talked. I did have a chat with Ira Cooper right after I opened this morning. He mentioned he was putting gas in his car at Martin's Texaco early last evening, when he saw deputy Beck casually following a pickup truck through town. The truck had Parker Well-Drilling on the door."

"That must be Clayton Parker from Jackson County," Jim said. "I've known Parker for a number of years. He's a good man. Wonder what he was doing over here? He drives that old pickup for work only. On a Sunday, he always drives the family's Lincoln SUV. What else did Ira see?"

Marvin leaned in closer, as if someone might overhear him. Jim was inwardly amused at how the druggist overdramatized everything he did. "The truck went on through town toward I-10. It wasn't long before Ira drove south on Main and finally saw

Beck's car in front of Burger Castle. The truck evidently went east on 1-10."

Jim nodded and made a mental note of Marvin's information. "Since our meeting with the sheriff, I've done a lot of thinking about how we three can best work together. You, being a druggist, are in touch with a great number of local folks. And with your natural talent for conversation, collect a lot of information."

Gardner smiled in agreement.

Jim continued, "That gives us a three-way approach to gathering facts as to what's going on with the Kellys in Danaville, the county, and at the farm. All of them have to come to town at one time or another to shop, get a haircut, buy farm supplies, or whatever. We may be able to learn something." The editor paused for a moment, then added, "You work from here, and I'll use my newspaper as the eyes and ears of the county. Most people like to talk to editors. The sheriff will do what he pleases because he's the sheriff. He may or may not share information about the Kellys that he discovers. He will, only when he gets in over his head, and he might. This situation is totally different than anything he's ever been involved in. For that matter, that's the case for all of us."

Jim Summers wasn't about to tell Marvin he was going to see the county attorney. He wanted to operate alone, with no obstacles thrown up by the druggist or the sheriff. He wanted to give Marvin the impression he was working closely with him, but in fact, the editor was doing his thing his way. Jim knew the Kelly farm mystery had a huge potential, possibly much larger than his imagination could generate. He didn't want anyone in his way.

Summers drank the last of his coffee and stood up. "Keep your eyes and ears open, Marvin; you're in a real good position. I've got to go. Thanks for the coffee."

The druggist rose from his chair with a slight smile on his face. As the editor was walking out, he went back to work in his pharmacy.

Jim walked north on Main Street, passing Hagan's Barbershop. He waved to Bo Hagan through the large glass front. Bo returned the wave as he continued working on a customer's hair. Summers then walked across the street to Fowler's Department Store. George Fowler was a friend—one that he could count on for discreetly discussing a particular community, political, or social problem.

The store was the largest in Danaville. George was a good merchandiser and known for his marketing ability and service. This combination had served him well. He was wealthy after thirty years of hard work. His community service was the envy of many other Danaville businesspeople.

Though George was sixty-two, he looked forty. He was five feet ten inches tall, but looked six feet. A full head of dark hair with gray streaks adorned his well-structured head and face with a square jaw, prominent nose, and deep-set blue eyes. His voice almost commanded one to listen when he spoke. Fowler was a deeply committed Christian. He was active in the First Methodist Church and a close friend to John Kelly. That was one of the reasons Summers wanted to visit him.

"Hi, Jim," George called out when the editor walked down an aisle toward the stairs that led up to the store office. Jim had not seen Fowler on another aisle helping one of his clerks stack boy's pants on a counter. The editor returned the greeting and walked around a large display of men's summer shirts over to where his friend stuck out his hand with a warm smile. "How've you been? Haven't seen you in several weeks," the store owner said.

"Hello, George. I've been hiding out, hoping that newspaper won't find me." They both laughed.

"What brings you to my humble store?"

"Oh, I just wanted to say hello and see how you were doing. I do have a question, however. Have you seen or talked to John Kelly lately?"

"Yes, in fact, I saw him and his family at church yesterday. Didn't get to talk with him, but my wife and I did say hello. Is there something wrong?"

"No, not really. I did an interview with him and his family a little over a week ago, which I included in a story on our county farmers. The interview was a little difficult because he seemed not to want to show me around the farm very much. He was his normal well-mannered self, but I got the distinct impression he was a little uptight."

George looked down, thinking about what Jim had said. "I didn't notice anything out of the ordinary yesterday except for one thing, now that I recall. After church, I noticed the family didn't visit with others as they usually do. They left right away."

Jim felt his question would be accepted by Fowler as only a concern for the family, rather than probing for a clue concerning the strange weather and what it might have done at the farm. The editor miscalculated George's keen mental perception.

"Is there some kind of problem?" he asked, feeling there was. The editor was quick to deny a problem. Fowler wondered. He knew how foxy and tenacious Jim was as a newspaper editor. Summers always had his radar on full power.

Jim had planted a seed in George's mind. It was just a matter of time until he called his close farmer friend to inquire about John and his family.

"Gotta go, George, my paper is calling me." As they shook hands, Summers said he'd like to buy lunch, perhaps Wednesday or Thursday. Fowler grinned and replied that was a good idea. The editor headed for the main exit on his way to see the county attorney.

CHAPTER TWENTY-ONE

RALPH TOBIAS STOOD up and walked around his desk, extending his hand as Jim Summers walked through the door. "Hi, Jim, it's good to see you. The last time we had a chance to talk was your interview of me about Mason County's case against the Williams boy and his shooting two of Ted Griffin's cows." Both men smiled. He motioned toward a large stuffed chair. "Take a seat and let's talk." Ralph took the other chair. "What can I do for you?"

"Before I explain why I'm here, I ask that our conversation be totally confidential. What I have to say is of great importance and magnitude."

Tobias blinked. His mind immediately switched gears. It was very clear the editor was not there for a social visit or some lightweight community problem. In a sober voice, the attorney said, "You have my word what you say here will stay here. It'll be treated as an attorney-client privilege, period."

Summers nodded his satisfaction. He laid out the details about the two storms and their relationship to the Kelly farm and the family, and what he had learned from the National Weather Service at Panama City. Ralph was in rapt attention. In fact, he asked his secretary to hold all calls.

The attorney's head was swimming as Jim related his visit to the farm and his attempt to extract a few details of the storm from

John Kelly without success. He added that Sheriff Bernam and Marvin Gardner had gone to the farm after seeing the unusual rainbow of the latest storm from downtown Danaville, and how John Kelly manipulated them from seeing anything except the immediate grounds and buildings. He explained to Tobias that was when he deduced that whatever had taken place, during or after the storm, did so out in the fields. The editor said he must get onto the property, or at least fly over it, and use his camera. He was sure there was something physical that he needed to see—and report. He went on to convince the attorney that he believed a divine event had occurred, or was in the process of occurring.

Jim looked directly into Tobias's eyes, and the attorney shifted his gaze to the floor. For a moment he was quiet, then he said, "Editor, this is almost a heart-stopper. It's hard to accept. It doesn't fit in with things we take for granted and accept on a day-to-day basis. Perhaps that's why it's so believable. The weather data alone makes it staggering."

The two men sat quietly, each thinking about the situation they faced.

"Ralph, can I get a court order to get onto the Kelly property as a reporter or whatever?"

"No, unless there is cause, such as a crime that was committed against you on the farm, or they were holding some type of property of yours and refused to give it up.

"Well, that leaves another possibility, which could be the best. What about flying over the farm with an airplane or helicopter? Photographing from the air?"

Tobias thought for a moment, and responded, "You have every right to fly either type aircraft over the farm, as long as you follow the rules set by the Federal Aviation Administration. I was a USAF Reserve A-10 pilot, and last flew in Desert Storm. That's been a number of years ago, and a few FAA rules might have changed. The pilot you hire will know the current rules. Just make sure you don't stir up John's livestock or flatten his crops," he said with a thin smile.

After more discussion about Summers's aerial reconnaissance plans, Tobias aired his growing concern about how people everywhere were going to react to the revelation of this act of God only three miles from Danaville. The control and safety of the citizens of this small town and Mason County were his first concern, but the larger issue was protecting the Kellys, their property, and dealing with the hordes of people that will surely surge into the area from all across the nation and foreign countries. The press alone will be a huge problem.

"You think reaction will be that strong?" Jim said. "All we have right now are some inexplicable and undeniable weather records and a family that is beginning to act a little strange. However, as I said before, something is on that farm."

The attorney was thinking way ahead of the editor. "Listen, there's no doubt that an event of great magnitude is unfolding in our backyard, and it'll soon be revealed. In fact, the sooner you make those photographs, the sooner we can start putting a comprehensive plan together. Some of the officials we contact will have to move fast because there's not much time left. Can you arrange your flyover for tomorrow? According to TV weather, it's supposed to be a clear day. I'll make a list of those who we think should be contacted ASAP, review it with you tonight or in the morning, then you and I will start making calls by three tomorrow afternoon. Sound okay?"

"Sounds workable. If I can get a plane set up in Panama City for 9:00 a.m., photographs could be made between nine thirty and ten o'clock. I can have prints by noon."

Ralph Tobias had a glint in his eyes. "That's great! I'll cancel the several appointments I have for the next two days. Let's get going."

ENRIQUE CRUZ WAS in a rather good mood on Monday morning. He was relieved to be free of Arlene and out of that house, now on his own. Though he had to return to pick up the remainder of his possessions the next day, it was a minor inconvenience. He had called Frank Bovitz soon after Arlene's edict, and given him the news. His boss had quickly made arrangements for a small apartment in a very nice neighborhood. It would be temporary until Enrique found something more elaborate to fit his new status as a protégé to both Bovitz, and most importantly, Alejo Gomez.

While at his desk reviewing some new customer orders, his boss called and asked him to come up right away. Five minutes later, Enrique walked into the reception area of Bovitz's office. The secretary smiled and said to go in.

"Hey, Enrique," Frank said in an upbeat tone. He got up with an outstretched hand and a grin. "How's my new 'free' man this morning? Did you sleep good last night?"

Cruz returned his boss's smile. "Frank, I feel like a new man." After a vigorous handshake, they went over to a well-furnished conference alcove, part of Bovitz's spacious office. Frank seated himself on one end of a leather-covered couch. He indicated for Enrique to sit in a plush chair on the opposite side of a large clear-glass coffee table.

"We'll have dinner at my house tomorrow night, about seven thirty. Kind of a celebration for your new life, also to brief you on a trip Alejo wants you to make up to Panama City and Pensacola for several days. I know this is sudden, but as of last night, we're now sitting on a fantastic Panama City gulf beach hotel and shopping mall deal that Alejo said he must have. Know what I mean? We're dealing with a surly pair of Conway brothers from Atlanta who own the property and want blood.

"You'll scout the property with a J. D. Poffer, and review our previous detailed evaluations of the area. Poffer is a local behind-the-scenes land investor, who is a business friend of Gomez's, and knows that the Conways are extremely greedy and run shady business deals. Afterward, you'll talk to the Conway brothers, and when they present their 'fantastic' deal, tell them what we will do. Poffer will give you the details.

"The objective is to purchase their prime beach property at our price. Alejo and his 'silent' partners could twist some arms and make a special deal to build the hotel. It'll be the largest on the gulf coast—connected to an upscale shopping mall and entertainment center. I'll have more details for you tomorrow night at dinner. You'll leave Wednesday morning. It's about a five-hour drive, and you could be there by 4:00 p.m. You have a suite waiting for you at the Surf-Side hotel. Now how about all that? We move fast, don't we?" Frank chuckled.

Enrique was good at masking his feelings, but he was dumbfounded at the suddenness of how his new relationship was evolving. "I'm impressed, Frank. It feels good to know I'm part of an efficient organization."

"By the way, Enrique. While in Panama City, you should call on the food purchasing officer at Tyndall Air Force Base. That'll cover your trip as far as Gelb Foods is concerned." Enrique nodded.

Bovitz rose from his chair and walked over to his desk. "I have several meetings today and tomorrow, so I'll see you at my house tomorrow night."

As Cruz was walking to the elevator, his mind was spinning with all the details of his trip that lay ahead of him. He had had no idea that his new venture would begin so suddenly. All he could think of was the power and money the association with Alejo Gomez and Frank Bovitz was going to bring him.

AT ABOUT THE same time, several miles away, Lyle, Teresa, and Arlene were getting their day in order. They expected Enrique to complete his move-out by Tuesday noon. In the meantime, Arlene was in process of contacting the principals of her three major clients to set up emergency meetings on Tuesday and Wednesday to assign the accounts to Marilyn Nobles. Meetings were set with Arlene's attorney and banker during the next two days to put all her holdings in a trust. She would have a discussion with her minister during the afternoon of that day. Teresa and Lyle would take her to all of her appointments and wait out of sight, except for the meeting with the minister—all three would see him together.

After lunch, Teresa telephoned her sister Carla. After four or five minutes, she handed the phone to her mother, who sat nearby. Arlene told her older daughter, granddaughter, and son-in-law that she must leave Tampa for a while, that she would stay in touch, and to trust her. She would explain everything as soon as possible. After ten minutes, she hung up, stood, and walked out of the room. Teresa squeezed Lyle's hand and followed her mother down the hall.

Lyle sat there thinking how touched he was by Arlene's loving toughness. She was giving up, for at least the foreseeable future, her home, her work, and part of her family. He wondered if he was as capable.

CLAYTON PARKER telephoned John Monday night to discuss the drilling rig and other equipment he wanted to use. John was all ears. Clayton explained that due to many unknowns, he wanted to use the larger of his two rigs. It was a 1999 Versa-Drill V-1000X, mounted on an International 2674 truck. He went on to explain it had ten wheels, was heavy, and needed room to maneuver. They would have to prepare access to the fields by removing the main gate behind the larger barn. John said he, Carew, and Red would have everything ready when he arrived. He added that if the driller could think of anything else they could do during the week to prepare for the rig, to be sure and call.

John knew they would lose a portion of the green beans, and no telling what other damage would happen to some of the other crops along the narrow main field road that led to the bean field. He suddenly realized that was of no consequence. It didn't matter; they were doing God's will. And after the discovery of what lies beneath the ground, the family's farming days were going to be over.

An uncountable mass of people will come to see the holy site and take mementos—dirt, anything. The farm's future existence would change. John knew the family's duty would be to protect the holy site. He prayed that Christians and Jews worldwide would rally to preserve God's work. After Reverend Butler has brought in special representatives from the Catholic, Protestant, and Jewish faiths, then they will identify and verify the evidence. He or Billy will call the governor and the White House for them to declare an unusual emergency and provide security for the farm and the surrounding area. The best that could be available at the very beginning would be the Florida National Guard, along with local and state law officers. Regular army troops would be available.

WADE BUTLER TOLD HIS WIFE he'd be in his study most of the day. Ruth knew what he had to do and said a little prayer for him. The clock was ticking. Time was definitely not on his side.

He checked his small desktop phone directory and found the number of his long-time friend, the Reverend Bill Durdin, the highly respected, world-wide evangelist and leader of The Light of Christ Crusade. Billy, as was called by everyone, had access to the Protestant, Roman Catholic and Jewish leaders. Wade knew that Billy would quickly understand the implication of what was happening at the Kelly farm, and how important time was. He would know the key clerics to contact and then organize a sanctioned body to witness the details of the miracle and protect its sanctity.

The reverend said a prayer as he dialed Billy's office.

"Good morning, The Light of Christ, may I help you?

Wade's hand was moist with perspiration as he gripped the phone. "Good morning. This is Minister Wade Butler, an old friend of Billy's. I have something extremely important to talk with him about. Is he in?"

"I think he's just finishing a staff meeting, let me connect you with his secretary," the receptionist said in a light, friendly voice.

A Ms. Chapman came on the line, listened to Wade, and asked him to wait a moment. He waited a lifetime, then a familiar voice said, "Well, well, well. Is this the preacher who used to brag about his fishing, and took me years ago and couldn't even catch his bait?" There was a chuckle on the line, and Wade immediately felt better.

"Hello, Billy. It's good to be talking to you again. Ruth and I hope your family's well. There's nothing more I'd like to do than have a long social conversation, but what I'm about to do is tell you something that will have precedent over everything you had planned for today, tomorrow, and perhaps for a long time to come.

Billy's mental homing device immediately locked on to his friend's words. He knew Wade well enough to know he had experienced something of magnitude. "I'm all ears, Wade. Let me tell my secretary that I'll be in isolation until further notice." A few seconds passed, then he was back on the line. "Go ahead, friend."

Wade carefully laid out the details of the storms and the Kelly farm event, how God's power was so evident and irrefutable, the evidence so unquestionable. He told Billy about John Kelly and his family's Christian faith, and how the farm was the epitome of their character. The minister told the evangelist about the drilling that was to take place in one week. After that, if not sooner, due to accidental discovery by some outsider, the event will become known by people everywhere, causing chaos and threatening the existence of the farm and the Kelly family.

As Billy listened, his mind was racing. An unusual feeling had come over him. He knew without question the Lord was in the process of sending a powerful message to the United States and the world, not from the Middle East, in general, or the Holy Land, but from a farm near a small town in northwest Florida—further proof that God ruled the earth and at any time, could use any part of it for his purposes.

Wade finished his explanation of the facts surrounding the unfolding events at the Kelly farm. He then told Billy the same thing he had told John Kelly, that in order to protect the Lord's work and the security of the Kelly family and their farm, his divine intervention must be validated. "We should contact the three major Western religions and have them send their best representatives at once. They should arrive before next Monday."

"I totally agree, Wade. I'll start moving immediately." He told his friend that he'd telephone him that evening with enough information for him to start making plans for receiving at least three people (but there could be several more) and provide housing for them. It would take three or four days for them to arrive, especially if one or two have to travel from Rome and Israel. "Further, these men will have to move fast, but I think the circumstances and God will motivate them." He added that his own motivation was higher than it had ever been. "We need to pray together right on the phone." Wade quickly agreed. Billy's prayer was short, but deeply moving. He asked the Lord to give them courage, wisdom, and understanding as they carried out his will.

After a few words of encouragement between the two of them, they hung up, each focusing on the large task that lay ahead.

The reverend then called the Kelly farm, and Granny answered the phone. "Hi, Granny, this is Wade Butler."

"Why, hello, Reverend Butler. It's good to hear your voice again," she said in her usual lilting voice.

"Hope you're doing well. Please have John call me when he has a moment."

"I surely will, Reverend. Tell Ruth I said hello."

CHAPTER TWENTY-TWO

JIM SUMMERS HAD called Bee Line Aviation in Panama City and rented a Cessna 172 and pilot for Tuesday morning. He would have to leave his home by 7:30 a.m. for the drive to the coast. The flight was scheduled for nine o'clock. It would take about twenty or twenty-five minutes of flight time to Danaville, possibly fifteen minutes over the farm, then twenty or twenty-five minutes back to Panama City. He should be back in his office by eleven thirty. Film processing would take an hour or less. Prints could be in the hands of county attorney Tobias by 1:30 p.m. All of this seemed very well-planned and efficient, but it was dependent on good photos. He must discover something on the Kelly farm.

The editor met Phil Tappan, a young flight instructor with Bee Line. He had already pre-flighted the 172 and was ready to go. Summers had brought two cameras with him and he checked them both. He affixed a big wide-angle lens to a 35 mm Nikon, his favorite. The other was an Olympus, a back up.

They lifted off at 8:55 and headed north. Jim had done some aerial photography before and appreciated the smooth handling of the Cessna by Tappan. Visibility was almost unlimited, and the pilot told him the few cumulous clouds had bases of three thousand feet. That meant Summers would have optimum shooting conditions at one thousand feet.

They were soon approaching Danaville. Jim checked his cameras for the second or third time. He had carefully briefed Tappan where the farm was located and how he wanted him to fly first across the center of the farm at right angles, then circle the entire property to the right, tightening the turns until they were near the center of the fields.

Summers was getting nervous the closer they got. Tappan had lowered the plane to one thousand feet, and the distant Kelly farm was pointed out to him. As the editor fixated on the buildings and fields, the plane was banked to the right, Tappan explaining he would fly about one mile to the east, then make a wide turn to the north, and then to the west, lining up the middle of the property for their first flyover.

The Kelly farm, viewed from the ground, was impressive in layout and detail. From the air, as the plane approached the property, the rows of crops and newly planted areas with the buildings and trees on the west side, near the county road, all looked like a miniature geographical model.

They were now flying directly over the farm. Jim was looking everywhere, but knew he'd have to be patient and scan one property segment at a time. As they passed over the buildings, the editor could see a man standing near the back of the big barn, looking up at them. The pilot said they'd make a 180-degree turn and fly back across the property. Summers readied his camera for a few over-the-nose shots of the county road, the house, and outbuildings as they approached.

After two more straight passes, they began their first circle around the entire farm. Now, Jim felt better as he could see ground detail much better out of the side window with the right wing down. He began to shoot, deciding he could later examine the photos under magnification. The plane turned a little tighter, carrying them over the middle of the crops.

The editor was staring down at what he thought was the center point of the crop fields when he noticed something. It looked like a vague circular pattern. He hurriedly put his camera to his eye and adjusted the zoom lens to six times magnification. He told the young pilot to continue turning around that point. Jim saw it was definitely a circular pattern, perhaps a hundred feet in diameter or larger. It was outlined by what appeared to be a dozen two-by-four posts. His heart was pumping hard. A post with a red strip of cloth marked the center of the circle. The circle was also slightly darker than the surrounding field.

He shot the rest of the film roll and told Tappan he had to reload. The pilot leveled the wings, then circled away for a minute or so, and turned back to better refine the circular pattern and give his passenger a better angle. Summers was excited. There could be no other reason for that circle and center post than to identify a location point, but for what? It was strange, he thought as he took another roll of film.

Jim soon told Tappan to head back. He was sure he had what he wanted. As the plane reversed the turn it had been in, it came around almost over the house, heading south. The editor noticed two men now stood in the yard watching the plane. As the 172 began a shallow climb to reach 2,500 feet, Summers knew he had something big.

Carew didn't pay much attention to the sound of the plane. On his way to the barn, he glanced up and saw a small high-wing airplane directly overhead, traveling west. It was lower than other planes that occasionally flew over. He shrugged and entered the barn. In several minutes, the plane was returning. He walked out of the barn in time to see it passing overhead, flying east. A little red flag began to raise itself in his mind. Whoever is in that plane is looking the farm over. It could be a sightseer, but he didn't think so.

At that time, John drove up on the pickup, returning from his trip to town. He got out of the truck, watching the plane as it disappeared over the trees. "It passed over town as I was preparing to leave Kessel's. It came from the south. Must be from Panama City."

"You know, John, I was thinking several days ago that someone might somehow get wind of what's happening here, and fly over. Maybe to make pictures. It wouldn't be too hard to find the circle."

"I think you're right, Carew." They walked around the barn to get a better view of the fields. "Look at it circling over the middle of the fields. No doubt they've spotted the circle and its center marker. I'm sure they're taking photos. I pray that whoever it is, will come to us first before making them public. I have a growing feeling it could very well be Jim Summers. When he was here to interview us for that story on farming, I got the distinct feeling he was trying to get a hint of what happened during and after the storm. He seemed to sense something. If it is him, I think he'll be more responsible and get in touch with me. We'll have to confide in him. I hope he's asked the pilot to keep the trip confidential . . . and that he will."

The plane stopped circling and headed toward them, then slowly turned toward the south. John saw it was blue and white, but couldn't make out the registration number on the rear fuselage. The farm boss thought he'd contact all of the flying schools in Panama City and possibly find who the plane belongs to and who rented it. He made a mental note to do that a little later, perhaps right after lunch. In the meantime, he wanted to join up with Red at the watermelon field and see how those three-week-old watermelons were coming along. In the meantime, Carew was putting up studding to frame the wall partitions in the barn. He had convinced John it would be wise to build eight rooms rather than six. Later that day, John and Red would help by nailing on the plywood sections to finish the walls. John had determined they would need more material and had suggested they go to a lumber yard in Dothan. He didn't want to raise any more questions than they already had. While in that Alabama city, they would purchase a load of foodstuffs. The large truck would be well loaded on its return trip.

WHEN PHIL TAPPAN parked the Cessna near Bee Line's hangar and cut the engine, Jim turned to him and said he'd like to talk about their flight. The young pilot looked a little puzzled. "Did I do what you wanted over the farm?"

"Oh sure," Jim answered. "In fact, you did great, but I want to tell you that the story I'm working on involving those farm fields is very confidential. I would greatly appreciate it if you said nothing about it to anyone, at least for a week or so. In fact, there's a good chance I'll want you to take me there again."

Tappan had an open, receptive expression on his face. "Why, sure, Mr. Summers. I have no reason to tell anyone. I'll do what you ask, and I'd like to work for you again, but if I may ask, what were you photographing? I mean, I was flying the plane and couldn't pay much attention to details on the ground. I was slow-flying the aircraft to give you more time to shoot. In a thirty-degree bank, with flaps down a little and the engine throttled back some, you have to be more precise in controlling the plane.

Jim unlatched his door to get some air. It was getting warm in the cockpit. "I can't say right now why I was making photographs of that farm field, but it's something important. What we did today is not unlawful or against FFA regulations, so don't worry about that," the editor said with a slight smile.

Summers shook Tappan's hand, thanked him, and walked over to Bee Line's office to pay for the flight.

On the way back to Danaville, Jim was elated he had discovered the circle at the Kelly farm, but at the same time, a slight shiver ran down his back. It validated his previous belief that something physical had occurred there during or after the storm. He was still in a state of awe at what he'd seen. It was apparent that he had made photos of a holy site—the weather records substantiated that.

As he neared Danaville, he anticipated developing the film. He knew he had fantastic pictures to show Tobias, and the attorney was going to fall out of his chair!

Jim parked in back of the newspaper building. He wasn't paranoid, but he didn't want Marvin Gardner or Sheriff Bernam to know what he was doing.

Summers was very satisfied with the crisp, clear prints. He phoned Tobias's office at 1:25 to let him know he'd be over after grabbing a sandwich. His secretary said Ralph would be in his office by two and was expecting him.

Summers arrived at the county attorney's office at 1:55, and Ralph was already in his office, waiting expectantly. It was evident to Jim that the attorney was pumped up. Jim held a large manila envelope, and as he sat down, Ralph's eyes were riveted to it. "Looks like you made a lot of pictures, Jim, did you find something interesting?"

"I sure did. You and I are going to have our hands full," he said, as he laid the envelope on the front of the desk. Tobias quickly reached and picked it up, opened it, and pulled out the photos and laid them in front of him. "I made five-by-seven prints so better detail can be seen. I was very lucky. I had a good pilot and my Nikon did its job."

"Jim, the quality of these pictures is superb, but tell me what I'm looking at on the ground."

Thirty minutes later, Tobias had been given all the details of the editor's flyover of the farm, and his interpretation of what his camera recorded. Ralph rose from his chair and started pacing around the room, with his hands in his pockets and his head down, his brain in overdrive. Jim didn't say anything for a long minute. He wanted the attorney to digest what he had been told and shown. Finally, Ralph sat down in his chair, exhaling audibly. "Man, this is beyond comprehension. It's staggering."

"That's right," Jim said.

"When whatever is in that field is revealed—and it will be— the Kellys and their farm will have to be protected from thousands of people who will come here to see the site. Most of them taking a handful of dirt or even part of a crop plant because they'll think it may heal them or enhance their spirituality," Ralph said. "In fact, Danaville and the entire county will need protection also."

"I agree. When you remember the first storm of a year ago with its odd rainbow, and compare the latest storm of two weeks ago with the same rainbow, they are exact duplicates. I checked with the National Weather Service, and they allowed me to review their tapes. The meteorologists proved to me that the storms were not generated by natural means. That's when I realized they were miracles. God wanted the Kellys to be his messengers. His message is in progress of being revealed at the farm as we speak. The photos show an area he marked in the center of the fields. I personally think the last rainbow was the pointer. The large circle was put there so the Kellys could mark the exact point to dig, thus the center stake."

"You think they're to dig up some object?"

"I sure do, and I believe it'll be very significant." Summers paused, then continued, "Ralph, we've got to discreetly contact state and national security people, including the White House and convince them they must move at a moment's notice. Can we pull that off? We also need to meet with John Kelly and tell him what we know, and convince him of the pending threat to his family, the farm, Danaville and the county, and so on."

"I have a few key political friends that would listen to me. Governor Clay Ashton, and one of the president's cabinet members, secretary of the Treasury, Phillip Beretti. In fact, Beretti and I were classmates at the University of Florida. I was a clerk in Governor Ashton's law firm when he was a top-notch litigator. We've been good friends since. I'm sure I can get the ear of each."

"I'm impressed," Jim said. "Those two aren't small potatoes. We have to move fast, though. You think you can contact them today? I have to return to the paper and check on tomorrow's edition, then I'll call John Kelly and ask him if you and I can come to his place early tonight for a talk."

The attorney's mind was fixed on the task ahead. "I'll start the process right away. It'll take a little while at the best. I'm going to ask they use a secure phone, if possible, to lessen the chance of unwanted ears hearing what I tell them. Let me know the time of our meeting with John."

"I'll call you as soon as I know something." With that, Summers picked up the envelope and hurried out the door.

It was a little after 3:00 p.m. and John was in the main barn, looking at the wall partitions Carew and Red were working on. They were doing a good job. Carew said the eight temporary rooms would be finished the next day. Red walked over by a door and picked up the ringing extension phone. "It's for you, John." He put the receiver on a nearby shelf, and as he walked back, said in a loud whisper, "It's that newspaperman, Summers."

John held up his hand as a signal to Carew to stop sawing. "Hello, Jim, what can I do for you?"

"Hi, John, this is Jim Summers. Hope all's well with you and the family. Ralph Tobias and I need to talk to you as soon as possible. It concerns you and your family's safety and the protection of your project."

With those last few words, John realized the editor knew some details of what they were doing, and he was now sure it had been him in that airplane earlier that day. Well, he thought, it had been just a matter of time anyway. Jim was smart. He was methodical and tenacious when pursuing facts. Having him as point man would be a good idea. He assumed the county attorney would coordinate the law enforcement for protection of his family and the farm. What Kelly didn't want to face was the probability of hordes of people swarming over his farm, utterly destroying it, and harming the family in the process. John knew the revelation of this divine event was going to be extremely emotional for people everywhere.

"Sara and I would like to hear what you have to say. Why don't you and Mr. Tobias come around seven?"

Jim phoned Tobias and said the meeting was set for seven. Ralph said he'd be standing on the courthouse steps at six thirty. He had several more telephone calls to make, but wanted to ride with Summers so they could talk on the way to and from the farm.

When Summers picked up Tobias, the attorney told him he finally got through to Governor Ashton. "Upon my request, Clay switched us to his phone 'scrambler' and we talked for a few minutes. I gave him just enough information to get his attention. He's going to send a very trustworthy aide from the Florida State Troopers, Captain Jack Stanton, to be here in the morning around nine o'clock. He'll be driving an unmarked car and dressed casually."

"Governor Ashton didn't waste any time. As you said, you must have gotten his attention."

THEY ARRIVED AT the farm about 6:50, and John came out onto the porch to meet them. He shook hands with each of his visitors, welcoming Tobias to his first visit. As Kelly showed them in, there was some light chitchat. When they entered the living room, Sara came in. "Why, hello, editor Summers, it's good to see you again." Jim smiled and nodded. She looked at Ralph. "Now I get to meet our county attorney for the first time."

She held out her hand, and he took it and said, "If I'd known just how pretty you are I would have found some excuse to have visited John before." She smiled as she gladly took his compliment.

They sat down, and Jim didn't waste a moment before he started talking. He first apologized for the flyover that morning, but explained he had an undeniable reason after earlier reviewing weather records of the two storms.

He told them the National Weather Service stated that neither storm was natural, their formation was unexplainable.

John and Sara were very surprised about the weather reports. They were quiet for a few moments, then John related that he and the family had thought each storm was somehow peculiar. However, the latest storm laid the sign of God in front of them— the experience of the hail and its pattern on the ground, and the permanent perfect circle in the bean field.

Jim and Ralph looked at each other in surprise. "What about the hail, John?" Jim said. "You mentioned a pattern, what do you mean?"

"The hail fell everywhere except on the crops. The cover of hailstones was along the access roads but stopped within six inches of the crops in all directions. It was an amazing sight," John said.

As the editor and the county attorney were sitting there dumbfounded, Kelly continued. He told them that a drilling operation would begin on Monday. He gave a rundown of the names of all the individuals involved in the exploration below the surface of the bean field. The family hoped to have representatives from the three major western religions arriving by Friday or Saturday. His revelation that extra sleeping quarters were being constructed in the barn and in the den of the house, and they may need more, was another surprise to his two visitors.

Jim was amazed at how much the Kellys understood the threat to them and were preparing to be under siege for a period of time after the news of the discovery spread throughout the country and the world. He and Ralph were also told that through Reverend Butler and Evangelist Billy Durdin, clerics from the three major Western religions would hopefully arrive soon for witnessing the bean-field "circle" and the drilling for discovery of whatever lay beneath the surface.

The Kellys were reminded by Summers that State Trooper Captain Stanton would arrive by nine o'clock the next morning to quickly assess the situation, familiarize himself with the farm layout, and report back to the governor by mid or late afternoon. Tobias told them he was in process of contacting the White House through his friend, secretary of the Treasury, Philip Beretti. Hopefully, he would accomplish that before noon.

With those closing comments, Summers and Tobias said good night and were shown out to the porch. Everyone shook hands and agreed they would stay in touch as required by need. After walking down the steps, the two men got into Jim's car and drove away. John and Sara went inside their soon-to-be-changed home, thinking about what lay ahead.

Summers and Tobias drove to the courthouse to check the attorney's phone answering machine. There were two messages, one from an aide of Governor Ashton. The governor had put State National Guard Major General Gerald Whitmire on standby, relative to a report from State Trooper Stanton tomorrow. The second message was from an assistant to Secretary Beretti. It instructed Ralph to call the secretary at ten the next morning. A phone number was given by the assistant, and then he hung up. Ralph was satisfied with the reaction he had gotten. The editor and the county attorney departed company for the night. It had been a very busy but fruitful day.

IT WAS 9:10 P.M. in Tampa. John thought he should call Lyle and fill him in on the latest events. Lyle was happy to hear from home. He knew everyone there was under a lot of stress, especially his dad, and it would become worse.

John told the details of what was going on, saying the tempo was picking up. He told Lyle about Jim Summers's flying over the farm and discovering the circle, then making photos. The editor revealed he'd seen the file tapes and other data of the two storms, along with a comprehensive briefing by National Weather Service meteorologists at the Panama City station. Both weathermen said the storms were not of natural origin. These two incidents really got Lyle's attention.

Lyle's dad further explained that Summers had teamed up with county attorney Ralph Tobias to work out a security plan for the family, Danaville, and the entire county. Tobias had already made contact with the governor and was working through the secretary of the Treasury for access to the president.

The last information he gave his son was the details about the several clerics who would arrive on Saturday or Sunday. This was being handled by Reverend Butler. It had to be done to validate the site and whatever they found beneath the surface. It would convince the world that the bean field was a holy shrine, perhaps the entire farm. Lyle thought for a couple of moments, and said with deep concern in his voice that they may have to give up the farm. John told his son that he and his mother were fully aware of that, but if that is God's will, so be it.

CHAPTER TWENTY-THREE

I T WAS NEAR 9:00 p.m. when the evangelist called. Wade was at his desk and quickly picked up the phone. He knew it was Billy and was eager to know what he had accomplished within the past several hours.

As usual, Billy's voice was positive and upbeat. "Hi, Wade. I've made some headway in putting together a highly qualified and respected group of clerics, two Americans, whom I know well, reverends Chase Griffin and Neil Claussen. I think you know Griffin. He said he met you a couple of years ago at a conference."

"Sure, I remember him," Butler said. "He's very well thought of by the Methodist ministry."

Durdin continued, "Claussen is a Baptist and a noted Bible-history scholar. There are two highly respected mideast religious scholars: Rabbi Jacob Metz in Jerusalem, and Father Keven Walsh in the Vatican. They all want to come, and I think as soon as they inform their peers, they'll be on the way. Let John Kelly know that all of these clerics will arrive by Saturday or Sunday. Details as to when, where, and what time will be forthcoming within the next twelve hours."

Butler appreciated Billy's quick work. No other minister, or as Billy would say, "preacher," knew as many key religious leaders. It was somewhat calming during this unusual spiritual undertaking to have Billy Durdin at his side.

"Hello, John. Sorry to call so late. I just heard from Billy Durdin and he's got key church representatives moving fast. We think there'll be six or more religious special clergy representatives arriving on Saturday or Sunday. Billy will be among them."

John momentarily felt overwhelmed, but quickly pushed that aside. There was much work ahead, and he would concentrate on that. God was running things, and that gave him the strength he needed.

"The family and I really appreciate you, Wade, and respect you."

The reverend was quiet for a few seconds, then spoke softly, "We all are family. We face life together and whatever else the Lord has in store for us. Thank you, John."

"By the way, our housing expansion is coming right along and the food supply is growing. We'll be ready for all of our guests by Saturday."

They spent a few minutes discussing the logistics of meeting the various arriving clergy at the Tallahassee or Panama City airport and bringing them to the farm. Wade said he'd soon know about who's coming and their individual schedules. John replied that he would arrange the transportation.

Upon hanging up the phone, John turned to Sara and told her what Wade had said. She felt better now that Reverend Butler, with the help of the highly respected evangelist Billy Durdin, was bringing in the special church clergy to inform the world that whatever is found would indeed be bona fide.

WEDNESDAY MORNING ARRIVED clear with a hint that the day would be warmer. John had not slept very well, as it seemed was the case the past few days.

Captain Stanton was due to arrive around nine, and John wanted to have the more important morning chores out of the way early. He knew he would have to show the captain every nook and cranny around the farm. The visit of the governor's representative was extremely important. His reconnaissance and recommendations to his boss would help the National Guard and all state law enforcement agencies in planning and executing a security plan for the farm and surrounding area.

Red was driving the big truck to Dothan again for more supplies. Sara had given him a list of foodstuffs to get, and John handed him a reminder note to pick up ten folding beds with mattresses, and several ten-gallon water containers from the army-navy surplus store on the west side of town. Kelly handed Red $800, smiled, and told him not to lose it. Red grinned and drove off.

John said a silent prayer of thanks for the financial help that had been extended to the farm. Lawrence Daniels, president of the Danaville Bank and Trust, and Paul's father, had worked out a financial package to the farm that would end up costing John and his family nothing. The bank president knew enough about events at the farm through his son to readily understand there would be many expenses and that John could not handle them alone.

Lawrence was also aware there could possibly be a kind of siege against the Kellys by thousands of people swarming the soon-to-be world famous farm. The family would need to be prepared for the worst.

AT A LITTLE after 9:00 a.m., a car stopped in front of the house. A man emerged, under six feet tall, 175 pounds, and had receding short-cropped hair. His prominent nose, deep-set eyes, and slightly jutted chin showed determination without a hint of arrogance. Captain Jack Stanton was a twenty-seven-year FHP veteran. He had been the chief of security for the governor's office since Ashton took office one and a half terms ago. The captain was an outstanding professional and was highly trusted by his boss.

Sara was in the side yard, checking her new roses, and heard a car door slam. She laid down the snips she was using and, taking off her light work gloves, walked around to the front of the house to meet the expected guest.

"Mrs. Kelly?" Stanton asked as she approached him.

"You must be Captain Stanton from the governor's office."

"That's me." He stuck out his hand, and Sara responded, "It's nice to meet you. You have a beautiful place here," he said as they shook hands.

Sara thanked him and said they had been looking forward to his arrival. As they walked up the front steps, she mentioned that the family was walking on eggshells, anticipating Monday's drilling start-up. They welcomed all the help they could get.

She showed him into the house, and as they went into the large foyer, John appeared. He apologized for being late, explaining that was the way farming was—it slowed everything to a walk. He greeted the governor's representative with a firm handshake and said how glad they were to have the state's help. John also mentioned that due to the implication the divine event could have on the nation and the world, there also would be a request today to Washington for federal help.

The captain was impressed with the Kellys. He thought both of them were very intelligent, honest, and sincere. It was evident John was of strong character and had enormous common sense. On the other hand, Stanton was a little on edge, not knowing what to expect as he examined the farm. Governor Ashton had briefed him on what Ralph Tobias had told him. Though the information was minimal, there was enough to let Stanton know he was now possibly in the midst of the greatest thing in his career or in his life.

They sat on the back porch drinking coffee, as John took thirty minutes briefing the captain on the status of the farm, the family, and their preparation to receive and house two or more dozen people for days, weeks, or longer, whatever the circumstances dictated. The captain nodded when Kelly mentioned they were working against very limited time. After a few questions by Stanton, they stood up to start the tour. Granny came out of the kitchen to say hello to their visitor. He liked her immediately and was further impressed by the Kellys.

Captain Stanton had brought a camera and a pocket-sized voice recorder, plus a notepad. John thought the governor's security man appeared to know what he wanted to accomplish.

They walked down the back porch steps and toward the main barn, their tour would start there. Carew and Red were hard at work, covering the wall framework of the temporary sleeping quarters with plywood sheets. Both men laid down their tools and walked over to meet the captain when John brought him in.

"Captain, these two are vital members of the family," John said with a smile. "The farm couldn't function without them."

Stanton shook hands with each of them. "Looks like you two are close to finishing this hotel," he said. "It looks great."

"Well, actually, we were just about to install the elevator," Carew said with his normal dry humor. The four men laughed heartedly. Carew's humor was appreciated. It came at a needed time.

John and the captain soon left the barn on the pickup truck, bound for the farm perimeter fences. After driving completely around the property, Kelly showed Stanton the retaining pond, and finally the bean field and its unmistakable circle. Jack Stanton's widened eyes revealed that what he was looking at was powerful and unexplainable. John patiently stood aside while the captain made photos from a number of angles along with a few diagrams in his notebook. As he walked the perimeter of the circle, he spoke into his recorder. He stooped at one point and compared the lighter and darker soil. Stanton felt butterflies in his stomach.

John told him about the local newspaper editor making aerial photos of the farm and especially the bean-field circle. The captain said he wanted to contact the editor right away.

As they drove back to the barn, both men were quiet. Finally, Stanton spoke, "John, I thought I'd seen it all in my twenty-five-plus years as a state lawman, but what has happened to date and what's going to happen Monday or Tuesday is beyond any man's comprehension."

Kelly muttered, "I know."

Sara and Granny had prepared an extravagant lunch in appreciation of Captain Stanton's time and effort. Carew and Red joined them. Before eating, the captain called Jim Summers and made an arrangement to stop by and pick up a set of the editor's photos to take back with his own to Tallahassee.

After enjoyable food and conversation regarding the next week or so, Stanton departed around two, having told John the governor's office would be in touch very soon, perhaps even as soon as that evening.

The family gathered on the back porch and discussed the day. John told them about his tour of the farm with Stanton. He felt the captain knew what he was doing, as he chose various points around the farm where the National Guard could set up security and bivouac.

ENRIQUE CRUZ WAS up early on Wednesday morning, preparing for his drive to Panama City. The evening before at Bovitz's home was a long one—much longer than he had anticipated. With only four hours' sleep, he was tired. Enrique had learned a lot, however, about Gomez and his small empire. Bovitz had had several drinks before, during, and after dinner. The more he drank, the more he talked. Enrique couldn't gauge what was fact and what wasn't, but he figured if 20 percent was fact, he now knew enough about the "association" that he would be a lifetime member. Though he was selfish and greedy, the thought of someone else controlling him was very uncomfortable. But he would have to adjust his thinking. He had no choice.

Bovitz emphasized that Gomez wanted the hotel deal, without failure. He was ready to go to any length to gain a foothold in Panama City. It could be a springboard for other deals in northwest Florida. Enrique knew what Frank meant and slowly nodded his head.

The Cuban finished packing, folded the maps he had been studying, and put them in his car with a suitcase and briefcase. The maps were put in the front passenger seat for easy access. When he had looked over the larger map of Florida's Panhandle, he traced I-10 from Tallahassee to Pensacola. He spotted the small town of Danaville about halfway between each city and fifty miles directly north of Panama City. Enrique recalled Lyle Kelly's family owned a big successful farm just north of Danaville. Arlene had mentioned several weeks ago that Teresa had visited there. He made a mental note to drive by and take a look at the farm after the hotel deal and a trip to Pensacola was completed. It wouldn't be out of his way as he returned to Tampa.

He topped off the car's gas tank at a nearby Texaco and headed east to connect with 1-275 North, which would feed into 1-75. A slight smile of anticipation crossed his face as he settled down for his five—to six-hour drive.

CHAPTER TWENTY-FOUR

C APTAIN STANTON HAD briefed Governor Ashton and Florida National Guard Commander Major General Gerald Whitmire, and was now eyeing the men in front of him as they quietly continued to study the photos. Finally, the governor spoke, "This situation is totally different than anything this state, and I must say, this country, has ever faced before."

The general rose from his chair and put on his hat. "I need to call a staff meeting, check with several of my field commanders and come back to you with an operations plan ASAP. We're working against time, and there's much to do."

"Let me have your overall plan in eight hours," Ashton said firmly. "We can fill in the small details later. Not only do we have the Kellys and their farm to protect, but many other people in Danaville and throughout our state. I've got to assume the White House has been advised by Ralph Tobias, the county attorney for Mason County. He and the local newspaper editor, Jim Summers, are working together. Summers took the aerial photos of the farm."

The general nodded and walked to the door, his military mind already locked onto the problem at hand.

Governor Ashton stood and looked out of his window. "Jack, call Tobias and tell him we'll be in contact within nine or ten hours with plans to position National Guard troops—ready to move when he deems necessary."

The captain left the governor's office with a racing mind—his thoughts reaching in every direction. He thought about the mass of traffic that would occur in northwest Florida, especially in and around Mason County, when people learn of the divine event on a farm near Danaville. His commanding officer Colonel Snyder of the Florida State Troopers needed to be briefed as soon as possible.

Carew walked up the back porch steps anticipating sitting down to one of Granny's famous fried chicken dinners. He and Red had worked furiously all afternoon on the eight sleeping quarters in the barn. They wanted to be finished by noon the next day. The two of them would then drive to Dothan to pick up a truckload of foodstuff to feed a growing number of Kelly family members, as they gathered at the farm for the drilling operation. Carew was tired, but he knew all of them had much more to do by Friday night.

Sara greeted him from the porch swing, "Hi, Carew, how's the Kelly hotel builder?"

Not having seen her, he was surprised. "Hey, Sara, I was lost in thought about the long list of things yet to do, and I'm having immense hunger pangs." They both smiled as he sat down in a nearby rocker. Carew always looked forward to conversing with Sara. She was warm and intelligent and showed a lot of interest in him.

As they were talking, Granny came out of the kitchen and announced that dinner was ready. She told them John would be down from his office shortly. Carew stood and walked to the door, turned, and swept his hand out and made a little bow. Sara and Granny were smiling as they walked past him into the kitchen.

John walked in as they were taking their seats at the table. "Hope everybody had a good day," he said. "Mama's table is a good place to end the work day and replenish our bodies and souls." The three of them looked up and smiled in agreement. He sat down, and while everyone held hands, he offered thanks.

They ate Granny's great fried chicken and discussed the preparation status for receiving, feeding, and bedding the expanded family and special guests. Granny and Sara had prepared the list of needed food and other expendable supplies with estimated costs. John had looked it over and added bedding items. The list had been turned over to Carew that morning, along with $2,500 in cash. He and Red would purchase the food items from a grocer-supply house in Dothan, which had been previously arranged by John. The bedding and various types of camping supplies, plus several large first aid kits, would be purchased from a large well-known military surplus store, also in that Alabama city. Several heavy-duty flashlights and small portable AM-FM radios, all with a supply of batteries, were included.

John reminded Carew that the Danaville Bank and Trust, through Lawrence Daniels, had donated $10,000 to the family for meeting expenses in carrying out this difficult mission for God. There would be more as needed. This arrangement had greatly relieved John of a major worry.

Sara asked what the latest count of people coming to stay at the farm during the exploration was. John said Reverend Butler had called about an hour before dinner and gave him the names of five clergy who would arrive on Saturday and Sunday. Wade said that his close friend, evangelist Billy Durdin, would be here and is responsible for bringing four special representatives of three major religions to the farm to observe the site and examine and verify whatever is recovered. They will also arrive on Saturday and Sunday."

John looked at an e-mail that Reverend Butler had sent two hours ago. "Here are the names of our important guests: Rev. Chase P. Griffin, the First United Methodist Church, Raleigh, North Carolina—a Bible historian with emphasis on miracles. Dr. Neil Claussen, the Southern Baptist Convention, Nashville, Tennessee—well-known author of many important historical works relating to the Old and New Testaments. Father Kevin Walsh, the Vatican—a biblical archaeologist and special emissary of Pope John Paul II. Rabbi Jacob Metz, professor of Jewish historical studies, Hebrew University in Jerusalem."

"Seems Reverend Durdin has put together an impressive group of clergy," Carew said.

"He knows God's work here on this farm must be unquestioned. This divine event will have a huge impact on the world, and these men will attest to its being factual," John replied.

"Reverend Butler said he would have the airline arrival times, and at which airport or airports, by late tomorrow. Then we'll know how to plan the pickups."

Carew nodded, and turned the conversation to the partitioning of the den. It would provide four additional sleeping accommodations. John suggested they do another accounting of how many beds were needed, with perhaps one or two extra if possible.

ENRIQUE ARRIVED IN PANAMA CITY late in the afternoon. Checking into his beach hotel, he decided to have an early dinner, call Bovitch, and then get a good night's sleep. He had an early-morning meeting with Alejo Gomez's associate land investor, J. D. Poffer, a man who had a reputation of driving a very hard bargain and who Gomez was counting on. After they reviewed the deal offered by Conway brothers, owners and developers of the hotel site, and going over Poffer's plan for squeezing the infamous Conways to induce them to lower their price, they were to have a business lunch with the brothers. Enrique knew the coming meeting could be tough and even ugly—a large amount of money was involved.

"Hello, Frank. Had a good trip up and an excellent dinner. You put me in a great hotel."

Bovitch was patient a few moments, letting his man feel good about his new station in life.

"I'm glad you like your accommodations, Enrique. People who belong to our small organization are always taken care of. As I told you last night, Poffer is a very good man—he's tough and well-connected in real estate. But as I told you last night, I want you to handle the meeting as we discussed. Poffer can play a part—you just protect our interests."

Enrique's boss wished him good luck and hung up. The Cuban had noticed Frank's brusque manner. He wondered if there was a problem. "Oh well," he thought. "I'll walk on the beach before turning in. That should help me sleep." He slipped on a pair of walking shorts, a tee shirt, and a pair of sandals, and went out the door.

AROUND NINE THIRTY on Thursday morning, Jim Summers was at his desk writing an editorial for Saturday's edition when the phone rang.

"Hi, Jim," Tobias said with his distinctive deep voice. "I just heard from Captain Stanton. He's faxing a copy of phase one of State National Guard Commander General Whitmire's plan of deployment for the guard throughout the state. We are to review it with John Kelly ASAP so he'll be on top of the details as they occur. Stanton said our local guard unit will be directed to set up a security perimeter around the farm. State troopers will be responsible for traffic control on all roads around Danaville, the farm and some other parts of the state."

"I got a return call from Treasury Secretary Beretti. He apprised President Brock of our situation, whereupon he called a meeting this morning with his national security advisor, the secretary of defense, and the attorney general. Beretti said we'd be contacted by 1:00 p.m. today."

The county attorney said they would take the fax and information from the White House to Kelly in early afternoon.

As Summers hung up the phone, he reflected how everything was moving at near warp speed; that Danaville, Mason County, the state of Florida, the nation, and the Western world in general, were about to experience a permanent change.

Another hour passed and Jim was just finishing his editorial when his extension rang. It was Ralph telling him the fax just arrived. Summers said he'd be right over.

On the way to Tobias's office, the editor mulled over how he could manage his newspaper, cover the gigantic, once-in-a-lifetime story unfolding around him, and help Tobias coordinate the security set-up for the farm and the county. The Kellys would need help in contending with the news media and obtrusive demands and threats made by people who would harm them.

He decided it best to take things one at a time and react according to the circumstances.

The county attorney was standing by his desk when Jim walked in. It was evident he was trying to control his excitement. "Come in, editor, I'm impressed with General Whitmire's fax. It's six pages of a very detailed plan for safeguarding the farm and surrounding environs." As the pages were handed to Summers, Tobias continued, "You'll note the number of National Guard troops that are assigned to the farm, and the placement of the central bivouac area. That'll be important to Kelly because he may have reason to change a few things."

"Especially setting up the mobile toilets and laying out pathways," Summers said. "With the farm's history and the pride John and his family have in it, they're going to be rather picky as to how everything is done. I can't blame them."

Ralph then picked up a yellow legal pad. "Whitehouse Chief of Staff, Carl Rollins called just before the fax came. He said the Defense Department has been in contact with Governor Ashton and National Guard General Whitmire. As of tonight, troops at Fort Bragg, North Carolina, and Fort Benning, Georgia, will be on standby for quick deployment as needed to this area and throughout the state.

"Captain Stanton will contact General Whitmire through our local National Guard commander Captain Ron Ackerman if additional troops are needed." Tobias tried to ease the tension by quipping that Ackerman owned and operated the Quality Auto Parts store in downtown Danaville. 'Ronnie' was a star running back for Danaville High School eighteen years ago, now he was going to command his infantry company in helping to provide security for the Kellys, and possibly, the county. "Marjorie and Ben Ackerman raised a fine son." Jim Summers smiled at Tobias's last comment.

Jim dialed the Kelly farm, and after several rings, Granny answered. "Hello, Granny, this is Jim Summers. Is John close by?"

"No, Jim, he's in the fields. Can I help?"

"Please get word to him that Ralph Tobias and I have some important information, and we'll be there in less than an hour."

Granny said she'd ring the back porch bell. That would bring him to the house in a hurry. Jim thanked her and put down the phone.

Tobias put the fax and his yellow notepad into his briefcase. "I've got to be in court in the morning, but it's a minor case. I have nothing on my calendar for Friday afternoon. After that, I don't think my legal services are going to be needed for at least an undetermined period of time. When the National Guard starts deploying on Monday morning, this town and county are going to be bug-eyed."

"You're right. We can expect disruption to businesses, schools—everything we can think of." The editor stood up and said, "Let's go to the farm."

LYLE, TERESA, AND Arlene had everything packed in the two cars and were ready for their trip to Tallahassee.

Arlene looked at her checklist and verified that all the important details were done regarding the house, her accounting business to be managed by her CPA friend Marilyn Nobles, and a financial plan with power of attorney for her banker, George Wilson, to pay bills, etc. She walked through the house, looking into every room, realizing it could be the last time she would see it for quite a while. Tears stung her eyes. All light switches, the stove, water heater, and air conditioner were checked again along with the empty refrigerator.

She knew she could count on her friends. Mark Zimmerman, her attorney, would be the key contact for her property and business matters.

"Well, everything is secure, and I guess we're ready to roll," Arlene said.

"Hopefully, you'll be back here before too long," Teresa put her arm around her mother's shoulder. "Think of all this as a blessing—that we all have each other, and more importantly, we have the Lord."

Arlene had a slight smile as she hugged her daughter. "I'm just feeling sorry for myself—I realize all of this is for a glorious purpose."

The three of them walked out of the house. Arlene locked the front door and walked down the front steps. Halfway to her car, she stopped, turned, and looked at her wonderful home with all of its comfortable familiarities.

They were soon on their way. Arlene and Teresa were in the lead car, and Lyle followed. The trip went without incident. After a couple of stops for lunch and gas, they arrived in Tallahassee around 3:30 p.m.

Prior to their departure from Tampa, Teresa told Lyle she and her mother had decided to stay in the Holiday Inn Express near the campus. That would afford them a chance for mother-daughter talk—especially under the circumstances. Lyle readily agreed.

It would be difficult to tell Bill Kraven, his roommate, that he was leaving school. Lyle knew that Bill would be surprised, disappointed, and would ask many questions. He would have to be very careful in how he answered. Lyle wanted to let Bill know how much he appreciated his friendship and wanted them to stay in touch.

Lyle and Teresa had planned to pack their clothes, books, and other personal items the next morning. He thought he could squeeze everything into his backseat and trunk.

After breaking his news to Bill, they would talk for a while, and then Lyle would return to the motel to pick up the ladies and find a place to eat dinner. He was hungry.

Bill was in the room when Lyle arrived. "Hey, farm boy. Where the heck have you been? When you called on Monday, I thought you'd be here Tuesday. When you didn't show up, I got a little worried. Is everything all right? The first thing I thought of was that you and Teresa tied the knot and were taking a $1.98 honeymoon."

"That's a nice thought, but we didn't get married. We were tied up with some important family business. And anyway, I would've laid out at least $5 for the honeymoon." Lyle grinned and walked over to his closet, opened it, and took out a number of clothes and laid them on his bed. He reached up to a shelf and took down an old suitcase which he never used for travel in public. It was also put on his bed.

Bill stood there with a puzzled look on his face. "What's going on, Lyle? You taking another trip?"

"Yes, Bill. Teresa and I are leaving FSU. We head for Danaville tomorrow right after lunch. She is staying overnight in a motel with her mother. I'm picking them up for dinner in a little while; then I'll come back here."

"You mean you two are leaving school for good? Why is her mother along? You won't be back? You're tossing in the towel on your degree? You and she have great grades. You've been on the dean's list every semester. It couldn't be money—you told me a year ago that your four years were paid for. The same with Teresa. Man, this is mind-boggling."

Lyle had known Bill was going to be upset and have many questions. He had a responsibility to tell him as much as possible—but no more. Perhaps when the news of the event became public, he would begin to understand.

"I should be back around nine, and we can talk a while then. I want you to know that I count you as a good friend, and I'd never do anything to hurt you. My life is in the midst of a gigantic change which I can't discuss. You'll know in a relatively short time what this is all about. Trust me."

Bill sat on his bed in a state of shock. He silently nodded his head, comprehending what Lyle was saying, but decided not to speak—he didn't know what to say at the moment.

Lyle, Teresa, and Arlene had dinner at Arrowhead, a good restaurant picked by Teresa—her mother was treating. Arlene seemed to be more relaxed during their excellent meal, and Teresa was beginning to show her laid-back humor. Lyle was feeling better about how things were going. He'd be glad to get home and join the family's preparation for the arrival of the scheduled visitors during the weekend and the beginning of the drilling operation on Monday.

The three of them arrived back at the hotel around eight o'clock. After talking for about thirty minutes, they decided they were tired. Lyle told Arlene good night, and Teresa accompanied him into the hall. They held each other for a few moments, each thankful they would be at the farm tomorrow. Teresa was proud of his "take charge" attitude along with his graciousness. Her love for him was inexplicable. She kissed him with passion, not wanting to let him go. Afterward, he reluctantly took a step back, still holding her hand, and wished her sweet dreams.

It was 8:40 when he walked into his dorm room. Bill was lying in bed reading, but quickly put his book aside. Lyle sat down in a chair, slipped his shoes off, and put his feet up on the end of his bed. He knew Bill was anxious to talk. After a few comments about their dinner and the Arrowhead Restaurant, the two roommates spent a little over an hour discussing their friendship and the importance of their families. But Lyle made sure he said nothing that would even hint why he and Teresa were resigning from school. He finally had to go to bed because his eyes were becoming heavy, and a busy tomorrow lay ahead. Teresa and Arlene were to be ready for hotel checkout by seven o'clock. After breakfast, Lyle would return to his dorm and finish packing and say goodbye to Bill. Arlene would take Teresa to her dorm and help her pack. They would meet for lunch at the main campus cafeteria and depart for Danaville from there. Lyle drifted off to sleep.

SUMMERS AND TOBIAS ARRIVED at the farm a little after 2:00 p.m., and John was waiting. "Come in, gentlemen," he said, as he met them at the door and shook their hands. "You must have some information from the governor. Carew and Red are not back from Dothan, so it'll have to be just me and Sara to hear what you've got." They all took seats in the living room. Sara walked in, smiled, and greeted the two visitors.

Tobias spoke first, "John, we've got a six-page fax from the governor's office that gives the basic deployment of National Guard members and state highway troopers for the farm and the county. Other plans are being completed to include certain areas of the state, if needed." The county attorney handed the fax to John for his perusal.

Summers spoke up, "We need your input regarding the suggested areas of security here on the farm, relative to the safety of your livestock, crops, and fences. The information you gave Captain Stanton, when he was here, and the photos he made were very useful to General Whitmire's planning staff. Do you feel comfortable with what you see spelled out in that fax?"

John was quiet for a moment as he looked at the National Guard initial security plan for his beloved farm. "This plan states that the Danaville National Guard Company B of the 132nd Infantry Battalion will have primary responsibility for safeguarding the farm and all of its family members. Isn't that unit commanded by Ronnie Ackerman?"

"Yes, it is," Ralph replied. "Captain Ronald F. Ackerman."

"He seems like a good man. It's like only yesterday that he was running wild on the high school football field; now, he's going to guard my family and our farm."

The editor eyed John and asked, "Do you feel comfortable with what's in that fax? I don't mean to be pushy, but we're to get back to Jack Stanton ASAP."

"I suppose so. I don't really understand how the military works, but I trust the governor and the National Guard—and you. I'm not too concerned about my property. I only want to preserve the bean-field site—it's holy ground, and nothing else can ever be more important."

Ralph got up, walked over, and looked down at John. "You mean you're giving up farming? You've got several generations of farming at this place."

"Yes," John said. "But my family is convinced that the Lord has had us in his plans for a long time. We can't and won't let him down. Our main purpose is to protect and preserve his holy work. He made it possible for my grandfather, Frank Kelly, to start this farm in 1926, and now God wants our help. We've all agreed to dedicate ourselves exclusively to his work."

Summers and Tobias had very respectful looks on their faces as they thought about John's words. He had made a huge impact on both men; for the first time, each of them felt they were part of something extraordinary, something that was larger and more important than anything they'd ever experienced.

"John, I've had contact with the White House," Tobias said. "The president and the secretary of defense, as well as other cabinet members, are on top of this and have contingency plans to support the National Guard, state by state, as needed. Regular troop units will initially be drawn from Fort Benning, Georgia, and Fort Bragg, North Carolina. It all depends how the public reacts to this powerful event."

Sara stole a glance at her husband and noticed he was looking out the window. Her heart went out to him. She knew he was trying to digest all this new information, along with the load of work yet to be done in preparing for Monday. He looked tired. In fact, she knew she must look the same because she felt tired. She silently asked the Lord to give strength to all of them.

The county attorney and the newspaper editor got up, thanked John and Sara, and walked toward the front door. "By the way, John, Jack Stanton will be here on Friday. Governor Ashton said to tell you the captain is to be your family's personal security chief. He will also coordinate with the military for any and all needs and/ or requests you may have."

John was impressed with the governor's concern for the Kelly family. He and Sara thanked their two visitors and told them they appreciated their help.

CHAPTER TWENTY-FIVE

JOHN WAS WALKING across the backyard, heading for the milking barn, when he saw Carew and Red pull into the driveway on their return from Dothan. It was nearing four o'clock—they had made good time. He waved and indicated for them to turn the big truck around, and he'd guide them back to the doors of the small barn. Carew soon had the vehicle positioned perfectly and switched off the engine.

"Everything go all right?" John asked as the two stepped from the truck. "Were you able to get all of the supplies?"

Carew grinned. "Look in the back of the truck—you'll see the answer. In fact, we had nearly $150 left over. Red and I almost stopped at a classy restaurant and had a huge meal, but I knew you'd be jealous, so we sacrificed and came straight home."

John smiled. He knew he had two of the finest farmhands and brothers in the entire state. He appreciated them retaining their humor during this time of unknowns. It was good for all of them.

They unloaded the truck, storing the foodstuff in a prepared area of the barn. Red unpacked the meat items from the bags of ice they had used for transport and put them into the large freezer. The two large walls of shelves were soon full of boxed cans, jars, and cartons of food that needed no refrigeration. Other large items, such as bags of flour and potatoes, were placed on wooden pallets on the floor. Provision had been made to protect all of the items from rodents in case they came around.

The cots, bedding, and other items for creature comforts were stored in a larger adjacent area so that all supplies were within easy access.

All of the temporary sleeping quarters would be set up Friday and Saturday. Portable bathing and toilet facilities had been placed in and around the main barn.

The three of them sat on a couple of workbenches outside the barn, resting their tired bodies after the strenuous unloading of the truck. They began discussing the sleeping arrangements for twenty-one to twenty-four people. John suggested that the Kelly ladies make a list of bed assignments to be given to all arrivals. Along with that would be a map of the farm—noting buildings and various facilities. This would be needed to facilitate efficient and safe movement around the premises, especially at night.

Soon, the conversation dwindled, and Red said he needed to head home. He told John, for the third time within the past week, that he and his family would move in on Sunday. John smiled and nodded his head to assure Red that would be fine. Carew stood up and gently slapped Red on the back and told him his wife and daughter would have first-class accommodations, but he'd have to sleep with the chickens. They all laughed, and Red, now relaxed, told them good night and walked to his car. John and Carew knew he had been uptight since the preparation for their visitors had started.

When the two of them walked into the kitchen, they were pleasantly surprised to see John's sister sitting at the breakfast table, talking to Sara and Granny. Pat was always upbeat. Her glass was perpetually half full. After a hug greeting, she said she had an invite from Sara, and there was no way she would miss the opportunity for one of Granny's meals. Granny laughed and retorted that her daughter was an excellent cook, but hated to clean the kitchen afterward—she never turned down a meal at the farm.

When asked about Paul, she said he was at a Lion's Club meeting and wouldn't be home 'til around nine. They always have dinner there, so she escaped her kitchen for the night.

Granny's dinner was enjoyed by all. Sara had baked a carrot cake which everyone oohed and ahhed over. The family was sitting relaxed, drinking coffee, when the phone rang. John reached behind him to a side table and picked it up.

He greeted Reverend Butler, and after exchanging a pleasantry or two, the reverend said Billy Durdin had sent the travel details with arrival schedules for the five clergy. All of them would be arriving via Delta Airlines at Panama City on Saturday and Sunday.

He would e-mail John with all the details within the next thirty minutes. The principal reason he called was to find out how everyone was doing. He told John it was natural that the family was under a lot of stress, and he emphasized the importance of putting that in the hands of the Lord.

John updated the reverend on the latest details at the farm: first, that they had brought in the first round of supplies and were finishing installing the sleeping accommodations; and second, that Summers and Tobias had been to the farm and briefed him and Sara on what action the National Guard and state troopers, through the governor's office, and the White House would take, starting late Sunday afternoon.

The reverend told John he wanted to meet each clergy member at the airport on both days. He not only felt it was the correct protocol, but he also strongly felt a need to do so. His associate minister would handle Sunday's service. John felt a sense of relief. This meant part of the transportation problem had been solved. However, he would send another car along with the reverend each day to ensure there would be only two passengers in each car, providing more comfort for the special guests.

"I really appreciate what you want to do, Wade. It'll be a big help," John said.

"Thanks, John, I'm happy to do it. I think the Lord appreciates it too."

ENRIQUE CRUZ'S EYES fluttered open to the sound of his wake-up call. He had slept fitfully, with thoughts of the day's upcoming meeting with the Conway brothers, a large real estate developer. His assignment by Alejo Gomez was to not give in to the brothers' price demand. The difficult part for him would be to counter the two property moguls' initial offer once, then draw the line—yet convince them they can't refuse the deal. Enrique had been briefed by Gomez and Frank Bovitz. They emphasized how hard-nosed the Conways were and their reputation for having ties with some strong-arm types in New York and New Jersey. It was rumored they usually got the price they wanted.

Cruz was still thinking about his adversaries-to-be when he drove up in front of J. D. Poffer's office. It was evident that Poffer was quite successful. His company, Poffer Properties, was housed in a beautiful large one-story white stucco building with a sienna-colored tile roof, designed like a Spanish casa. Set off by stately palms and great landscaping, it was very impressive. Enrique yearned for position and money. Looking at Poffer's place of business pushed his desire up another notch—he would do almost anything to become powerful and wealthy.

"May I help you, sir?" said the very attractive, dark-haired woman sitting behind a large reception desk. Enrique was glancing around and was stunned at the beautiful large room.

"I'm sorry. I was admiring your outstanding quarters, outside and inside. They're beautiful."

The woman smiled warmly. "Why, thank you very much. We're kinda partial to them ourselves. Are you Mr. Cruz? Mr. Poffer instructed me to expect a gentleman at about this time."

Enrique felt important as he answered to the affirmative. She asked him to have a seat while she informed her boss.

He sank into a plush leather chair and continued to visually soak up his surroundings.

"Mr. Cruz, I'll show you to Mr. Poffer's office."

Enrique looked around to see the receptionist standing at a door, smiling at him.

He stood up and followed her through the door and down a wide hallway. There were lighted paintings on each wall. They looked expensive. They arrived at double doors; she opened one, and they entered.

"Well, Mr. Cruz, welcome to Panama City Beach," Poffer said in a low-pitched assertive voice as he stuck out his hand.

Their handshake told Enrique that J. D. Poffer was aggressive in everything he did. Enrique's hand felt like it had been crushed. "Thank you, Mr. Poffer, it's a real pleasure to meet you. Mr. Gomez sends his best regards."

"That ol' tightwad knows 'best regards' cost him nothing. If I can sew up this beach property deal—with your help, of course," he replied as he looked hard into Enrique's eyes. "He'll owe me a nice commission, a very nice commission. By the way, call me J. D."

He waved the Cuban to a large couch facing an ebony coffee table. Poffer sat across from him. On the table was a large portfolio. "I'd better give you the highlights of what we'll be discussing with the Conway brothers. We've got about thirty minutes before we have to leave for their hotel. Let's make tracks." He reached and opened the file.

Enrique sat back in his chair, waiting for J. D.'s briefing.

Poffer explained that the Conway brothers wanted $250 million for sixteen acres. Ten of those, for $175 million, were prime property, being located on the water. The remaining six acres, for $75 million, were located directly across Highway 98.

The property was just west of Panama City Beach and currently consisted of a bunch of old beach houses and several small motels and restaurants in need of a lot of repair. The Conways twisted a few arms, squeezed out a few dollars, and got the county and city to condemn most of the structures. Owners of the few remaining buildings were willing to take fifty cents on the dollar, as evaluated by the Bay County Board of Realtors, to escape their problem.

Many upright real estate sales companies and property developers despised the strong-arm tactics of the Conways, Poffer emphasized.

Their large, well-funded company was known in the industry by the big-timers, as the "blitzkrieg boys." They'd try just about anything to make a deal. One of their favorite ploys was trying to convince the potential buyer that they wanted only to make a minimal margin on their investment. Then, the longer a customer would hold out, the nastier the brothers would get.

J. D. was worked up. He reminded Enrique that the strategy was to counteroffer 10 percent less.

The Cuban's mind was racing. He couldn't tell J. D. that his orders from Gomez and Bovitch, explicitly spelled out a simple strategy—listen to the Conways quote their price, then make a nonnegotiable offer of 20 percent less. Gomez had told him, "They may turn purple and exhale fire, but they'll have to take our offer. I have too much on them. Just tell the brothers you represent an organization that is going to wire transfer the money to their account by noon Friday. We have their account number. Don't reveal who you represent. Just tell them it's a large influential organization. That ought to get their attention."

"Poffer is going to explode," Enrique thought, "but I can't worry about that. Once he finds out that his commission will be somewhat larger than he expects, he'll cool down."

J. D. got out of his chair, picked up the file, and put it in his briefcase. "Let's go face the dragons."

They arrived at the Conway's hotel five minutes ahead of their ten o'clock meeting. J. D. had said the "confrontation" would be in a small conference room located on the ground floor. He led the way with a determined stride—as if to say "Let's get on with the business at hand."

Enrique was a little nervous but determined not to let it show. Underneath his first assignment was a deep desire to learn how to be tough and assertive and use people for his personal gain. He wanted to become important fast. The only way to do that, he thought, was to intimidate people and run over them when needed. But first, he had to establish a dominant reputation. This upcoming meeting would be the springboard to his future.

As Poffer reached the meeting room door, it opened, and out stepped an attractive lady, perhaps in her midthirties. She was well dressed in a conservative pleated medium gray skirt and navy blue blazer. Her dark hair framed an oval face, accented with large expressive eyes. J. D. had met her once before. She was a special assistant to the Conways, and a tigress. He wanted nothing to do with her and hoped she had no prominent role in the meeting.

"Why, hello, Mr. Poffer, It's good to see you again. I was just going to the lobby to watch for you and lead you back." She locked her eyes on Enrique. "This must be Mr. Cruz."

J. D. replied in his strong voice, "Nice to see you, Ms. Russo. Yes, this is Enrique Cruz, representing the highly interested private investment group in Tampa." They shook her hand.

She smiled. "Welcome to you both. Sam Conway and his brother Calvin are waiting." Poffer wasn't impressed by her last comment. It was arrogant. She reflected the personality of her two bosses.

The Conways were standing at the small conference table when Ms. Russo and the two guests walked in. Sam Conway, the older brother by two years, walked around the table with hand outstretched to Poffer. "Well, J. D., you and I talked just ten days ago, now here we are again, ready to consummate a great deal for all of us, eh?"

J. D. didn't say anything. He just turned toward Enrique, signaling to the Conways that he was the man to deal with. Poffer was there to make sure all technical matters were made clear to Cruz. The brothers glanced at each other with narrowed eyes.

Calvin broke his silence and said, "Let's sit down and get comfortable. This may take a little while, and if anyone wants coffee, soda, or whatever, Ms. Russo will be happy to provide it." Enrique stole a glance at her and she had a thin, false smile on her face. He didn't trust her.

There was conversation about most everything: politics, sports, the stock market, and last but not least, a few strong comments about beautiful Panama City Beach—its business growth and its future. Poffer and Cruz knew the brothers were trying to set the stage for a frontal attack. Cruz was ready, but he counted on J. D.'s knowledge and no-nonsense disposition.

When Poffer saw the Conways lean toward each other and briefly whisper, he knew they were ready to start their assault.

"Enrique," Sam said rather sharply, "it's a mystery to me that your group, company, or whatever sends only one man to this important meeting, whose experience in high-level financial transactions is, at best, very limited. The people you represent would better serve their interests by having sent a major player." Sam glanced at Cal, then back at Enrique—he had a look of haughtiness.

There was dead silence for a few seconds, then Enrique stood up and looked at each brother. J. D. started to say something, but Enrique held up his hand for him to hold his comment. "Excuse me, J. D., I'd like to say something about that disparaging remark. My people briefed me thoroughly about each of you and your company. I've been privy to your track record, details on your major transactions, and the several run-ins you've had with the IRS and the State Real Estate Board; plus, we have contact with principals in several companies you have done business with, and you have a questionable history. We are going to do business together. You have something to sell, and we want to buy. I propose we get on with it without beating around the bushes."

Even J. D. was surprised at Enrique's toughness. It sure wasn't lost on the Conways. They seemed stunned. Poffer was laughing inside.

"We have studied your offer of sale for the beach property, and J. D. furnished us with a very detailed ten-year market analysis of Panama City Beach as it grows westward. Comparative property values have been run and we now feel confident our evaluation is well within acceptable limits."

Cal Conway was still smarting from Enrique's directness. *No one talks to the Conway brothers that way*, he thought. "Sounds to me like you have already determined what you will pay," he said in a razor-sharp voice.

"We have done what any smart investor would do," Enrique said. "We measured the value of your property to derive a fair price."

"A fair price?" Cal asked. "You think our price isn't fair?"

Cal's face was the color of a deep sunburn. Sam stood up with his brother and had a scowl on his face.

Enrique looked directly into the eyes of each Conway. "No, I don't," he answered. "It didn't take us long to realize that you two padded your profit quite well. We won't pay your price, but we will, however, pay a fair price you can't and won't refuse."

The brothers looked at each other questioningly. "What do you mean by that?" Sam asked.

J. D. turned his head and looked at Enrique but tried to hide his surprise. Enrique had not said anything to him about Alejo making a special offer with "muscle" behind it.

The Cuban continued, "I mean that your price of $150 million for the described sixteen acres in your proposal of ten days ago is out of the question. We know from irrefutable sources just how you set the value of your property—how many people you literally ran over and officials you paid off to acquire it. We have sworn affidavits with individuals' names, and copies of agreements along with any payoffs involved. Our attorneys stand ready to file charges against you tomorrow morning if so instructed."

The three people across the table from Enrique and J. D. had sat back down. Cal, Sam, and Ms. Russo were quiet, although the brothers were evidently about to burst with anger.

"Gentlemen, my organization will wire transfer $120 million to your primary bank at ten in the morning, with instructions to the recipient bank to hold the check until J. D. and I receive a formal notice of sale, no later than twelve noon," Enrique said. "The amount I quoted represents a 20 percent reduction of your original quote."

Poffer kept his outward calm, but he was getting angry at Enrique for not telling him about Gomez's dictated amount he was going to pay for the property—$120 million. "And we've told them they have no choice. What a piece of business," he thought.

He was determined to demand a higher commission—Alejo had promised a $250,000 fee to J. D. when the negotiated sales price with Conway brothers was $150 million, less a 10 percent discount, or $135 million total. Now the final dictated price by Gomez would pay the Conways $120 million. J. D. was under the impression that his commission would be much less. He was very disappointed.

Cal stood and pointed at Enrique and half-shouted, "Who are you to threaten us if we don't accept your offer?"

Enrique answered, "Cal, we have informed you and your brother exactly what is and what will be. If you intend to contest our offer, then it's going to hurt, if not destroy, your company. I'd advise you to take the $120 million. It's fair and equitable, Cal, and I expect your bill of sale by noon tomorrow. I will forward it to our attorney for review."

With that, Cruz and Poffer walked out of the conference room. Cal and Sam Conway and their assistant sat there feeling like they had been broadsided by an eighteen-wheel trailer truck!

As the two walked toward the hotel lobby, J. D. said they needed to go somewhere and talk. Enrique knew Poffer wanted some answers, and he would provide as many as he could.

They walked outside the hotel and spotted a large coffee shop across the street on a corner. Both were quiet as they strolled along. Finally, Poffer spoke, "I've never experienced anything quite like that meeting. I thought I was tough, but you sure surprised me with what you said and how you said it. You could at least have told me what the new plan was—how it affected me, regarding my commission, etc."

Cruz responded in a low-key manner. "I was instructed not to share the strategy or my tactics with anyone, including you. Sorry for the surprise."

They went into the coffee shop and found a booth in the back, away from the large front window. After they ordered coffee, J. D. confronted Enrique. "Mr. Gomez guaranteed me $250,000 commission upon the purchase of the Conway property. Since we discounted their price an additional 10 percent, where does that leave me?"

"J. D., you did an excellent job carrying out the evaluation and marketing research on the Conway property. Because of your good work, Alejo is going to pay you $500,000—you've earned it."

Poffer looked hard into the Cuban's dark, intense eyes and saw he was serious. "To say the least, I'm speechless. Alejo has my gratitude. I also appreciate the good word you put in for me."

"Keep in mind, J. D., that if the Conways try to fight our 'offer' we are prepared to destroy their company. We may need your assistance."

"That won't be a problem," Poffer said.

After about fifteen minutes of lighter conversation, with J. D. saying he would steer Enrique to a few outstanding real estate developers that he knew well, they walked back to the hotel and J. D.'s car. They saw no sign of the Conways.

Enrique returned to his room, phoned Frank Bovitz, and gave him every detail of the meeting. Bovitz was extremely pleased and congratulated Cruz, saying he would pass on the good news to Alejo right away. The money would be wired to the Conways' bank the next morning.

When Enrique hung up the phone, he lay back on the bed and congratulated himself. He had carried out his first assignment for Gomez and Bovitz, and he felt really good. The Cuban knew he would receive a nice bonus for his work—the first of many to come, he thought. He was on his way to attaining the status he had wanted for a long time.

Cruz was a stickler for detail. The day-timer notebook he'd brought with him was key to his daily regimen. Names, titles, job descriptions, places, and dates were entered on every new business call he made. He had planned to contact his Gelb Foods customer base in Panama City, Pensacola, several military installations, and Tallahassee when he headed back to Tampa.

He wanted to stop in Danaville and check out the Kelly farm on Sunday or Monday as he drove to Tallahassee. Enrique still suspected Lyle Kelly and Teresa had caused Arlene to humiliate him. He was glad to be out of the family, but his ego had been bruised, and he wouldn't forget it.

CHAPTER TWENTY-SIX

S HERIFF BERNAM DIDN'T go into Gardner's Drugstore very often, so when Marvin saw the large lawman striding through the store toward him, he knew it had to do with the Kellys. "Mornin', Sheriff. It's good to see you."

Claude Bernam was an effective sheriff, but not long on diplomacy—except at election time. "The same here, Marvin."

"What can I do for you?" Gardner stepped out of the pharmacy and shook hands with the sheriff.

"Oh, nothing. I left my car at Peel's Shell for an oil change, thought I'd drop over and chat for a few minutes."

"Well, good. Let's sit and have some coffee." Marvin didn't waste any time to bring up one of his favorite subjects. "Have you heard anything at all lately about the Kellys or the farm?"

Bernam took a sip of coffee, and looked over his shoulder as a couple of people walked by. "Deputy Beck was on regular patrol on 77 and had turned around at the county line for his return trip. When he pulled back onto the highway, he fell in behind a familiar looking two-and-a-half-ton truck. As he trailed along about a hundred feet behind, he realized it belonged to the Kellys. He noticed the back was open and full of stacked cartons and other items. Pulling a little closer, he could see that in the cartons were mostly foodstuffs along with metal-framed one-man type military-style beds. Beck could even make out stacked mattresses.

He finally passed the truck, blew his horn, waved, and increased his speed toward Danaville."

Marvin had sat up in his chair and began to lean on his elbows toward Bernam, as if to ensure he heard every detail. "Why would the Kellys be trucking in food and bedding? They have three hundred acres of vegetables along with livestock, and a very large house."

"Well, it seems to me they're expecting a lot of company," the sheriff replied. "I have a feeling that's been growing stronger lately that something strange happened on that farm during the storm, and the family has been quietly circling the wagons to protect whatever the 'something' is. Carew Hinson and Red Reddington were on that truck, and they were coming from Dothan. That's the most likely place within a one—or two-hour trip where they could buy a large quantity of food and military surplus bedding. I'm going to have Deputy Beck contact grocer suppliers and military surplus stores in that area and see if he can turn up something."

"There must be something we can do in the meantime, Claude. Whatever is on that farm could have an impact on Danaville and the whole county."

"Yeah, that's what worries me. I think I oughta talk to Jim Summers and see if he has any ideas. Time is working against us. I'm sure he's in his office now. His car was parked in front of his office when I passed there on my way to the Shell station. Let me talk to him alone. If he has a bead on something concrete, being a newspaper man, he may want to keep it to himself. I'll get back in touch ASAP."

Gardner was disappointed. He wanted to be in the lead pack whenever something of substance was found regarding the Kelly farm. But he knew that the sheriff would feel more comfortable working one-on-one when asking a newspaperman questions.

"Be sure you let me know if Summers reveals anything of importance," Marvin said. "Remember, the three of us agreed to work together in finding out what's happening at the Kellys."

Bernam grunted an okay as he walked toward the front door.

The editor's only office window provided a view of the intersection of Main Street and Railroad Avenue. It gave Jim a chance to keep an eye on some of the comings and goings of downtown Danaville. However, most of the time, he was glued to his computer or in the pressroom with his two-man crew, battling another edition of the news off the presses.

Summers had just finished talking to Ralph Tobias. Putting the phone down, he swiveled his chair around to look out his office window and think about what the county attorney had just told him. The first thing he saw was Sheriff Bernam parking his blue-and-white in front of the newspaper office.

"Wonder what's on his mind," Jim thought. "I hope this isn't another attempt by him to pick my brain."

A few moments later, the sheriff came to the open door of his office. Jim motioned for him to come in. "Hey, editor, what's going to be your lead story this Saturday?" Bertram said with a big grin.

"Hi, Claude, have a seat. The *Mason County News* won't have any earth-shaking news this weekend. Everything is kinda quiet around the county." Summers's mind raced ahead, and he added to himself, "But next Wednesday's edition will be overflowing with the greatest news in the newspaper's history. The national press will have beaten us to the draw by Monday night or Tuesday morning, but we'll have much better information than they will." Out loud, he asked, "Want some coffee?"

Bernam got a serious look on his face and said, "No thanks, Jim. I came by to tell you what Deputy Beck discovered yesterday on 77, just south of the Jackson County line." The sheriff related the details of the deputy trailing the Kelly's big truck returning to the farm, evidently from Dothan, loaded with enough food and bedding to take care of a number of people.

Jim listened intently and knew immediately that he now had to brief Claude about all the details of the event at the Kellys and what was to happen during the next few days. It was just as well. The sheriff and his deputies would be needed. After about fifteen minutes of details, Claude sat quietly, looking out of the window, trying to digest all that he had just heard.

"Would you have Captain Stanton get in touch with me?" he said. "You and Ralph know him and have his full support. I would think you could get through to him right away. I need to brief my deputies as soon as I can round them up."

"I'll do that within the hour, right after I inform Tobias that you now know the major details of what's going on, and that you'll be talking to Stanton."

The sheriff stood, picked up his hat, walked to the doorway, and paused, looking back at Summers. "This is big—real big." Then he walked out

IT WAS LATE Thursday afternoon when John entered the kitchen from the back porch. Sara, sitting at the table peeling potatoes, looked up and gave her husband a beautiful smile that was an elixir to his tired body. It had been a long busy day. He, Carew, and Red had hurried the last details of the sleeping spaces in the barn, and had turned their attention to cutting the wall sections for the four spaces in the den. They would install them the next morning.

After hugging and kissing Sara, he asked, "Where's Mama?

"She's putting away the extra towels and other bath items the guys got in Dothan. How're all the preparations for Monday coming along?"

He related the current status of everything, and added there was a huge task ahead of them, and a lot of people involved. Sara nodded in agreement.

The phone rang and John walked over and picked it up. It was Clayton Parker. John was glad the well driller had called— he had made a mental note earlier in the day to call him, but it had slipped his mind. Clayton was his expansive self as he greeted John, and said he hoped his family was well and in good spirits. John thanked Parker, and then they discussed the large task facing them, commencing Monday morning. Clayton said he and his top drilling operator were ready, and would be there late Sunday afternoon.

John assured him there would be no problem in moving the large drilling rig to the bean field. It was crossing the softer ground to reach the center of the circle that was the potential problem. Both men agreed that rain would complicate things. After a few more words, they bid each other good night and hung up.

Five minutes later, Jim Summers called to give John the news about Deputy Beck's spotting the Kelly's large truck the day before, filled with food and other items, on the way to the farm from Dothan. John wasn't very surprised. He had been thinking for a few days that the family's activities would be discovered, one after another. He prayed that the general public wouldn't learn the details of the divine event until the drilling had been finished.

Summers went on to explain what was shaping up at the present. "Jack Stanton will arrive tomorrow evening. He has a room at the Comfort Inn and will want to see you on Saturday morning. He wants to have Captain Ackerman present so you three can review all contingencies. I think Tobias and I ought to be present—he acting as the eyes and ears of the Feds so he can keep the secretary of defense informed on an as-needed basis, and me so I'll know how to plan for press coverage of the drilling and recovery activities on Monday and Tuesday."

"Tell Stanton I'll be happy to meet with him and Ackerman tomorrow around 9:00 a.m. along with you and Ralph," John said.

The editor was quiet for a moment, reviewing all the ongoing details in his mind, then asked, "Do you have enough people to meet and pick up the five clergy members that are due Saturday and Sunday?"

"Yes. Reverend Butler will drive to Panama City on both days and meet the planes. Would you ask Sheriff Bernam to furnish a deputy to drive the reverend each day to indicate security for our guests?"

"That's a good idea," Summers said. "I'll speak to him at once." Since joining the Kellys in their preparation for drilling in the bean field, Jim had been very impressed with John's ability to absorb a lot of varied information and act on it with common-sense planning. A very bright man, he thought. Jim respected him. A few more moments of conversation, then John thanked the editor for his help, wished him a good evening, and hung up.

Carew walked in soon after, and the four of them sat down to dinner. "One more day and we start changing our dining habits and schedules," Granny said. "Sara and I agree we'll have to use this table and the dining room table together in order to seat everyone at the same time."

"Everyone may not be eating at the same time due to various things that will be going on for some of our family at most any hour during each day," John said. "We really don't know what to expect, so we stay flexible. Starting tomorrow evening, we'll have at least three more diners—Lyle and Teresa and her mother, Arlene. Pat and Paul will be here on Saturday along with three of the clergy. Dick and Ann Kessel, plus the two remaining clerics, will arrive on Sunday." John smiled at his mother and his wife. "You two better add several more leaves to the large dining table." They all laughed.

Carew added, "There is always the mobile table, sawhorses, and plywood—easy to make." The laughter was extended.

Sheriff Bernam got to his office just before 7:45 p.m. He would have a few minutes to collect his thoughts and get his emotions in hand before his deputies arrived. The kind of information that Summers had given him was awesome. Claude had not attended church very often through the years, and never gave religion much thought. But the occurrence at the Kelly farm was having an increasing effect on him—one unlike any he had had before.

Bernam had left his secretary's outer door open as well as his door. He heard several sets of boot heels clicking on the marble floor toward the open door of his office. In several moments, his deputies would be surprised beyond any explanation—the same as he was.

Dan Beck led the other four deputies into the sheriff's office, and said, "Hey, Sheriff, isn't eight o'clock at night an odd time to have a staff meeting?" Dan was smiling as were the others, but they quickly saw their boss looked very serious. There was sudden quiet in the room. The deputies had a feeling that something big was brewing.

Claude briefly looked at each man and said, "Guys, I know it's unusual for us to have a meeting at night, but the circumstances demand we do so. When I tell you what's up, you'll understand the timing."

Fifteen minutes later, all of the deputies were sitting quietly, looking at nothing in particular, each trying to comprehend what they had just heard.

"I won't keep you any longer. I know each of you is going to do some soul-searching, but try not to let it affect your duty. Three of you return to your shift, but all of you stay alert and be prepared for some long hours starting Sunday evening or Monday morning. Remember, say nothing to anyone about what's going on. The public will know soon enough. In the meantime, I'll be coordinating with a Captain Jack Stanton of the Florida State Troopers. He is a special envoy of the governor. As soon as I'm briefed by him, I'll let you all know what's expected of us."

Beck hung back when the others walked out. He waited a moment until his deputies had gone. When he looked at the sheriff, their eyes met and did not waver. "What is it, Dan?" Bernam asked with a furrowed brow.

"I'd sure like to work side-by-side with you on this, Claude. This thing has gotta be the biggest happening in this country, ever. I'd like to be real close to all the action as it unfolds. Don't forget that I spotted the Kelly truck coming from Dothan yesterday, and what it was carrying—now we know. I'm already involved in the details of this development."

The sheriff got out of his chair and walked around his desk and stopped about two feet in front of Beck, staring into his eyes. "Dan, I know you're about to jump out of your boots to be in a high-profile position as all of this unfolds, but this particular happening is not a run-of-the-mill law enforcement issue, it's a phenomenon—a miracle—that requires all of us to be respectful and aware of who's really in charge. There'll be no office or public politics involved in what we do. I will not allow you to use any of this as a personal stepladder for your career."

Dan shifted slightly back and forth, from one foot to the other. It was evident that the sheriff had been deeply affected by the event at the Kelly farm. It was clear to the deputy there would be no way for him to gain personal recognition of being a close partner of Claude Bernam's. His only hope for ever being noticed as an important part of the sheriff's office would be an unexpected piece of luck.

"Okay, Claude. I understand." With that, Beck put on his hat and walked out, knowing that he was more or less on his own as a lawman.

FRIDAY BROKE AS a gray, overcast morning. After breakfast, John walked out to the back porch and surveyed the sky. The early weather report predicted a 20 percent chance of rain until late Saturday afternoon, then clear skies through Monday. Knowing how unpredictable weather could be, he silently asked God to keep the ground dry until the drilling was finished.

He looked out at the fields, then at the barns and the other buildings. Turning, his gaze swept through the large, magnificent oaks, and took in the pond and pasture beyond. He then walked to the other end of the porch and observed the expansive manicured lawn with shrubs and flowers, shaded in part by more oaks. What a beautiful statement made by all the Kellys through the years. A tear of love ran down his cheek.

"Well," he thought, "what is happening to the Kelly family today is God's plan. He has allowed us to use this land from the day Grandpa Frank stuck his plow in the ground for the first time. Now, he is reclaiming this farm for a greater purpose that will soon become apparent to all of us.

John and his family strongly agreed that giving up farming and dedicating themselves to carrying out whatever the Lord led them to do would be an honor and privilege. In fact, he felt throughout all the years of hard work and love for the three hundred acres that there had been only one purpose for this special place—the wondrous work of God that was unfolding now, moment by moment.

He was so deep in his thoughts he didn't hear Sara walk up. "Everything okay, dear?" Her husband nodded his head, and put his arm around her waist. "You seemed a little tense last night, and very quiet at breakfast," she said.

"I think I passed over a deep chasm this morning. I've just experienced a feeling of releasing my lock-grip on the farm for the old reasons, and grasping the hand of the Lord for the new reasons he is now revealing to us."

She pulled him to her and buried her face in his chest. "I think we all have the same feeling."

"I'd better hook up with Carew and bring in the plywood and studding for the sleeping compartments in the den. We'll use the front porch to do most all of our sawing of the lumber with a skill saw. We can have the job done in four or five hours. That ought to make Mama happier."

"Me too," Sara said with a smile.

John walked out to the main barn to find Carew. He heard hammering and knew his top hand was putting finishing touches on the original eight sleeping compartments located in the large building.

John was impressed at the work Carew and Red had done on the compartments in the barn. Whoever occupied the living spaces for whatever time was required should feel comfortable and have adequate privacy, he thought.

"Howdy, Mr. Carpenter, have you seen a farmer by the name of Carew, or another by the name of Red?"

Carew looked at John, who had a big grin on his face. "Yes, I saw both of them packing Carew's car and mumbling about how they couldn't wait to flee their slave-driver boss." Both men broke into a hearty laugh—a laugh they needed.

John walked over to his best friend, put a hand on his shoulder, and said, "Can you wrap this up in short order so you and I can start in the den?"

"Sure can. I'll be finished here in about fifteen minutes, then we'll take that lumber there"—he pointed with the hammer in his hand—"to the front porch."

Accommodations for their scheduled visitors would soon be complete.

CHAPTER TWENTY-SEVEN

LYLE AND BILL talked a short while on Friday morning before Bill's nine o'clock class. It would be to no avail to pursue questioning his departing roommate about what was going on at the farm, so he spent the time telling Lyle how great it had been sharing a room with him these past two years. Lyle readily agreed, and emphasized that they would get together in the not-distant-future. That seemed to placate Bill's feelings.

He glanced at his watch and grudgingly got up and held out his hand. Lyle brushed the hand away and put his arms around Bill's shoulders. He responded, and they shared a big bear hug. With that, Lyle told him, "We'll pray for each other and keep in touch."

"Take care, Lyle. I'll miss you." With that, Bill Kraven opened the door and walked out. Lyle stood looking around the room, thinking how it had been a huge piece of their lives for two years.

Lyle called Teresa and told her he had finished loading his car and would be over in fifteen minutes. She told him she was all packed, and laughingly said she was waiting for her slave to arrive and load her things into her mother's car. He told her his pay scale was very high, and to have her checkbook ready because he was on his way.

It was evident that Teresa and Arlene were in much better spirits than the night before. That pleased Lyle. There were many things ahead of all of them, and they must keep a positive and trusting outlook.

Lyle arrived within a short while, and the loading of Arlene's car went smoothly. Lyle remarked that they should lease a large truck to accommodate Teresa's "stuff." The two women gave him a look of pretended, animated anger.

Teresa had said a tearful goodbye to Doris Coffer, her roommate; both of them promising to stay in touch. Lyle had said to Bill Kraven that he would know in the near future the reason he and Teresa were leaving school; Teresa said the same to Doris.

The two fully loaded cars departed the campus and drove to Chili's, a favorite restaurant for the college crowd. After a relatively quick lunch, they were ready to head west to Danaville.

Before rising from the table, Arlene put out her hands to Teresa and Lyle. They each responded, and as they held hands, she spoke in an even, soft voice to Lyle, "I have to admit that I'm nervous and yet thrilled about meeting your family and seeing the farm. You two are going to have to stick close by me, enforce my courage until I settle down, and I will."

"Believe me, Arlene," Lyle said. "Like I told you before, you'll instantly be accepted by the family as soon as they meet you, just as I did." He lightly squeezed her hand and smiled. She relaxed and returned his smile.

Teresa was also smiling. "Let's hit the road. We should be there by a little after 2:00 p.m. I can't wait."

Traffic was moderate on 1-10, and they were driving north on Danaville's main street at one forty-five. Another five minutes or so and they would be home. Arlene was impressed at how pretty the town was.

John and Carew were just finishing their work in the den when Granny appeared at the doorway and told her son that two cars just parked in front of the house. Sara came down the hall, heading for the front door. "John, Carew, come on. Let's welcome the kids and give Arlene a special greeting," she said in an excited voice.

Everyone went out to the front porch and down the steps to give a warm homecoming to all three.

John hugged Teresa first, while Sara warmly welcomed Arlene. Granny and Lyle held each other while he kissed her on the cheek. John turned to Arlene, took her hand, and told her how much they had looked forward to her coming, and she must understand she was now a bona fide family member. Sara kissed her son and her daughter-in-law-to-be. Carew and Red hugged Lyle and Teresa, and shook Arlene's hand. It was indeed a loving homecoming.

Arlene was touched by all the warmth that was emanating from her new family and the feeling of total acceptance. Her anxiety completely disappeared. She said a silent thank-you to God.

All of them went into the house. Arlene's eyes had been constantly moving since they drove up, taking in every detail. She was extremely impressed at what she saw. It was a beautiful setting; the house and grounds, with the beautiful oaks, all emphasized God's power. She was sure the aura of his presence was all around her. Arlene was comforted.

Sara went over to Arlene and told her John would like to take her on a short tour of the house and grounds a little later when she was settled in. Arlene smiled and said she was looking forward to it. In the meantime, Lyle, Carew, and Red would unload the cars.

After dinner, when everyone was in the living room talking, John excused himself and went up to his office to make several phone calls—the first was to Reverend Butler. "Hi, Wade. Hope all's going well with you and Ruth."

"Everything is as it should be, John. We're fine, just standing barefooted on pins and needles, waiting for the 'discovery.'"

"That's one reason I love and respect that man," John thought. "He has a great sense of humor, but is respectful as to how he uses it."

Wade continued, "The family okay? I hope Lyle, Teresa, and her mother had a good trip from Tampa."

"As you know, things are beginning to pick up speed. The kids, along with Arlene—Teresa's mother that I told you about—got here about 2:00 p.m. Of course, three clerics are due tomorrow and two on Sunday. By the way, did Sheriff Bernam assign a deputy to accompany you when picking them up?"

"Oh yes. The sheriff himself is going with me both days—Delta out of Atlanta, arriving at 10:30 a.m. tomorrow; and Delta again, at 1:23 p.m. on Sunday. Our two foreign men of God, one from Rome and the other from Israel, will be on the Sunday flight," the reverend said.

John was pleased that Bernam had chosen to accompany the reverend, rather than send a deputy. It was more in keeping with the status of the arriving clerics.

The farmer told Butler about the meeting the next morning at the farm with Captain Jack Stanton, Jim Summers, Ralph Tobias, and National Guard Captain Ron Ackerman, covering all aspects of security for every area of the farm and the family, with emphasis on the visiting five men of God. The reverend listened intently and was heartened by what he heard. As they were wrapping up their conversation, Butler told John he would like to come out Saturday night and get together with him and the three visiting Protestant ministers. John didn't ask why. He knew whatever Wade had in mind would be important.

The next call John made was to Doc McNally. He tried his home, and luckily he was in. His wife asked John to wait a moment. "Hello, farmer, how in the world are you?" Doc said exuberantly. "You and the family must be enjoying good health. I haven't seen any of you in a while."

"We're all doing well, Doc. I hope you and your wife are doing likewise. If you have ten minutes or so, I'd like to bring you up-to-date on what's happening with us and the farm." John had gotten Doc's attention.

"You take as much time as you need." Doc knew John well enough to feel there was something important brewing at the Kellys.

John began telling Doc the details of the past two and a half weeks at the farm. He told of the first and second storms, the rainbows, and about the peculiar hail pattern. When he described the bean-field circle and its darker soil, Doc sucked in his breath.

John then brought the doctor up-to-date on preparations for security of the farm, the family, and the county.

There was only silence from the phone for a moment, then Doc responded in almost a whisper, "John, this is breathtaking. It has all kinds of ramifications for us and for the world."

"That's right, Doc. We don't know just how people are going to react. Reverend Butler and I think some will come here to see the site and participate in a unique religious experience. The others will want to collect souvenirs or items for monetary gain—ending up destroying the site. Even riots could break out. All of this could spread throughout the state, the nation, even most parts of the world."

"That means a lot of people could get hurt . . . or worse," Doc added.

"Exactly," John said. "Mason County citizens and those folks that will be flooding into this area will be candidates for medical help at some stage. According to our local National Guard commander Captain Ron Ackerman, the local guard unit is comprised of one infantry company. That's about 120 men which will be deployed around the farm. It has limited medical capability, with usually two medics and several corpsmen. They must first react to need among their own. There's no way they could also take on a number of civilian injuries."

"I think I can help solve a potential problem, John. I'll contact a few other doctors who are in position to react positively to an idea that is forming in my old head. I'll just mention briefly that I'm sure a team of multifaceted medical personnel can be set up to treat a wide range of trauma and other needs. I'll be back in touch with you tomorrow before five o'clock with a detailed plan. I'd like to think we won't have very many problems starting Monday evening and lasting however long the mass of people keep coming. But it may not work out that way."

John thanked Doc and hung up. He thought how fortunate he and the family were to have so many caring and capable friends. "God bless 'em all," he said.

Forty-five minutes had elapsed when John rejoined everyone in the living room.

"Well, the nomad returns," Lyle said with a smile.

John returned his son's smile, and faced the group. "Had to make a couple of calls to check on the preparation for tomorrow and Monday. It's going to be a busy day tomorrow. Lyle, Carew, and I will have a 9:00 a.m. meeting with Summers, Tobias, Stanford, and Ackerman. Captain Jack Stanton of the Florida State Troopers, and Captain Ron Ackerman of our local National Guard unit will brief us on the security plan worked out by National Guard Commanding General Whitmire through Governor Ashton's office for us, the farm—especially the bean field—and the county."

Everyone in the room had been impressed by John's leadership since the beginning of the huge event that was unfolding. They were even more impressed by him now, as the exploration was about to begin. He seemed to have grown stronger. They knew that God was at work in John.

The next thirty minutes or so were spent in discussing the arriving clerics. Three would get to the farm around noon the next day; the remaining two arriving at about 3:00 p.m. Lyle asked if there were any kosher food items available for Rabbi Metz.

John assured Lyle and the others there was indeed kosher food available. Reverend Butler had taken care of that himself. Sara said she had a kosher cookbook that Pat donated from her large book collection.

It wasn't long before talk about bedtime began. Teresa and her mother would share a bedroom, and Lyle would have his old room for at least the night, then would move to the barn. Pat and Paul Daniels would take Lyle's room starting Saturday evening. The two clerics arriving tomorrow, Rev. Chase Griffin and Dr. Neil Claussen, will occupy two of the five cubicles in the den. Billy Durdin, Fr. Kevin Walsh, and Rabbi Jacob Metz would occupy the other three. When John mentioned the accommodations to Reverend Butler, the reverend thought them very acceptable. With that, everyone said good night.

GRANNY HAD THREE willing breakfast chefs ready to lend a hand when called upon. As Sara had learned, her mother-in-law, in a most loving way, ran the kitchen with a creative discipline. She welcomed help, but only when there were many diners at her table. So, except for Sara and sometimes Teresa, the kitchen ballet, as John had called them once before, danced flawlessly. Arlene sat comfortably and enjoyed the show.

In a short while, John and Carew came in from tending the livestock and chickens. Granny knew John wanted to show Arlene the bean field before his four guests arrived for the 9:00 a.m. meeting. "It's time to eat. Teresa, tell Lyle breakfast is ready." Just at that moment, Lyle walked in, apologizing. He had overslept and had been shaving.

Breakfast was great and everyone complimented Granny and Sara on their culinary skills. Arlene had never sat down to a real "country" breakfast such as was served—eggs to order; bacon, sausage, or ham; red-eye gravy; grits; wonderful biscuits; three cereals to choose from; mixed fruit; and milk, coffee or tea. She correctly assumed that farmwork helped keep off the pounds.

Soon after, John, Lyle, Teresa, and Arlene drove out to the bean field. On the way out, John gave Arlene the details of how the hail had abruptly stopped before falling on any of the crops, and the discovery of the perfect circle in the bean field. He knew Lyle had told her about the phenomenon, but John had a need to tell her what he had experienced. Arlene was all ears, and hearing about the event from John, who had been wrestling with preparation for the pending exploration, magnified her feeling of awe.

John soon parked the truck and they got out and stood looking toward the center of the bean field. Lyle stood beside Arlene and pointed. "Do you see those posts way out there?"

She looked and finally spotted some of them. "Yes," she answered. The four of them walked down the rows of beans until reaching the nearest post. She saw the other posts leading off to the left and right, making a circular pattern. Then she looked down, and it didn't take but a moment to see the outer edge of the darker soil. Arlene realized at once this was made by God's hands. Goose bumps appeared on her arms.

Teresa moved over to her mother. "Isn't this powerful?"

"It's beyond my ability to describe my feeling," Arlene replied quietly.

John pointed to the center post and told her that's where the drilling would start on Monday. The four of them stood there, wondering what lay beneath the surface.

Upon returning to the house, John went to find Carew. He wanted to make sure the electric fans had been placed in the barn cubicles along with the portable toilets along a far wall.

Carew was helping Red place the drinking water dispensers in the cubicles along with disposable cups. "How about the ice storage?" John asked.

"We have twenty-five one-hundred-pound bags under sawdust in the small barn. Don't know how long it'll last, but it's a start," Carew said.

"Yeah, we almost wiped out the Graceville ice plant," Red added.

John reminded Carew that they had a meeting in about twenty-five minutes. Their four guests should be arriving soon.

JOHN WALKED THROUGH the kitchen and saw Sara making a large urn of coffee for the meeting. He went over and put his arms around her waist. "John Kelly, can't you see my hands are full right now?"

"That's what I was counting on," he said into her ear.

She sat the pitcher of water down and turned around with a smile and sparkling eyes. "You have an important meeting in a few minutes. You'd better scoot," she said.

"Just wanted to say I love you." He smiled and walked out.

"Mama, please tell Lyle that our company has arrived. He's on the back porch with Teresa and Arlene," John said as he went through the living room toward the front door.

Granny replied she would be happy to do so and headed down the main hall, walked through the sun room and kitchen, and out onto the porch. As she told Lyle about the arriving company, Carew walked up the back steps. Lyle looked at Teresa and reminded her that the meeting could take a while. She smiled and told him to go learn as much as he could—it was important. With that, he and Carew went to help the senior Kelly greet the visitors.

John, Lyle, and Carew walked up to the two cars, just as Jim Summers and Ralph Tobias were getting out of the lead vehicle, and Jack Stanton and Ron Ackerman were emerging from the other car. They all shook hands and said hello. The only one not well-known by the Kelly members was National Guard Captain Ron Ackerman. He was warmly greeted and welcomed to the farm. John made a point to greet State Trooper Captain Jack Stanton and introduce him to Kyle. John and Stanton had developed respect for each other during their first meeting.

"Ron, I hope you don't take offense at my comment," John said, "but I remember you ran for a lot of touchdowns when you played tailback for Danaville High and Florida State University, and now, sixteen years later, you're an army captain and National Guard commanding officer of an infantry unit in Danaville."

Ackerman grinned. "John, in spite of my football days, I'm where I want to be. I'm in my hometown, and I can contribute to the National Guard. Fortune has smiled on me so far."

Jim Summers said he thought he could speak for a great number of Danaville citizens that Ackerman was highly respected, thus, the very man for the job ahead. Ralph Tobias and John nodded in agreement. Not having known Ackerman before the previous evening, Jack Stanton looked on attentively. Lyle and Carew also were interested in the point being made.

"I appreciate your comments, gentlemen, but when Captain Stanton and I brief you later, you'll see that we have dual responsibility to General Whitmire, commander of the Florida National Guard, and to Governor Ashton," Ackerman said.

"Well, gentlemen, let's go in out of this heat, get comfortable, and start things moving," John said. They went up the steps and through the double doors into the handsome old house.

The seven men went into the living room, and John more or less directed who sat where so that the four visitors were facing the three Kellys. That would make conversing easier.

John said he wanted his wife to come in and say hello before they got started. He walked out of the room and returned in several moments with beautiful Sara. She graciously welcomed the four visitors and was introduced to Ron Ackerman, the only one she had not met before. Sara told him the family was very thankful that his troops would be providing security for the family and the farm. They would be in all of their prayers. The captain thanked her and said all prayers would be welcomed.

Before beginning the meeting, John pointed over to a corner where the large coffee urn was sitting on a table cart, and said for everyone to help themselves. Four of the seven men took the offer, then settled back into their chairs.

Jack Stanton opened his briefcase, took out sets of papers, and passed them to everyone. "These are copies of the overall plan of operations for the deployment and placement of troops here at the farm, commencing at 1700 hours . . . uh . . . 5:00 p.m. on Sunday, tomorrow. The plan incorporates details, such as troop conduct toward American civilians, who, rather than being just curious, may become aggressive and try to penetrate our defensive perimeter. There is no doubt there will be some people who will be passionately out of control. Those will be handled as fairly as possible, but force will be used if needed. Troops will have power of federal arrest. As news of this event spreads, there could be those even from other countries who would attempt to steal whatever the exploration reveals. Think about it, the 'find' will be priceless to certain people." With that, Stanton turned to Ackerman. "All yours, Captain."

Ron Ackerman looked and conducted himself like a military man, but at the same time, was relaxed and folksy. He was, as the cliché goes, "a born leader," and highly respected by his men and by the Danaville community.

The captain stayed seated. Making eye contact with everyone, he continued relating the National Guard operational plan. "I will make a general call-up early this evening for our company to report to the armory at 0900 hours tomorrow. They will be carefully briefed regarding the respectful handling of civilians—but if push comes to shove and there's a threat to the troops' safety, or that of any of your family, special guests, or property, they will do whatever is necessary to control the situation."

Ackerman took a sip of coffee and continued, "Captain Stanton toured the farm a week ago and recorded strategic points on the outer perimeter of the property, as well as the inner perimeter around the bean field. From his notes and photos, I've chosen the pond area for our general bivouac. We have 120 men in our company, and I think that will be adequate to do the job. If we find we need additional troops, General Whitmire has arranged for us to draw them from a National Guard armored battalion in Panama City. The same goes for additional food supplies and any medical supplies and care that may be needed."

"Dr. Ken McNally," John said, "a friend and our family physician, is at this moment working on a plan, along with other doctors, that will provide a large medical triage group comprised of complementary specialties. They would be located at our small hospital in Danaville—a little over three miles away. Doc's to call me tonight and give me details."

"That's a good move," Stanton said. "If things get real rough, we would at least have comprehensive medical help."

The National Guard company commander looked at John. "That eases my mind somewhat. We have only three medics of limited capability. I'd like to suggest we get our hands on a medevac helicopter. It's only three and a half miles from the farm to the hospital—just a few minutes away." He turned his eyes on Stanton. "I don't have the rank to pull it off solo—I'd need more persuasion up the line by larger brass than I have."

All of them thought Ackerman's suggestion was the way to go. Stanton rose and got another coffee. "Otherwise," he said, smiling at the NG captain. "I need to talk to your ultimate boss, General Whitmire, and let him push the buttons."

"Something like that," Ackerman replied with a slight smile.

"I'll get on it immediately. We need the chopper and a pair of trauma medics to go with it. They're well trained. If we're lucky, perhaps one could be in place at the hospital within two days."

Jack Stanton told them that the state was providing a large number of troopers for traffic control. Mostly in Mason County, with contingents in surrounding counties. Local county and city law enforcement officers would be used also.

The meeting was soon concluded and everyone went their way, feeling that the powerful, unusual circumstance that had brought them together had bonded them forever. John, Lyle, and Carew stood on the porch, watching the two cars drive away. John was already thinking about the three clerics due to arrive at noon.

CHAPTER TWENTY-EIGHT

REVEREND BUTLER FELT a little strange riding with Sheriff Bernam in his dark blue unmarked Victoria Ford. But he was pleased the sheriff had suggested this arrangement. It was much more formal than his driving the three church VIPs to Danaville and the farm in his smaller four-door Toyota by himself.

"Reverend, I very seldom have anyone to ride in the front seat of this car. But now, to have an outstanding Danaville preacher as a passenger is a big privilege."

Wade laughed. "Just wait until we pick up our guests today and tomorrow, then you'll really have a privilege." Bernam also laughed.

The sheriff asked what the visiting clerics would do if something unusual was found during the exploration. The reverend said it was not a case of "if," but a case of "when," and went on to explain what he meant. With Bernam asking questions as Butler talked, time went by, and they soon were crossing the North Bay Bridge, nearing Panama City.

When they parked at the airport, it was 10:05 a.m. They entered the main terminal and walked over to a bank of TV monitors, located near Delta's ticketing counter. The reverend soon spotted that the arriving flight from Atlanta was on time. He and Bernam walked to the designated gate and waited, along with ten or twelve other people. A Delta 737 soon pulled up to their gate ramp.

Wade was a little nervous. Meeting his close friend Billy Durdin, along with two other well-known, learned clerics, was a unique experience.

This was the beginning of bringing five outstanding men of God to the farm to confirm the truth of what happened at the farm, and what was about to happen. He glanced at the sheriff and noticed that even he seemed edgy.

Deplaning passengers began to emerge from the ramp into the gate reception area. Butler spotted Billy Durdin, the taller of the two men walking with him. Durdin saw Wade and he smiled and waved, and turned his head to tell his two cleric companions his minister friend was waiting. "Hello, Wade. It's really good to see you again."

"Same here, Billy. The Kelly family and I have been eagerly looking forward to the arrival of all of you. As you know, two more are due tomorrow."

Billy turned and put his hand gently on the arm of one of the gentlemen beside him. "Rev. Wade Butler, this is Rev. Chase Griffin, one of the associate ministers of the First United Methodist Church of Raleigh, North Carolina." Griffin was in his late fifties, of medium height, and had a shock of pure white hair. Durdin put his other hand on the arm of the second man and said, "This other friend of mine is Dr. Neil Claussen of the Southern Baptist Convention in Nashville, Tennessee." Dr. Claussen was a little younger, somewhat short and slightly over two hundred pounds, with receding dark hair. They all shook hands and warmly greeted each other.

"Now, gentlemen, I want you to meet a very important man in our community—Sheriff Claude Bernam," Butler said. Claude was an imposing figure at well over six feet, in his crisp tan uniform trimmed in royal blue. "He volunteered to drive us and be our official escort." The three visiting clerics shook Claude's hand and warmly exclaimed that they were happy to meet him. The sheriff felt good.

On their way to the baggage claim area, a number of people in the terminal stared at the four men in suits, and the big uniformed lawman walking along and talking together.

Butler told the clerics that the sheriff had arranged for one of his deputies to meet them at baggage claim, and the officer would load their bags into his patrol car, assuring space and comfort for everyone. Not knowing how long they would be staying at the farm, each cleric had brought more than one bag. They were introduced to Deputy Charlie Williams, and they thanked him profusely for his assistance. The three visitors were truly impressed with the reception they had received. The deputy followed the sheriff's car as they exited the airport and drove north to Danaville and the farm.

During the drive, Billy asked Wade to give them an overview of how the preparations for the security and the exploration were preceding. As Wade was finalizing the details, the car entered the Danaville city limits. After observing Main Street and a dozen blocks or so of quaint homes and yards, they began to see pastures and fields. The conversation turned to questions about Danaville and Mason County. Reverend Griffin and Dr. Claussen wanted to know details about the entire community, but the sheriff had slowed the car to make the turn into the farm. They would continue their conversation later.

"I'm very impressed," Dr. Claussen said. "This is a beautiful farm!"

Reverend Griffin added, "It's totally idyllic. I see what you meant, Wade, when you said the Kellys attribute their success to God's help. It's evident."

The sheriff parked the car in front of the house, and all five men got out. Deputy Williams parked right behind the sheriff's car, got out and stood by, ready to unload the luggage.

"JIM, THIS IS Marvin. You, the sheriff, and I met a week ago in Varnum, and we agreed to stay in touch with each other in gathering information about the Kelly farm.

The editor collected his thoughts from Marvin Gardner's excited outburst on the phone. "Yes, we did say we'd keep our ears open to anything people might say about the storms and the family, and pass it along to each other. What's up, Marvin?"

"I was walking out of my store about ten minutes ago, and I saw Sheriff Bernam's personal Crown Victoria Ford headed north. He was driving, and the odd thing was, Reverend Butler was in the front seat with three other men in the back. Couldn't tell who it was in the back, but they had suits on. And," he stressed, "a deputy was following them in his patrol car."

That would be the clerics, Jim thought. *I can't tell Marvin anything, the time is too critical. He'd spread it all over town within several hours. He'll begin to learn things late tomorrow afternoon, anyway, when the National Guard convoys out to the farm.*

"Well, Marvin, I have no idea what that was all about. It may be some out-of-town church officials here for a meeting with Butler, and the sheriff was providing transportation—perhaps for sightseeing or something like that."

"Jim, I don't buy that. I think I'm getting the run-around, even from you. Claude was in my store just two days ago, and when he left, he said he'd get back to me if he stumbled onto something. I'm going to drive by the farm right now and see if that's where those two cars ended up."

Summers mentally counted to ten, and spoke, "Perhaps it would be better if you wait until you see the sheriff again and ask him about what you saw, or—"

"No," Gardner interrupted. "I know there's something big going on at that farm, and since no one wants to tell me what it is, I'll find out myself." With that, he hung up.

Jim dialed the farm. After four rings, Lyle answered. The editor briefly told him what the problem was, and asked him to get the sheriff on the line. It took three or four minutes before the bass voice of the sheriff said, "Hello." He was on John Kelly's cordless phone, which Lyle had taken to him because they had just arrived and everyone was outside getting acquainted.

When Jim related what Marvin had told him, Bernam knew what had to be done. He would intercept Gardner, carefully explain the situation at the farm, and tell him that he could not say anything to anyone until the word was officially released by the Kellys and the State of Florida National Guard. In this situation, Marvin "Motor Mouth" Gardner could get some people panicked and/or hurt with rumors and innuendo. The sheriff knew he would have to warn Marvin that he would arrest him if he persisted in playing detective and talking.

Bernam walked over to Deputy Williams and told him to unload the baggage and put it on the edge of the driveway. "Drive back toward town and intercept Marvin Gardner. Tell him to please return to his store, and that I will be there within an hour and explain things to him. Be firm but reasonable. Call me on my cell if there's a problem."

Deputy Williams unloaded his car and drove off.

ELEVEN KELLYS AND kin assembled at the farm that morning to greet the three clerics. Pat and Paul Daniels and Dick and Ann Kessel had come from Danaville to join the family about an hour before the VIPs arrived. With the presence of Reverend Butler and Sheriff Bernam, the number increased to thirteen. A little later, Jim Summers, Ralph Tobias, and Jack Stanton would arrive and complete the total of the reception party at sixteen—the number that formed the closed family circle.

The clerics showed great appreciation and love for the greeting they received. It was so apparent the Kelly family were unique Christians.

John told them the family and their friends were honored to have such men of God come and help them through this awesome time. He emphasized that all of them together would be experiencing the completion of a great act by the Lord. It had started with the second storm and will continue with the drilling exploration—an experience that will be unparalleled forever, one that has brought them together to do his will.

Billy Durdin assured the group that he and his two cleric brothers, as well as the two others due the next day, were honored to come to this special place and witness the completion of this great event. It was the calling of their lives.

John invited all of them inside, where they would soon have lunch. He told the three special guests they would be taken to the bean field whenever they were ready. In the meantime, everyone took turns talking to the three VIPs.

Deputy Williams had driven only a mile south from the Kelly farm turnoff when he spotted an oncoming car that looked like Gardner's. He had seen Marvin's maroon Buick several times and knew there was only one in Danaville. Carl turned on his flashing lights and slowed. Marvin was surprised and also slowed, but when he had stopped on the road shoulder, his car had slightly passed the patrol car approximately one hundred feet.

The deputy made a U-turn and pulled up behind the Buick. By the time he had walked up to Gardner's car, the pharmacist had recognized Carl, opened his door, and gotten out. "Hey, Carl, what's the problem? I wasn't speeding."

"Oh, I know, Mr. Gardner. I stopped you to give you a message from the sheriff."

Marvin squinted at the deputy in the midday sun. "A message from Sheriff Bernam delivered personally by his deputy on Highway 77 in the middle of the day?'

"Yes, sir. He wants you to return to your store, and he'll be there within an hour."

"Were you just now at the Kellys? Were you trailing his car through town about twenty minutes ago, and Wade Butler and three other men were with him?"

"Yes, sir, but right now it's important you return to your store and wait on him."

Marvin got into his car and said, "Okay, Carl, I'm doing it under protest. His explanation better be extraordinarily good, or I'm going to make a lot of noise to the county commissioners." With that, he made a U-turn and headed south.

Deputy Williams also turned and followed the Buick, but no closer than a quarter of a mile.

THE FAMILY KNEW how much Granny liked control of the kitchen, and they gave her plenty of space as they walked through or stood and talked to her. The current circumstances changed that, however. With nineteen people to consume a large, well laid-out buffet lunch, she was more than agreeable to have Sara, Teresa, and Arlene to assist her. The logistics were formidable, but were overcome with relative ease by the four women.

Lunch was served and everyone was impressed with the selections and taste of the food. Clerics Durdin, Griffin, and Claussen, along with Wade and Ruth Butler, John and Sara, and Dick and Ann Kessel, sat at the dining room table. The others sat at one of the five tables that had been set up in the large hall and the sunroom. No one had a desire to sit on the huge back porch because of the heat. Summers, Tobias, and Stanton sat in the sunroom, with a chair that was to be occupied by Sheriff Bernam. However, he had to go to Danaville and talk to Marvin Gardner.

Billy Durdin had been briefed days ago by Wade Butler about the storm, the hail, and the rainbow, along with the appearance of the bean-field circle. At that time, Durdin passed the information on to the four clerics that he knew well. They in turn told their various religious bodies, who quickly urged them to travel to the Kelly farm. Even though all of this was done and they were now on the scene with a commitment, Billy and his associates wanted to hear John give them as much detail as possible.

"John, would you give Dr. Claussen, Reverend Griffin, and me a step-by-step description of what's happened since that last storm hit the farm and the 'circle' appeared? It will be helpful to us in our work."

The memory of every detail was indelibly stamped on John's mind. He desperately wanted to be of help to the clerics.

"I'll be glad to," John said with a slight smile. He started by detailing the first storm, almost a year ago, so that comparisons could be made to the one two weeks ago. When he explained the hail pattern on the ground, the three guests listened intently, their eyes locked onto John's face. There were a few questions and a few minutes of discussion. John then told about the discovery of the bean-field circle, and the way it changed coloration. After that, there was more discussion, then it was suggested they visit the site. He commented that it had to be seen to feel the impact.

"The only vehicle we use to go into the fields is my old pickup truck, so I'll have two of you in the cab with me, and the other two will have to ride in the back." He looked at his guests and saw smiles.

Durdin looked at his old friend Wade Butler. "I remember my dad would let me ride in the back of his pickup when I was a kid. Wade, let's be kids again." Butler grinned, and said he was all for it.

Everyone laughed and got up. The clerics were shown to the den with its newly installed cubicles where they could change clothes. Their luggage was neatly arranged against a wall. Ruth Wade had brought a change for her husband. John went to his room to slip into a pair of jeans and a khaki shirt. Lyle suggested Reverend Butler use his room.

The ladies gathered in the kitchen to talk. Summers, Tobias, and Stanton, having seen the circle, moved into the living room to continue their discussion regarding the timing of a press release to the major wire services and all major television broadcasters—the networks as well as cable news channels.

Captain Stanton requested that they inform the governor and General Whitmire prior to releasing any information to the public. He further stated that he felt a press release could have all kinds of implications with people everywhere. It must be carefully worded to reveal the details of the event in a reverent way. Stanton looked at Summers and Tobias and asked if that sounded acceptable. Both of them readily agreed that it did.

The editor was very impressed with Jack Stanton.

Ralph Tobias said they must also coordinate with the White House and do nothing until the secretary of defense knew all details of what was going on and why.

Stanton reminded the editor and the county attorney that the governor's office and the Defense Department were already communicating.

When the clerics and John had changed into casual clothes, they climbed aboard the pickup and headed for the bean field. All of them, even John, had a feeling of expectancy.

They soon arrived at the holy site and parked. Everyone quieted down and stared when John pointed to the posts in the distance. "This is God's special place," he said.

They got out of the truck and walked out to the nearest post and saw the darker edge of the circle. The clerics had a feeling of a powerful presence—like none any of them had ever experienced.

Durdin said, "As much as I've seen, experienced, and been directly involved in, doing work for the Lord throughout the world, I've never felt so humble, so near him."

They stared at the center post and wondered what lay underneath.

After a very heart-felt prayer by Reverend Griffin, asking God to provide them with understanding and dedication to his purpose, the five men walked back to the truck, got in, and drove to the house. No one said a word.

John suggested they pick up Lyle, Carew, and Reverend Butler, and show the entire farm to their special guests. Everyone agreed. It was only practical that with such an important work going on, the clerics had a little more knowledge about the farm.

The three new passengers were soon aboard and the tour underway. John drove the farm perimeter, showing the beautiful spring crops as they marched row after row, field after field—then a visit to the retaining pond, the dairy barn and milk cooler, pigsties and shelters, plus the large chicken yard and house. The last part of the tour was a walk through the two barns and equipment buildings that housed the two tractors and all of the equipment they towed. The clerics enjoyed seeing all of the farm, but so did the four family members who were along—they never tired of seeing the Kelly legacy.

WHEN SHERIFF BERNAM parked in front of Gardner's Drugstore, he didn't relish what he had to do, but it was important and he was determined. There was too much at stake to allow

Marvin to poke around and run his mouth. On top of that, the sheriff had to miss that great lunch at the Kellys.

"Hello, Marvin," the sheriff said as he walked up to the pharmacy counter.

Gardner turned and looked over his glasses at Bernam. "Well, well," the pharmacist said, "if it isn't the Royal Mountie of Mason County. What can I do for you?" Marvin wasn't smiling.

Bernam looked Marvin directly in the eyes. "I have to talk to you. Would you please come to my car with me? It's very important."

The pharmacist looked at his watch, as if his time was limited, then looked at his tech assistant. "I'll be back in a few minutes," he said. He followed the sheriff outside and got into the blue-and-white patrol car. Marvin felt humiliated.

Sheriff Bernam pushed his big body behind the steering wheel and looked at Gardner. "Marvin, I want you to listen to me and not talk. What I have to say is extremely important to the well-being of this town, the county, and way beyond." Then, for the next twenty minutes or so, Bernam laid out the details to the pharmacist about what had happened to date at the Kellys and what would transpire during the next few days. When the sheriff finished, there was dead silence as they both looked straight ahead, unaware of people walking by on the sidewalk in front of them.

"I don't know what to say," Marvin finally said. "All this is hard to digest. I had a feeling something strange was going on, but nothing ever like this."

The sheriff continued to say nothing for a few moments, then spoke, "Marvin, you must sit on this until at least Jim Summers's press release is distributed to the media. By then, our community will know something big is in the works, and they'll be reacting."

"I understand," he said almost inaudibly. "I would do nothing to impede the safety of our community. Claude, I would ask only one favor. Would you talk to John and ask him if I can come to the farm when the exploration is finished?"

Bernam looked across at Gardner with a hint of a smile. "I'll do my best. In the meantime, be patient. Thanks for your understanding and help."

The sheriff cranked the car—a signal the meeting was over—and Gardner got out and walked toward his store.

THE BALANCE OF Saturday afternoon at the farm was more relaxed than had been the morning. After about an hour on the back porch, the majority of the family and guests began to dwindle—the seven women strolled down to the pond and through the beautiful yard. John, the visiting VIP clerics, Reverend Butler, Lyle, Carew, Dick Kessel, Paul Daniels, and Jack Stanton gathered in the living room to discuss the important activities to take place starting the next day and continuing beyond the exploration and discovery.

Summers and Tobias had to return to Danaville. The editor needed to work on an outline for the press release to have whenever it became due. He wanted it ready to the point that all he had to do was drop in the date, time, and descriptive information, and location of the happening. Also, he would prepare a list of recipients, taken from a communications source guide he kept in his small library. Jim had a number of newspaper editor friends throughout the state and the South. Some of them he would call personally. They could be helpful.

Tobias went to his office to check his e-mail and voice mail and pick up his car. Then he would go home to his wife and two teenage sons. He had not shared the details with them about what was occurring at the Kelly farm because teenagers, under the best of circumstances, tended to talk. If he had told Marie only, she would have wanted to tell their sons what was going on. It had been hard to keep the information to himself but now he would sit his family down and inform them of the powerful unfolding story. They would then decide what they needed to do for their security. Ralph knew they would be welcome to stay at the farm. He would have to convince Marie and the boys it was the prudent thing to do.

Ralph told his wife the day before that they had been invited to the farm on Sunday for a unique worship service conducted by several out-of-town clerics visiting the farm. Reverend Butler would also be there. After a light lunch, everyone would stay and greet a Catholic priest and a Rabbi, when they arrived in midafternoon. She questioned why such a service was being held there with all the different clerics—and why was Reverend Butler involved when he was the minister at the First Methodist Church? He told her it was for a very special occasion, and that he could tell her no more. She was extremely puzzled, but she trusted her husband.

Ralph was convinced that being in the midst of such a select religious group and very near the site of God's powerful work would have an enormous spiritual effect on his family. When all of the details were revealed to his wife and sons, they would experience a great change in their lives. The reason for security would become clear.

At about 8:00 p.m., Granny told John he had a call from Doc McNally. He walked to the living room doorway and motioned across the room for Jack Stanton to join him. The captain had been talking with Lyle, Teresa, and Arlene, but excused himself, got out of his chair, and picked his way across the large semicrowded room, and joined John at the door.

"I want you to sit in on a phone call from Doc McNally and hear what he has to say to both of us regarding his plan for setting up an emergency medical center in Danaville. Let's go up to my office. I've got a speaker phone, and we can relax and have a good conversation."

As they started up the stairs, Stanton said, "I'm sure glad to hear that something is already in the works. I've been concerned with the limited military medical services we have currently. The situation has been discussed at length with General Whitmire, and he was to confer with Fort Benning to see if they could send a MASH unit with extra staff if our situation becomes ugly in any way."

John was pleased that Stanton was on top of a need that dictated attention from the governor's office. He felt Doc was about to tell them that the details were already in motion. "Hi, Doc. Sorry to keep you waiting, but I've got Captain Jack Stanton, the governor's security chief, here, and we're on my speaker phone." Doc and the captain exchanged greetings.

"Well, John, I've had good luck in getting a group of excellent doctors and staff together who wish to participate. The group to draw from will include general surgeons, orthopedics, cardiologists, anesthesiologists, and both surgical and general-care nurses.

"They'll bring along all kinds of surgical and treatment equipment, nursing supplies, and medications. The Mason County Hospital will be the general trauma center. For any extreme cases that need protracted specialized treatment, the chief of surgery of the Southeast Alabama Medical Center in Dothan is working on a plan to have available a number of helicopters from Camp Rucker to carry out rescue missions for injured people from the farm or elsewhere in the county and transport them to our hospital, or for anyone that needs complex care from here to Dothan or elsewhere."

John and the captain were impressed. "Doc, we can never thank you enough for what you're doing," John said.

"Why, John, our purpose is to treat injured people, if it comes to that—and the Lord knows I hope it doesn't—and if needed, to take our care to any level that's required."

Stanton, who had been taking notes, broke in. "Doc, I'll be in touch with the governor's office ASAP and inform them what you're doing. They will want to assist in any way possible. General Whitmire, commander of the state's National Guard, will be involved also. On the other side of the coin, Ralph Tobias, the county attorney, has already set up contact with the White House. The Defense Department has already set up liaison with Whitmire, and there will be support from our national military and other agencies."

"John, I've one other call to make. When years start piling on, bedtime comes a bit earlier. I appreciate and am trying to understand what you're dealing with, and I feel certain that we all are going to be deeply involved. Good night to you both."

CHAPTER TWENTY-NINE

ENRIQUE CRUZ HAD contacted two Gelb Food customers in Panama City on Friday morning before departing for Pensacola. He was still smiling about the part he played for Gomez and Bovitz in the victory over the Conway brothers. His ego had been greatly massaged by his Tampa bosses, and he felt almost invincible.

The Cuban was scheduled to meet at 3:00 p.m. with a Lieutenant Commander Vance, the food procurement officer of the huge naval air station—a great potential account for Gelb.

Another contact he was to make in Pensacola was investment banker James E. Dalton. Though it would be a Friday evening, J. D. Poffer had known Dalton for several years, and on occasion, had done business with him. J. D. told Enrique it would be wise for him to talk to him, and in time, meet him personally. He told Enrique he would call the banker and have him expect a call from a Mr. Cruz at 7:00 p.m.

Dalton had an "inside" reputation for putting together all kinds of investment deals—many had left a trail of questions, but the banker was gifted in providing no answers.

After wolfing down a cheeseburger, Enrique headed west on Highway 98. He was surprised at the beauty of the coast, both the undeveloped and developed areas. The number of beautiful high-rise condos and shopping centers were the kind of properties he wanted to get involved in. It was easy to see that Florida's Panhandle gulf coast was probably one of the best—anywhere.

The meeting with Lieutenant Commander Vance went well, and after about an hour, they shook hands. Enrique thanked the officer for the opportunity to quote on a year's supply of a variety of foods with the understanding that if all went well Gelb would be invited to renew the quote for another year. Cruz went out the door smiling.

Enrique knew that Bovitz would make some contacts, "persuade" a few people—even twist a few arms, if needed—and present the best price and service plan to Lieutenant Commander Vance.

In order to celebrate a good week in his new position and the day's good call on the U.S. Navy, Enrique had an early dinner of filet mignon at one of Pensacola's best steak houses which allowed cigars in a special businessman's dining room. Feeling very important, he ordered an expensive Cuban brand after dinner and puffed on it for thirty minutes or so. He got a few looks from several business types—just what he wanted.

Cruz returned to his hotel room by 6:50 p.m. He mused at the thought that he'd call at exactly seven o'clock and impress investment banker Dalton with his punctuality.

"James Dalton speaking," said the slightly raspy voice.

"Hello, Mr. Dalton, this is Enrique Cruz, an acquaintance of J. D. Poffer."

"Oh yes, Mr. Cruz, J. D. asked if I would mind talking to you. He mentioned you are connected with an investment group in Tampa. What's the name of your organization?"

Enrique hesitated a moment, then answered, "I can't tell you that, Mr. Dalton. The principals, who are all very successful men, have an agreement to never divulge their identities so as to better facilitate a wider range of business opportunities."

"That's a bit strange. I know of certain companies or philanthropic organizations that have one or two unknown partners or participants, but not one where ALL of its members are unknown."

"Well, it's the way we carry out our business. The lower-level management staff, such as myself, are known and can be easily contacted," Enrique said.

Dalton was quiet for a moment, then cleared his throat. "I owe J. D. Poffer a couple of favors, so I'll pass a lead on to you. There's a gentleman in Tallahassee by the name of Gordon Malloy. He's a very successful real estate developer. His latest project is located south of Danaville, off Highway 77, near Crystal Lake. It will be a large, well-planned three-thousand-acre residential community. Though he has much of his financing, he needs much more. I suggest you get in touch with him on Monday. Gordon doesn't waste time—he moves fast. You can use me as a reference—that'll get you in the front door."

Enrique's mind was racing. Much of the real estate development business was foreign to him, but he could bluff his way past part of it and get on the phone with J. D. for technical help. "I certainly don't want to impose on your weekend, but I'd like to meet you personally before I leave for Tallahassee on Sunday."

"I'm sorry, Mr. Cruz," Dalton said. "My wife and I are going out of town tomorrow. We leave in the morning for Cleveland to see our daughter. I'll look forward to meeting you at another time."

"Thanks for the tip, Mr. Dalton. I'll follow up on it, and let you know how things turn out."

"Please tell J. D. I send my best regards, and I hope to see him soon. Good night, Mr. Cruz."

Upon hanging up the phone, Enrique started thinking how very peculiar that Danaville suddenly had a double meaning to him. He was curious about Teresa's boyfriend Lyle Kelly, his family, and the farm that Arlene had mentioned to him months earlier. When he and Teresa came to Tampa a week ago, Enrique remembered he caught bits and pieces of conversation—as if a conspiracy were in progress. The way Arlene tossed him out wasn't her style. He was sure Lyle and Teresa had been part of it. But he was happy to be rid of Arlene. She had actually done him a favor—it hadn't cost him a dime.

Something was still eating at him, and he wanted to confront Lyle Kelly. Cruz decided to drive to Danaville the next afternoon, check into a motel, see the town, and find the farm. If time allowed on Sunday, he would drive south on Highway 77 and try to find the area near Crystal Lake to be developed by Gordon Malloy. It would show the real estate mogul, when they met, that Cruz was a stickler for detail. He would drive on to Tallahassee late Sunday afternoon, call Malloy on Monday morning, and hope for a quick appointment to meet him personally.

Things were moving rapidly, the Cuban thought. He was pumped up. He called J. D. in Panama City and luckily caught him at home

"Hate to bother you this late, J. D., but I just had an interesting talk with Jim Dalton. He was cautious but helpful. Gave me a solid tip about Gordon Malloy, a developer in Tallahassee. Do you know him?"

Poffer was in a good mood—still thinking about the $500,000 he'd made on the Conway brothers deal. He told Enrique that Malloy had a good record and was a hard-nosed business man, and to be conservative and cautious when talking to him. J. D. emphasized to Enrique that if any technical details came up, to not commit on anything without contacting him. "Just appear laid back and do things quietly. Sell Malloy that you're smart."

Enrique related Jim Dalton's message to J. D., that he sent his best regards. J. D. said it would be smart to keep good relations with the banker.

They talked for another several moments, then called it a night. Cruz took a shower, watched the news, and went to bed, thinking about Danaville—and Lyle Kelly.

JOHN, LYLE, AND Carew, along with Sara, Teresa, and Arlene, gave everyone several stapled-together sheets of information—a map of the farm boundary, plus locations of all buildings, fences, and gates. Facilities such as toilets, water for drinking and bathing, and ice storage in the smaller barn along with first aid supplies, flashlights, and several small portable AM-FM radios were also listed.

Everyone was very complimentary on the accommodations, knowing the farm was not the Ritz Carlton, or some other four-star hotel. But given the occasion, and the uncertainty of the next several days or perhaps even weeks, they were thankful for the planning and action taken so far by the family. All of them looked forward to the arrival of the National Guard the next afternoon, but it gave some of them the feeling that the farm was becoming the Alamo. However, the overriding strong conviction shared by everyone was that God was in charge, and it calmed their nervous feeling of facing the unknown.

It wasn't long after showing the guests their temporary home that the house and the large barn became quieter and lights began to disappear. Everyone was thinking about Sunday—the first day of final preparation for beginning the exploration. Prayers were said and eyes closed in sleep.

Sunday morning came with overcast skies, and according to a radio weather report while John was shaving, there was a 40 percent chance of rain until midafternoon. Skies would be clearing by late afternoon. John hoped there would be little or no rain because Clayton Parker would arrive around 4:00 or 5:00 p.m. with his huge drilling rig, and a soaked, soft ground could cause a big problem.

It was 5:00 a.m. as John dressed. He had asked Lyle and Carew the night before to meet him in the backyard by five. Sara looked at her husband as he was tying his shoes. "Where did the night go?" she asked with a yawn.

"I asked myself the same question," he replied. "I think there's a thief around here that steals hours, especially for the past two weeks or so." He smiled, then stooped and kissed her. "Gotta go and get the day started. Lyle and Carew are probably waiting." With that, he left the room. He knew that his mama, Sara, and most of the other women would be real busy cooking and serving breakfast, and then almost at once, start preparing lunch.

"Did you guys cheat and get up early?" John said when he walked out of the kitchen onto the back porch and saw them sitting on the steps. Lyle looked around and saw his dad standing on the top step, with a grin on his face. He and Carew looked at each other and slowly shook their heads. With that, the three of them went to tend the livestock and feed the chickens. John said he wanted to check the ice supply in the smaller barn to see how it was holding up under the sawdust.

Lyle looked around at the large backyard and counted eight cars. There would be fourteen to sixteen by the end of the day. He likened it to a small auto sales lot. Great-grandpa Frank Kelly could have never imagined what was happening at the beloved farm that he started many years ago. He and Grandpa Seth would turn over in their graves if they knew the farm would soon be greatly downsized or totally cease production. There were no choices.

It was almost seven thirty when breakfast was over. Everyone spread out in small groups or singles to take care of various things or to see some more of the farm. Carew was more than willing to answer questions. A few went down to the pond just to reflect on what was happening around them and to them. All would meet on the back porch around nine forty-five for worship. They were looking forward to hearing the well-known clerics.

Lyle, Teresa, and Arlene walked slowly down the long drive to the main gate. "You know, Mother, it's been a joy to see you react so positively to God's presence that keeps constantly growing all around us and the farm."

"I can't explain it, but I've never felt more at ease with myself and all of the people that I've talked to anywhere or any time. I'm so happy you two convinced me to come. There is no doubt that God was speaking through you and Lyle."

John was pleased to see the arrival of Jim Summers and the Tobias and Reddington families. The editor was single with no children. He felt it important to continue to run the newspaper, given the opportunity, and be able to follow various activities related to the huge story ready to break at the farm. It was incumbent on him that he keep the county, the state, and perhaps the nation, aware of the facts. He would be at the farm as much as possible.

Tobias wanted to work closely with Jack Stanton in coordinating all state and federal security plans and actions by the governor's office. His close friend U.S. Secretary of the Treasury

Philip Beretti had not only been his contact with the White House and Defense Department, but had also put him in touch with the U.S. attorney general's office. Gerald L. Scott, an assistant attorney general, had been assigned to work with Ralph on an as-needed basis to ensure that any and all arrests or other actions taken against those who trespassed the farm boundaries, damaged the property, caused harm to persons, or tried to take any portion of the holy site would be prosecuted on an international basis if needed. Other than security for his family, this was another important reason to stay at the farm. He would call County Judge Harper that night and tell him he had to be absent for a few days. The judge would figure out why by Tuesday morning.

Red, Jenny, and their two young daughters arrived about 8:30 a.m. This would give them a chance to move their things into two of the barn temporary quarters, meet all the new guests, and be ready for the worship. Lyle and Carew helped both families get settled.

ENRIQUE ARRIVED IN Danaville around 5:00 p.m. on Saturday. He checked into the Holiday Inn Express on Highway 77 just south of downtown. He asked the young desk clerk a few questions about the town. She was very polite and had a good personality. Her answers were informative. When he told her he was from Tampa and wanted to look the town over, she responded that Danaville was a speck compared to his hometown, but there was a lot to offer in all of Mason County. He added it was small but very pretty and restful looking.

When he asked about Crystal Lake, she told him it was about twenty-five miles south on 77. She added that it was a beautiful lake and very popular, but there were other nice lakes around.

He went up to his room and put his bags on the bed. He'd shower and eat later. Right now he wanted to drive south and see where the "Garden of Eden" was that Malloy was developing.

The Cuban drove for twenty-five minutes and finally saw a recent clearing through the trees on the right, a distance of about a quarter of a mile. There was a large, attractive sign that read A

Gordon Malloy Residential Development near a wide blacktop road that led to the area. It was evident there were many acres that had already been cleared and in the process of being graded. "Well," he thought, "this is proof that Malloy has his development under way. He ought to be impressed when I tell him I've already checked it out."

Enrique turned his car around and drove back to the highway. He wanted to see Crystal Lake, so he turned to the left and headed south again for a few minutes. Soon, there was an improved road on the right with a sign stating Crystal Lake. Within a short distance, he spotted the large sky-blue lake with a white-sand shoreline. It was beautiful. He was sure that part of Malloy's development was located at or very near the lake.

Returning to his motel, he slowed just south of Danaville to get a better look at a moderate-sized lake on the right, near 1-10. It had a park with a sign Blue Lake. But he had other things on his mind. Enrique decided he would rise early the next morning and do a little inquiring and drive around for a while, looking the town over, and then find the Kelly farm and see what the possibilities were of getting onto the property. He had no idea what was happening there. It didn't matter. He only thought of Lyle, Teresa, and Arlene.

When he entered the lobby of the hotel, he wanted to talk to the new desk clerk, a young man, but had to wait while a couple checked in. He sat across the room and read that day's edition of the *Mason County News*. Not much in it, he thought. It was just a small-town newspaper with local news that was foreign to him. Still, he found it interesting. He had an indescribable feeling that he was supposed to be here. Soon, the clerk finished with the couple and Enrique went over and asked a few casual questions about the community.

The young man was happy to talk about Danaville. It was his hometown, and he liked to inform people about the "hub of northwest Florida," as the locals called it, with a certain amount of belief that it was a true statement. Upon being asked if he knew the Kellys, he said no, he'd never met them personally.

ENRIQUE WOKE UP hungry the next morning. The continental breakfast laid out buffet style in the dining area on the main floor didn't appeal to him. He wanted eggs and bacon. The young woman desk clerk that had been on duty the day before was there, and gave him a smiling, "Good morning."

She told him the location of a nice café that served a good breakfast. It was almost 8:00 a.m. when he walked into Martha's and took a seat. The motel clerk was right—the food and coffee were good. The place wasn't very busy, and Lavern, the fifty-plus-looking waitress who was probably only forty, was friendly and talkative. He introduced himself, hoping to learn more about the community, especially the Kelly farm and the family.

Lavern was happy to talk about Danaville and Mason County. She told the Cuban about places to see, such as Falling Waters State Park and some of the handsome old homes along with the antique and specialty stores downtown.

Several customers came in and she started to go greet them, but she hesitated long enough to hurriedly answer his last question.

When asked about the Kellys, Lavern quickly said he couldn't miss the farm. Just drive north on 77, about three miles, and turn right on County Road 26. It would lead him right to the farm. She said he'd know it when he saw it. With that, she smiled and went to greet her new customers.

Enrique left Lavern a $10 tip. His breakfast cost $5.95. He wanted to be remembered as a big spender—by everyone.

He went out to his car and drove about a block and pulled into a gas station for a fill-up. In a few moments, a blue-and-white county sheriff's car pulled into the other lane of pumps. When the officer got out, Enrique was impressed with the man's size.

He turned back to check how the gas pump was doing. His tank was near full. He momentarily forgot about the officer. A few seconds later, an even-toned voice said, "Excuse me, sir."

Enrique turned to see the big lawman standing about four feet away. "Yes, officer?" He said. He felt intimidated, but concentrated on not showing it.

"I noticed your car has a Hillsborough County license plate. Just wanted to know how things are in Tampa. I was there a couple of years ago and thought it was a real nice city."

Cruz wasn't sure why the deputy sheriff was talking to him. Maybe it was a slow morning, being Sunday. He noticed the officer's name tag over his right shirt pocket read "Dan Beck," and his badge had the words "Chief Deputy" cresting the gold star over the left pocket.

"Yes, Deputy, I'm from Tampa. I'm the marketing manager for Gelb Foods, who has a large operation there. I have customers in northwest Florida that I call on from time to time." *Almost the truth*, Enrique thought, *but he doesn't need to know everything.*

Beck looked at Enrique directly in the eyes. The Cuban felt as if the deputy was trying to see inside of him—as if he was searching for something.

"Oh, you don't owe me an explanation. I'm not checking you out. I just wanted to say howdy and offer you assistance if you need anything while in our community." Dan had negative vibes about this man from Tampa and planned to keep an eye on him until he left town, hopefully before 5:00 p.m. If he stayed longer, he might find it very interesting in and around Danaville. "I hope you enjoy Danaville." With that, Beck went back to his car.

Enrique went inside and paid for the gas. When he drove from the station, he turned north on 77, having decided to drive to the farm. He'd satisfy his curiosity, return to the hotel, check out, and head for Tallahassee.

Being Sunday, there wasn't much traffic. He thought the downtown area was quaint, just as Lavern, the waitress, had said. Even the railroad track that ran east and west through the center of the business district was not a visual blight.

After passing many attractive old homes and some remodeled ones, Cruz began to enter into the countryside. He soon noticed beautiful farm fields on his right, realizing they must be part of the Kellys' land. The Cuban slowed and soon spotted the County Road 26 marker. He turned right and was amazed at the symmetry of the fields. Beyond, sitting on a slight rise, almost hidden by spreading oak trees, was a very large and handsome old farmhouse. Enrique was impressed. He wished he could see more of the farm, but saw many cars parked under the trees to the right of the house. There must be some important function going on, and he didn't want to get involved and become known. Though he'd like to confront Lyle, Cruz knew he was in the enemy's camp, and that would be impossible—at least, for the moment. After turning the car around, he headed back toward town, driving slowly, looking to his left along the farm boundary, watching for the end or corner of the fields to see if there was a path or road running from the highway along the south perimeter fence line. He saw an old rutted road, mostly covered with weeds, running down the shoulder toward some trees. *That might work*, he thought.

As he entered Danaville's northern city limit, there was a sudden noise from the engine. It surprised Enrique so much that he jumped and almost lost control of the car. He had been deep in thought about the farm and what he had seen. He was jealous, and his ego was still smarting from the repudiation he received from Arlene, Teresa, and probably the instigator of it all, Lyle Kelly.

There was a thump or two, then a sharp slapping sound, then nothing. The car's engine stopped right away. He pulled over to the wide shoulder and parked. Enrique knew he had a major problem—there was a feeling of helplessness.

He pulled the hood release and got out of the car. There was no sign or sound of an overheated engine. Raising the hood and looking at the silent, useless engine, he had no idea what to look for. His experience with automobiles was zero. The Cuban's eyes fell on the main drive pulley, the air-conditioner, and alternator pulleys. There was no drive belt. It had broken, and he guessed, was lying on the road behind him in several pieces. It was 10:23 Sunday morning, and he was marooned. There was hardly any traffic, but he had to try to flag someone down. Before doing that he knelt down and looked under the car, which provided nothing. Enrique then looked at the road behind the car and immediately spotted an object that looked like a piece of the belt, lying almost on the edge of the pavement. It was about one hundred feet away. He walked back to the object, and it was a major piece of the belt. Picking it up, it dawned on him it served no purpose, whereupon he tossed it away.

As he was walking back to the car, two vehicles passed, headed south, but made no effort to stop. The Cuban saw a car heading north, and at first didn't recognize it, but at a second look, saw it was a county deputy. The car slowed, and as it cruised by, he saw that it was Deputy Beck behind the wheel. Enrique thought, in his situation, he would accept help from Satan himself.

Beck made a U-turn and drove up and stopped behind Enrique's car. "What's up, my Tampa friend?" the deputy said, as he walked up. "Did one of America's finer mid-sized cars call it quits?"

Cruz nodded his head and walked around to the front of the car with the lawman. "Yeah, it's the serpentine drive belt," Beck said. "It powers everything—you lose it, the car dies immediately."

"Can someone in Danaville tow it in and fix it?"

"Not today. I can call Otis Smith. He'll tow it to his garage and fix it tomorrow. If Ackerman Auto Parts in town doesn't have the belt in stock, he'll get one from Panama City, or Dothan, Alabama. It may take until late afternoon before your car is ready to roll."

Enrique looked into the nearby woods and quietly said, "Whatever it takes, Deputy Beck."

"Since we are here in the wilderness together, and I want to help you out, I'd kinda like to know who I'm talking to. People from around here all have names and they like to use them, out of respect."

"Enrique S. Cruz, born in Cuba, now an American citizen."

Dan Beck could see that Cruz was in a bad mood and appeared not to like him.

CHAPTER THIRTY

I T WAS TIME for the worship service. Even with the gray clouds, it was a very special day. The sun was shining in everyone's heart. As the twenty or so gathered on the large back porch, they all had a feeling of a powerful presence unlike anything they had ever experienced in their lives.

Rev. Billy Durdin opened the service with an eloquent inspiring prayer. Dr. Claussen followed with a short talk about the reason they were all brought to the farm, and what may be expected of them.

Sara and Pat led the group in several hymns, followed with a powerful, moving sermon by Reverend Griffin. He preached about the immeasurable power of God, and pointed to many dramatic examples in the Bible and recent history. Griffin emphasized that the Lord was speaking clearly to them all.

The service was the most unique and touching that any of them had ever experienced—that applied to the four clerics as well.

As the light rain began to fall, everyone's high spirits was alive and well. John and Lyle looked at each other, hoping the rainfall would be minimal. They both thought of Clayton Parker and his big drilling rig arriving about 4:00 p.m. A real soggy ground would not be conducive to its crossing the bean field.

Just as planned, the worship service was finished about eleven, and lunch was served right away. John and everyone else wanted

Reverend Butler and Sheriff Bernam to have a relaxed lunch before departing for Panama City. Butler and Sheriff Bernam finished early and excused themselves. It was 11:50 a.m.—plenty of time for their rendezvous with Father Walsh and Rabbi Metz when they stepped off the plane at 1:30 p.m. or so.

Again with Deputy Williams following in his patrol car, Reverend Butler and Sheriff Bernam made the trip south on Highway 77, as they had done the day before. They arrived at the airport with thirty minutes to spare.

Father Kevin Walsh and Rabbi Jacob Metz were easy to spot coming up the ramp. The priest wore the traditional black suit and shirt with the stark white collar. The rabbi was dressed in a dark blue suit, very light blue shirt, and a maroon tie. A black yarmulke sat tightly on the back of his head. Walsh was tall and thin. His white hair belied his forty-six years. Metz was in his fifties and a little under six feet in height. A head of thick black hair set off a ruddy face with dark eyes.

They readily saw their two greeters, and picked their way through a group of people. Reverend Butler intercepted them. He smiled and stuck out his hand. Father Walsh had been walking slightly ahead of the rabbi and grasped the reverend's hand with a return smile. "It's a pleasure to meet you, Father Walsh," Butler said. "The sheriff and I represent the Kelly family and welcome you and Rabbi Metz." Butler switched his attention to the rabbi. "And you, Rabbi Metz, your reputation precedes you. We are indeed happy to have you with us." The rabbi smiled as they shook hands vigorously.

"This is our county sheriff, Claude Bernam. He and one of his deputies will drive and escort us to Danaville and the Kelly farm."

Upon collecting their luggage, the two cars headed to Danaville. Butler could see that both of their religious VIPs were tired, although they were enthusiastic and happy to be on the final leg of their long journey from Italy and Israel.

Reverend Butler's mind was working fast. He reflected on the almost inexplicable events of the past two and a half weeks. Now, sitting in the car with him were two very respected religious representatives, who would soon join the other clerics and himself at the farm, all working together in interpreting and protecting God's plan.

Father Walsh and Rabbi Metz thanked Sheriff Bernam for driving and escorting them. The sheriff told them it was an honor. He added that this was the highlight of his career. That pleased both visitors.

As he had done with the clerics the day before, Butler related the latest details at the farm. The priest and the rabbi concentrated on every word.

The two guests absorbed the beautiful North Bay as they crossed the bridge, heading toward their destination. The countryside was tranquil with pine trees, a few farm fields and a pretty lake or two.

Danaville was quiet and peaceful on that Sunday morning as the two cars proceeded along Main Street toward the Kelly farm. Butler and Sheriff Bernam were thinking that by that night or the next morning, the Mason County seat was going to be full of excited, apprehensive, and fearful citizens. The reverend knew that at the very best, the knowledge of what was going on at the Kelly farm would spread quickly throughout the United States and the world.

John was thankful the light rain had stopped; the skies looked brighter, which gave him hope that the ground would be relatively dry by evening. He had estimated their new VIP guests would be there before 3:00 p.m. Everyone at the farm was hanging around talking—in the house, on the back porch, and front porch.

Lyle and Carew were sitting on the front steps discussing all the things that were to take place within the next few hours. The sheriff's car, with deputy Williams following in his patrol car, suddenly appeared, coming down County Road 26. Lyle went into the house and told his dad and the others that their company was arriving. Teresa, Arlene, and Pat walked over to join the two men, and they all went out the front door, to greet their guests.

The two cars pulled up as the family, the three clerics, and other guests gathered around to welcome the two religious VIPs from Europe and the Middle East.

Carew looked at their new guests as they were being greeted, and knew that in about an hour, Clayton Parker would drive up with his huge mobile drilling rig. An hour after that, the National Guard would arrive. The priest and the rabbi would have very little time to get their feet on the ground before a lot of excitement would begin.

After he was introduced by John to the new arrivals, Carew pulled him aside and mentioned that time was moving fast. John nodded and said their guests had been told what was to happen, but he would review the timeframe with them again.

Father Walsh and Rabbi Metz were mesmerized by the great reception they had received. They were further impressed by the magnificent farm house and the surrounding grounds and buildings.

DEPUTY BECK WAS successful in reaching Otis Smith at home, and the auto repairman said he'd be there within thirty minutes. Beck and Enrique made small talk while waiting for the tow truck.

"Deputy, what's so special about the Kelly farm?"

Beck was silent for a moment. He didn't want the Cuban to know what was currently happening at the farm, and what was about to happen.

"Well, it's a significant farm because of the family. Four generations of Kellys have made that farm a great success with hard work, love, and respect for others."

"Do you know Lyle Kelly?"

The deputy was surprised that Enrique had asked about John's son. *How had he come up with the name*, he wondered.

"Yes, I know him well. So does almost everyone in Mason County. Do you know him?"

"He goes with Teresa, my ex-stepdaughter," Cruz replied.

Beck was really surprised at that statement. *Of all the people that know Lyle Kelly,* he thought, *here's a Cuban from Tampa, standing in front of me, whose ex-stepdaughter is Lyle's girlfriend.* He couldn't say anything about her being at the farm with Lyle. Beck also wondered if Cruz knew her mother was also there. "Is that the reason you came to Danaville?" he asked.

It was obvious that Enrique looked uncomfortable. "Well, not exactly. I was on my way to Tallahassee on business and stopped off just to see the farm I had heard so much about from Teresa." He didn't say anything about the property development near Crystal Lake—that would remain confidential.

The deputy wondered what the real reason was for Cruz's being here. Did he expect to see Lyle or Teresa, or meet the family? Beck didn't think the family was part of the Cuban's motivation. He felt relatively sure it was Lyle he wanted to see— why only him? Had there been a run-in between them, and he wanted some kind of retribution? It evidently had not been too long since Teresa's mother left Enrique, and Beck guessed that the Cuban didn't know she was at the farm this very minute. The deputy was pretty sure he was looking at a man who could cause a problem. He'd have to keep a close eye on him.

An old Ford tow truck approached from Danaville, slowed, and made a U-turn in front of them, pulled to the shoulder of the road, then backed up in front of Enrique's car.

Smith was a direct, no-nonsense man. After he looked at the car and hooked it to his truck, Enrique asked if there was a rental car he could drive while waiting for his car to be repaired. The mechanic said he had an old Jeep Cherokee that was in fair shape. He'd rent it for twenty bucks a day, less the gas. That satisfied Cruz.

When they reached the garage, Smith said he'd know the next morning around nine how long it would take to get a new belt and install it. With luck, he should have the car ready by two o'clock at the latest. He went into his little office and got the keys to the Cherokee and handed them to Enrique and told him he could pay him later. With that, the Cuban thanked Beck for his help and climbed into the Cherokee and drove off.

Deputy Beck got into his car and sat there thinking about all the things that were going on, and the big events that would start later in the day. He had a lot to do. He and all four of his deputies were on twenty-four-hour call.

When Otis had locked his garage and passed the deputy on his way home, Beck started his car and drove toward the Holiday

Inn. He wanted to see if the Cuban was there. The old Cherokee was parked in a guest slot near the front of the building, so he headed toward a subsandwich shop for an early lunch. It was going to be a long day.

JOHN LOOKED AT his watch and noted it was almost 4:00 p.m. Clayton could be there at any time. He looked around him, and everyone appeared calm and in good spirits. They seemed to be anticipating the beginning steps to finding the answer to God's mystery in the bean field. What he saw and felt around him was very encouraging.

All of the religious VIPs were in the sunroom along with Brandon Cook, the geologist. It was evident that Rabbi Metz was very much at ease and seemed pleased to be among the five Christian clerics—like them, he was excited to be a witness and perhaps contribute to the forthcoming exploration and discovery of God's work.

The senior Kelly walked over to one of the open French doors to the sunroom. He stood there for a few moments, listening to the discussion. Brandon Cook was referring to a book as he spoke. It was a geological history of the Middle East for the past two thousand years. Cook had shown John the volume several days ago, and explained that the structure of the book rested on a biblical and archaeological foundation, consisting of many facts and carefully weighed theory. Brandon had written the book ten years ago. It had been widely studied by Christian and Jewish biblical historians and archaeologists. It was evident that the five clerics in the sunroom were very attentive to the geologist's comments about his work.

At 4:10 p.m., Jack Stanton and Ralph Tobias told John that Parker had just turned off County Road 26 into the farm entrance. John went to the sunroom doorway and told the clerics and the geologist that the well driller had arrived. Word spread quickly throughout the house and everyone went outside to view the large drilling rig—the tool that would retrieve whatever God had planted in the bean field.

Lyle, Carew, and Red had been strolling under the oaks in the front yard, talking about the coming days, when they saw the big vehicle approaching the main entrance to the farm—a car was following. They trotted toward the driveway to intercept Clayton Parker and his rig as it slowed and made the turn into the farm. Parker stopped the rig as Lyle approached and stepped up on the running board. The well driller stuck his hand out of the window, and the two men shook hands. "Good to meet you, Mr. Parker, I'm Lyle Kelly."

"I figured that," he replied. "You look a lot like your dad."

Lyle grinned and nodded his head. "You and your rig are very welcome. Everyone has been looking forward to your arrival. Is that your wife driving the car?"

"Sure is. She's part of the package."

Lyle instantly liked Parker. He had a relaxed, positive manner laced with humor. Young Kelly looked at the car and waved. She waved back. He stepped to the ground. "You know where the main gate to the fields is. Just pull around to the right, on the side driveway—it's almost a straight shot. Carew, Red, and I will walk alongside, and if needed, help you line up with the gate to the fields."

"Sounds good to me," Parker said. He put the thirty-ton dark blue rig in gear and started moving forward—it was impressive, with ten wheels supporting a 1999 Peterbilt chassis driven by a 300 HP diesel engine. A 515 HP Caterpillar engine was mounted on the rear deck for all drilling operations. It carried a large derrick structure, lying across the forty-five-plus length of the chassis and over the cab. It would be raised upright and positioned precisely over the drilling spot within the next hour or two, ready for use the next morning. Everyone was keenly aware that time was tightly compressed—the National Guard was due to arrive within the hour.

Clayton stopped the drilling rig about ten feet in front of the wide main field gate, cut the engine, and dismounted from the high cab. Most of the group gathered around to get a close view of the large, strange truck with its rugged-looking structure and technical equipment. John met him and they shook hands vigorously. He told the crowd that Parker and his wife were now part of the family. Parker's wife, Emily, was working her way toward her husband, while being hugged and shaking hands. She finally moved to his side. Both of them felt good about their acceptance by everyone.

Since it was almost time for the National Guard to arrive, John suggested it might be better for everyone if they gathered in or near the house until Captain Ackerman had deployed his troop to the preplanned locations.

While they began to move off, the clerics had walked up near the drilling rig and moved slowly around it as they looked closely at every major feature. John and Clayton came over and joined them.

Rabbi Metz turned and looked at everyone, then swept his arm toward the rig. "This is a tool of the Lord. He has sanctioned this machine to discover his work."

The others stood for a moment, thinking about his statement. They were all caught up in the enormity of what lay ahead. They finally drifted toward the house, deep in conversation. John told Clayton he would ride with him to the bean field. Lyle, Carew, and Red would follow in the pickup.

The diesel roared to life and they eased the large drilling rig through the gate and straight down the access road to the fields, at slow speed.

"We're gonna need a mud collection pit about twenty by thirty feet and about three feet deep before we start drilling," Parker said as he glanced over at John. "We pump a drilling fluid down the drill pipe into the drill bit to lubricate and cool the bit. The fluid, along with the drilled dirt, is forced under pressure back up the hole to the surface, dumping the mud and debris into a prepared ditch leading to the pit."

"I'll have Carew and Red attach a set of plows to the big tractor. They'll break up the ground and use a scraper to remove the dirt. It'll be done before you're ready to start drilling. We aim to please. You tell us what you need and we'll provide." Parker chuckled and started gearing down as they approached the bean field.

Parker soon stopped the rig, letting it idle. He had told John about the special three-foot by eight-foot wheel pads he had strapped on back of the rig to lay down for traversing the soft field. A softer surface meant a possible disastrous bog down for the extremely heavy vehicle. Precaution was in order. He and John stepped down to the ground, and when the three inexperienced drilling crewmen walked up, Parker smiled and told them they had just volunteered for a little job. He explained their task. Lyle looked up at the truck bed to where the two stacks of wheel pads were tied down. Rolling his eyes, he looked at Carew and Red. All five men laughed. Another bit of tension was released.

AS SOON AS Enrique returned to his hotel room, he slumped into a chair, propped his feet on the edge of the bed, and sat for a few minutes reviewing his day, trying to relieve his frustration.

He picked up the phone and dialed Frank Bovitch, not only wanting an ally to talk to but also to bring his boss up-to-date on the details of checking out Gordon Malloy's Crystal Lake development. The explanation to Frank about his car trouble and his forced stay over in Danaville got no comment other than, "That's tough luck, Enrique. Get to Tallahassee as soon you can, and call me after you talk to Malloy. I've gotta go now, good luck." Cruz held the dead phone while thinking Bovitch's attitude toward him was crass and disrespectful. He slammed the phone back on its cradle with a feeling that his bosses were using him without intention of letting him in on the inner circle. His Latin anger was heating up.

Enrique decided to take a shower, then return to Martha's for lunch. After that, he'd drive around town and see some of the old homes, maybe see a movie. "A hick town, a hick deputy sheriff. What else could happen?" he wondered.

Later, after an unappetizing lunch, Enrique drove two blocks on Main Street to the Star movie theater and parked nearby. It didn't appear there were many people at the early matinee that had started fifteen minutes earlier. The feature was a Bruce Willis film. He anticipated the movie would take his mind off his troubles for about two hours.

The teenage girl in the ticket booth told him the next movie was at 3:10 p.m. He decided he would return at three.

The Cuban got into the Cherokee rental and decided to see the town. He cruised around the commercial center, drove north on Main for several blocks, then turned west into the major residential area, cruising up and down residential streets. He looked at homes—some that were very handsome and old, others that had been remodeled and beautiful. He wasn't really looking. He was just killing time.

Enrique remembered that the hotel desk clerk had told him about Falling Waters State Park and drew a rough map for him. Why not? Enrique thought. Maybe it would be an interesting place to see, plus using up some of his two-hour wait for the movie.

He found the park without much trouble and walked around, exploring the paths and the wooden crossovers, and finally, a view of a deep chasm where the falls, located above, dropped freely when there was more water than at present. There had been little rain during the past two weeks. Only a small trickle of water was visible.

His thoughts were still on Bovitch's short, curt conversation, and he was also wondering if Lyle Kelly was at the farm. He walked to the Cherokee and climbed in. As he drove back, he took a longer look at a golf course he had passed on the way to the park. He assumed that was the Danaville "country club."

The drive back to town and the Star Theater took only a few minutes. Enrique parked the car almost in the same spot as before. It was 2:55 p.m.—enough time to stroll past two storefronts to look in the windows of a furniture store. After wasting another five or so minutes, he turned back to the theatre. The $2.50 charge for a ticket and $1.50 for a large tub of popcorn were shocking. It cost at least twice that in Tampa.

The theater had about two dozen people in an auditorium that could seat 250-300 people. Certainly not the attendance found in one of Tampa's super multitheater centers. But the Star was comfortable. It was difficult for the Cuban to concentrate on the movie. It was over at ten minutes until five, and he walked out, squinting at the late-afternoon sun.

He heard a siren coming from his left and turned his head to see a county sheriff's patrol car approaching, leading three National Guard Humvees and a number of large troop trucks. The people who were still emerging from the theater stopped and looked also. Within seconds, the deputy's car and Humvees passed, followed by twelve trucks, all going north, with troops wearing full combat gear in most of them. Everyone was surprised and had questioning looks on their faces. One man near Cruz was heard to say the guard would not be going out on drill late on Sunday—they would normally be coming in after a weekend exercise; the troops had to return to their jobs on Monday morning. Another noticeable thing by some in the crowd was the serious way the soldiers looked.

Enrique observed that several cars had pulled over and stopped as the convoy roared by, and the drivers got out to watch the trucks pass. Bringing up the rear were two county deputy sheriff patrol cars—the last car was driven by Chief Deputy Beck.

The Cuban walked quickly to his rental car, backed it around, and headed north. He was determined to find out what was going on. He estimated the convoy was a quarter mile ahead. He'd keep this distance so as not to be too obvious. For some inexplicable reason, he felt they were going to the Kelly farm. He had a strange feeling.

While Enrique kept his distance from the convoy at a constant thirty-five miles per hour, he was chastising himself for his stupidity. From the high he had in Panama City four days ago from sealing the deal with the Conway brothers and a good sale to the navy in Pensacola for Gelb Foods, he now felt as if he had stepped off a cliff into a void.

When he saw Deputy Beck slowing his car, he realized the National Guard convoy was approaching the Kelly farm. "That's where they're going," he thought. "Why? It would have to be for a very important reason. There must be some kind of threat. But what or who could it be?" As he was trying to process those thoughts through his mind, he failed to notice that Beck had stopped on the road shoulder. Enrique realized the deputy had recognized the Cherokee, so he pulled in behind the blue-and-white patrol car.

Deputy Beck got out of his car and walked back to the Cuban. "I guess the National Guard got your attention when they passed through town; and I can understand your curiosity, but you can't go to the farm. That's off-limits to everyone."

"What's the deal, Deputy? What's happening? It's got to be something big. What is it?"

Dan Beck looked directly into Enrique's eyes. "You'll know in a short while, but now is not the time. I want you to go back to town, pick up your car tomorrow, and if possible, drive on to Tallahassee."

"What do you mean 'if possible'?"

"There are things that could occur that would prevent local citizens and others from being able to move around freely—for security and safety reasons."

Enrique looked at Beck for a moment and realized this was out of his control and he had no options. "Okay, Deputy, I know I have no other choice but to go back to town, right?"

"That's about it," the deputy said.

KARL AND TISHA PASTERNAK had been visiting their son and daughter-in-law in Varnum and were headed north on 77 toward home.

"Aren't those two county patrol cars ahead, following some army trucks?" Tish asked.

"Yep," Karl replied. "There's another car between us and the county mounties. We'll just follow along and see what's going on."

They saw the tailing deputy's blue-and-white car pull over and turn on its flashing lights, meaning for the following car to stop. Karl thought they were to stop also, but as he slowed, the deputy had gotten out of his car and waved to Karl to pass. He then walked back to the car which he had pulled over. When the Pasternaks drove by, they recognized Deputy Dan Beck talking to a stranger.

"Wonder what that was all about? And, Tish, since we're on a slight curve, can you see far enough ahead to see how many trucks there are?"

"Why, Karl, they're turning onto County Road 26, our road—there must be twelve or fourteen of them. It's the National Guard." She was getting more excited by the moment.

They were now slowing little by little, now down to ten miles per hour, as the trucks and the deputy's car ahead prepared to turn right. When Karl finally made the turn, the deputy ahead stopped. The Pasternaks followed suit. The deputy strolled to their car.

"Hello, Mr. and Mrs. Pasternak." The deputy touched his hat as he greeted them.

"Hi, Milton," Karl said. "What in the world is happening at the Kellys?" Pasternak was looking past Deputy Milton Walls, watching the lead trucks, about half a mile distant, turning into the entrance of the farm. "Why the National Guard and why the Kellys?" Karl was stunned—as was Tisha.

The deputy looked a little embarrassed, as he shifted his weight from one foot to the other. "Mr. Pasternak, I've known you and Mrs. Pasternak for a long time. I went to high school with your son and we graduated together, six years ago. I can't, however, tell y'all what's going on. It's highly classified right now, but you'll know within at least two days. Since your house is about a half a mile or so beyond the Kellys, you'll see the National Guard patrolling the farm's perimeter roads, and a number of guard posts will be in place around the entire property. You'll find that one of those posts will be located adjacent to your house."

"Your place will be guarded also because of possible problems with the curious, or even those people that mean to intrude on the farm and try to either destroy or steal something. I don't even know what that would be, but we'll all know in due time."

Karl and Tisha were listening intently, with fixed eyes on the deputy's face. Karl finally spoke, "You mean there's been a discovery of some kind that's worth a lot of money—or is it a big threat of some kind?"

"Oh, something like that, I suppose. I do know, however, that you two will have to stay around your place until more is known—and I don't know when that will be. The Kellys, through the National Guard, will make sure you'll have enough food and anything else you'll need until it's possible for you to move around freely and safely."

Pasternak and his wife looked at each other with a reluctant acceptance. "It appears we don't have much of a choice," he said.

"I'm sorry you've been caught in an unusual situation, but it's bigger than all of us. I or any of the other deputies will help you in any way we can. Just call us." With that, he handed Karl a card with the sheriff's office and emergency phone numbers, and returned to his idling car. He pulled over to the narrow shoulder and allowed the Pasternaks to proceed home. He waved as they passed.

After putting the car in the garage, they entered the house, and Karl went directly to the phone and called his son, then several friends. The word began to spread.

CHAPTER THIRTY-ONE

THE FARM FAMILY and guests were excited and nervous when the police car escort led the three Humvees, with Captain Ackerman, two second lieutenants, four sergeants, and the large troop trucks through the main entrance. All fifteen National Guard vehicles pulled around the house, made a left turn, and drove about two hundred yards to the pond and started parking nearby, side-by-side. The soldiers, with packs and weapons, began to jump from the trucks and immediately formed into four platoons consisting of thirty men each. They stood at ease in ranks, waiting for their CO to make a few remarks, along with his aides—a second lieutenant, a first sergeant, and the four lieutenant platoon leaders. Within minutes, the troops would set up their bivouac. Dispersal to their preplanned posts would begin by seven o'clock.

John, Captain Stanton, Ralph Tobias, Jim Summers, and Lyle went out to the pond to greet Captain Ackerman.

The National Guard commanding officer was all military business, unlike walking into his auto parts store on a weekday, where he was just an everyday businessman—quite a contrast. The assignment he was to carry out was far different from any that he had faced before.

John, Summers, and Daniels listened as Ackerman, Stanton, and Tobias talked about the perimeter guard posts that had been picked by Captain Stanton two weeks previously and agreed upon later by the National Guard commander.

Captain Ackerman detailed to the group his plan of rotating the troops at twenty guard posts every four hours—twenty-four hours a day. Each of the twenty posts would be manned by two men per shift. At any time, there would be forty soldiers stationed equally distant along the perimeter fence around the farm. Continual patrolling of the perimeter road would also be done by vehicle, each with two or four men each. With that, Ackerman excused himself and walked toward one of his lieutenants and his first sergeant, who had been standing a short distance away, waiting for him to finish talking to the farm group.

Soon, the soldiers were moving like a synchronized machine, unloading equipment, marking off areas for tents, mess facilities, and setting up portable toilets and bathing facilities.

John and the others stood quietly and watched the activity. They were very impressed by the National Guard.

They started back to the house, and as the group walked along talking, John was thinking about the impact of the drama being played out on his farm. The thoughts that he had had ten days ago had magnified. It was inevitable—the farm was in transition. No longer would its purpose be to produce food.

He thought about his dad and his grandfather—how they would react to this amazing event, and the enormous sacrifice the family had to make. John knew without any hesitation they would give the farm to God for his purpose.

When he and the others returned to the house, He reassured the family that Captain Ackerman and his National Guard members were in the process of setting up a well-planned security wall that would protect the farm. It was obvious to him that everyone there was in a positive frame of mind—their outlook boosted his faith and lessened his apprehension.

Jack Stanton and Ralph Tobias were quick to accept John's invitation to accompany him to the bean field. He wanted to see how the placement of the drilling rig was progressing, and to offer Parker help, if needed.

A few minutes later, John parked the pickup on the access road adjacent to the spot where the rig entered the bean field. The twin wide tracks of flattened bean plants marked the path of where the large vehicle had rolled on the wheel pads to its destination—approximately 150 yards away. The three of them saw that Parker had raised the derrick into its vertical drilling position.

"Hi, Clayton, how're things going?" John said as they walked up. The big well driller turned around from the side of the rig and pointed to his helpers.

"With eager beavers like these three, everything's in good shape. I sure feel bad we had to mess up a lot of bean plants when we brought the rig in."

"That's the least of my concerns. Looks like you and the guys did a good job," John said.

As he, Stanton, and Tobias walked around the impressive drilling rig, looking it over, John gave Lyle, Carew, and Red details of the National Guard move-in, and its preparation for deployment before sunset. They were impressed.

Parker wiped his hands on a rag he took from a front fender of the rig, then walked over and stuck out his hand to John, then to the other two. Parker's handshakes were vigorous, to say the least. "I'm totally convinced that this will be the most important drilling project that any man, anywhere, will ever be involved in," he said.

"That's for sure, Clayton. That's for sure," John said. "When do you think you'll be able to start drilling tomorrow?"

"What about right after breakfast?" Clayton answered with a question. "I've briefed my crew, and the drilling will be straightforward and uncomplicated, unless we hit an unforeseen obstacle." He paused for a moment and nodded at the six men around him. "We should do fine."

"Sounds great," John said as he looked at everyone. They were nodding in agreement, all smiling in expectation.

Stanton spoke up, "Even though the drilling hasn't started and we believe very little, if anything, is known about this project

by outsiders, Captain Ackerman and I believe a guard detail should
be put on the drilling rig, starting this evening. There'll be two
guards here, changed out every four hours, starting at sundown."

No one had any questions, so John said it was dinnertime,
and they would start their significant work for the Lord the next
morning right after breakfast. Parker announced he was ready for
dinner. The seven men rode back to the house, hungry and tired.
It was almost 7:00 p.m., about thirty minutes before sundown.
They knew the Guard would be posting their first shift soon. As
the pickup passed through the main gate to the house, all eyes
looked to the right through the trees toward the pond. Though it
was approximately two hundred yards from the house, they could
see soldiers setting up tents and doing other tasks as they worked
on completing their bivouac.

IT HAD BEEN an emotional day for everyone at the farm. They
sat around in different rooms, quietly talking as they ate their dinner.
The five clerics had split up. Each one would sit with a different
group for a while, then rotate to another location. They wanted to
know everyone better. The family and the others felt a strong
bond with them.

After dinner, Lyle and Teresa were sitting in the swing at the
far end of the long front porch, isolated from the others, a place
they could talk quietly about their feelings for each other, and
again, about the coming events.

He asked about Arlene. Teresa said her mother was doing
great and had really found herself within the family—she seemed
at peace, even with all the unknowns of the coming days.

Teresa told him with moist eyes that her love for him was
greater than ever. He felt as if his heart would burst. They wanted
to get married very soon. They would get their blood tests from
Doc McNally and their marriage through Ralph Tobias.

AROUND NINE THIRTY, everyone began to slowly prepare
for bed. Those assigned to the barn drifted out the back door and
disappeared to their sleeping quarters.

Rev. Billy Durdin had announced there would be an early thirty-minute prayer service conducted by him and the other clerics on the back porch right after breakfast. It would be to consecrate efforts toward discovery of God's message. This meant an early breakfast preparation for Granny and the other women. John had already told his mother and Sara that Parker thought the rig would be ready to start drilling by nine or so.

It had been determined by John, Clayton, Stanton, and Tobias that other than the clerics, only geologist Brandon Cook and Jim Summers would be present at the start of the drilling. The others would come when the core sampling was completed.

ON THE WAY back to town, after Deputy Beck had stopped him from following the National Guard convoy, Enrique began to notice a slight smell of something getting hot. He didn't know much about cars, but he did look at the instrument panel and right away noticed the temperature gauge needle pointing to hot. There was a Chevron gas station on a corner near downtown Danaville. He pulled in and parked in front of one of the service bays.

The attendant was a young man in his midtwenties, evidently running the station by himself on that slow Sunday. Cruz got out of the car as the young service attendant walked up. "Smells like you've lost the engine coolant," he said. "Pull the hood release."

As Enrique reached back into the car, he found the small lever and unlatched the hood, he asked, "You think it's serious?" He felt his frustration growing, as he looked at the dirty engine and then to where the attendant was taking the filler cap off the coolant reservoir. It was empty. The radiator was almost empty also. The young man found the feeder hose to the radiator had come loose and the strong-smelling coolant fluid had quickly leaked out, some spilling on the hot engine block. He said he thought the hose connection had been leaking for some time and had finally worked free.

"Will it take long to fix this thing?" Enrique asked.

"Not really. I think I can put the hose back on with a new clamp, and it'll do just fine."

"It's a rental from Otis Smith's garage," Cruz said.

The young man cocked his head to one side as he looked at Cruz. "I've never known Otis to have a good, dependable rental car."

It wasn't long before the coolant reservoir hose was repaired and new fluid added. Enrique wasn't in a hurry. He had nothing to do except go to his hotel—and he wasn't in the mood for that.

When he asked the attendant what was the cost for his services, the young man said he would charge for the coolant only. Enrique pulled out a fifty-dollar bill and handed it to him.

"My name is Enrique Cruz. What's your name?"

"George Rustin," the young man said. "But, Mr. Cruz, this is way too much money."

"No, it's what I want to give, and I want you to have it." Enrique again felt important as the young attendant looked at him with obvious respect.

"Okay, Mr. Cruz, I truly appreciate it—I'm happy I could be of help."

Enrique asked if he had seen the National Guard convoy when it came through town a little earlier. George said he and two customers watched the trucks loaded with troops pass by. All of them thought it strange the guard would be going north, late on Sunday afternoon. They were all aware the armory was located on the south side of town.

"What if I told you the Guard went to the Kelly farm?" Cruz said.

"Kelly farm? What would they go there for? How do you know they did?"

The Cuban explained how he trailed the convoy at a distance, after the last truck and the rear escort sheriff patrol cars had cleared downtown—how Deputy Beck had seen he was being followed, and stopped him, sending him back to town. Enrique said he looked again as he swung his car around and was sure the troops were turning into the farm.

Rustin stared at Cruz with a slight gaping mouth. He said nothing for several seconds; then he spoke with intensity, "There must be something terribly wrong at the Kellys. Maybe it's a UFO or something like that."

AT THAT MOMENT, Marvin Gardner drove in, in his big Buick. Attendant Rustin asked Enrique to wait until he said hello to one of his regular customers. Gardner got out of his car, went to the pump, and prepared to put gas in his car. George hurried into the station and turned on the pump. As Marvin was standing there waiting for his tank to fill, he looked over at Enrique, who was about twenty feet away, and smiled in greeting. The Cuban halfway nodded in return and reached up and pulled down the hood of the Cherokee. He was uncomfortable. His response to people he didn't know was slow and careful. His conceit could make him distant and aloof.

Enrique didn't like standing there beside his rental car, killing time, but he wanted to talk to George again. He leaned against the driver's door and focused his attention on Main Street, and tried to relax.

"Excuse me, but are you Mr. Cruz?" Enrique turned around and saw that the man who had been refueling the Buick had walked up.

"Yes," he answered cautiously.

Marvin stuck out his hand and stepped closer. "I'm Marvin Gardner. I run Gardner's drugstore on Main Street, a block south of the railroad track."

Cruz's interest suddenly increased. *Here's a man who has a little stature in this dump*, Enrique thought. *It might be to my advantage to hear what he has to say. But he evidently wants something. I'll listen and see where it leads.*

They shook hands, and Gardner continued talking. "I ran into Otis Smith at Martha's Café about an hour ago. He doesn't get many out-of-towners coming into his garage, so he told me a little about you. When he said Deputy Beck assisted you with your car up near the Kelly farm, and that you had stayed in town last night, I wondered if you have some connection with the Kellys." Marvin knew what was going on at the farm, and he would bide his time until the story broke through the news media within two or three days. In fact, he had received several phone calls at home around 5:30 p.m. from friends about the north-bound National Guard convoy.

The question in Gardner's mind was why this stranger from Tampa stopped in Danaville on this particular weekend, and drive out to the farm before the National Guard arrived.

Cruz considered the question for a few seconds, then responded that he had heard outstanding comments about the unique family and farm. And since he was on his way to Tallahassee, he decided to stop over and see them. It was only curiosity.

The druggist knew it didn't take staying overnight just to go see a farm from the road. It was evident the Cuban had not been invited. His story was weak—real weak.

As much as Gardner would like to be at the farm, he was in lock-step with the sheriff and was honoring his agreement. His priority was to find out as much as he could about Cruz and inform Bernam.

Enrique didn't care for the pharmacist's attitude, but listening to him, he began to realize there might be a way to get onto the farm, regardless of the National Guard and whoever else. The Cuban remembered a little used rutted road that turned off to the right just before reaching the southwest corner of the farm perimeter. There were pine trees and brush where he could possibly hide the car, about a hundred yards or so from Highway 77. His pulse quickened as he thought about revenge.

CHAPTER THIRTY-TWO

"WOULD YOU LIKE to have dinner with me? There's a nice restaurant on Highway 90 only two miles from here. It has great seafood." Marvin wanted to talk more to the Cuban. *Good food always loosens the tongue*, he thought. He sensed that the man standing in front of him, not making eye contact, had some kind of personal interest in the Kellys, and it may not be friendly.

"No thanks," Enrique said. "I need to make some telephone calls and then turn in early. I'm tired."

"I'm disappointed. How about breakfast in the morning?"

"Look, I hate to be blunt, but I really don't want this to go any further. As soon as I pick up my car tomorrow, I'm leaving this place and heading for Tallahassee."

The pharmacist knew that by then, things may be so chaotic around Danaville that the Cuban would find it difficult to leave town. All roads could be clogged with traffic from all directions, trying to get to the Kelly farm. He stood there for a few seconds. When he saw Cruz was not moving, Gardner turned and walked to his car, wondering why the strange man from Tampa continued to lean against the Cherokee with his head down. Marvin felt he was helping Sheriff Bernam and the Kellys by keeping an eye on the Cuban. He planned to contact Bernam and give him a heads-up about Cruz.

After Gardner drove away, Enrique walked over to the service store where Rustin was preparing to close for the night. He had said the station closed earlier on Sunday night.

He wanted to get onto the farm and find Lyle Kelly. The longer he thought about it, the more intent he became on getting satisfaction for the way he was treated a week ago by Arlene, Teresa, and Lyle. Cruz was unaware that Arlene was at the farm; he assumed she was in Tampa, but he had a feeling that Teresa was there with Lyle. The Cuban blamed Lyle for his being kicked out of "his" house. It was a huge insult to him. He was glad to be free of Arlene and Teresa. Lyle was the target for his anger. He felt a real need to confront young Kelly and extract vengeance. Enrique's egocentric mind was pushing him away from reality and toward deep trouble.

Rustin looked up from the register, where he was counting the day's receipts, preparing to close up for the night. "I saw Mr. Gardner leave. Hope everything's okay."

"Oh yeah, he's a nosy one—I don't think we'll be talking again. Say, I'd like to offer you a chance to make some real money tonight."

Rustin looked at Enrique closely. "What do I have to do?"

Cruz knew by the question that the attendant might be interested.

"It's important that I go to the Kelly farm tonight. I need your help, and I'll pay you $250. All you have to do is rent your car to me for several hours. I'll have it back to you by 1:00 or 2:00 a.m. I can't drive my rental—it would be easily recognized; the county deputies will be patrolling up and down 77, for sure. You told me you had a Ford Explorer. No one would connect me to that vehicle. I'll take very good care of it. In fact, I'll up the amount to three hundred. And I'll leave you the keys to the Cherokee. I'll take it back to Otis tomorrow."

"Mr. Cruz, what're you talking about? Why the Kelly farm? According to a customer who was traveling south on 77, he was stopped by a deputy sheriff while the National Guard convoy was turning onto County Road 26. My customer said he had a pretty good view down the county road and was positive the trucks were turning in to the farm."

Enrique smiled slightly. "He's right. The Guard is there and, by now, probably crawling all over the place. Why? I don't know. Maybe the Kellys are allowing them to carry out some kind of exercise. I know I must go there tonight, regardless. I only need transportation to and from the farm."

"There's no way you can get into that place," Rustin said. "You know there are troops everywhere. How do you think you can get past them, going in and coming out?" He sat on the corner of a small desk. "Whatever is going on at that farm has got to be big—real big. And I don't think it has anything to do with a military face-off with an invading enemy."

George looked out the large front window and saw a number of cars headed north on Main Street. They had to be going to check out the farm. It was early Sunday evening and unusual for people to be out driving. The news was spreading around Danaville, and curiosity was growing. He stole a glance at the Cuban, who had also watched the cars go by.

"Why are you so desperate to go to the farm tonight? Why don't you call whoever it is you want to meet with?" Rustin asked. "It seems to me that you're not expected out there."

"I can't talk about why. It's a personal matter."

Enrique saw Rustin's thin interest dissolving. Evidently, the Cuban had misjudged the young man—thinking he would jump at the money offer with few questions. But George had proven to be cautious. It was obvious to Enrique that he would have to carry out his plan alone. He had initially planned to get to Lyle without help, but when he met Rustin, there was a possibility he had found a partner. Now, it was back to square one.

He would drive the Cherokee to the farm, sneak in, and find Lyle. Cruz was aware the odds against his succeeding were formidable, but there was an indescribable feeling urging him on. His ever-present anger at people that he had controlled for years and had lain just beneath the surface was now in front of him. Young Kelly would now be the recipient of it.

"No, Mr. Cruz, I'm not your man. I appreciate the money offer, but all I want to do is go home, eat supper, and watch TV. No offense, but I don't want to rent my car." When George looked at Enrique's face and eyes, he saw an intensity that hadn't been there earlier. It gave him an uncomfortable feeling about the man.

Enrique didn't like to be turned down by anyone. It was an affront to his ego. He moved to the door, and as he pushed it open, he turned and looked at Rustin directly in the eyes. "I was just giving you a chance to make some money tonight, but I can handle things alone—I really don't need any help." With that, the Cuban walked out to the Cherokee and drove off.

George finished closing up and went home. His mind was straining to sort out just what it was that Cruz was up to and if someone at the farm was in danger.

Rustin thought he should call Gardner and tell him about the Cuban's determination to sneak onto the farm and confront someone—that it was very evident Cruz was carrying a grudge against. As soon as he walked into his house, George phoned the pharmacist.

ENRIQUE PICKED UP a hamburger and fries on the way to the Holiday Inn. After getting a Coke at a hallway dispenser, he went to his room. It was several minutes before eight. He wanted to depart for the farm around nine. He turned on the TV, sat down, and ate. Even his so-called dinner was repugnant.

Cruz sat there, oblivious to the blaring TV, too preoccupied with his upcoming mission. He was aware that his odds of failure were great, and his future with Gelb Foods—as well as, more significantly, with Bovitz and Gomez "Enterprises"—would be finished. "Oh well," he thought, "my feeling of having been made a lackey by my two bosses has proven to be true." Enrique was through with them, one way or the other.

When preparing to leave Tampa, he had unconsciously packed a pair of dark blue jeans and a black long-sleeved button-down shirt, which he changed into, thinking they would make him a little more difficult to spot in the dark. He opened his large overnight bag, unzipped a side panel, and took out a small .25-caliber automatic pistol, which would fit unnoticed in one of his pants pockets. He had taken a course in handguns several years ago and was knowledgeable in their use.

At almost nine o'clock, Enrique stepped out into the hall. When he closed the door, he had a fleeting thought that he may never open it again.

TWO MILES FROM the hotel, Marvin Gardner had just put down his phone after finally talking to Sheriff Bernam. Marvin was still angry. He had initially called the sheriff's home at 7:10 p.m. and left a message. A call to the sheriff's office only produced another answering machine. It was total frustration for Gardner. Time was ticking, and Marvin had a strong feeling that the Cuban was going to the farm at any time. In fact, he could be on his way at this moment. The sheriff finally called at five after nine.

The pharmacist quickly gave Bernam a rundown of his conversation with the Cuban. The sheriff was all ears, and said he and his deputies would quickly put out a net and pick up Cruz before he got to the farm. He reminded Marvin that the National Guard was well deployed, and it would be a miracle if Cruz got through their perimeter. Bernam thanked Gardner and hung up. Marvin felt like he had made a large contribution toward the safety of the Kellys and the farm. He sat down in his den and turned on the television. He wondered when news of the huge event would hit all the networks and newspapers Monday night, Tuesday morning or evening, or surely by Wednesday morning.

Gardner had not told his wife all of the details of what was going on. Barbara was a worrier. His plan was to feed her information bit by bit so she would handle the total impact more evenly.

Meanwhile, Sheriff Bernam had not wasted a moment. He contacted Beck and told him to put his deputies on red-alert patrol. Beck described the Jeep Cherokee and the Cuban in detail, and told his men to intercept the suspect ASAP.

When Dan Beck got the call from Sheriff Bernam, he smiled slightly because the news about Cruz did not surprise him. The deputy's observation skills had raised a couple of red flags from the moment he first talked to Cruz. It shouldn't be difficult to find the curious Cuban. He was not cunning enough to become a real threat to any member of the Kelly family. The National Guard security perimeter was too tight for anyone to penetrate.

Chief Deputy Beck contacted his four men and laid out the situation, describing Cruz and the rental car he was driving. Beck told them to split up their patrol coverage—two deputies on 77 north of County Road 26, and two south. He would freelance from downtown Danaville to the farm and elsewhere, if needed.

CRUZ GOT INTO his old rental, turned out of the hotel parking lot onto Main Street, and pointed it north toward the farm.

AFTER TALKING TO his deputies, Beck left his apartment and drove downtown on 90, turning south on Main to the Holiday Inn. That would be his starting point once he established the Cuban had indeed departed. Seeing no sign of the Cherokee at the hotel, the deputy went north.

ENRIQUE CROSSED THE midtown railroad tracks and drove at a moderate speed toward the Kelly farm. There was a surprising number of vehicles on the road, going and coming, but he paid no attention because of his total fixation on his destination. He had planned to turn onto the narrow, old dirt road he had spotted earlier in the day on his way back to town from the farm. It ran down a sloping embankment and disappeared beyond a large stand of tall pine trees. Cruz thought it would be a good hiding place and fairly close to the farm.

He would pull over to the wide highway shoulder and park ten or fifteen feet before reaching his turn-off. Sitting there with his lights off, he'd wait for a long gap in the traffic, then drive down the road and park as far into the trees as possible. Cruz had estimated he would be approximately a quarter of a mile from the farm's south boundary fence and another mile from the house. He would have to walk through the fields, guessing the direction to the house. It would take at least an hour, but he was determined.

MEANWHILE, DAN CALLED the sheriff on his cell phone. They had agreed to use phones rather than radios to keep the lid on what was unfolding. The deputy related what was happening, and that he thought the Cuban was now driving to the farm. Bernam said he'd stand by, and told Beck to call him just as soon as they caught Cruz—he would come to the scene, wherever that may be. Dan knew the Cuban would have to park the Cherokee out of sight, somewhere off 77. Since Cruz didn't know the territory, and had had no time to do any scouting, he would be hard pressed to come up with a good place to hide his car.

Beck and his deputies knew just about every square foot of Mason County. His mind was sifting through all the possible places the Cuban might choose, and it suddenly dawned on him that an old narrow, old logging road led off to the right from 77, winding through large trees. He called two of his deputies for assistance, telling them to arrive quietly. He was less than two miles from the old road. Beck would approach the turn-off slowly, dousing his lights just before leaving the highway.

The chief deputy was approximately one hundred yards from the turn-off when he spotted a darkened car moving down the highway shoulder slope toward the trees. 'That's him,' he thought, with some relief. Beck cut his lights, slowed to almost a crawl, and as the patrol car followed the rutted road, he hit the redial button on his cell phone. The sheriff was relieved when his chief deputy briefed him. Bernam said he was on his way.

Enrique could hardly see what was in front of him once he drove under the large pines. The road turned just ahead, which was good he thought. The Cherokee would be hard to spot from the highway. He finally parked and was preoccupied with thinking about his walk to the farm and what he would do when he got there. Suddenly, he was startled when the bright lights of Beck's car flooded the Cherokee and surrounding area.

"Please get out of your car, Mr. Cruz. This is deputy Dan Beck, we need to talk." The amplified words of the deputy's voice sounded loudly from the patrol car's speaker.

The Cuban was totally surprised. Sweating profusely, he exited the Cherokee, wondering how the deputy had found him. Enrique's head throbbed and he felt like the earth had opened up and swallowed him. He slowly got out of the old road rental car and stood looking toward the deputy. It was impossible to see anything because of the lights. His mind was spinning. Cruz now realized that the life he had envisioned of position and money was now destroyed, because of his hate for Lyle Kelly, Arlene and Teresa, even the entire Kelly family. On top of that, it was evident that Frank Bovitz and Alejo Gomez had used him for the Panama City Beach property deal and wanted nothing to do with him. He also realized how much of a mess his life was and how wasted he felt.

Beck walked up and shined a flashlight into the Cuban's face and carefully over his body. "Would you care to tell me what you're doing in this lonely stretch of posted woods at this time of night?"

"I'm not quite certain," Enrique answered in a subdued voice, as he turned his head and looked off into the night in the direction of the farm.

The chief deputy saw that Cruz was very disturbed and perhaps psychotic. All of them would have to handle the Cuban carefully and try to find out what was driving his behavior.

Beck told Enrique to turn around and then handcuffed him. The deputy patted down Cruz and suddenly stopped and extracted a small automatic pistol from his right pants pocket. 'Well, this magnifies the seriousness of his trouble,' Beck thought. "Do you have a permit to carry this pistol, Mr. Cruz?

"No," Enrique mumbled,

Deputy Beck reached into his shirt pocket and took out a small laminated card, and read the Cuban his Miranda rights. Sheriff Bernam, along with deputies Walls and Williams, walked up and waited until Beck finished.

"Good Job Dan," Bernam said in a soft, low-pitched voice as he stopped at his chief deputy's side. After a few seconds of silence, the sheriff spoke to Enrique. "You've got certain rights, Mr. Cruz, and we'll make sure you are not deprived of them. As deputy Beck just read to you, you don't have to answer any questions until you are represented by an attorney. In the meantime, there're several things I'd like to ask about that would be helpful to our investigation.

"Such as?" Cruz asked quietly. He had already resigned himself to the worst—he didn't care what happened now.

"You met and talked with George Rustin earlier this evening?"

"I had car trouble and he fixed it. We talked, just like people do in such situations."

The sheriff leaned against the Cherokee, and after a short pause, continued, "Didn't you offer Rustin money to drive you to the Kelly farm, perhaps so that you would not be seen on the way out here?"

Except for the crickets, there was a long moment of silence.

"Mr. Cruz, did you hear me?"

"Yes, sheriff, I heard you. I offered the young man two hundred and fifty dollars. He turned me down, so here I am."

"George Rustin is a good young man. He used good judgement," Bernam said.

"I found this automatic on him," Beck said as he handed it to the sheriff.

Bernam looked at it closely. "Were you planning to shoot someone at the farm?

"I'm not sure what I was going to do."

"Mr. Cruz, two of my deputies here are going to take you to the country jail. You'll be held in custody for the time being. An investigation will start immediately. You may contact your attorney first thing in the morning."

Enrique's mind had almost shut down. He knew he was now in a deep hole with no way out and would tell them anything they wanted to know. He had no attorney and wasn't interested in trying to attain one. Somewhere in the back of his mind, he remembered he would be furnished legal counsel by the court. It didn't make any difference to him.

Deputies Williams and Walls walked Cruz over to a patrol car and put him in the backseat. It took a moment for him to get his cuffed hands positioned so that he could sit without total discomfort. Both doors locked with only outside access. He looked at the steel mesh screen between him and the front seat and felt totally trapped as he sank deeper into his depression. Williams got in and carefully backed past the sheriff's car, turned into an open space and drove out toward 77. Deputy Walls trailed behind.

Beck walked over to the Cherokee and opened the driver's door. His eyes examined the interior, but the only thing he found was a folded sheet of paper lying on the passenger side of the front seat. He picked it up and saw that it was a sheet of Holiday Inn stationery with a badly drawn map on it. The deputy turned and handed it to the sheriff. "Look like this excuse for a map was the extent of the Cuban's planning."

"Well, it appears he had a fairly good memory. Having been up 77 as far as Country Road 26 only once, and probably still only thinking about sneaking onto the farm at that time, he remembered the old road. Keep it with the pistol as evidence. From what you told me about your conversation with him earlier, he's a strange one. His reluctance to demand an attorney immediately is odd, and he didn't hesitate to answer my questions. He's educated and evidently has a good job in Tampa—you said as a manager of some kind, with a food distribution company, didn't you?"

The deputy nodded. "Yeah, when I told him this morning that I was just trying to get to know him a little, he responded sparingly, then turned away. He's a cold fish."

"Tell your men to keep his arrest quiet for now. Also, nothing is to be said to any of the Kellys until I say so. You and I will determine when to contact his company. Now, I'm going home and go to bed. It's been a long one. You and your men get as much rest as you can. Additional state troopers will be here in the morning to give us a hand.

CHAPTER THIRTY-THREE

T HE OVERCAST THAT had draped itself over the farm
through the day had disappeared by sundown. The night
was clear and the air held a slight scent of Sara's roses as
she and John stood on the front porch, having a private moment
together before going to bed.

They were discussing the inevitable coming marriage of Lyle
and Teresa. How they would work it into the awesome event
taking place around them, after the discovery. John was convinced
that even the wedding of their son was to be an important piece of
God's holy mosaic.

Sara was looking at her husband and holding his hand. All of
a sudden, he snapped his head to the left, toward the yard and
sky. "Look at that!" he exclaimed as he squeezed her hand and
gently pulled her toward the porch steps. "Another one!"

"What's wrong, John? What did you see?"

"Meteors," he said excitedly.

As they started down the steps to the yard, Sara exclaimed,
"Oh, John, there goes another one! It's so bright!"

They stood there watching a number of the streaking lights
cross the sky, feeling it was God's sign that He was watching over
the family and the farm. Soon the meteors waned and the sky was
still. John and Sara hugged each other and said in a reverent
whisper, "Thank you, Lord." With that, they went into the house

and to bed. The next day was going to be significant—the drilling would start.

The house and barn were quiet. The family and guests were each confronting their thoughts about Monday, or they were already asleep.

THE FARM AWOKE very early on Monday morning. Few of the family and guests had slept well, in anticipation of what the day held for them. There were a number of yawns and baggy eyes at the six o'clock breakfast, but they were still reverently upbeat.

Everyone hurriedly ate and gathered on the back porch for the prayer service. The atmosphere was filled with expectations and open hearts. While sitting there waiting for the service to start, each was thinking about the family and farm. They watched as a National Guard olive-drab truck came from the bivouac area and turned into the main gate toward the drilling rig to retrieve the last two guards of the third and last posting at the rig overnight. For a moment, all eyes on the porch were fixed on the vehicle's helmeted driver and his companion. The group appreciated the presence of the young soldiers—many of them well-known in the community by the farm family and guests.

All six clerics were standing off to one side of the gathering, talking quietly among themselves. They soon stopped, and Reverend Butler stepped in front of everyone. He held up his arms and turned his hands slightly outward. A hush fell on the back porch. Butler was eloquent as he prayed, pledging the hearts, souls, and energy of them all to the Lord. He ended by asking for blessings on the visiting clerics and their dedication to this holy work.

Reverends Billy Durdin, Chase Griffin, and Dr. Claussen, had a different but inspirational prayer relating to the history of the Kelly family and its unshakeable faith through four generations of hard work in developing the farm. Father Walsh talked a few minutes about the miracle that had occurred in the bean field, and how it would leave a holy, indelible mark on the souls of all of them and people throughout the world. The priest blessed them in Latin, then smiled and sat down.

Rabbi Metz stepped forward. He looked warmly at his new friends, knowing the bond they all shared was watched over by the same God. Everyone on the back porch had liked the rabbi instantly when they met him the day before.

He wore a black satin yarmulke on his head. His stature and warm personality commanded their attention. He explained that a head covering symbolized man's submission to God, reminding him there is someone above him. Metz then told them about the three prayers: morning prayer ("*shacharit*"), afternoon prayer ("*minchah*"), and evening prayer ("*ma'ariv*"). He further explained that most prayers are recited while sitting; some of them are said while standing. Generally, one stands for the more important parts of the prayer, as a sign of respect, and faces east toward Jerusalem. The rabbi then invited them all to join him in a Shacharit to the God that belonged to all of them. They all stood and faced east as he recited a beautiful prayer in English.

After the service, some of them stayed on the back porch while others drifted down onto the backyard. They wanted to see the drilling rig crew and observers depart for the bean field. All of them were excited.

JOHN APOLOGIZED TO his passengers about their transportation to the drilling site, but it was more practical. They all were quick to let him know it was a plush arrangement compared to some experiences they had gone through in other parts of the world. There was a chuckle or two as they walked out to the pickup and the large truck. All of them were dressed in work clothes or rugged casuals. Hats were also included.

Carew and Red had loaded several large ice chests with bottled water and canned soda. Lunch would be brought out to them later. Two portable toilets were put on site during the last evening. A large canvas canopy stretched over an aluminum-pipe frame would be erected immediately after arriving at the rig. Folding chairs were included.

John, Father Walsh, and Durdin got into the cab of the pickup, while Butler, Griffin, Claussen, and Rabbi Metz climbed into the back.

Carew, Lyle, and Stanton sat in the cab of the truck, with Parker, Cook, Summers, and Red in the rear.

The two trucks started moving off slowly. John and Carew didn't want to overly jostle their passengers. All of the others staying behind waved and gave shouts of encouragement. Those in the two trucks waved back.

CLAYTON PARKER WAS extremely pumped up for the job at hand—by far the largest challenge he or any driller would ever face. His preplanning had been thorough, and with geologist Brandon Cook standing by, Parker was ready to start drilling into the unknown. He was the first out of the big truck when Carew stopped behind the pickup.

When the passengers got out of the vehicles, they stood and looked at the large dark blue rig with its upraised derrick, a monolithic symbol poised to reach into the depths of the earth for God's message. All of them knew the ground they stood on was hallowed, and it touched their souls mightily.

Everyone had been made aware that the drilling process and preparation of the hole for exploration would take one and a half to two days. Parker and Cook had explained there might not be a cave. But whatever God wanted them to find was buried in the ground, and they had a strong feeling that a cave was involved because the Florida Geological Survey map of the area indicated limestone strata lying thirty to fifty feet beneath the bean-field drilling site. But the entire group at the farm wanted to spend the first day at the drilling site to watch the exploratory drilling and proof of a cave. After that, most of them, especially the ladies, would retire to the house until they were told the drilling was completed and Lyle was ready to descend into the hole.

Carew, Lyle, and Red unloaded the aluminum canopy structure and its canvas cover, which had been bought at the military surplus store in Dothan, along with the truckload of other supplies for everyone at the farm. It didn't take long to bolt the frame together and secure the canvas top. The twenty-four-by-twenty-four-foot canopy would provide a much-needed shaded rest area. It also had roll-down side flaps for the late-day sun. After placing the ice chests, chairs, and other items under the canopy, they joined Parker in finalizing the rig for start-up.

John, Reverend Griffin, and Father Walsh were standing near the rig derrick, talking and looking down at the spot that the small exploratory drill bit would soon bore into. John looked around at everyone as they quietly chatted—some standing in the early-morning sun; others sitting under the canopy. His eyes scanned the distant fence line about three-quarters of a mile away, and he spotted a National Guard truck moving slowly along the perimeter road and, faintly, two soldiers manning a guard post. They were evidently changing guards. "God bless them," he thought.

"John, everything has been checked, and we're ready to start down with the smaller bit for soil sampling and recording the depth of the limestone," Parker said.

The senior Kelly smiled and said, "Clayton, God and all of us"—he swept his hand toward the awaiting people behind him—"are counting on your expertise."

The 3-7/8-inch bit was spun into the ground at a few minutes after 9:00 a.m. The small-bit stem was fitted with a core barrel to collect samples of soil, rock, and, finally, the expected limestone. Due to its size, the bit would sink at a relatively rapid speed, and Brandon Cook had agreed with Parker to pull the drill pipe and bit with the core barrel at three depths: ten and twenty feet, and when they hit the limestone. They would examine the core samples to see if the formations were as expected.

Cook had guessed that the top of the limestone strata would be at a depth of thirty to thirty-five feet.

It didn't take long before the drilling stem was pulled up from the hole for the first time, and the core barrel was checked. Cook saw that it was only heavy orange-red clay and nodded okay. The pipe was lowered, and the drilling continued.

The second pullout occurred forty-five minutes later. Another clay sample showed no extraordinary change, but there was some sign of limestone. Cook knew they were nearing their target. A second pipe section was added, and drilling resumed. After ten feet, the bit impacted substantially on what Parker and Cook knew was the top of the limestone strata. The depth was twenty-seven and a half feet. Cook shrugged and said he was happy it was no deeper. The string was pulled, and upon examining the core barrel, it was confirmed that they were ready to change to the thirty-six-inch bit with its 4-1/2-inch drill pipe.

Parker pulled out his cell phone and called his close and trusted friend, Charlie Kent, the owner of a drill-pipe supply and metal-fabricating company fifteen miles away in Jackson County. Kent had been expecting the call. He and Parker had talked the day before. Parker told him he needed two fifteen-foot sections of thirty-two-inch steel casing welded together. He also told him to weld six, six-by-eight-by-two-inch lifting ears with two-inch holes equally distant around the outside diameter, and within two to three inches of one end of the casing. The ears would provide cable attachment points for the crane.

The rig was now ready to drill again. This would be the "serious phase," as Parker aptly put it. Rev. Billy Durdin asked everyone to move in closer for prayer. They formed a semicircle, standing silently approximately twenty feet from and staring at the currently most important spot on earth—a small hole under a huge suspended thirty-six-inch drill bit.

Durdin prayed fervently, thanking God for choosing all of them to witness his glorious power and purpose. The other clerics kept their heads bowed for a few moments longer, and softly echoed Billy's thankfulness.

After a chorus of 'amens,' the crowd watched transfixed as Parker started the rotary and lowered the rotating bit. Several minutes went by and darkened soil mixed with drilling fluid began exiting the large hole as a mud slurry under pressure fron the rig deck-mounted mud pump, and followed an excavation trench to a large, previously prepared collection pit located off to one side of the drilling rig.

Drilling was slower because of the size of the huge bit. It put a larger load on the rotary power and pipe string—all measured in torque. When the bit reached the limestone, the load would increase.

Two hours later, at a depth of twenty-seven and a half feet, the drill stem shuddered somewhat as the thirty-six-inch bit struck the limestone. Parker shut the rig down to tell his crew and John that they were ready for the more difficult drilling phase.

John suggested it would be a good time to have lunch. Everyone was in favor of eating and reflecting on the next few hours. Parker, Lyle, Carew, and Red were happy to rest for thirty or forty minutes.

The crowd gathered under the large canopy to serve themselves from a long table covered with sandwiches, fruit, salads, and drinks. A smaller canopy was a few feet away. It had been jury-rigged by John, Jack Stanton, and Lyle, using a large tarpaulin and some two-by-fours brought from the house. The two shelters were appreciated by everyone, especially while eating their lunch. About half of them sat on the ground with no complaints.

John was sitting with Sara, Granny, Teresa, and Arlene. While they talked, he was reflecting on the well-being of the livestock. He, Lyle, Carew, and Red were rising one hour earlier each morning to feed and milk the cows and turn them out to pasture, and then feed the hogs and chickens. Except for what was necessary for daily consumption, a large amount of milk and eggs was being disposed of daily in excavations in the southeast corner of the fields. Jack Stanton had convinced John on Saturday that it would be hazardous to leave the secure farm perimeter with a load of milk and eggs for the market when they didn't know what trouble may arise from the events at the farm. Captain Ackerman agreed, and John had to accept the reality of the situation.

Perhaps after the family's mission had reached a conclusion, he thought, except for farming, their routine would return, but have a different character. Milk-and-egg sales would continue. The bean-field site would become a shrine to God; the surrounding fields converted to parking spaces and parks. John had even thought of keeping twenty acres for pasture, and adding more cows and chickens.

Sheriff Bernam had driven up and parked behind the large farm truck. With long strides, the big man headed for the shade and food.

Sara looked past John and Captain Ackerman, who was sitting nearby, and saw the lawman. She patted her husband lightly on the knee and tilted her head toward the approaching sheriff. He got to his feet and went to greet him. John offered his hand and smiled when Bernam walked up. "We've been expecting you. Now we have you, Captain Stanton, and Captain Ackerman all here together. We feel safer already!" The sheriff laughed along with those nearby. "Get yourself some lunch and come join our little group."

Bernam said hello to Sara and the others. "I would've been here earlier, but something rather important came up." He glanced across at Arlene, thinking if she only knew what that 'something' was. "I'm not going to turn down free food. I'll be right back."

Jim Summers appeared with a couple of cameras and a photo equipment bag suspended from his neck and shoulder. He had been busy using a small voice recorder interviewing Parker whenever the well driller had a few moments in between operating the rig. Summers was shooting the entire drilling operation as it went along.

Granny asked him to get some lunch and join them.

The editor smiled at her and said he had to return to the rig soon. Jim told John that he needed to talk to him for a moment. John got up, and the two walked just outside the canopy into the sunlight.

"A press release should be made to all wire services, starting with the International Press Network, just as soon as we are ready to recover whatever it is that's in the ground," Summers said. "Parker said it could be by late tomorrow afternoon. As you know, I'm a stringer for IPN, and due to the magnitude of what's happening, it's incumbent for me to make a timely report. Also, it will help dispel the rumors that are now spreading in our community. Everyone on the farm will be surprised at the reaction this is going to cause among people everywhere. I believe thousands of people from everywhere are going to start showing up here soon after the story is broken by the mass news media. All of them will want to see the holy site, and many will try to do so by any means possible."

John was silent for a moment. He didn't know anything about how the news business worked, but he trusted the editor—they had become close friends. "How long do you think it will take after you file before the news appears on television?"

"I think the networks and the cable news companies will be running the story immediately as a cut-in news bulletin, then on all regular late evening news shows. Also, news people from everywhere, in the United States and throughout the world, will appear soon. Some, starting with nearby TV stations, arriving first; then the three major network and cable news people in New York will be arriving by late afternoon." Summers smiled slightly. "Foreign news people will follow soon thereafter. As I said to you the other day, you and the family—even me—had better get ready for constant, bothersome interviews by many over-zealous newshounds. It'll be rough."

"We've talked about this a little, and it makes us uneasy. But I think everyone on this farm understands there are rough days ahead," John said.

"That's very true." Summers replied. "It looks as if Parker and his crew have finished their lunch and are just about ready to start drilling the big hole. I need to talk to him before he gets busy." The editor picked up his gear and started to move off.

John put his broad-brimmed hat on. "I'd like to talk to him myself." The two of them walked toward the rig.

Parker was checking the mud pump and compressor before starting the rotary that turned the huge bit. John and the editor walked up just as Parker turned and saw them. He gave them a big grin. "Fellas, everything's about ready to start with the big push."

"I think everyone's ready. They're anxious," John said with a smile.

Summers told Clayton he wanted to record a short interview with him before the drilling began. The big well driller wiped his hands, and the two of them walked toward the cab where there was a little shade.

John leaned against the side of the rig, partially in the shade, and thought about his ride to the bean field on the rig with Parker the day before. He had learned a lot about this big, burly man who loved his work and people. Clayton Parker and his wife had no children, but had a rather large family consisting of his customers, neighbors, children in general, and most of all, their church friends. John admired him.

When Parker had finished talking to Summers, he walked over to John and told him that he had ordered the casing. Kent would deliver it the next day around noon, and Cal Owens, his associate, would be bringing a truck-mounted crane to off-load and place the casing—if they could get through the growing automobile traffic. He'd been monitoring his radio and knew the roads were crowded. Parker added that he had told Jack Stanton about the expected delivery. The state trooper captain assured him that immediate plans would be made to escort Kent's trailer truck and crane from his shop to the farm with four to six state patrol cars.

John was relieved. Stanton had told him earlier that morning that the automobile traffic of the curious was increasing steadily on all roads to and around the farm. Many troopers were now working all roads in the immediate area and were on standby to spread their traffic control to 1-10 when needed.

When everyone understood that the drilling would not be completed until the next day, about half of the group chose to return to the house and wait until the hole was complete and the casing set. Those remaining, including the clerics, gathered around the drilling site, approximately twenty-five feet away. Parker had earlier told them it was best to use caution around a working drilling rig.

Soon, the thirty-six-inch bit started rotating into the ground. Everyone stared at the developing large hole, while silently praying.

Ralph Tobias and Jack Stanton joined Kelly and Summers as they watched the drill bit vanish on its way to finding the unknown.

"How long will it take to reach the limestone?" Tobias asked

"Parker estimates the twenty-seven feet will take about two hours," John answered. "The large bit travels slower—even in sand and clay. The limestone will be much more difficult. Once it makes contact with the top of the strata, he plans to let it turn until the limestone is indented evenly. Then it will be pulled and replaced with a twenty-eight-inch carbide bit. The smaller diameter hole will leave a four-inch ledge in the limestone for the casing to sit on when it's cemented into place. He thinks it could take from four to six hours to penetrate the limestone into the cave, depending on its depth and compactness. Parker and Cook think the ceiling will be no more than ten to fifteen feet deep. Pass the word to everyone that the drilling will cease for the day about sundown and resume at seven o'clock in the morning. Maybe we'll hit the cave by noon or so."

"John, how in the world can you remember all of those details?" Summers asked.

"Because this means so very much to me and my family, to all of you. And Parker's planning and hard work, along with that of everyone, is the key to reaching and recovering whatever is down there; and he's deeply dedicated to preventing anything going wrong. He said the Lord is guiding his every move. And he is."

At approximately 5:20 p.m., the bit made contact with the limestone. Lyle and Carew had just finished clearing out the mud pileup that had collected in the drain channel from the drilling hole to the mud pit. They walked up beside Parker, who was watching the hydraulic pressure indicator, when he suddenly made an adjustment to the rotary RPM.

"That's it! We're on top of the formation."

Red joined them as Parker glanced over his shoulder at his three crewmen. "We'll let it cut into the stone for five minutes or so. The indention will help center the twenty-eight-inch bit when we start it up in the morning. Tomorrow's gonna be an interesting day," he said with a grin. "We'll start about 7:00 a.m." After another several minutes, he shut down the rig.

PARKER, LYLE, CAREW, AND RED were tired. It had been a long first day, both physically and emotionally. Of course, everyone at the farm shared that condition, especially on the emotional side. They knew that if everything went well the next day, the Lord's purpose would be revealed to them.

The group enjoyed a good late meal that the ladies had prepared. Because of the events and their timing, all of them talked quietly as they ate, seeming to keep their energies reserved for the next day—and beyond.

After an announcement by Reverend Butler that a short fifteen—or twenty-minute prayer gathering would be held the next morning at six o'clock, he commented that when they reached the cave, it would be a major step toward the most important day in their lives and those of people everywhere. They all sat silently for several moments, reflecting on his words, then began to go on separate ways to visit in twos and threes, or take a shower and get some sleep—if possible.

John had asked Jack Stanton, Ralph Tobias, and Captain Ackerman to meet with him on the front porch after dinner. He wanted to get a detailed update from Stanton on what was happening on the nearby roads. Ackerman would fill him in on the perimeter guards and any incidents with outsiders that had already occurred and what could be expected tomorrow or the day after, and especially after Jim Summers filed the news releases. Tobias was to brief all of them on the latest word from Washington. His friend, Treasury Secretary Beretti, had telephoned him about fifteen minutes before dinner.

After fifteen minutes, John felt more at ease regarding the state of security for the holy site and everyone on the farm.

He was extremely interested when Tobias told him and the other two that Beretti confirmed that President Burke and his cabinet were focused on the unfolding event at the farm. Secretary of Defense Weston, coordinating with Secretary of State Kasmin, the NSA, the attorney general, and the FBI, had a two-hour meeting and constructed a basic plan that could be initiated immediately. As things unfold, additional planning and action would be carried out. The FBI was immediately sending a small special tactical unit to work with local and state law enforcement—even the National Guard. The county attorney looked over at Stanton and Captain Ackerman. They both nodded affirmatively.

After bidding each other good night, they headed for their respective quarters. John spotted Sara, Lyle, and Teresa coming out of the living room, headed for the stairs. He discreetly turned them back into the large room, and spent several minutes telling them about his short meeting on the front porch. They were impressed at how fast things were happening and with who was involved. With that, they all called it a day and went upstairs— each of the two couples holding hands.

CHAPTER THIRTY-FOUR

T UESDAY MORNING ARRIVED with an overcast sky. The weather forecast the night before had predicted light scattered showers until late afternoon. Parker was thankful there was no predicted heavy rain. He knew the Lord would protect the drilling operation, and was humming quietly as he and his three-man crew headed for the bean field.

After breakfast and a short prayer service, everyone prepared hopefully for the day. Most of the group would be there to support the drilling crew when the rig started drilling through the limestone—and would be there when the bit broke into the cave—even if it took all day. They knew the casing would then be lowered into the hole and cemented into place, and then Lyle would descend into the depths to find what was waiting for all of them and the world.

It was almost 7:15 a.m. when Parker started the rotary turning. Careful monitoring of the hydraulic pressure on the drill stem and mud pump was crucial. A broken bit would not be welcome—and it would cost a lot of time.

The bit was stopped every fifteen or twenty minutes, and lifted slightly off the limestone for several minutes for it to cool. Parker was doing all he could to avoid a problem.

Rate of sink, or penetration speed, was very good—nearly four feet per hour. The elapsed time since starting at seven fifteen had been two hours and thirty-five minutes. The drill-bit had traveled almost nine feet.

Cook stepped over beside Parker. He put his hand on the big well driller's shoulder and said he had a gut feeling they were more than halfway there. Clayton smiled and told the geologist they were making good time. He prayed that they could keep up the pace.

It was 10:20 a.m. when the bit was shut down to cool again. The depth was ten feet and eight inches. The geologist examined a handful of return mud, washing away the drilling fluid in order to closely examine bits of limestone. He nodded slightly as he showed it to Parker, who was pleased that the stone was not unusually hard.

The geologist commented he thought they'd punch through the cave ceiling not long after lunch. Parker smiled and started the rotary again.

Jim Summers knew the importance of keeping a chronological record of all activities regarding the event and retrieval of God's gift now lying below the ground. He knew he would be the conduit for the initial information given to the press.

The editor had been consistently taking photos and interviewing various individuals of the group, especially the clerics, the drilling crew, and John, Tobias, Stanton, and Ackerman. John was the glue that kept everything and everyone together—the immediate and extended family, as well as those welcomed guests that were contributing to understanding God's plan for all of them. The more Jim Summers watched and talked to John Kelly, the more he was convinced the man was unique and immensely gifted in his day-to-day relationship with family and people in general. In Jim's mind, John was the embodiment of a Christian. He set examples by his deeds and evident love for people, winning their respect and attracting them to him.

Parker told his three-man crew to feel free to take individual rests by rotation for the next hour or so. He thought it best that no less than two of them stayed close to the rig. They grinned and gave him a thumbs-up sign. Clayton Parker loved to work hard, and he also had a great sense of humor. He laughed, turned to his rig, and started the rotary turning again. Carew and Red looked at Lyle, telling him to get lost for a while. He did a little bow, turned, and walked toward the canopies.

WHEN LYLE WALKED UNDER THE large canopy and its welcome block of shade, Teresa rose out of her chair and met him. She was happy to see him and showed it. After a whispered exchange of a loving greeting, they walked over to where she had been sitting with Arlene, Pat Daniels, and Granny.

"Well, well, well," Granny said. "My favorite well-driller grandson has come to see how we hard-working chair-sitters are doing."

All of them laughed—even others sitting or standing nearby, who heard Granny, joined in. Lyle stepped over, held out his hand, and she stood up, and they hugged.

"I love you, Granny," he said as he looked into her bright blue eyes. She kissed him on the cheek.

"You'd better, otherwise, no more carrot or pound cake for you, for a long time—perhaps for a day or two." Everyone had inched a little closer, enjoying Granny's sharp wit. Her intelligence, love, and great sense of humor drew people to her.

Lyle talked to Arlene and his Aunt Pat for a few moments, gave each a small hug, and turned his attention again to Teresa. They walked over to the smaller canopy which at the moment was unoccupied. He looked into one of the large ice chests and pulled out two cold bottles of water. They sat in folding chairs and were quiet for a moment, each focusing their thoughts toward the other, and toward Lyle's imminent down-hole exploration.

They had recently discussed their marriage plans with their parents and Reverend Butler. It was agreed the ceremony would be held in the house as soon as possible, depending on the unfolding event—perhaps within a week or ten days. Everyone that was now sharing the experience of God's work would attend the wedding.

Lyle and Teresa knew that within the next two days after Summers filed the news release, their plans may have to be changed to contend with some large obstacles. But both being positive minded, they were sure things would work out.

She squeezed his hand. "Lyle, I know you're constantly thinking about going down into that hole. I'll be praying for you every second."

"I know you will." He lifted her hand and kissed it. "I'll need your prayers and those of everyone here. But I'm confident of my mission, and anxious to get started. God wants me to succeed. Am I nervous? No. Other than having a huge flock of butterflies in my stomach, I'm rock-solid calm." Smiling, he stood and pulled her up. "I've got to return to the rig and let Carew or Red have his work break. Parker and Cook think we're getting close to breaking through the limestone. Perhaps in less than two hours. I'll talk to you again after we set the casing and cement it into place. It'll take about two or two and a half hours to dry. That means it could be about 5:00 or 5:30 p.m. before I descend. There'll still be two hours of light."

"I love you so very much, Lyle, and I'm so proud of you."

"And I love you, more than I can adequately express," he answered. "I'll come back here after the cement is poured, and we'll have a couple of hours to relax and talk. It's now the hottest part of the day—stay in the shade with your mom and the others." He winked at her and walked toward the rig.

AT APPROXIMATELY 1:05 P.M., Clayton got a call from Charlie Kent on his cell phone, telling him that he and Cal Owens, following in his truck crane, were about twenty-five minutes away; that is, if the heavy traffic continued to give way to the flashing lights and sirens of their trooper escort. The well driller was pleased that Kent was on schedule. Clayton had told him that someone would meet them at the farm entrance gate and lead them back to the bean field.

Parker then told his crew and John that the casing would be arriving soon. It would be a good time to have a fast lunch and be ready to help Kent and Owens back their trucks across the wheel pads to the drill site. While Parker shut down the rig, John motioned to Stanton and Tobias and walked in their direction. He asked them to meet the two special heavy vehicles at the farm's main entrance and guide them to the bean field. They hurried away.

Lunch consisted of sandwiches, potato salad, and fruit—good, but quickly eaten. Parker and his crew returned to the rig just as the faint sound of diesel truck engines came to them from the access road to the farm fields.

"Well, men, there they are," Parker said. "Kent and the casing will head in first; then Owens will follow. Lay the wheel pads just like we did for the drill rig. Carew, you and Red do that. Lyle will show them the parking positions I pointed out. I'll keep drilling and shut down if you need me."

The bit was soon turning again. Parker glanced at his watch and noted it was 1:55 p.m. Even if things went well and they soon drilled into the cave, pulled out the stem and bit, lifted the casing and eased it into the hole, and cemented the casing into place, it would probably be too-near nightfall to send Lyle down. The well-driller had already determined there must be enough light to ensure a safe operation. Lyle would have two flashlights that would suffice during his descent into and ascent from the hole and while in the cave, but adequate light on the surface around the rig and the hole entrance was the most important—especially if there was an emergency. Parker would have to see how the next two or three hours played out.

Within forty minutes, Kent's trailer truck had reached its predetermined parking spot, with the rear end of the trailer within twenty feet of the rig and at a right angle to the hole. In another thirty minutes, the truck crane was parked opposite the rear of Kent's trailer at about the same distance from the hole, its crane pointing at the casing. When time came to off-load the large steel pipe and set it in the hole, Parker felt there would be no appreciable problem.

The drill bit broke through the ceiling of the cave at 2:23 p.m. The hydraulic pressure decreased, and the rotary speeded up. Parker quickly shut everything down. Carew and Red were nearby and immediately saw his excitement. They knew they had hit the target. Red trotted toward Kent's truck cab where Lyle, Kent, and Owens were talking. He shouted out, "Hey, guys, the eagle has landed!"

With smiles on their faces, they intercepted Red, and the four of them went to the rig in a hurry. Parker was wiping his hands on an old rag and grinned. "Well, we did it without breaking a drill bit." He patted the rig's control panel. "Old blue came through with flying colors." All six men stood there in silence for several moments, each thanking God.

All the others quickly appeared at the drill site, smiling and congratulating Parker and his popular three-man crew. Their mood was noticeably upbeat. All six clerics were there—several staring at the hole with a trace of wonder on their faces, the others with bowed heads.

At the moment, the growing, distinctive sound of a helicopter was heard by all of them. They looked to the south and saw that it was perhaps a quarter of a mile away, flying straight toward the rig.

John was standing beside Brandon Cook and Jim Summers, as they watched the blue and white helicopter slow down and pass slowly off to the left side of the bean field. John guessed it was at an altitude of four hundred to five hundred feet, and keeping a distance of about two hundred yards as it began to circle around the drilling site.

"It's WPCF-TV News," the editor said. "Someone called and convinced them to come take a look. They're taping us right now, and I'm sure they now know there's something very unusual here. The newsman or newswoman in that chopper smells a scoop. It won't be but a few minutes before they head back to their station and start preparing a story. Right now, they're fishing, but will present the beginning of an investigative report tonight on the six o'clock news, that will keep viewers in several counties glued to their TVs for the next day or days—others will jump in their cars and come this way. The 'flying reporters' will be back tomorrow, hammering away. It's important that we move fast—get them to delay for at least twenty-four to thirty-six hours until I file the general news release—to prevent them from pouring gasoline on the already smoldering rumors that are beginning to spread. They don't realize they're looking at the biggest story that's ever happened in this country."

John looked at the circling helicopter again. "I think you're right. We've got to keep them quiet, at least for tonight, and hopefully, until tomorrow night. But if they force the issue, we'll have to take what comes, and keep going."

"I'm going over to one of the canopies, sit in the shade, and call WPCF's station manager and lay out the general facts to him about what's going on—how and why we need his cooperation and how Governor Ashton and President Burke are already taking action," the editor said. "Then, ask Ralph Tobias to call Washington and ask Secretary Beretti to inform the White House we need an immediate no-fly zone established over the farm. The Federal Aviation Agency will have to handle that, but they'll need to be urged by the president to move fast."

John looked at the circling helicopter, with the big WPCF NEWS logo on its fuselage, and headed over to the rig to tell Lyle and Parker about what Summers was doing. After that, he would tell Sara and the others at the canopies. Those at the house would be told that night how curiosity and rumors were quickly spreading.

In the meantime, the helicopter made two more circles around the farm, then turned south toward Panama City.

It wasn't long before Summers returned and told John that he had talked to WPCF's news director and station manager. He said that although they initially balked and emphasized they were within their rights to follow up story leads as they developed. Both TV station executives were told why details of the farm events had to be guarded for the next day or so; the editor emphasized that the governor and the president were involved. That got their attention, and they relented.

Summers added another detail—that he agreed to allow WPCF access to the site immediately after the initial news release. He looked at John and said he hoped that was acceptable. Kelly nodded and put his hand on Summers's shoulder, smiled, and told him all of the press-coverage details were his bailiwick alone.

THE DRILL STEM AND LARGE bit were retrieved, dismantled, and stowed. Parker retracted the stabilizer outriggers and moved the rig forward fifteen feet or so to provide more working room for the crane.

He conferred with Kent and Owens for several minutes, with Owens assuring the well driller his crane would have no trouble handling the thirty-foot casing. The rugged lifting mast on the four-ton truck had a maximum capacity of eight thousand pounds; the casing weighed approximately four thousand pounds. He attached four-foot cables to the six lifting ears of the casing and hooked those to a two-foot-wide inverted heavy steel cone with six connectors at the end of the main lifting line of the crane. The arrangement ensured that the casing would hang exactly perpendicular when moved over the hole.

Carew and Red helped Owens secure all the lines to the casing. Kent got into his truck and slowly drove it forward after the casing was lifted to approximately a forty-five-degree angle, allowing its bottom end to slowly slide off the trailer bed. The crane continued lifting the big steel pipe until it slowly swung free of the ground and hung vertically, approximately one foot off the ground, making it easier for alignment with the hole. The maximum length the crane could handle was thirty-seven feet, thus leaving a five-foot clearance at the top of the mast—close, but workable. Owens slowly backed the crane and the hanging casing toward the target. Carew and Red stopped him exactly over the hole. They were now ready to lower the casing. It was 3:25 p.m.

Lyle, Carew, and Red stood at equal distance around the casing, with their gloved hands lightly on its surface. They would try to prevent the big piece of pipe from sliding down one side of the hole, keeping it centered so that its lower end didn't shave off large amounts of soil.

Owens would lower the casing very slowly to its resting place on top of the limestone. He and Parker had discussed the casing load factor with Brandon Cook, who felt the density of the stone was compact enough to provide adequate support. But this was pure educated speculation, nothing more.

As he stood off to one side of the busy area around the crane and rig, John was so focused on the preparation of the casing he was startled when Sara's voice broke through his concentration. She had quietly walked up and stood beside him.

"It's amazing when I think how our minds and daily work activities were totally consumed by this farm until a little over two weeks ago. Now, we're standing in the middle of our 'used to be' beautiful bean field, doing God's work and praying that we succeed, knowing our farming days have passed." He looked down into her upturned eyes, smiled, and reached for her hand.

"Just think, my wonderful wife, out of all the people in the world, the Lord chose our family. The feeling is wonderfully beyond description."

Parker's deep voice asked everyone please to keep back twenty-five or thirty feet from the suspended casing. They readily cooperated and stood attentively, silently praying as the pipe moved slowly downward into the hole.

The casing wobbled slightly two or three times as it descended, but Lyle, Carew, and Red managed to keep the lower end of the nearly two-ton steel tube from shaving the side of the hole. Within twenty minutes, it stopped moving.

It had come to rest on the limestone ledge. Getting signals from Parker, Owens still held tension on the cables to make sure the heavy load wasn't suddenly dumped on the limestone base. That would only increase the pressure on the limestone and possibly cause it to crumble and seriously damage the hole into the cave.

Parker said he was satisfied with events so far.

The casing stood in the hole with about two feet protruding above ground level, which he had earlier predicted.

All of the onlookers were thrilled to be witnessing these lasts steps of preparing the hole for Lyle's exploration. It was nearly 4:00 p.m. There were about three and a half hours of useable daylight left. It was estimated by Parker that filling the slight space surrounding the casing from the bottom up with cement would take about an hour. That would leave two-plus hours for it to set hard enough for the cables to be unhooked and prepare for Lyle's descent.

Parker, John, Lyle, and Jim Summers gathered for a few moments to discuss whether to start the exploration just before nightfall.

"Jack Stanton talked to Captain Ackerman a couple of hours ago and was offered the use of several floodlights mounted on stanchions that we could use on the ground to light up the surrounding area, especially the drilling area," John said.

Parker nodded his head. "And the rig is equipped with several lights. I think we'll be fine. Lyle won't have to worry about the time of day anyway, because it's dark all the time where he'll be. He'll have a big flashlight and a lantern anyway. Right now, me and the crew will connect up the pressure lines for injecting the cement into the hole, and get on with it."

The other three men readily agreed with Parker to keep things moving and explore the hole as soon as the cement had set and the casing was totally stable.

CHAPTER THIRTY-FIVE

"THE SHERIFF SAID I was to take you to the farm if you still want to go, Marvin," said Chief Deputy Beck. "The traffic is steadily growing and becoming a major problem everywhere. Have you looked outside lately? Anyway, about the only way you're going to make it is to ride with me. When can you be ready?"

Gardner's heart leaped into his throat. He couldn't talk for one of his rare silent moments. "I'll be ready in thirty minutes," Marvin finally said. "By the way, can you bring me back tonight?"

Beck was silent for a few seconds, then spoke wearily, "I suppose so, Marvin, but I'll have to drop you off at the farm, return to patrol for several hours, then pick you up afterward. It might be ten or a little after. I'll be by your place in thirty or forty minutes."

Gardner depressed the phone cradle button, then dialed home. He told his wife he had to go to the Kelly farm and would be home late. Even though she asked why, he was evasive, not wanting to tell her just yet what was going on. She was the nervous type, and he didn't want to upset her with even the few details he knew of what was happening at the Kellys.

He had had a strange feeling a week ago when the sheriff gave him a little information about the unusual event that was occurring at the farm. The pharmacist was really keyed up. He was about to be allowed into the Kelly circle.

Marvin told his assistant pharmacist and the young soda-fountain operator that he would be out the rest of the day and asked them to lock up at nine.

MARVIN HAD BEEN in front of his drugstore for ten minutes, pacing around, anxiously waiting. Several people had walked by and spoke to the well-known druggist. They readily noticed his keyed-up manner, which was more than usual.

At 5:05, Deputy Beck pulled up and stopped his blue-and-white patrol car in the street.

The pharmacist quickly got into Beck's car, and they drove north. Gardner had to concentrate on not talking fast. He was fully aware that the deputy didn't particularly care for him, and had many times in the past let him know it. However, Marvin was surprised when Beck was friendly and talkative. In fact, the druggist was speechless when the deputy told him that God was at work at the Kelly farm and it would soon affect the world.

"What do you mean, Dan? Is this about a religious happening, maybe a miracle?" His last question was just a wild guess.

"Yeah, I've not seen the bean field where this is, but Sheriff Bernam has. He said it's powerful, that if anyone ever had doubts about there being a God, this will change their mind and heart in a split second."

"Has it affected you?"

Beck nodded almost imperceptibly, but said nothing.

As they left the city limits, Marvin was surprised at the increasing number of cars moving slowly ahead of them. Beck switched on his flashers, and the traffic slowly pulled over onto the road shoulder when they could squeeze in between other parked cars. But it was slow going anyway. There was a state trooper standing on the highway center stripe every two hundred yards or so, trying to urge traffic on in both directions.

The patrol car began to approach the farm fields, and later, County Road 26. Traffic was nearly bumper-to-bumper. Of those people who had parked on the shoulder, most all were out of their cars, standing, talking, and looking at the farm. Some were standing on car tops, using binoculars.

"Most of Danaville and Graceville must be out here," Marvin said excitedly. "The sheriff told me that Jim Summers has yet to contact the various news services. Wow! What will it be like then?"

"It may get rough around here," the deputy said. He acknowledged the two troopers that were standing at the intersection as he turned onto County Road 26. They waved him on.

Off to the right, near the farm fence line, were two National Guard members manning one of the many perimeter-guard posts. Gardner noticed they were well armed and dressed in full-battle gear. It was another sign to him that the magnitude of the events taking place at the farm was growing. A small shudder ran down his back.

They soon turned into the main gate of the farm. Another state trooper was parked just inside the gate on the side of the road. Two more guardsmen were outside, between the gate and County Road 26. As Gardner looked in the distance toward the house and the surrounding grounds, he saw no other security people, but he knew they must be everywhere. He would learn a lot in the next few hours.

Beck stopped the car on the side driveway with a view of the two barns. Marvin was surprised at the great number of cars that were parked under and around the trees.

He got out of the car; and before closing the door, leaned back in. "Did you say three or four hours?"

"Yep, as you saw, all of us peace officers have our hands full."

"Okay, just checking. One more thing, what happened to that Cuban fella? I called his motel and they said someone checked him out. That seems odd. Is he ill, or did something else happen to him?"

"Marvin, I can't get into that. I have to go. See you around 9:30 or 10:00 p.m."

With that, the deputy turned his car around and drove off. The pharmacist stood there momentarily and remembered he had sized up the Cuban on Sunday when they talked and felt there was something stirring in the shadows. "Oh well," he thought. "I'll deal with that later."

He was mildly surprised to see the sheriff's car. It was parked near the driveway. "Claude's always ready to leave in a hurry if needed," he thought as he walked toward the large back porch of the house.

Granny called out in her distinctive, always cheerful voice, "Welcome to the farm, Marvin. Come join our back-porch discussion." Along with Granny were Arlene, Pat Daniels, and Ruth Tobias.

Gardner waved and climbed the eight steps two at a time to join them, but not to stay very long. He was anxious to see the bean field and the rig.

After introductions, he looked at Arlene for a moment and started to speak. He wanted her and everyone on the porch to know that Enrique Cruz was in town, or had been there. The pharmacist thought the news would embellish his standing. He had no idea it would set off a myriad of negative emotions affecting Arlene, Teresa, and Lyle, and to a lesser extent, the entire family. He could wait until later. His mind was currently focused on what was continuing to unfold in the center of the farm.

Gardner visited a short while, then told Granny he would like to go to the bean field. She knew that was the main reason he had come to the farm, and picked up a cell phone lying in the swing beside her and dialed John.

"Hello, dear, everything still going okay? Good. Deputy Beck brought Marvin Gardner out. He'd like to come see the field and the operation. All right, I'll tell him." She turned to Gardner. "Jim Summers will be here on the old pickup in a few minutes, you'll soon be able to see the most important place in the world. Perhaps later tonight all of us will see whatever it is the Lord has left there for us to find."

All four women understood when Gardner suddenly got up, said he'd see them later, and moved toward the steps to intercept the editor when he drove through the gate. They knew he was keyed up and anxious to see the holy site.

Summers soon arrived, and Marvin eagerly climbed into the truck. With Marvin talking excitedly, the editor turned the pickup around and headed toward the drill site.

Later, when John had shown a part of the circle's edge to Gardner and told him about its size, he was left in mild shock, and as the others, was in awe of what he saw. He understood now the gigantic impact this would make on everyone and their lives. He felt inadequate and weak at first, but now a tinge of revitalization crept into his mind.

Gardner was impressed with the huge drill rig and the truck crane with its cable still attached to a large pipe protruding from the ground. John told him the drilling was finished and Parker was about ready to pump cement into the hole around the casing. In three or so hours, it would be dry enough for Lyle to descend into the cave.

The pharmacist went to church fairly regularly, but he had never gotten into religion as a lot of his friends and acquaintances had. He had a distinct feeling that was going to change.

John excused himself to go talk with Lyle. Marvin walked over to the canopies. All but six or seven of the thirty-two people at the farm were gathered under the canopies to relax and get something to eat while waiting for the big moment when Lyle would be lowered into the black hole. As he walked up, many verbally welcomed him; some waved. He acknowledged them, but headed directly toward Sheriff Bernam.

"Thanks, Claude. I appreciate your help in getting me here. This is breathtaking," he said as he looked around.

"Glad to do it. I always try to keep a promise—now more than ever."

Marvin looked at him for a moment and immediately understood that the sheriff had changed also. There seemed to be a charge of electricity in the air.

THE SUN BEGAN to cast lengthened shadows as the day waned. The Kelly immediate family members—John, Sara, Lyle, Teresa, Arlene, Pat, Paul, Carew, and Red—were sitting together with the six clerics, all involved in quiet conversation. A reverent atmosphere prevailed.

Lyle and Teresa were sitting a little to one side of the family, engrossed in a conversation of their own. Everyone understood and left them alone. They were well aware that Lyle's eminent mission was indescribably unique—one that could never be duplicated. Everyone knew he felt a huge burden. Personal prayers were constantly being said for him. He was reassuring his future bride he would be all right, and that God would be helping him to complete his task. She knew he was right, but still worried about him.

Each of the clerics looked over at the young man and knew of no other person, except a few from the biblical days, who had had a larger burden on his shoulders. All of them, separately and quietly, asked God to guide and protect him.

Time moved along, and finally, Parker got up, looked around at the group, and said, "Well, folks, we're gonna get Lyle into a harness, give him some tools, and send him down the hole. He should be ready to go in thirty minutes or so. Though it's less than an hour 'til sundown, we'll go ahead and set up the generator and light stanchions Captain Ackerman loaned us, and have plenty of light to work by when nightfall comes."

Everyone got out of their chairs, put away soiled paper plates, cups, and napkins, and began to move slowly over to the rig area, preparing for this most important time in their lives. All of them were expectant and keyed up.

Parker had devised an old parachute harness for Lyle. Its straps would comfortably support his seat and torso, leaving his arms and legs free so he could manipulate himself, working with his hands and feet as needed. The suspension cable would be hooked over his head to a three-foot strap attached over each shoulder.

Lyle was equipped with a large flashlight and a battery-powered box lantern, a twelve-foot length of three-eighths-inch nylon rope, a small military folding shovel, short mountain climber's pickaxe, hard hat, a pair of industrial gloves, and a pair of headphones with a small boom mike, very similar to a pilot's headset.

When Parker examined the surface cement around the casing, he was satisfied with its hardness. The casing was stable. He asked

Owens to release the restraining cables, removing them from the casing, and prepare a safety hook on the end of the hoisting line for Lyle's harness. After attaching all the equipment to the harness and putting on his hat and gloves, he was ready.

Teresa was standing several feet away, watching Lyle. He walked over and hugged her, and they kissed, neither one aware of all the eyes fixed upon them. She was quietly crying. He whispered that he loved her and he'd be back soon.

All the clerics moved in closely around Lyle. They each put their right hand on his head or shoulders and fervently asked God to bless him.

While the six religious leaders were praying for Lyle, John and Sara stood close by, holding hands and thinking about their son. They loved him deeply and were very proud that it would be him that retrieved God's gift. John had had a strong feeling for a long time that the Lord had special plans for Lyle.

Carew and Red pulled the nearby dangling hoisting line over and snapped the hook onto Lyle's shoulder straps. Owens engaged the hoist and slowly lifted him off the ground to a height of three feet. Lyle's two co-workers were on each side of him, with their hands on his legs. They positioned him over the casing, making sure the hoist line and Lyle were perfectly centered over the thirty-six-inch hole. Lyle waved and smiled as he was lowered and slowly sank into the unknown.

Lyle had no outward fear of what lay below as he descended. He had turned on his flashlight a few moments before and now played its beam down the pipe, but couldn't yet see the bottom of the casing—or where it sat on the limestone shoulder.

"Hey, Lyle, how you doing?" Parker asked in his distinct bass voice. The sound coming through the headset was very clear.

"Fine, Clayton. I'm guessing I'm about halfway there. I think I'm just beginning to see the base of the casing."

"You've gone about fifteen feet. You should be at the base in about two minutes."

Lyle played the beam of his light downward, and it picked up the hole in the limestone. "Better slow me down a little more,

Clayton. I'm almost there." The descent slowed to a stop just as Lyle's feet touched the rough edge of the entrance hole in the limestone. "I'm there. This twenty-eight-inch hole is going to be a tight fit, but I'll make it. We'll have to go slow."

"You tell me how much, and we'll do it." Lyle entered the ominous black hole very slowly. The wall of the hole was fairly smooth. There were small places where crumbling had occurred, but overall, the bit had done a good job. He glanced at the base of the casing as he passed by. It was sitting on the stone rim perfectly. "I've got about eight or ten feet to go. I can barely make out the cave floor. The best that I can tell is it looks like there's a pile of wet rubble that collected under the hole. Okay, my legs are through the ceiling, and I'm about six or eight feet above the gunk—it looks like a huge pile of mud and small pieces of limestone."

"We'll continue slowly until you're just above the 'gunk,' as you call it. Before lowering yourself onto the pile, take a good look and describe what you see." Parker tried to not let his voice show his tenseness.

Lyle moved the beam of the flashlight around the cave. "This space is fairly large, and except for the mound directly below me, which is approximately eight to ten feet in diameter, the floor is rather flat. The cave is rather smooth and void of formation irregularities, unlike the caves I saw in Jackson County years ago. In fact, this space doesn't look much like a cave. It doesn't look old. I think I'll switch to the lantern. The flashlight is not quite bright enough. I see a part of the wall on the far end that seems to have an indention that's in shadow."

From time to time, Parker would put his hand over the phone mouthpiece and relay Lyle's remarks to the crowd. They were totally focused on what he said.

"We'll let you down easy-like so that you can test your footing. If it's too soft and deep, we can send down some planking for you to make enough of a covering over the soft stuff to allow you to move around under the ceiling hole more easily."

"Okay, but hold up until I take a look around with my bigger light." He unhooked the battery-powered lantern from his harness chest strap and pointed it to the far end of the cave where he had seen a darker shadow, indicating an alcove or at least a recessed area. *Sure enough, there is an alcove*, he thought. His pulse quickened.

"Clayton, I'm going to check out the far end of the cave—about thirty feet away. I'll test my footing on the mound beneath me, then we'll go from there."

Lyle's feet touched the mound. He first thought it was too soft, but as he sank into its surface, it became firmer, and it was soon apparent that if he stood on it, the muddy gunk would only go up halfway to his knees. He could handle that, and told Clayton he was moving off the mound toward the shadow to get a better angle of light from the lantern.

He disconnected himself from the hoist cable and uncoiled more of the phone line to make it easier to move around. As he neared the alcove and pointed the light into its darker area, he saw a large jar or urn. His heart was pounding and cold shivers ran up his back.

"I've found something, Clayton." Lyle slowly moved to within three feet of his find. Under the beam of the bright light, it appeared to be made of clay. It was about twenty-eight inches high and twelve inches in diameter. Its surface was smooth, but it looked ancient, and was sealed with a dome-shaped lid.

Parker held his breath for a moment, then asked, "What is it?"

Lyle carefully described his find.

Parker briefed everyone about what Lyle had discovered. All of them wore quizzical looks and quietly commented to each other, wondering what the significance of a clay jar or its contents might be.

The clerics had huddled and were discussing what the significance of the jar could possibly be, though it did bring to mind a significant religious historical mystery that involved clay jars. Reverends Griffin and Claussen and Rabbi Metz all thought of the two-thousand-year-old Dead Sea Scrolls and how they were found in jars, initially discovered fifty-four years ago in caves at Qumran very near the Dead Sea—but that was in the Middle

East, not in Florida. They thought Lyle's discovery strange and very much like that time.

Rabbi Metz was very knowledgeable about the Dead Sea Scrolls. Some of his work at the Hebrew University in Jerusalem encompassed teaching the history of various important collected Jewish antiquities, and studying the bits and pieces of the mysterious scrolls. They could be seen in the Rockefeller Museum in Jerusalem.

"Is the jar very heavy?" Parker asked Lyle.

"No, I estimate it weighs about twenty to twenty-five pounds. It sure gave me goose bumps when I picked it up." He was enveloped by a feeling of a great power as he handled the jar. He was totally aware that his life and Teresa's and that of his family was now headed in an irreversible direction, controlled by the Lord.

"We've got to figure out a safe way to bring the jar up." Parker was silent for a few moments, then continued, "I have several heavy burlap sacks on the rig—they just might be the ticket. I'll add some weight and send them down with some additional nylon rope. I suggest you wrap the jar tightly with one sack and then put it into the other one for lifting."

Lyle agreed with Parker's idea, and sat down to wait on the bags to arrive. He turned off the lantern to preserve its nine-volt battery, and changed to the flashlight.

The darkness, except for the narrow beam of the smaller light, was thick and heavy. Its quietness was total, except for the magnified sound of his breathing. He looked at his watch. Only three minutes had passed since Clayton had talked to him.

While waiting on Clayton, John came on the line. "How're you making out, Lyle?"

"I'm doing okay, Dad. This experience is making a huge impression on me. It's very different down here, even for a cave. I have a feeling this place hasn't been here very long. You know what I mean?"

"I do. More than likely, it hasn't. Here's Parker. I think he and Carew are ready to send the bags down. Take care, and we'll see you soon."

Lyle carried the jar over to the edge of the mound and sat it on the cave floor.

Parker's voice boomed in his ears. "Lyle, we're sending the stuff down. I think it'll pass by the hoist cable okay, so be ready."

Lyle climbed up onto the mound and stared up at the hole, about twelve feet away. He shined the flashlight upward and soon saw the small perpendicular bundle emerge from the hole. He reached up and grabbed it and told Parker it had arrived. Pulling the bundle and its slackened line, he left the mound and knelt on the floor beside the jar. The jar was carefully laid on its side on one of the large spread-out burlap bags. After unwinding the lengths of nylon rope, he slowly rolled the jar across the bag, gathering the burlap until it was encased in a sort of cylinder. After tightly binding the wrapping with one of the ropes, he sat the jar upright into the other bag. He then bound the outer bag with another length of rope, making it hang vertically. The bundle was then attached to the suspended rope and centered under the hole in the ceiling.

"It's ready, Clayton, haul away."

"We're gonna take it nice 'n' easy," Parker replied. "Here goes."

Lyle watched it slowly disappear into the hole, and then hooked the hoisting cable to his harness. As he was waiting to be lifted to the surface, he shined the flashlight around, trying to file away in his brain's memory cells as much detail of the cave as possible. He was still trying to absorb the reality that he was experiencing.

Within several minutes, Parker exclaimed, "We've got it, Lyle. Give me several minutes, and we'll haul you up."

When the bundle was pulled out of the hole and set on the ground adjacent to the casing, the crowd politely applauded and moved a few steps closer to the hole, staring at the burlap-covered jar, knowing it would be only a short while before they saw God's work.

"Are you ready, Lyle?" Parker asked. "We'll go very slow, especially through the limestone."

"Haul away," young Kelly replied. "I'd like to see more light and have more space."

A few minutes later, his head appeared above the rim of the casing. Everyone cheered and called out, "Atta boy, Lyle, way to go. God bless you, Lyle."

He faintly smiled and gave a small wave. While Carew and Red were helping him out of the harness and patting him on the back, Teresa came over and hugged him. "I'm so proud of you," she whispered.

"It's really great to step out of that black hole and see you," he said.

John, Sara, Teresa, Parker, Carew, Red, and all of the six clerics encircled Lyle and Teresa. They wanted to pay homage to the man who had discovered and first touched God's gift to them and the world.

Reverend Butler asked everyone to join him as he said a prayer of thanks to the Lord for the safe and successful mission Lyle had accomplished, and to give them all wisdom in understanding the purpose of the jar and its contents.

John then suggested they move the burlap-covered jar over to one of the floodlight stanchions so that all details could be examined closely as they unwrapped and opened it.

Parker picked up the bundle and went toward the nearest light, about twenty-five feet away, with everyone following closely.

Carew had picked up an eight-by-twelve-foot tarpaulin that was left over when the canopies were erected. It was spread on the ground for the jar to rest on. Parker sat it down as the clerics, John, Lyle, and all the others stood close by.

Parker cut away the burlap. Once that was done, they all inched forward to get a better view of the light sienna brown jar. John suggested that several of the clerics examine the lid and see how best to lift it off.

Billy Durdin asked Rabbi Metz, Father Walsh, and Reverend Butler to handle that task. The three of them stepped forward, and in a solemn manner, kneeled around it, each carefully examining the lid rim. They agreed there seemed to be some kind of seal where the lid rested on the slight shoulder of the jar. Rabbi Metz put his hands on the lid and tried twisting and lifting it simultaneously. It wouldn't move.

The rabbi leaned closer and looked carefully at the rim of the lid where it met the shoulder of the jar. "I see a bead of what appears to be wax of some kind. It's almost the same color as the jar, very hard to see at first glance. Does anyone have a knife?"

Parker came over and handed Metz a large open pocket knife. The rabbi started working the blade around the bottom of the lid, and soon a hard substance began to flake off. After a couple of minutes, the knife was laid aside, and he again grasped the lid. After one try, he lifted it off and laid it beside the jar. Everyone was very quiet and totally attentive.

The rabbi looked around at the other clerics and at John. He pointed at the open jar. "May I?" his raised eyebrows asked.

"Go ahead, Jacob, bring out whatever is in there," Durdin said.

Jim Summers moved in close and continued clicking away with his Nikon.

Reverends Butler, Claussen, and Griffin, and Father Walsh got down on a knee or squatted on each side of the rabbi so they wouldn't block the view of the group behind them. Metz could see the top of a bundle about ten inches from the top of the jar. He reached into the wide mouth of the jar and carefully lifted it out. It was a rolled-up object, about eight inches in diameter and about twelve inches long, and heavy.

"It's a scroll of some kind," the rabbi said. "It's metallic. It appears to be copper, and it seems in good shape. In fact, it's very similar to the lone copper scroll found along with the Dead Sea Scrolls at Qumran, ;years before. The other clerics were in agreement, as Metz laid it carefully on the tarpaulin beside the jar.

MARVIN GARDNER WAS trying to digest all of the day's events and was almost in a trance. He had witnessed a clay jar from God being brought out of the ground, and its contents extracted and displayed before all of them. His mind was spinning. It was difficult to process the magnitude of the events. He knew there was more to come, and like all the other witnesses, he was aware his life would now be totally different.

He put aside his previous thought of telling Lyle, Teresa, and the others about Enrique being in town. The pharmacist realized now that was not his responsibility, and neither would it be right. But he did think the family needed to know, and he wanted to convince the sheriff they be told.

Gardner left the crowd around Rabbi Metz and walked toward the canopies where Sheriff Bernam was standing off to one side, talking on his cell phone. As Marvin walked up, the sheriff made a "just a moment" sign and continued talking. After ten seconds or so, he lowered the phone and put it on his belt clip. "How're you doing, Marvin?"

"It's amazing, sheriff. I'm euphoric, but at the same time I'm on edge, not knowing where all this is going."

Bernam looked at the pharmacist and replied, "When I saw you earlier, I knew this atmosphere had enveloped you like it has all of us. We are changed for the rest of our lives."

The sheriff was very perceptive and had a strong feeling that Gardner had something else on his mind. "What's bothering you, Marvin? Something you want to say?"

"Yes, I do. There've been so many things happening the past few days—some of them got lost in the mix—but there is one in particular that bothers me: Enrique Cruz. I think you should inform Lyle, Teresa, her mother and John that he's been in town for two or three days."

Bernam looked directly into Gardner's eyes and said nothing for several seconds. "I've thought about it, but things have changed regarding Cruz. The timing is not good now to be telling them about him and what has taken place."

"What do you mean?" The pharmacist asked with wide eyes.

The sheriff felt he owed Marvin an explanation because of his cooperation in keeping quiet the past three days about activities at the farm. Given the timing of all recent events, and the soon-to-be news release to the world, he knew Gardner could be trusted.

"He was picked up last night in the woods just south of the farm, acting very suspiciously. He had pistol on him and couldn't explain what his intentions were. He's now in jail and will be held until we can figure out what his problem is and what he had in mind. I offered him a call to his company and to an attorney this morning. He said he had no desire to contact either."

Marvin had been hanging onto every word. It was apparent the sheriff was letting him in on some very classified information. The pharmacist knew that he'd never share it with anyone. "What will happen next?"

"Since this is sort of an odd case, I don't know. Cruz told me this morning that he'd been married to Arlene, the mother of Lyle's fiancée, Teresa. He claims she turned him out, and Teresa and Lyle were responsible. I have a hunch he was out for some kind of revenge—for whatever reason—and it probably was directed at all three. The man is desperate and it's evident he has some large psychological problem. Perhaps he's had one for a long time."

They talked for several minutes more, then the sheriff said he had to pick up Jim Summers so that the editor could file the initial press release about the miracle.

The sheriff soon met Summers and they walked directly to the blue and white patrol car parked behind all the other vehicles under the trees. Within two hours, the world would begin to learn about the awesome event at the Kelly farm.

EACH OF THE clerics was recalling the level of his knowledge of the Dead Sea Scrolls. Rabbi Metz was the most knowledgeable, but Reverend Claussen and Father Walsh had had also extensively studied the scrolls over the years.

They reflected on the find in front of them—a clay jar containing a copper scroll, brought up from a Florida cave—the similarity to the Qumran discovery was staggering.

All of them remembered that the original copper scroll, discovered in Cave 3 near Qumran, had been on a rock shelf, along with many other jars that held the largest single cache of important biblical scrolls found in any of the other caves. That

lone copper scroll was an accounting of many treasures and
their locations. The treasures were never found, but reference
was made to a second copper scroll which was never found.
Could this be it?

The rabbi could readily see that the scroll in front of him was
in very good condition. The fact that the copper showed no
oxidation was not only a good sign but was also amazing. The
absence of a patina was proof to Metz that the scroll was not old.
He was convinced it had been recently made by God and placed
into the cave.

Everyone was transfixed as they listened to the Rabbi and
watched as he continued to slowly unroll the miracle scroll, carefully
looking it over. He was in tears from his joy as he felt the cool
copper in his hands, knowing it was God's work. He looked at
some of the clerics around him, along with John, Sara, Lyle, and
Teresa, and saw they too were wiping their eyes. A Hebrew dialect
was used in writing the scroll, and Metz saw immediately that it
was an accounting of items, with comments and locations, but
needed careful scrutiny and interpretation

"This must be guarded with our lives. I suggest that all of you
come by and see it up close, then we should put it in a safe place
under lock and key until it can be deciphered and fully understood.
I suggest we invite one or two Dead Sea Scroll scholars, perhaps
from Jerusalem or elsewhere." Everyone agreed with the rabbi.

As the large group slowly filed by and looked down at the
partially opened scroll, with its dull sheen reflecting the nearby
stanchion floodlight, John, Jack Stanton, Reverend Butler, and
the other clerics gathered off to one side to talk.

John spoke first, "Captain Stanton and I have concluded that
the scroll and jar should be put in a large lockable metal footlocker
I have. It's in a storage room located in the smaller barn. It'll be
much more secure there."

"I'll speak to Captain Ackerman and request a two—or four-
man around-the-clock guard to be posted at the barn," Stanton
said. "I think the scroll should be escorted from here to the barn
by the clerics and two National Guard troopers as an honor guard.

We could use the big truck." He looked around, and when he saw approval on all the faces, he pulled out his cell phone, called Ackerman, and got an immediate okay.

It was 8:40. The day had been long and emotionally draining for everyone. Parker and Carew had placed a temporary cover on the casing opening, making sure it was rainproof. Though it had been overcast since midafternoon, the latest weather report forecast no rain overnight. But the big well driller had learned the hard way that Mother Nature wasn't always predictable.

Everyone headed for the house, leaving the posted National Guard troops to secure the site.

CHAPTER THIRTY-SIX

I T TOOK THE sheriff and the editor about forty-five minutes to reach Railroad Avenue and the *Mason County News* office. Normally, that trip would have been no more than ten minutes or so.

Both men had been surprised at the traffic on 77, and in Danaville it had become much worse. Various license plates from Jackson, Bay, and Holmes counties, and a number of Alabama cars, were spotted. "I hate to think what this is going to be like after you send that press release," Bernam remarked. "How long will this take?"

"Well, I need to process a few photos and scan three or four to send with the release. It shouldn't take long to put the facts of the find into the format I've prepared. I'd say an hour, or an hour and a half."

"You said in the car that this will be filed with the International Press Network, and they take it from there?"

"That's right. They won't ignore this story, even though it comes from a small-town newspaper in northwest Florida. This release is going to turn on the news media's lights all over the country. And I expect to receive some immediate calls for confirmation. I'm including my cell phone number in the release."

The sheriff sat down and picked up a recent fishing magazine. "Well, I hope you haven't put too much of a load on yourself."

Summers walked down the hall to his photo lab and started processing the roll of film that contained shots of jar being pulled up, unwrapped, and opened, and several views of Rabbi Metz unrolling a portion of the scroll.

Claude had looked through a second magazine, put it down, and glanced at his watch. It was a little past 9:30 p.m., and he suddenly realized he was tired—real tired. It would probably be after midnight before he got home, and more than likely he would only get a few hours' sleep.

He thought, "Here I sit, waiting for the world to be told about God's awesome acts, and I should be out making contact with other lawmen. Maybe I can hurry Jim along." The sheriff got up and walked down the hall until he saw a closed door with "Lab" painted on it in a semihaphazard style. He rapped lightly on the old wood. "Hey, Jim, can I come in?"

The door opened, and Summers smiled. "Sorry, Claude. I sometimes get carried away when I'm in here and forget everything else. Come on in."

Bernam chuckled. "Seems to me you've got a bird in the hand, editor. Every time things get rough, or you get tired of being around people, you can just duck in here."

Summers walked over to a table where about a dozen or so three-by-five-inch color prints lay. "Actually, I do that every great once in a while," he said with a slight smile on his face.

The sheriff was impressed with the sharp, detailed photos. "I hope they look as good as they do now when they're received by the International Press Network."

"IPN has first-class computer equipment, and the several photos I send will be sharp. It won't take long now to get everything together and send it to the eyes and ears of the world."

They returned to the Jim's office and he sat down at his impressive-looking computer with a large monitor screen. It was flanked by a scanner and printer. Bernam looked on as Summers opened a folder, took out three pages of notes, and laid them beside his keyboard. He turned on the computer and brought up a previously prepared e-mail news bulletin format and typed in information from his notes and added the New York address of the International Press Network with an alert to the night manager. The editor then scanned three photos and made them as attachments to the completed news bulletin and sent the story on its way.

Letting out a long sigh, Summers turned to the sheriff. "Well, that's it. Once they feel the story has merit, I think they'll send it on to their 240 worldwide news bureaus, asking them to stand by until they get solid confirmation."

"How long will it be, you suppose, before the phone starts ringing?" Bernam asked.

"I don't think it'll be very long. I have a feeling there'll be a few doubtful but curious callers first, but it'll pick up soon after. I did state in the release that the airspace over the farm is off-limits to all aircraft, per the FAA. That in itself will raise some hackles and help to slow down the overaggressive newshound types."

"Just like any profession, the news media has those that go to extremes," the sheriff commented.

"Yep, there're all kinds out there, and it may get ugly at times for all of us."

"Jim, you can't handle all the phone inquiries and face-to-face confrontations that are going to take place."

Summers looked at the sheriff for a few seconds, then responded, "Claude, I'm going to do all I can to work with the media, but our first priority, as I see it, is to protect the family and all events occurring on that farm."

"There's one thing about all this," Bernam said. "We've got a great group of dedicated people working together. That sure makes me feel good."

"Me too. I suddenly realized, on the day I flew over the farm, taking pictures of that circle, that my life had changed forever. I knew that I had truly become one of God's servants."

"I feel the same way, and everyone at the farm does too," the sheriff said as he raised his big body out of his chair and stood. While stretching and stifling a yawn, he remarked, "I'd better check in with my deputies and see how they're doing."

"While you're doing that, I'll call John, Stanton, and Tobias and let them know the press release has been sent. Stanton will notify the governor, and Tobias, the White House. I have a cot, bedding, and a small fridge and hot plate in a back room—I sometimes do my best work late at night—so I'll stay here to receive phone calls. It's going to be a long hectic day tomorrow."

"I'm going home and sleep for a while. If push comes to shove, call me; otherwise, I'll be here by seven. By then you'll know whether to stay here, or if I can take you back to the farm."

With that, the sheriff left for home.

"WHA . . . WHAT'S THIS?" Ceci Chan exclaimed as she read the e-mail news release from Danaville, Florida, on her computer screen. She brought up the photo attachments and said, "Wow!" After printing the five pages, Ceci grabbed them and hurried down the hall to Tom Gordon's office. It was 10:50 p.m., eastern time.

"Take a look at this," she said as she barged into her boss's office, holding the pages out to him.

Gordon was the night managing editor and a seasoned newsman. As a fifty-five-year-old, he had thirty years in the news business—eleven years with IPN. He had seen it all, in twelve years as a correspondent and seven as an editor for a Midwest daily. Of average height and slightly portly, Gordon was balding, had a calm face and manner, but had a well-known dedication to the print-news business. He was highly regarded in his profession.

"What do you have, Ceci?" he asked, halfway interested as he took the pages.

"This just came in from a biweekly-newspaper editor in Danaville, Florida, wherever that is, in the northwest part of the state, I think. His name is James E. Summers."

Gordon read the report and carefully looked at the photos. He stood up, still looking down at the pages spread before him. "This is a grabber! Tell the staff there'll be a meeting in the conference room in two minutes."

As Chan left the room, He was already focused on the task ahead. Tom had reported wars, disasters, and homicides, but like reporters for centuries before him, had done nothing like the news release on his desk. The key to the facts, as outlined in the details presented by editor Summers, was the revelation that Florida Governor Ashton was active in preparing to protect the Kelly family and the holy site. Also, and even more important, was how President Burke had committed his support. "This is the biggest happening ever in this country's history," Gordon thought.

Gino Antonelli, an editor, along with three writers—Bert Layton, Jerry Spacek, and David Baer—walked in. Ceci hurriedly followed ten seconds later. All of the staff except her had quizzical looks on their faces; it was very rare that they had such a quickly called staff meeting.

Gordon was sitting quietly in his chair at the head of the table, looking down at an open folder with several pages as his staff found a place along each side and sat down.

"What's up, Tom? Something big in the works?" Gino asked.

He looked up, removed his reading glasses, and scanned the faces of each of his staff. "We've just received an extremely important news release from a small town in northwest Florida called Danaville. The editor, James Summers, of the *Mason County News*, a biweekly, sent the story to us for national and international distribution. There are three good color photos along with a very cryptic yet informative description of a miracle that occurred two and a half weeks ago. They managed to keep it quiet 'til this afternoon, when they discovered a copper scroll. This event is shattering. But my guess is, it's just the beginning. Each one of you carefully look at this information."

He passed the folder to writer Jerry Spacek. After few moments of silent study, he passed the folder to Gino Antonelli, who carefully studied the material, then passed it on. All of them reflected on what they had read and seen.

"The story is well documented and proven by these photos and believed by the White House and the governor of Florida," David Baer said. "It's solid."

All of them agreed.

Gordon stood up and started walking slowly around the table. "We have to write a lead headline and story and get it on the wire to all major papers within the hour. That means before midnight, Eastern Time. It'll make most morning editions if it's no more than five hundred words. Put a 'more to follow' tag on it. You guys decide who'll write it. As per usual, I want to eyeball it before Ceci sends it. Gino, stand by with me while I call Summers." He stopped and looked at the others and said, "Let's go!"

Antonelli followed Gordon over to his desk and took a chair, while the others hurried out.

Tom pressed the conference-call button and dialed the *Mason County News*. It only rang twice, then a strong, confident voice said, "Jim Summers."

"Mr. Summers, this is Tom Gordon at the International Press Network in New York. Gino Antonelli, one of our editors is here with me. We're totally amazed at the release we received from you less than an hour ago. I don't have to tell you how huge the news is and what an impact it's going to make. It's now being prepared for immediate distribution. Hopefully it'll make most major morning papers."

"It's nice to talk with you, Mr. Gordon. All of those on the farm realize the implications involved, and are ready to deal with them. They are fully aware that most anything could happen once the nation reads their newspaper or watches the TV news. I estimate the timeline to be twenty-four to thirty-six hours before masses of people start showing up in Danaville, trying to get to the farm, with all kind of agendas. It'll continue to get worse as days go by."

"We'll work with you any way we can, Mr. Summers. IPN will send a lead newsman from our Atlanta bureau, with one or two support people yet to be determined. I want to come also."

Jim told them that hotel accommodations or housing of any kind was very limited and would soon disappear once the national and international news media started flooding in. Hotels in Panama City, Pensacola, Tallahassee, or Dothan, Alabama, would be available, but transportation to Danaville and the farm would be a huge problem—unless they chartered a helicopter and found a place to set down near the farm.

Gordon commented he would look into that possibility. Also, he and his crew weren't beyond using army half-shelters or even all-weather sleeping bags and camping in some field or whatever—he'd done it before in his career, as had the others, even under life-threatening circumstances.

Before hanging up, Summers told the IPN editor that all press representatives would be issued ID badges by the State of Florida at the farm's main entrance gate when they presented their credentials.

Gordon said he understood, and that he was looking forward to meeting him and the Kelly family. Summers wished him luck on his trip to the farm and put the phone down.

IT WAS LATE when John, Jack Stanton, and Ralph Tobias heard from Summers. He told them the news release had been sent to the International Press Network, and they had confirmed receipt and were in the process of routing it to the national and international news media.

Tobias immediately called his contact number at the White House, and Stanton got in touch with the governor. Things were moving.

John got the immediate family together, along with the others that were still up, and told them that the news was now out of the bag—it would be widely known by a majority of Americans by early or mid-morning. According to Summers, a few all-night TV news stations probably would have a "breaking news" announcement between one or two in the morning.

The intense feeling of the events increased among all of them. But they were thankful that people everywhere would soon know of God's work, though it could inevitably lead to various threatening problems for the farm.

The senior Kelly had received word earlier from Jack Stanton that six FBI agents had checked into a motel right off I-10 on 77. They would monitor the overall security situation for the farm, and any foreign visitors, including any international representatives of the press, and keep the attorney general and the secretary of defense informed. John wondered how they were going to get around. But then realized the FBI always had the means at their disposal.

It was 11:45 p.m. when John walked out of his office and got into bed. Sara had been asleep since eleven. Other than a few faint car horns on 77, everything was quiet. Though he was very tired, he prayed that all the things his family had done and those things they were to do would please God. Sleep came quickly to him.

THE ATMOSPHERE WITHIN the news departments of the major newspapers was one of complete mayhem. Some of the Eastern papers had received the IPN release at the last moment, their night editors barely making their deadlines for the morning editions and inserting the fantastic story onto their front page. Others would have to wait until their next edition—they were scooped. Those in the Central, Mountain, and Pacific Time zones had plenty of time to place the story in a careful, eye-appealing layout, leading the front page with a bold headline and one or two photographs. The large newspapers were quickly making plans to get their best reporters to the site as soon as possible. Smaller papers would line up freelancers or various news bureaus located in Florida, Alabama, or Georgia.

The three major TV networks and cable news companies, received the story and immediately put it on air as major breaking news. Midnight wasn't a choice time for news of that magnitude—most of their East Coast primetime viewers were in bed. But it was a start, and the early-morning news programs would reach millions. All of them were already contacting their daytime producers and editors, and scrambling to get their field news people to the Kelly farm as soon as possible.

Because the International Press Network had given Jim Summers's name, address, phone number, and e-mail address as their source, his phone started ringing right after he dozed off. He knew there would be phone calls, but not so soon and not so many, that late.

Jim answered the first one, cautiously—not knowing quite what to expect. He had decided to hold off answering any questions until the next day. Sleep would be hard to come by, but he was determined to get as much as possible.

"Hello, Mr. Summers. This is Dave Parker of the *New York Clarion*. I apologize for the late call, but your release is awesome, and you realize, being a newspaperman, how important time is to a story—especially this one."

"Mr. Parker, I'd really like to accommodate you, but frankly, I'm too tired to talk right now." The editor saw his other two lines light up. "Please call back after eight in the morning. There'll be several of us to accept calls then."

"But I need information now." Parker's voice had a slight edge to it. "Surely you understand how big your story is."

"Yes, I understand how big my story is. I'm deeply involved in it. Call back in the morning."

Jim hung up and punched one of the blinking buttons. It was the *Miami Sun* wanting more details, etc. After taking two more calls, he realized he had made a big mistake by allowing IPN to tag their release with his name and telephone number—a big mistake. He hadn't realized how tired he was. Without letting his conscience get in the way, he pulled the phone connection plug and went to bed. He dozed on and off for two hours and woke up at 2:50 a.m., wide-eyed and frustrated.

CHAPTER THIRTY-SEVEN

TUESDAY NIGHT, WHEN Enrique had not heard from the attorney again, he realized that Frank Bovitch and Alejo Gomez had abandoned him. They had used him to help seal the Panama City Beach deal and pretended his other calls in northwest Florida were important. It was now clear he had been used and discarded—he was on his own.

"Why am I in jail?" His thoughts were whirling, making him dizzy. "I was doing nothing wrong when they arrested me. Okay, so I was carrying a gun—they can't prove anything. Everyone is against me. It all started when that Lyle kid came into my home with Teresa and convinced Arlene to run me off. I've got to get out of this hole and go to the farm." The Cuban's psyche continued to crumble.

Deputy Williams, who was on jail duty for a few more hours, was sitting at his desk, working a crossword puzzle and drinking coffee. He was suddenly startled by loud cries from his only prisoner. He quickly left his desk, failing to put his revolver in the drawer, and unlocked the master security door to the cell block, and hurriedly walked to the Cuban's cell.

Cruz, on his cot, was moaning loudly and holding his right side. The deputy was tense and very nervous. He had never experienced a wailing prisoner with a medical emergency.

Williams asked what was wrong as he unlocked the door and walked into the cell. Enrique exclaimed in grunts, between clenched teeth, that he was having sharp pains. The deputy immediately thought of appendicitis, and was momentarily uncertain what to do. He walked a few steps toward the cot, trying to calm his prisoner down.

The Cuban suddenly leaped off the cot and drove his body into the officer, knocking him back into the cell bars with such a surprising force that his head struck the steel doorframe and he was badly dazed. Williams slipped to the floor, tried to reach for his prisoner's leg, but missed. Cruz bent over and yanked the revolver out of the deputy's holster, his mind focused only on getting out of jail and finding Lyle Kelly.

He had made no plans as to how he would accomplish the latter. He was breathing hard as he went through the open cell door and ran down the hall, past several empty cells, and through the master security door into the office section of the jail. He stopped for a moment to get his bearings, then stepped into a large hallway, where a stairway led down to the main floor.

At that time, Chief Deputy Beck, having remembered a pair of new boots he had left beside his desk, wanted to pick them up before returning to duty. He entered the main entrance of the jail just as a man he did not recognize at first came running down the stairs, holding a revolver. As Beck pulled his gun, he recognized the Cuban and yelled for him to halt. Enrique saw the deputy and ran harder, coming directly toward the deputy. Before Beck could set himself, the Cuban smashed into him, spinning the officer aside.

Just as Cruz neared the jail's main entrance, the deputy yelled again for the Cuban to halt. Beck knew he must not let the frantic prisoner get to the street while holding a pistol. He fired his .9 mm automatic, the bullet striking Enrique in the right hip—bringing him down as he crashed through the double doors. The deputy ran up to the closing doors cautiously, and looking through the glass, saw the Cuban on the far side of the walkway, trying to get up. Beck, crouching, pushed through one of the doors.

Cruz turned around in a sitting position and smiled at the deputy. "What's the matter, Beck, have you lost your touch?" He was holding the pistol in his left hand down by his side. His right hand was on his hip wound.

"Put the gun down, Enrique," Beck said. "Don't be foolish. We can still work things out. Your wound needs attention."

The Cuban said nothing for a few seconds, but his eyes were wide open and intense. His expression was that of a wounded wild animal. Beck knew that Enrique was making a decision, and it would be extreme and final unless the deputy could wound him again.

"Life's not worth living around pompous, successful deadbeats," Enrique said. With that, he fired, the bullet buzzing past the deputy's right ear.

Beck fired, trying to hit Cruz in his gun arm or shoulder, but his round hit the extended pistol, and ironically, ricocheted into Cruz's chest—he was dead within ten seconds.

This was the second man the deputy had shot during his career. The first, seven years before in Varnum, wounded a belligerent drunk who had attacked him with a large knife. Shooting the Cuban had him shaking. He had not been trying to kill him, yet fate had ruled otherwise. Beck checked Cruz's pulse, knowing he was gone.

Deputy Williams ran up with drying blood on the side of his neck from a small head wound. He was still a little wobbly. "Oh gosh, Dan, I'm so sorry, so very sorry. I'm to blame for all this."

"Don't worry, we'll sort it all out. What's done is done. A great many law officers acting in good faith have made mistakes." He reached over and put his hand on Williams's shoulder. "Let's sit down and you can brief me just as soon as I call 911 for an ambulance, and then the sheriff and the coroner."

There were two long wrought-iron benches flanking the wide front entrance to the jail. Beck and Williams sat down on one about fifteen feet from the body. The chief deputy took out his cell phone and dialed 911 for an ambulance. He then called Bernam, who was on his way home from Summers' office. After that, he contacted Dr. Pelser, the county coroner, waking him up. It was then 11:30 p.m.

When the sheriff answered, he remarked that he had just been about to phone and check in before getting a few hours' sleep. Dan broke the news to him about the attempted escape and the subsequent shooting. Bernam said in a very serious voice that he'd be there in seven or eight minutes.

Beck then turned to Williams. "Turn your head and let me see the extent of the cut."

"Aw, Dan, it'll be okay. Other than a bump and a slight headache, it's nothing."

He looked at what appeared to be about a one-inch cut on top of a slight bump behind his left ear. "It doesn't look too serious."

Dan could hear the sheriff's siren about three blocks away, and farther, the ambulance. He looked at three bystanders and saw two other people walking up. "Sorry, folks, but you'll have to leave. This area is off-limits to the public." He turned to Williams. "Bernam will be here in about ten minutes. Tell me what happened upstairs."

Williams swallowed hard. "If I had not been so startled when I heard his screams, I know I would've put my piece in the desk drawer, per SOP, before checking on Cruz, but I didn't." When I got to his cell, he was lying on his bunk, his knees drawn up, holding his right side. I thought he might be having appendicitis. I went in and stopped several feet from him. In a second or two, he came off that bunk like a wild bull and drove me into the steel door. The next thing I knew, I was on the floor and he was gone—and so was my revolver." He nodded toward Enrique's body. "My failure caused that."

"Not necessarily," Beck replied. "I believe he still would have tried to go through you, one way or another—he was desperate. If you left your revolver in that desk drawer, more than likely he would have quickly searched for and found it, and the same sequence of events would have played out."

Williams stared down at the sidewalk while a tear slowly rolled down his cheek. He felt down—way down—but Beck made sense. He knew he would have to face a hearing. He could only hope for the best.

Sheriff Bernam parked in his space behind the jail and walked out the front door, just as the EMS ambulance drove up in front. At about the same time, the coroner Pelser pulled up.

The sheriff didn't say anything to Beck or Williams as he went over to the body. After a moment, he turned around with a tight face and looked at Beck. "What happened?"

Chief Deputy Beck gave his boss all the details. Sheriff Bernam was silent for several moments, then said the shooting was justifiable. The two deputies didn't feel any better—they were still feeling anguish, and would do so for a long time.

Dr. Pelser made a cursory examination of the scene and Enrique's body, then informed Bernam he'd do a comprehensive a little later

The EMS specialists put the covered body onto a gurney and rolled it out to the ambulance. Pelser told the sheriff that he'd check with him in the morning as to what would be the final disposition of Cruz. He and whichever undertaker was to be involved should know as soon as practical. Bernam said he would call Gelb Foods the next morning and hopefully tie up those loose ends. The coroner bid them good night and left.

"The Cuban really became unwound," Bernam said. "There were hints of it before tonight, and I concluded he was just a tightly wound ball of string with a few frazzles. One just never knows. Tomorrow's going to challenge all of us. An awful lot people who are just curious, and many others with all kinds of needs and dark agendas, are gathering around us. We've got to be on our toes, and that's difficult when we're all so tired."

The sheriff said he had been bothered as to why Cruz had evidently wanted to kill Lyle and perhaps Teresa and Arlene, her mother—what the connection was between them all. He told Beck and Williams he had called Gelb Foods in Tampa, the day before and found that Enrique's boss was a Frank Bovitz. The Gelb vice president was tight-lipped, but was made aware that if push came to shove the sheriff could subpoena him for a deposition. That made him a bit more cooperative.

Bovitz told the sheriff that Cruz had recently been turned out of his home by his wife, Arlene, her daughter, Teresa, and her boyfriend, Lyle. Bovitz couldn't remember Lyle's last name, but that was immaterial to Bernam. He had the information he wanted.

The sheriff then told his two men that when he met Teresa and Arlene for the first time on Saturday at the farm they used the last name Carter—the name of Arlene's first husband, who was deceased.

"Are you going to tell them all about Cruz, what he was planning and what happened to him?" Beck asked Bernam.

"I don't have a choice. I'll do it in the morning. The news is going to hit them hard. All of them will have a feeling that they contributed to Enrique's actions and death. I've got to convince them that the man had lost his equilibrium, went off the deep end. I'll also ask Arlene about his people, who to contact, and so on."

The three lawmen got up and walked inside, preparatory to going their way for the night. Beck told Williams he'd take him home. He could pick up his car tomorrow. The junior deputy didn't refuse the offer.

The empty jail building was locked for the night. Beck would forward the emergency phone number to his car until 6:00 a.m., then change it back. Another deputy would be on duty then.

Bernam and the two deputies walked to the rear parking lot to their cars. "Dan, do you feel like finishing up tonight? Want to go home and rest?" the sheriff asked.

"No, Claude, I don't think so. I'm better off working. Anyway, we're in a strain for manpower."

"Okay, men, I'll be in touch with you tomorrow. After the trip to the farm, I'll notify Bovitz at Gelb Foods and inform him about Cruz. Maybe they would take care of the expenses of transporting the body to Tampa and his burial—if that's where his people are. I'm sure Arlene will know."

WEDNESDAY MORNING WAS slow in coming. Many hadn't slept well. The night was spent dozing on and off, thinking about the copper scroll and its discovery.

Billy Durdin had told them that Rabbi Metz, along with the Reverend Father Walsh and Reverend Griffin, would hold a short meeting on the back porch or in the backyard at 7:00 a.m., right after breakfast. They would talk about the copper scroll locked up in the smaller barn and its possible relationship to the scroll found as part of the Dead Sea Scrolls about fifty-four years ago.

After a quick breakfast, as they were gathering for the meeting, two helicopters showed up. One—gray and white with a black-and-red Dothan, Alabama, television station logo—slowly circled the farm just outside the set boundary, its cameras undoubtedly running. The other, dark blue with no logo, just ID numbers, came from the southeast toward the farm house, made a slight turn toward the expansive front yard, slowed, and began to descend for a landing.

"It's all right, folks. They're two FBI agents. I got word earlier that they were on the way," Jack Stanton said as he was coming down the back steps to join all the others. "They're going to be our guests for a while. We'll be right back." He, John, and Tobias walked around the house to go meet them.

Two men were exiting the helicopter as John and Stanton walked around the house and down the wide driveway toward the landing area. The engine was idling as the agents quickly walked away from the craft. As soon as the men were well clear, its long rotating blades speeded up; and it quickly lifted off, gained altitude, and headed south.

John noted that both agents were dressed casually, but had side arms on their belts. One was wearing sunglasses. Just like the movies, he thought with a trace of a smile.

"Welcome to the Kelly farm, gentlemen," John said as the five of them met near the front driveway. "This is Captain Jack Stanton from the governor's office, Ralph Tobias, the county attorney, and I'm John Kelly."

As they shook hands, the taller of the two FBI men, who looked a little older than the other and was slightly balding with a ruddy face, smiled and spoke, "That's Agent James Nelson, and I'm Del Magee, senior agent in charge of our squad. We're from the Atlanta office. Four others are in town and will be contacting the sheriff shortly."

Nelson was about five feet ten inches tall, had thick red hair, and a youngish face with light freckles. He grinned broadly and said he was happy to meet John, Tobias, and the captain. He quickly added he was from a farming family in Iowa and was impressed at the looks of the Kelly farm. John responded that he now knew why he admired the young man so much. They all laughed, and the senior Kelly invited them to meet his family, gesturing toward the house. As they walked, Stanton gave them a quick general-status briefing. They listened attentively, knowing there would be more explicit detail a little later.

When they turned toward the backyard, the agents were surprised to see such a large group of people standing on and around the back porch. Magee and Nelson had had only a short briefing by their Atlanta office director because of time limitations, and really didn't know many details about the bean-field discovery or the large number of people involved.

Everyone openly welcomed them. Neither agent had been greeted like that on any assignment they had ever worked. They would soon learn just how different their greeters were and how different this assignment was—the biggest and most important in their career.

They acknowledged the crowd and shook hands with the immediate family and the clerics. Breakfast was offered but refused, Agent Magee saying they had eaten earlier. John surmised they must have gotten out of bed before daylight.

Soon, Billy Durdin opened the group meeting with a prayer, asking God to be patient with them as they searched for the meaning within the scroll and continued to carry out his purpose.

John liked to refer to the large group, gathered together in the backyard, as the "extended Kelly family." They had happily accepted that status. Everyone was expectant as Rabbi Metz, Reverend Griffin, and Father Walsh faced the crowd. A subtle applause of appreciation broke out from the family. Rabbi Metz smiled and held up his hand, and with the other two clerics, nodded his head in recognition of their loving gesture, thanking them.

The three religious representatives spent about twenty minutes presenting facts and figures about the initial discovery of the Dead Sea Scrolls in 1947, found in eleven caves around Qumran, very near the Dead Sea.

Reverend Griffin spoke first. He said that in early 1947, an Arab Bedouin discovered a cave located near Qumran, a community about twenty-five miles east of Jerusalem and very near the Dead Sea. It contained seven two-thousand-year-old major biblical scrolls stored in large clay jars. This startled Bible scholars everywhere. But as ten additional caves were discovered over the next twenty years, each yielding the same kind of scrolls in jars, the race spread among religious academicians to digest the great finds of the first Bible-related writings.

All of the discovered scrolls yielded a vast amount of Old Testament books and references that would make up parts of the New Testament, especially the four gospels, all written on papyrus, leather, parchment, and clay—all except one!

Griffin paused for a moment and scanned the crowd. They were all very quiet and still—totally absorbed in his words.

Everyone leaned forward when Griffin mentioned the copper scroll. He told of its discovery in Cave 3 on March 20, 1952, about one and a half miles north of Qumran. Eight more caves holding scrolls would be discovered around Qumran, but not another copper scroll. The special scroll was significant because the text was hammered on almost pure copper—one of a kind. It was not in a jar on the cave floor, as the others, but alone, on a carved-out shelf, leaning against the wall in two parts. Age had left its mark.

Griffin turned to Father Walsh. The reverend father from Rome was liked by all at the farm. His voice was soft, but he held one's attention when speaking. The reverend's quick, dry sense of humor never overrode his serious side. He gave his audience a short insight as to the information the scroll contained.

It was engraved with a form of Hebrew, listing sixty-four locations where great treasures were hidden, usually beginning with a phrase such as "In such and such location," then an amount of valuables was listed, most of it being gold and silver in large quantities—extremely large. But some jewelry, perfume, and ritual clothing were included.

An example would be the listing of over four thousand talents of gold and silver to be found in cave number three. A talent was a unit of weight that equaled about 75 lbs.

Father Walsh paused a few seconds to let that sink in. He continued by saying that when added up, all the listed treasure in all the caves was between 58 and 174 tons of gold and silver— the latter amount estimated to be $1.5 billion at current prices, but much more in intrinsic value today. Did it exist? If so, who did it belong to? It was never found, but why was the detailed list meticulously engraved on a copper scroll, a surface that would last a long time?

The group was stunned. Some had heard a few details about the Dead Sea Scrolls; others had not.

The reverend father looked over at Rabbi Metz and nodded.

Metz was in his element. He loved to teach, and before him was an eager class, ready for his words. He smiled and started talking in his rich, deep voice, saying that the Dead Sea Copper Scroll, approximately one foot wide and eight feet long, but now in a number of pieces, resides in the Archaeological Museum of Amman, Jordan.

All of the other scrolls comprise about 830 documents, formed from eighty-thousand-plus individual scroll fragments, and are cared for by the "Shrine of the Book," the annex of Jerusalem's Israel Museum.

He told his audience he would begin trying to decipher the script on the newly recovered copper scroll within the next hour, explaining that it was most important to determine, as soon as possible, what God wanted them to do.

They would prepare a place on the floor of the barn with blankets for padding, helping to protect the scroll when it is unrolled. Summers wanted to make sequential photos of the columns of text as well as overall views. The other clerics would witness all facets of handling and recording the text. Reverend Butler furnished a tape recorder to Metz.

The rabbi said it was his impression that the Copper Scroll in the barn, about 150 feet away, was somehow connected to the Dead Sea Copper Scroll. A code was discovered in the text of the latter, indicating more details were continued in a second scroll which was hidden in a detached location. It was never found.

They all looked at each other in bewilderment and back at him, immediately concluding that the scroll in the barn could hold the continuing code.

Looking upward, Metz raised his hands with palms up and asked God for his blessing, then told everyone it was time to go to work. He and the other religious leaders with John, Sara, Lyle, Teresa, Carew, and Summers walked toward the barn.

CHAPTER THIRTY-EIGHT

J UST AS THE first helicopter that morning was departing, another one, plus two light airplanes, took its place. The circling air traffic was growing.

Granny and several others stopped and watched the aircraft until it disappeared behind the large trees. Slightly shaking her head, she commented to the others with a smile that they could just as well be looking at giant dragonflies flitting about. With that said, she, Arlene, and Pat went into the house.

A few minutes before 10:00 a.m., another helicopter appeared from the east, and just before reaching the farm boundary, turned to the north, and began to slowly descend across County Road 26. It landed in an abandoned pasture that belonged to the Pasternaks.

Captain Ackerman was standing on the north side of the bivouac area with one of his platoon leaders, watching the chopper land. He had received a call from Jack Stanton about an hour before that a TV reporting team from Fox News was given permission by the Pasternaks to land on their farm. Ackerman saw that the craft had no logo and knew it must be a charter. Following a request from Stanton, he told the sergeant to send four men to thank the Pasternaks and escort the news team back to the farm.

The captain knew other TV news people from the major networks would start showing up soon, along with those from five or six major newspapers. The foreign news organizations would follow within a day or so. Stanton, Summers, John, and Tobias all agreed that would be the limit. Though news was traveling at warp speed, Summers had contacted IPN again and requested they send out a notification to the domestic and foreign "sensational" press, prohibiting their entry onto the farm.

Several minor confrontations had occurred the day before with people trying to drive or walk along on County Road 26 and the outer east perimeter road; some of them making nasty remarks to the troops at their posts along the fences. If some passions got out of hand from the growing horde of people for whatever reason, or an outright attempt to access the holy site was made, Ackerman prayed that his troops could keep the lid on without anyone getting hurt.

Jim Summers had talked to Gordon again at approximately 3:00 a.m. Wednesday morning, four hours after sending the news release and getting the phone call from the IPN night managing editor.

"This is Summers. I couldn't handle all the calls that were coming in, so I pulled the plug and went to bed. But I'm too jacked up to sleep, and I feel all the calls should be answered."

"Glad that you called, Jim. I started to suggest when I called you that you let us handle all inquiries. I'm sorry I didn't. I know you have your hands full. Why don't you put a message on your answering machine to call IPN for information?"

Summers was relieved. "I appreciate your help, and you're right, this small-town editor has all he can handle."

"I look forward to meeting you. I'll be there, hopefully, before noon." When Rogers hung up, he sat for a moment, thinking about the events on that farm outside of Danaville, Florida. He had an inexplicable feeling that she should get there as soon as possible.

He was not only needed, but he also wanted to be part of the mystery drama being played out. Tom had earlier called and chartered a Lear jet from a company IPN used frequently. He and Gino Antonelli would depart Newark at 8:20 a.m. for Panama City. A helicopter would be waiting there for the twenty-five-minute trip to the farm.

He walked down the hall to the communications department. After briefing Ceci Chan about relieving Jim Summers from the flood of phone inquiries, they collaborated on a fact sheet that she typed, which would serve as a script with which to brief the various print, radio, and television news people when they called. As Tom was returning to his office, he felt he was being guided by an unseen power in everything he was doing—it was strange.

There was a large storage room at the end of the hall. It held several compact hand-carried or survival backpacks with necessary items for living outdoors. They were called disaster kits for covering plane crashes, earthquakes, hurricanes, and other disasters in isolated areas. The kits had only enough military food packs for four days. Rogers wasn't sure what they may encounter around the farm, but he was used to the unexpected.

He had a feeling, however, that this would be a "first."

ON WEDNESDAY MORNING, Sheriff Bernam, after three and a half hours of sleep, picked his way to the farm with the help of the state troopers along 77. It took almost fifty minutes from his house. It was 8:10 when he was waved through the main gate. He dreaded having to tell the Kellys about Enrique's attempt to sneak onto the farm and confront Lyle with the evident intent to kill him, and perhaps, Teresa and Arlene. But the toughest part would be telling them about the Cuban's death.

After parking his car on the side yard under the trees, he walked to the back porch. There were a number of people there, sitting and talking.

"Hi, Sheriff," Granny called out. "Come join us."

Bernam made a slight wave and nodded to the group. He climbed the steps and went over and sat down in a chair next to Granny, Arlene, and Pat. The others were talking among themselves, a few going into the kitchen and coming out with coffee.

"How about some coffee and a doughnut?" Arlene asked. "I'd be happy to get it for you."

It was hard for the sheriff to look into her eyes. "No thanks, ma'am. I've had two cups already—I'm trying to cut back." He was real uncomfortable trying to act as if everything was normal. He chatted a few moments with them, but was anxious to get his unpleasant duty over with. "Excuse me, Granny. Is John around? I need to talk with him."

"He's in the small barn with the clerics, Sara, Lyle and Teresa, and others. Rabbi Metz is trying to interpret the scroll. Go out there and tell them hello."

The sheriff got up, thanked Granny, forced a smile at Arlene, nodded at Pat, and then headed for the barn.

When Bernam walked up, he spoke to the National Guard man on duty, "Mornin', Private. All of you are doing a great job."

"Thanks, Sheriff. This is a strange assignment, but we've been told it's probably the most important we'll ever have."

"I think that's right, Private. I think that's absolutely right. You have a good day." Bernam opened the door and stepped into the storage room. Though the room had no outside window, it was bright with two overhead lights and one of the floodlights from the drilling site. John and the others were standing around the opened scroll, which was lying on a couple of blankets to accommodate its approximately eight-foot length. Rabbi Metz was on his knees, bent over the holy copper treasure, with a large magnifying glass in one hand and a small tape-recorder in the other.

All of them were so intent on what Metz was saying they did not look around when the sheriff entered. He stopped when he saw the dull sheen of the metal. It momentarily took his breath away to know he was looking at an exclusive work of God.

The sheriff eased up close behind John and whispered, "I need to talk to you. Would you step outside with me?"

John turned and looked at Bernam and saw a serious glint in his eyes. "Sure, Claude, let's go."

When they got outside, the sheriff quickly gave John general details about Enrique's arrest and death. John was speechless for a few moments, then reacted. "That's a very pitiful situation. I didn't know him, but it's sad when a human being's mind or whatever self-destructs. I know my family is going to be shocked, especially Arlene and Teresa. You go on to the house and stand by, and I'll get Sara, Lyle, and Teresa and meet you in two or three minutes."

"After you give them the news, I'll have some questions, and I'm sure they will too—especially Arlene and Teresa."

As the three of them walked toward the house, Lyle couldn't hold his curiosity. "What's going on, Dad? Why did Sheriff Bernam come and get you?"

"I'd rather wait until we meet the sheriff, Arlene, and Granny in the living room, then the sheriff will explain everything." Sara and John looked at each other very briefly. Lyle and Teresa didn't notice because their eyes were locked together. Both of them had a vague unspoken feeling it had something to do with Enrique. Teresa reached for Lyle's hand and didn't let go until they reached the porch and joined the sheriff and Arlene.

A few of the others, seeming to know something heavy might be in the works, continued their conversations and pretended to pay little attention to the Kellys as they went into the house.

After they entered the living room, John asked everyone to sit down as he closed the doors. "The sheriff wants to brief you on a serious matter that recently occurred."

Bernam looked at Arlene for a moment. She too felt it might have something to do with Enrique—but how and what? She glanced at Teresa and mentally set herself for some kind of bad news.

"Enrique Cruz, the man you recently separated from, was in Danaville over the weekend." Arlene, Teresa, and Lyle traded wide-eyed looks. The sheriff continued, "Deputy Beck met him early on Sunday morning at a gas station in town. Beck was friendly, but Mr. Cruz seemed on the defensive. Before noon, it happened that he had driven out to the farm—I suppose for a look—then, on the way back to town, had car trouble. My chief deputy came by and arranged to have his car towed in, again noticing a slight hostility."

Lyle had a feeling he knew why Enrique had come to Danaville, and it wasn't just to see the farm to satisfy a curiosity. When he had first met Cruz, there was an immediate feeling that the man was a psycho, but he had kept it pretty well hidden. According to Teresa and Arlene, he had changed for the worse over the past two years. Having been around him on a daily basis, Arlene had told Teresa and Lyle that although Enrique never laid a hand on her in anger, his meanness had been growing over the years when they were alone. She wanted peace in her life, so she turned him out. Lyle's future mother-in-law was now genuinely happy with her new family.

"Where is he now?" Lyle asked.

"He was arrested Sunday night about nine forty-five as he was preparing to sneak onto the farm near the south boundary fence off 77," Bernam replied. "He was carrying a small pistol, and later confessed he was going to confront you. It was apparent to me that the man intended to kill all three of you."

The sheriff glanced at Arlene and Teresa. Both of them sat there quietly, looking down. Lyle got up and walked over to the windows.

It was difficult for Bernam to continue, but it was part of his job to sometimes bear shocking news. "Lyle, I think it best that you come sit by Teresa and Arlene and let me tell the rest of this story." The three of them looked a little puzzled. Lyle had a feeling something bad was coming, but said nothing as he sat down by Teresa and took her hand.

"Late last night, he faked severe sickness and overpowered a deputy. As he was running out of the jail with the deputy's pistol, he refused to stop when warned twice to halt by Chief Deputy Beck, who had just entered the building. Mr. Cruz was just nearing the main entrance doors when Deputy Beck shot him in the right hip, bringing him down to hopefully save his life."

John looked at Sara. Her eyes glistened as she squeezed his hand and looked over at Lyle, Teresa, and Arlene. Granny's heart also went out to them, especially Arlene and Teresa who had borne the brunt of Enrique's insulting personality for years.

"The tough part of my report to you," Bernam continued, "is that when Beck went through the door, he confronted Mr. Cruz, sitting on the sidewalk, leaning against a hedge. When the chief deputy told him to put down his gun, Mr. Cruz fired at Beck, the bullet just missing his head. Beck had no choice but to defend himself and fired, trying to hit Enrique's gun arm, but the bullet hit his gun, and ironically, ricocheted into his chest, killing him within ten seconds. The county is very sorry when these circumstances arise. We regret the loss of life, but reality is reality. It will happen again sometime in the future, no matter how hard we try to prevent it."

The room was quiet for several moments, then Arlene raised her head, and wiping her eyes, said, "Sheriff, I don't for one minute blame the deputy or you. When I married Enrique, he was a nice but quiet man. But after three years, I noticed quite a change. And as the years went by, he became more distant and demeaning. I didn't love him. I guess, like so many others, I refused to admit our marriage had long since failed. I'm so sorry he died, but that's in the hands of the Lord."

She walked over and shook Bernam's hand. Everyone in the room thought she was a strong woman. Teresa hugged her mother, then Lyle, Granny, Sara, and John—in that order. They all thanked the sheriff for his report. Bernam was glad it was over.

John felt the need to say something before they left the room. "You know, I believe that God controls every aspect of life. He has been guiding all the events prior to and during the recovery of the scroll, and all the way to its use for his purpose that we are involved in. No person or persons will stand in his way. Evil people will have no part in our work for him. Praise the Lord." All of them, including Sheriff Bernam, said "amen."

As Bernam, John, Sara, and Granny were leaving the room, the sheriff asked Arlene if he could have a minute, and she was quick to say, "Yes." All the others went out, leaving Lyle and Teresa sitting on one of the couches in deep conversation.

"Arlene, I need your help. I need to know who to contact in order to finalize the disposition of Enrique's body."

She looked at him with her lips slightly quivering. "I know I should take care of that, but I can't."

"I understand the situation, I really do, Arlene. I'm more than glad to handle matters."

"Thank you, Sheriff, I appreciate that very much. He has a brother and an uncle in Miami," she said. "I would talk to his uncle, his father's brother. Enrique and his brother were not close." Bernam noted who to call, and then thanked her, again giving his condolences. Arlene touched his arm and smiled up at him, then joined Teresa and Lyle.

He remembered that he must call Bovitz and tell him about Enrique. He picked up his hat and went to join John, Sara, and Granny.

ON WEDNESDAY MORNING, the major television networks in New York, along with a cable news company in Atlanta, were all desperately tying to get television news teams, their own or that of one of their regional stations, to Danaville. They were incensed that Fox News was already on the scene, having sent a three-man crew from a Tallahassee affiliate early that morning—it was only forty-five to fifty minutes by helicopter.

It wasn't easy getting newscasters, cameramen, and sound engineers with their equipment to a small rural town in northwest Florida. The networks could draw on regional stations for most stories—but this one called for their "A" team. The closest airports that could handle medium corporate-sized jets, and possibly offer charter helicopters, were Dothan, Alabama, or Panama City, Tallahassee, and Pensacola, Florida.

Corporate insider information and gossip constantly traveled back and forth between these broadcast giants and their affiliates. It wasn't unusual for middle-level personnel and a few management types, even broadcast personalities, to move from one network to another. Competition was fierce for scooping a big story. The Kelly farm could be the biggest ever.

It was almost 10:00 a.m. when the Lear began its descent to Panama City Regional Airport. Tom Gordon and Gino Antonelli would meet their Atlanta bureau man at the corporate terminal, rendezvous with their chartered helicopter, and make the twenty-five-minute trip to the Kelly farm.

Gordon looked over at Antonelli. "Does it feel to you like we are entering into a completely different dimension—one we've never been in before?"

His editor slowly nodded his head. "Yes, it sure does."

TERESA AND ARLENE sat in the living room after the others had left and quietly discussed the tragedy. Arlene said a person couldn't live with another for ten-plus years, in spite of tensions, without leaving a little part of herself with the other. She felt sad that Enrique died the way he did, but he had been prevented from possibly killing her, Teresa, and her future son-in-law. She thanked God for that. But regardless of her emotional state, it was very clear to her now that she had a new life—she had been reborn. It would take a while to work out her future, but she felt very positive. She knew the Lord would guide her.

Lyle was thankful that Teresa and Arlene would now be safer, although he and the other family members wondered how the farm events would play out. It could get much worse before it settled down to a stable condition. He thought there was a lot to happen yet.

He went from the negative to the positive by mentioning to Arlene that he and Teresa wanted to get married within the next several days, perhaps on Monday—five days away—if events allowed. They had discussed how their marriage would be truly unique, with a special meaning, by holding the ceremony adjacent to the entrance of the holy cave. Each of them felt it would please God. Lyle had talked to Reverend Butler. He said he would be honored to perform the ceremony.

Teresa moved closer to Lyle, pulling his hand to her mouth and kissing it. He put his arm around her and grinned at Arlene. He said that he had talked to Ralph Tobias about the marriage license. Tobias said he'd take care of it. He would get the county clerk to waive the rule of both parties having to sign the application in the presence of the clerk or an assistant. He'd make sure the county received a copy for their files.

Given the extremes of the morning, the emotions of the three of them had been stretched like a rubber band, and they were drained.

"Let's go to the kitchen and talk to Mom and Granny," Lyle said. "Then I'll go see what's going on in the barn."

They got up and walked toward the aroma of frying chicken.

MOST PEOPLE ACROSS the county had seen and heard the TV and radio special news bulletins Tuesday night, between 9:00 p.m. and midnight, depending on their time zone. They had a difficult time sleeping afterward. Many on the East Coast were unaware of the miracle until Wednesday morning when they looked at the front page of their newspaper or turned on their television or radio to be awed by the story. Only the three photos that were originally sent by Summers to IPN appeared on the front page of all newspapers and on the television news leads. But they were phenomenal.

Phones were ringing constantly at every radio and television station and newspaper across the country. The media explained they didn't have any additional information, that the story was just developing, and they were expecting more details soon. Some people were upset, screaming epithets and accusing the stations and papers of holding back additional details. Other callers, those belonging to extremist religions, cults, and atheist groups, claimed it all was a scare tactic of mainstream religions to recruit members. Some of those callers vowed to take action against the Kelly farm and all others that would perpetrate what they referred to as the "fictional event."

Upon hearing from Jim Summers immediately after he sent the press release to IPN, the clerics called their respective seniors and reported the details of the discovery of the copper scroll. The Light of Christ Crusade immediately started prayer groups. The Methodists and Southern Baptists were joyously awed, and called for special worship services. The Vatican was astonished. The pope would hold a High Mass in St Peter's Square Thursday at noon, Rome time. The worldwide Catholic Church would hold a special mass as soon as possible after Pope Paul's service.

REVERENDS DURDIN, GRIFFIN, and Claussen, and Father Walsh, told their brethren that Rabbi Metz would attempt to decipher the scroll the following morning. The other clerics would immediately tell their respective leaders of all details as they developed.

The rabbi called Jerusalem around midnight (8:00 a.m. there),_and talked with two fellow rabbis that he had worked with—one, involved with the Israel Antiquities Authority; and the other, Jerusalem's Israel Museum. They were shocked, and at first, speechless; but with a quiet reverent tone, told Metz their prayers were with him, the other clerics, and the Kelly family.

CHAPTER THIRTY-NINE

MARVIN GARDNER WAS perplexed as he looked from behind the pharmacy counter at the growing number of people in his store. The soda fountain's six stools were occupied, as were the four booths. He counted nine others who were waiting to sit and order, or just standing around in front of the magazine stand, thumbing through everything on display in spite of a sign stating Do Not Read These Publications Without Purchasing.

The pharmacist was uptight, but knew he had to be tactful—and careful. Two or three of them looked a little rough, and he didn't want any problems in his store, or elsewhere. There were six state troopers, along with a Mason County deputy, patrolling downtown Danaville. But with all the outsiders pouring in, the eating establishments and most stores and sidewalks were teeming with people. Many cars crawled in heavy traffic, looking for a parking place. Marvin realized his staff of three could never keep an eye on all of them. Some of the bad ones could steal him poor before he managed to call a trooper. But he was determined to protect his business.

All the merchants were aware that they were prime targets for souvenir hunters. Whether it was clothing, hardware, shoes, auto parts, toys, or many other items—like the old expression "anything that's not nailed down"—it was obvious that Danaville could be picked clean. A portion of the crowd was there for one reason: to take something from near the Kelly farm to keep as proof that they were there, or to sell it back home as a "blessed" item to some person who could not come to the area.

There were many others who had come carrying their Bibles, only hoping to get access to the holy site, or at least near enough to feel the atmosphere of God's power that had enveloped the farm, and pay homage to him.

Just as it was at Lourdes, France, and other historical miracle sites, there would be many desperately sick and crippled people to come from all over the country—and perhaps from other countries—hoping and praying to be cured.

Some people were forming small groups in and outside the drugstore, praying as well as singing.

Across the street, a large rotund perspiring man had crawled up on the top of his or someone else's car, and was preaching, holding a well-worn Bible in his hand. He was passionate, and many had gathered around, seemingly interested in what he was saying.

A middle-aged blind man playing an old accordion was being led slowly through the sidewalk crowd by a nine—or ten-year-old girl holding an open glass jar. It had a one-dollar bill and a few coins in it.

The six state troopers were patrolling downtown on foot. They had to keep their eyes open and keep in touch with each other by radio. Most of the people on the sidewalks seemed to be courteous, some were not.

As Marvin was literally sweating in his crowded drugstore, he telephoned Fowler's Department Store. George Fowler told him that his place was not as crowded as it had been earlier, but he expected more people at any time. He commented that he never thought he would see a traffic jam on Danaville's streets, or people elbow to elbow on the sidewalks. The town almost had an eerie carnival atmosphere. Gardner agreed and told him to keep in touch.

The pharmacist turned back to his problem. His employees, Carla and Mary Beth, were frantically working behind the soda fountain, trying to fill all the orders. They weren't keeping pace, and some of the crowd was showing impatience.

As much as Gardner didn't like heated confrontation, he knew he had to step in and try to gain some order. He couldn't afford to let things get out of hand. Leaving the confines of the pharmacy, he picked his way to the front of the store. Some of the crowd moved aside to let him pass; others were less well-mannered. In fact, they seem to test him. They didn't know that he owned the place, and couldn't have cared less.

"People, please give me your attention." A few of them stopped talking, but the others ignored him. He raised his voice a few more decibels. "People! I own this drugstore, and you must listen to me!" The noise died down quickly when everyone saw that it was the owner speaking. They also noted that he seemed a little out of sorts.

"Gardner's Drugstore always appreciates its customers, but today, there are just too many of you in here at one time. I must ask about half of you to step outside and give us a little more room and a chance to better serve you. It's up to you. Either that, or I lock the doors."

They realized then he was serious, and if they wanted a place to cool off and have something to eat or drink, they'd better follow his edict. So, slowly and begrudgingly, about a dozen of them went outside, but stood around near the entrance, talking loudly and blocking the sidewalk.

Marvin thought that was much better, but he felt the calm would probably be short-lived. He was well aware that if he did lock up, there was a good chance the rowdy ones would break into his store and loot it. He would have to ensure that all controlled drugs were secured in the special locker, and then he would hope for the best.

SUMMERS CONCLUDED HIS DETAILED PHOTO shoot of the Copper Scroll, section by section, as it was slowly unrolled. He also had photographed the clerics as they were gathered around Rabbi Metz and the scroll to show skeptics that the discovery was verifiable by highly respected men of God and was indeed a miracle. Some of the photos would be released to the press along with comments from Metz late that afternoon, but no detailed information regarding the scroll text. That would remain classified.

The Fox TV crew was the first to come onto the farm. Captain Ackerman's troop led them to the editor, who gave them a briefing regarding what had occurred so far, and a general layout of the farm. Upon being asked about the cave site, Summers said he would have one of the family show them where it was. But he suggested they first go to the barn—perhaps tape the clerics as they witnessed the Rabbi deciphering the scroll.

What he didn't tell them, however, was that Rabbi Metz would almost be whispering, as he read and commented in Hebrew into a hand-held recorder. His voice would be unintelligible to them. The rabbi and the other clerics had earlier agreed that all text on the scroll would be kept classified by them and perhaps two or three others, yet to be determined, until it was safe to publicize it.

Summers led them over to the barn, introduced them to everyone, and left. He wanted to talk to Ackerman about the other arriving news media people.

The editor noted it was almost 11:15 a.m. as he walked toward the National Guard bivouac area to see Captain Ackerman. He passed the back porch and nodded at the group who were sitting and talking.

A helicopter was circling the farm boundary while another was flying east, just outside the north farm perimeter toward the Pasternaks. It soon descended and landed in their pasture, which had been designated for helicopters transporting members of the news media. The editor was pretty sure that it was the IPN people. Tom Gordon had called him from Panama City about an hour earlier.

Jack Stanton had asked Ackerman to keep a couple of National Guard members there during daylight hours to check everyone that landed—ensuring they were news media people.

When Summers arrived at the bivouac, the National Guard Captain met him with a slight grin and a handshake. "Well, well. My troops and their little tent city are finally going to get some long-deserved press coverage," Ackerman said.

"You bet," Summers replied with a smile. "I promise you'll get plenty of press. By the way, I think the helicopter that just landed has three men from the International Press Network that I want to talk to. They'll be the key news people that I'll work with. You might say they'll be my coordinators with the worldwide news media."

"You want my guys to give them a little extra security and see to their living needs, like eating and sleeping?" Ackerman asked.

"That would be greatly appreciated, Ron. Their boss is Tom Gordon."

"I'll send the same four soldiers that met the Fox crew earlier, then assign a full-time two-man security team to Mr. Rogers and his crew."

"That's great. I'll stick around and meet them here."

While waiting for the troops to return with Gordon and his IPN team, Summers had a chance to look around the bivouac area. He was impressed at how exact the encampment was laid out. He noticed the mess tent, a structure approximately fifteen by thirty feet, its sides rolled up to ease the noontime heat. The mess crew was readying lunch to be served at twelve. There were a few off-duty soldiers already hanging around, ready to jump into line when the mess sergeant rang the "clanger."

All of the perimeter guards that had finished their shift at 6:00 a.m. were still in their bunks. They would be fed at 2:00 p.m.

The editor looked at the cows in the pasture, beyond the fence which was fifty or so yards beyond the bivouac. The ten or twelve grazing cows seemed oblivious to all the goings on around the farm, especially their National Guard neighbors.

When Jim turned from looking at the cows, he saw three civilians coming toward him. Their four-man escort had dropped off near the mess tent.

"Mr. Summers?" Tom Gordon asked as he and his two companions walked up.

"That's me," Jim said with a smile. "And you must be the night guru of IPN." They shook hands and immediately liked and respected each other. "I know you three must be tired. You're usually in bed at this time of day."

"We wouldn't have been able to sleep anyway. We've looked forward to being here. In fact, it's an honor," Rogers said. He then introduced Gino Antonelli and Bret Hughes of the Atlanta bureau. Summers suggested they walk to the house and meet the senior Kelly. He explained that John Kelly was the family patriarch, holding everything together and protecting the farm during this trying time.

Just as all the other first-time visitors, Rogers and the other two IPN newsmen were extremely impressed with the farm grounds and the large classic house.

Without yet getting into all of the details regarding the events transpiring at this special place, Rogers, Antonelli, and Hughes were already sensing an inexplicable power that enveloped them.

Lunch was being served as the four of them reached the house. John, Sara, Lyle, and Teresa were coming from the barn. The clerics and the Fox news team followed not far behind. They all met at the back porch steps and were introduced by Summers to the newcomers

The three-man IPN team was warmly welcomed by the family and clerics. Gordon had known that a Fox pick-up team from Tallahassee had preceded his crew by three hours. But Summers had already requested, and Rogers had agreed, that IPN be the official worldwide source for all news coming from the farm. That had pleased Gordon, not only because he would be the one speaking for the Kellys and the continuation of events but he could also keep all media people on a short leash, helping to control the integrity of this great historical, holy happening. He was truly humbled. Even now, he knew it was the most important assignment he had ever had.

After introductions and a few moments of conversation, John suggested they join all the others for lunch. They went up the steps and slowly filed through the kitchen door into the large breakfast area, passing two long buffet tables laden with salads, soup, and sandwiches. This was a far different time for Tom Gordon and would be for all other newsmen coming to the farm.

Sheriff Bernam and Chief Deputy Beck met in the sheriff's office at 11:00 a.m. with four of the six FBI agents that had arrived in Danaville the night before. Jack Stanford had told the sheriff earlier that the team leader of the six, Agent Magee, along with another agent, would be at the farm early that morning to get a status report and to brief him, Captain Ackerman, John Kelly, and the clerics.

Agent Frank Modes was second-in-command to Del Magee. He would do the same as his boss—listen to the sheriff, then brief him about the FBI's concerns.

Bernam welcomed the agents and asked them to please have a seat. Rhodes remained standing. He was over six feet tall, somewhat slim, and his prominent chin, cheekbones, and nose, set off by deep-set dark eyes, gave him an intense look. Yet when he spoke, his voice was low in pitch and volume. He introduced each of his men, then got right on to business.

"Sheriff, we've been informed to some extent, based on early, limited information, about what has occurred at the farm, but we're in the dark regarding what's now happening and what you and the state troopers are doing. We've seen the crowds and experienced the traffic from the motel to the court house, and it's obvious that problem is going to continue to grow, probably on a multistate basis. Please give us all the details of where things stand at the moment. When you've finished, I'll brief you two on the concerns we have."

The sheriff was impressed. He looked at Rhodes for a moment, thinking how straightforward the man was—not a wasted word. Bernam followed suit.

It took about ten minutes to give Rhodes and his three agents a complete rundown of all the things that had occurred on the farm and in town since the storm. He included an overall Kelly-family profile.

When the sheriff had finished, Rhodes and his agents sat quietly for a moment, digesting the enormity of what had happened at the farm. They were astonished, but tried to keep a calm facade. However, both county lawmen could read awe in the four agents' faces.

Agent Rhodes had been leaning against a table in a corner of the rather large office. He straightened up and walked over near the sheriff's desk.

"I want to pass on some information to you from the FBI in Washington regarding bad guys who probably will show up in Danaville and/or the farm in the next one to three days—it could even be later. But we need to prepare quickly. It's according to what group it is and where they're coming from. Living space and roads around here are quickly becoming crowded. Moving around is difficult. More and more religious and nonreligious people will abandon their vehicles and walk—even cross-country—to get here. We have to keep in mind that most of them are very desperate, for whatever reason. In addition to the news media coming and going, the skies will be full of other helicopters and airplanes. We know the Federal Aviation Agency has the farm perimeter under a no-fly zone, but that won't make any difference to some. We want to emphasize that we believe there will be a major incident, from the ground or from the air. The masses of people are gathering in Danaville and the closer surrounding towns, some trying to reach the farm for many dark reasons. For example, one contingent could be militant atheists, wanting to disprove God's miracle. Another could be various cults. But the real threat is Muslim terrorists, being much more dangerous. They would want to destroy the discovery site and the copper scroll, or take the scroll and hold it for ransom from the three major Western religions. That would take more time to plan and execute by them. But we believe their arrogance would be much larger than the reality of their chance of success. Those people don't march to the drumbeat of reason. They are cold-blooded killers and their plans are based on jihad—a holy war. We'll have to make all contingencies. Even if they knew they wouldn't have a chance, they might try it, if for no other reason than to die as martyrs to please their Allah." Agent Rhodes sat down and was quiet, a sign that he had finished for the time being.

Bernam leaned forward and put his elbows on the table, and his fingertips together to his pursed lips. "What can my deputies and I do to help prevent the growing chaos from getting totally out of hand, and to protect the farm, the Kelly family, and more importantly, the holy site and the copper scroll?"

"The FBI wants you and your deputies, along with Captain Stanton of the Florida State Troopers and Captain Ackerman of the National Guard, to work with us in order to establish and carry out an overall plan for identifying certain individuals, surveillance of same, and preventing any attempted aggression."

"Will I still have control of my deputies and discharge my duties as given to me by the county?" Bernam asked.

"Certainly, but the way things are quickly changing in this county as of this moment, it seems to me your responsibility is ballooning. Your usual identifiable clear-cut day-to-day duties would be the same, but your workload is growing fast by the hour."

"Wouldn't trying to identify bad individuals of any kind be like finding the proverbial needle in this growing mass of people?" the sheriff asked.

Rhodes replied, "It'll be difficult, especially due to their number. But we have a plus working for us. This is happening in a rural area—much better than a city. It's very hard to move around unnoticed in this town and surrounding area—and to hide. You and your men know every square foot of this county. That's a big plus."

"In normal times, we can spot general troublemakers a mile away," Bernam said. "But we're going to lean on you for the make-up or identification keys to the American religious anarchists, and more importantly, the radical Muslim terrorists. We know there are basics, such as darker skin, black hair, and dark eyes, but there are many American citizens of Arab or some Middle Eastern background with those same physical traits. I'm sure there will be many that are good citizens and dedicated Christians. We'll do all we can, but it'll be tough, and require a load of man hours to separate the good from the bad."

Rhodes nodded at another agent. "Agent Charles Krause has had a number of years following the deadly activities of Arab and other radical Muslim terrorists in Beirut, the World Trade Center, Berlin, Yemen, Israel, several airliners, and so on. He knows how they think. Chuck, tell these gentlemen what we'll likely have to deal with, and some of the things we've already put into play."

Agent Krause showed his German genes with his blond hair and steel blue eyes. At age forty, he had the body of an athlete, but showed a laid-back demeanor in speech and movement.

"The other agents and I discussed our tasks last night and again this morning, regarding the task at hand. After assessing the location of the holy site, the fields, farm buildings, and house in relation to Danaville and the surrounding countryside, there are several things we need to do rather quickly."

Krause told Bernam and Deputy Beck that the first thing would be to get all law officers and National Guard personnel to check the identification of only very suspicious-looking and acting adults in Danaville, around the farm, and on all roads leading into the area. Look at driver's license, social security, voter registration, even a credit card. It would be a judgment call, but it could put pressure on those that would commit aggression toward the farm. That might be enough to make them feel vulnerable, and they'd do something that would require them to be detained—whether they be American antireligious fanatics or some other group.

Krause added that he felt the Moslem terrorists would use one or two helicopters at night for their attempt to destroy the holy site, and try to locate the copper scroll. That would give them more flexibility and speed. They could use an airplane and try to drop explosives, but he was convinced that would be their last choice. The terrorists had no chance to pull it off, and any attempt could turn out to be bloody—many people could get hurt. They would be dealing with extremists of the worst kind.

While talking, the agent was moving around the room. Though he held several five-by-seven-inch note cards, he seldom referred to them. "This morning at 7:10, we received confirmation from the Department of The Army regarding our earlier request for four attack helicopters with full operational back-up from Fort Rucker, near Dothan, Alabama. Four A64 Delta Apaches will arrive at the farm around 4:00 p.m. Agent Magee, our boss, Captain

Stanton, and National Guard Captain Ackerman will arrange deployment."

He went into detail as to how Ackerman would work out a defense patrol plan with the pilots, saying the four Apaches would rotate two-hour shifts, from thirty minutes before sunset until thirty minutes after sunrise, utilizing one or two aircraft per shift. The pilots and crew would sleep in two shifts during the day.

Sheriff Bernam tried not to show his amazement, as did Beck, but they were astounded at what they had heard from Rhodes, and especially Krause. Although they had worked alongside FBI and ATF agents on one or two much-lesser occasions before, they had never been exposed to such fast action and detailed planning. To say the least, they were very impressed. Bernam fully understood how serious the FBI was to protect the farm by employing the Apache helicopters. Their responsibility was to totally repel any attack on the holy site or any attempt to destroy or take the copper scroll

"Agent Krause, I presume the Apache helicopter has radar, but what kind of firepower does it have?" the sheriff asked.

"It has Doppler radar that is classified, but it can see everything a long way off. Its armament consists of a rocket pod on each of its short wings with fifteen 2.75-inch general purpose rockets each. The real kicker is that it also carries four Hellfire laser-guided rockets on each wing. Everything else is classified, but it can take on and deal with much more than we're asking it to do. We wanted insurance, and now we have it."

Deputy Beck got up from the metal folding chair and stretched his large body somewhat. "Excuse me, gentlemen, but that chair was designed for smaller folks."

There were a few smiles as he stepped over to a wall and leaned against it. He held his hand up, indicating he had more to say.

"Do you fellas expect the terrorists to come from the Middle East? If so, won't it take a number of days for them to make plans and get over here? If they're first-timers to our country, it seems to me they'll need a lot of inside help."

"No, we believe there have been cells of radical Muslim terrorists in this country for a long time," Krause answered. "They're almost invisible. Some are citizens; others have green cards, which is a type of work permit for a limited time. Those particular ones presented a valid passport upon their initial entry into the United States. Some, if not many, are here illegally, but know their way around. They are extremely difficult to find. Most Muslims are not Arabs."

Agent Rhodes then said that almost an hour and a half ago, the Federal Aviation Agency had issued a revised no-fly zone for the farm to the U.S. Air Traffic Control and to every helicopter fixed-base and corporate operator within a five-hundred-mile radius of Danaville. The new NF zone would be a five-mile radius around the farm, applying to any type of aircraft, to be effective starting thirty minutes before sundown until thirty minutes after sunrise each day until further notice.

"When they approach the farm, whether one or two aircraft, they'll easily be spotted at a minimum of eight to ten miles," Krause added. "One or two laser-guided Hellfire rockets will do the job, depending on the number of aircraft. I think it's safe to say they won't get any closer to the farm boundary than one or two miles."

"How can we be sure the aircraft that appears on the Apache's radar screen are the terrorists?" Bernam asked.

"It or them—there could be two aircraft—will be flying full bore, just above the treetops without running lights. No legal aircraft would ever fly without lights or fly that low cross-country. Both are against federal regulations and reflect a stealthy operation. Our guys will know when the terrorists are coming." Krause crossed his arms and said, "That's it."

Agent Rhodes arose and commented it was time to get to work. Everyone shook hands, and the agents started filing out. Rhodes lingered a moment and spoke to Bernam, "I would like to assign two of these agents to work with you and Chief Deputy Beck, if you agree. I think it would be helpful all the way around. You'd be in charge, except for federal matters, then they'd report to me. But all information would be shared."

"Sounds like a good idea," the sheriff replied.

"The four of us have a number of calls to make back at the motel. I'll send agents Cumbie and Serito over around 4:00 p.m."

"That'll work," Bernam said.

CHAPTER FORTY

JOHN, LYLE, STANTON, Tobias, Summers, Captain Ackerman, the clerics, and the other men of the family had just been briefed by FBI agents Magee and Nelson. All of them, just as Sheriff Bernam and Deputy Beck had been, were amazed at the extent of planning and operation that the FBI had already put into motion.

It was near 12:30 when they all filed into the house for lunch. John, Carew, and Tobias were following several of the clerics. John overheard Reverend Griffin and Father Walsh discussing their concerns regarding the possibility of injury and death occurring while the holy site and the Copper Scroll were being protected.

Billy Durdin was just ahead, and he also overheard the conversation. He turned and said quietly to his two brother clerics, as he put a hand on an arm of each of them, "Be at peace, dear brothers, God has picked this family and us to protect his great work. It will tear at our hearts, but we must do what we must do." They nodded their heads and said "amen" as they reached out and touched Billy on his arms. John looked at Carew and Tobias— they also had drawn strength from Billy's words.

After lunch, all of the family members that could do so squeezed into the barn storeroom to look at the scroll once again and hear Rabbi Metz as he explained the text on the rolled-out length of copper. Everyone had been excitedly anticipating the moment.

There was a big floor fan in one of the back corners of the room, but it did little to lessen the heat. The floodlight was on, turned toward Metz and the scroll, away from the crowd.

The crowd had stopped talking as they entered the room, but Billy Durdin held up his hand and asked everyone to bow his head. He prayed that all of them would soon fully understand God's purpose, and dedicate themselves to holding all they see and hear in the sanctity of the barn storeroom as a secret until that purpose was served.

They all said "amen," with full knowledge that the information they were to soon learn from the scroll would never be divulged by them until it had served God's plan.

Billy looked around from one to another. "God will let us know when, you can be sure." He looked at the rabbi and nodded, giving him his cue.

Rabbi Metz smiled and said that he was humbled by what he had discovered in the scroll. He stated the entire document was written in modern-day Hebrew and not the difficult early form of the language—a square-form script with a mix of Aramaic and flavor of Egyptian hieroglyphs—as in the first copper scroll.

It was evident to everyone that the rabbi was thrilled as he further explained the indented letters on the scroll were precisely and neatly done, making it easy to read. He then produced a spiral notebook with the gist of the scroll text in English that he had recorded earlier.

Metz said the scroll lying before them contained the kind of information as was on the first copper scroll—an accounting of treasures and their locations. The difference being that the treasures listed in the first scroll were in sixty-four designated buried locations. But after years of searching by many scientific people, nothing was ever found. The second scroll designated only twenty-eight locations. The rabbi said he'd give them more information about those locations later.

He explained that two thousand years ago in the Middle East, weight was measured in biblical talents. One talent equaled about seventy-six pounds. He reminded everyone that the estimated total weight of gold and silver bars, along with other items on the first Copper Scroll list of treasures was 160 tons—today, this would have been worth approximately $1.5 billion.

Every eye in the room was glued to the rabbi's face as he paused to carefully examine his notes.

"My dear friends, this scroll," he said as he indicated it slightly with his hand, "not only lists descriptions of treasures and their weights, it gives their locations in very specific terms. And my memory tells me that the locations are not connected to the old sites set forth in the first copper scroll. I have determined that the twenty-eight sets of numbers are the coordinates in latitude and longitude of each site, located in somewhat the same area where the Dead Sea Scrolls were found."

There were slight murmurs and exhaling of breaths as the meaning of what they had just heard sank in.

"Otherwise, the coordinates as set down on this scroll means the Lord is pointing out the treasure to us. All that is needed is a Global Positioning System. It is known as a GPS, a hand-held electronic instrument that, when the coordinates are keyed in, receives its information from a satellite and shows the user exactly where that spot is."

Another stirring rippled through the packed room. The large group was now well aware that the Lord had prepared the way. It was up to them and other followers to ensure his plan was carried out.

"The treasures to be found are staggering, if my math is correct. The twenty-eight sites hold a total of more than 1,000 tons of gold and silver, worth at least $80 billion.

"I'm sure the total intrinsic value, based on how the treasures came to be, would be much more than that."

A stunned silence hung over everyone. It was a staggering, incomprehensible amount. But more importantly, all of them wondered what God's purpose could be.

"I must reiterate what Reverend Durdin said," Metz commented. "This copper scroll and the information it contains is undoubtedly the most important news, perhaps in the past two thousand years. It must be kept a secret by all of us. You'll notice the news media was not allowed to attend this meeting. Any hint of the magnitude of the details you now know about the scroll must be kept from them and anyone else. If it were to leak out, there would be worldwide chaos. God's work would be compromised and totally destroyed."

All of them were in full accord with the rabbi.

FBI agents Magee and Nelson were at the briefing to learn all that was possible about the scroll and the plans of the family and clerics in preparing its shipment to Israel. They were totally awed by what they learned and their expected road ahead.

The security and transport of the copper scroll would be in their hands along with many FBI personnel and other U.S. security agencies. No details would be given to the news media, other than general information about the scroll, from the farm to its final destination. They would work closely with the Israeli Secret Service, the Mossad. All of these things needed to be set in motion immediately.

Rabbi Metz, Father Walsh, Reverend Griffin, and the other clerics stood together. Father Walsh informed the crowd that a search-and-recovery team would be set up immediately to locate and recover all treasures. The team was to be comprised of scholars from learned institutions, with expertise in linguistics, history, theology, archaeology, engineering, and metallurgy.

The rabbi added there were complex instructions at the end of the scroll, explaining what was to be done with the treasures—the culmination of God's purpose for his divine intervention. A special and highly trusted financial management group would be organized to handle all the complex details. He emphasized to all of them that they would be briefed on that as soon as possible.

The meeting was concluded with prayer, and as before, the crowd moved slowly around the copper scroll, their eyes locked on to the unique work of God. They knew there was only a short while before it would be sent to the Holy Land. Most of them would never see it again, and they wanted to remember its every detail.

Soon, the barn was almost empty. The rabbi, with the help of Reverends Durdin and Claussen, rolled up the scroll and replaced it on top of the thick folded blanket inside the footlocker, and locked it. The jar was wrapped in another blanker and laid behind the footlocker.

As the three clerics left the barn, two National Guardsmen locked the large main door and took their normal guard positions.

BY THE SECOND day after the worldwide press release was sent by IPN, there had been a larger influx of the media than had been expected. The head count so far stood at twenty-six. The foreign press would start appearing that evening or by noon the next day. Summers and Gordon had earlier agreed to invite only several of the best-known European media services from Rome, Germany, and Britain. Three of the most experienced and trusted members of the Israeli press would be contacted by Rabbi Metz. He had said they would be a key in timing, measuring, and informing the world of what was going on in Israel.

All other media types, both from the United States and worldwide, would be refused access. They would have to depend on pool reporters, yet to be organized, for their information.

Gordon would have his people in New York send a bulletin within the hour, stating such information to the worldwide news media. He and Summers hoped it would help them get control of a growing problem.

Carew and Red had tried to accommodate all the requests for transportation to the bean field, but found it was impossible to be chauffeurs for the media. After taking several reporters to the site, the two farm hands would return to find several others wanting to go. Carew announced to several of the media to spread the word to their cohorts that there would be transportation only twice a day, 10:00 a.m. and 3:00 p.m.

The media people didn't like to be managed by outsiders, but they had no choice, unless they took Carew's suggestion and walk to and from the bean field.

He and Red still had to tend the livestock—milk the cows, wash down the milking-house floor, and feed the pigs. Lyle helped with the farmwork when not involved with his dad in some of the meetings with the clerics, National Guard, FBI, and others. Teresa and Pat had volunteered to feed the chickens and gather the eggs.

The loading of the unusable milk and eggs and transporting them to the pit once a day was handled by National Guard members. Captain Ackerman had volunteered three men to John three days ago. The senior Kelly was thankful for the help.

Parker, Owens, and Kent were securing the temporary casing cover to make it safe and rainproof. There would be a very wide concrete apron and a lockable steel hatch designed and put into place as soon as possible. The canopies would be left in place for the time being.

The drill rig, crane, and flat-bed truck had been moved to a secondary field access road. Only the tractor was left to cover the mud pit and smooth the ground around the holy site. The site would continue to be lighted at night—powered by a skid-mounted diesel engine.

Two of Captain Ackerman's squads had cleared two, two-hundred-by-two-hundred-foot spaces in the fields for heliports—one inside the farm's south boundary, and the other inside the north boundary, about three thousand feet apart. Part of a corn field and watermelon field, were destroyed, but that was unimportant now—there was now a much larger purpose for the farm.

At 3:55 p.m., four helicopters in formation were seen approaching from the north. Everyone knew they were the Apaches as promised by the army. Captain Ackerman had been in touch with Ft. Rucker, covering details about the planned operation.

The Apaches, now at five hundred feet, banked to the left and split up—two, continuing to the south for their approach and touchdown, the other two made a right 180-degree turn to the north as they descended to their temporary home. A humvee was waiting at each landing site with Ackerman in one and one of his lieutenants in the other. They would brief each two-man Apache crew.

The National Guard captain was aware that a convoy of six army supply and ground crew vehicles, including a refueling truck, was to arrive around 5:00 p.m. It had departed Ft. Rucker at 2:30 p.m., knowing the road would be clogged with traffic.

All of the family members and guests stopped whatever they were doing and watched the olive drab helicopters descend. They knew the four aircraft, with guns and rockets, were to protect them, the holy site, the scroll, and the farm—but they were not looking forward to their having to be used. Everyone hoped things stayed relatively quiet.

REVERENDS BILLY DURDIN and Chase Griffin, Rabbi Metz, and the other clerics informed John that after dinner they would like to reveal God's instructions on the scroll to everyone. He knew that had been on the family's mind since the list and locations on the scroll had been revealed that morning. The senior Kelly spread the word.

Granny, Sara, and Arlene told those in the house and on the porch that dinner would be ready at five thirty or so. Granny jokingly said that with helicopters buzzing around and army trucks arriving, somehow they'd work dinner in. People nearby laughed. They all needed a little humor—it relieved their tension

It was 4:50 p.m. and the army convoy was arriving after an almost three-hour trip to the farm, from a distance of forty miles or so. They were quickly guided by National Guard personnel out to the helicopters. The army and the National Guard were focused on their task—family members that were on the back porch and in the yard were impressed by what they were seeing.

Dinner was announced, and after Reverend Griffin said grace, everyone lined up and soon was enjoying his meal. As they ate, most of the conversation among the various small collections of diners was about the coming meeting with the clerics. All of them were anticipating the meeting.

At approximately five forty-five, the large family group didn't waste much time in finding a place on the back porch to sit. The clerics were sitting, facing their audience. Billy Durdin gave a prayer asking the Lord to help all of them understand his purpose in defining what was to be done with the immense treasure, and give each of them the strength and courage not to share their knowledge with any outsiders until the proper time. He then turned to Rabbi Metz, and with a smile, said it was all his.

The rabbi stood and opened his spiral notebook, looked out over his loving adopted family, and began. His audience was focused.

"My brothers and sisters," he began. "Please understand what I tell you will be the gist, in very general terms, of what I interpreted from the scroll regarding God's instructions. You'll receive much more detail in the near future. I want the document's text carefully examined by a small, trusted translation team of Bible-language scholars in Jerusalem. An objective agreement on the scroll text is crucial."

He said the Lord had specified that the treasure was to be apportioned to various parts of the world to directly help people overcome circumstantial poverty and disease. If part or the entire population of any people were held in political and/or spiritual bondage, every possible effort must be made to free them. He paused and looked over the audience. They were very still, and were looking at him intently.

He continued by telling them God was very clear about how the treasure was to be managed. A special group of his servants, chosen by those who found the scroll in his special place, would secure the treasure and make all arrangements through the different nations to carry out his will. Emphasis was put on the importance of not turning over the treasure to any third party. Control was the key, the rabbi told them.

All of them were staring at John, Lyle, Carew, Red, and Parker, knowing that they were who God wanted to carry out his wishes. John was looking down at his hands, deep in thought.

"John, would you like to say something?" the rabbi said.

The senior Kelly rose from his chair and moved to the front and faced the family.

"I've been in awe since we saw the rainbow, the hail on the ground, and the circle in the bean field several weeks ago. The Lord pointed us in the right direction, and two days ago we found his fantastic gift and message. Now, he's told us what we are to do. It's going to be a huge job, and we are all in this together."

The crowd got up at once as Sara started singing "Amazing Grace" in her beautiful alto voice. Several others joined in. Soon everyone was singing. The famous hymn grew in heart and volume.

After the singing, as everyone was sitting down, John motioned for Lyle and the other three to come join him.

"These men did all of the 'heavy lifting.' All I did was walk around and watch, saying yes, no, maybe so, or I don't know. They truly inspired me with their ingenuity and very hard work. At the same time, Lyle, Carew, and Red managed to tend the livestock and get the milking done. Others helped when possible. Parker here did a magnificent job of handling the drilling operation, with Carew and Red helping. And of course, Lyle has the unique honor of having gone into the Lord's special cave and discovering the copper scroll. He accomplished something no other man has done, or will ever do again. What he did was very special for God and all of his servants here on this porch."

The porch erupted in applause, with several called-out compliments and amens. There were many smiles and thumbs up.

"I am deeply amazed and humbled," John said as he looked around at the clerics. "I count on you heavily."

All of them, looking at him with understanding, nodded.

"There are many details to take care of as soon as possible. The first thing is to arrange for the scroll to be taken to Israel. As Rabbi Metz said, it needs to be studied to have a consensus from linguists of its contents. He and the other clerics told me this afternoon that an arrangement will be made with a carefully selected team of scholars and engineers, sworn to secrecy, to find and collect the treasure and secure it. A clandestine financial management organization would be set up to directly assign the gifts to the carefully designated recipients. I and the others here by my side, along with the clerics, will review all proposed steps by the various responsible groups. Our job, then, would be to decide a course of action, following God's plan without exception."

Pat turned to Sara, smiled, and whispered, "He doesn't sound like John the farmer. He sounds like a lawyer."

Sara nodded and whispered back, "John feels strongly about his Kelly lineage and the farm. But he knows now that both have been in the Lord's plans from the start. He's totally dedicated to helping it all work—for the world and for the farm."

The meeting ended with a prayer, and everyone went his way. John, Lyle, Carew, Red, and Parker stayed on the porch with the clerics and discussed the preparations for sending the scroll to Israel and the fulfillment of its instructions.

IT WAS ALMOST 6:30 p.m. when the phone's ringing jolted Bernam from his sleep. Fifteen minutes before, he had pushed back in his high-backed leather chair and took one of his "recharge naps." He had told his deputies the naps refreshed him. Lately, he needed all the refreshing he could get.

"Sheriff Bernam," he said, still clearing his head.

"Claude, this is Marvin. I need your help, and I think the other stores on Main do too."

"You're not the first one to call, Marvin. I'm aware of the growing crowd, and it'll probably get bigger, but right now my office and the state troopers don't have a quick fix. We're working on it, but it may take two or three days to move most of those people out.

"Well, it's been a bad afternoon, and the crowd's growing. Some of them are rowdy, and I'm afraid there's going to be some real trouble, though most of them seem to be decent, religious people.

"Captain Stanton is assigning six additional troopers for Danaville. He said that General Whitmire has ordered two additional National Guard platoons from Panama City to be divided between Danaville and the farm. But it will be morning before all of them are in place."

"I'm closing up. I have to protect my employees and the interior of my store. All of my restricted drugs and cash are locked up in the safe. Everything else is secure only by the locks on the doors. We'll see what tomorrow brings. Good night."

Bernam knew Marvin was frustrated and very nervous about his store, his employees, and himself and the Danaville citizens in general. But the situation was not a quick-fix one. The sheriff knew they would have more manpower relatively soon, but for now, he and Jack Stanford had to make do with the resources that were on hand and the two platoons that were on the way.

He was about to leave the office and get something to eat when the phone rang. The sheriff let out a sigh and picked it up.

"Sheriff Bernam, this is Agent Cumbie. The two hours Agent Serito and I spent in your office late this afternoon were very constructive. You were very helpful in furnishing details about Danaville and the county."

"Thank you, Mr. Cumbie. I'm always happy to help the FBI."

"I've got some information that Captain Stanton gave us about twenty minutes ago. There are reports of huge traffic tie-ups in Jacksonville, Tampa, St. Petersburg, Orlando, and Tallahassee. A number of altercations have occurred in all of those cities. Several people have been seriously injured. Much of it is driven by frustration and short tempers over traffic jams. There have been some cases of looting because of the shortage of police in the business districts and residential areas—they are all on the main feeder roads and freeways. The same thing is happening in cities across the country."

"I guess we all expected something like this would happen," Bernam said, "but not to the extent that's unfolding. Jack Stanton told me that the governor is calling out all National Guard units to assist law officers across the state. I'm sure other states are doing the same."

"That's all I have at the moment, Sheriff. Keep us posted about the traffic and people screening. As we discussed, there'll be additional help by morning. Agent Serito and I will see you then."

With that, both men hung up.

Bernam called his chief deputy. Beck was in his car, checking with his deputies. They were spread out from I-10 to north of the farm on State 77. The deputy told his boss that traffic and people were everywhere, and his few men and the state troopers were barely able to keep 77 open—the going was extremely slow. Several arrests had been made, and they were expecting more. The Mason County Agriculture Center was being used as a large holding cell for all apprehended lawbreakers.

The sheriff grabbed his hat and headed for home to eat. He'd sleep for three or four hours, then relieve his chief deputy by midnight.

CHAPTER FORTY-ONE

A T 6:45 P.M., two of the four Apaches rose out of the fields on an easterly heading. After one mile, one would turn and fly north and start the first phase of a two-mile radius. The other Apache set up a one quarter-mile 360-degree pattern until the first aircraft was halfway around the preplanned two-mile radius, then it followed—each now ninety degrees from the other.

Everyone had been anticipating the first patrol flight and stood transfixed, watching the strange-looking helicopters moving through the late-afternoon sky. They said a little prayer for each two-man crew and their flight-support personnel on the ground. Some of the onlookers had a hint of butterflies in their stomachs.

"All of the folks here and within two miles or so are going to get tired of hearing those helicopters eleven or twelve hours a day," John said to Agent Magee and Jack Stanton. "But it's a small price to pay—they just may be needed."

"You're right," Magee said. "As I said earlier this morning, Agent Krause believes there's a better-than-even chance that the Muslim terrorists will show up. Destroying the holy site and/or taking the copper scroll, or even trying and failing, would make them martyrs. They're big on that stuff, and they hate all of us from the West—especially Christians, Jews, and our God."

Many of the news media were following the Apaches with still
and video cameras. Some of the still cameras had enormous
telephoto lens. The photographers must have wanted to see the
beards on the pilots' faces.

Nightfall came and the family began to adjust to the helicopters
and the ebb and flow of the sound of their engines as they flew
around the farm. They were far enough away that the noise wasn't
overbearing.

Many of them were watching television in the living room,
following various stations, especially Fox News, as they would
cut into their regular programming from time to time with an update
on the situation at the farm and its effect in the United States and
throughout the world. Fox and two other national broadcasters
had flown in small up-link TV dishes by helicopter that afternoon,
tying in to power at the Pasternaks', and were transmitting farm
coverage via satellite directly to New York.

Arlene watched a segment of news about traffic and other
problems occurring in most Florida cities, one being Tampa. She
tried to discreetly dry her eyes as she thought about how she
came to be at the farm. She silently thanked God. Lyle and Teresa
sat nearby. All three watched and listened in silence.

LATE THURSDAY NIGHT, around eleven thirty, seven radical
cultists calling themselves Sepas, from some mystical place called
the Mountain of Fire, had been caught by two guards as they
were cutting through the east perimeter fence.

At first, they balked and tried to back down the guards, and
though several of them had handguns and one pulled out a stick
of dynamite from several in his belt, the guards raised their M-
16s, with one of them talking into his headset radio, calling for
backup. At that time, the older man, who seemed to be in charge,
fired his pistol at the guardsman who was using his radio. Luckily,
the badly aimed shot only nicked him in the side, just above his
web belt.

In turn, the other guard shot the cultist in the upper left chest
at the collar-bone level. He hit the ground hard. The wounded

guardsman fired a burst over the other individuals' heads. They stood frozen for a moment, and when they saw quickly approaching headlights, they put down their weapons and the dynamite.

The slightly wounded guardsman and the seriously wounded Sepa cult leader were loaded into a Humvee, while four additional NG members herded the other cultists into the back of a one-and-a-half-ton truck. They posted two new guards on the fence line, and wasted no time in returning to the bivouac area.

An army medevac helicopter had been consigned to the Danaville Hospital, with two medics. Captain Ackerman called for assistance, giving a description of the wounds. They were lifting off within five to six minutes. The medevac pilot had been briefed upon starting his assignment that he would signal with his IFF—Identification, Friend, or Foe—instrument as soon as they were airborne to forewarn the Apaches of who he was and the purpose of his mission.

The medevac chopper pilot spotted one of the Apaches approximately one mile off to his right as he made an approach to a clearing just north of the bivouac area. About a dozen National Guard members had formed a large circle with flashlights, providing a safe landing area. Soon, the two wounded men were aboard and headed for Danaville.

There were two other attempts by other extremist types; they were caught and arrested at the perimeter fence line in two locations about a mile apart. There was no gunfire, but a few weapons and a wire cutter were confiscated. After that, things quieted down for the night.

A LIGHT RAIN began to fall around 5:00 a.m. on Friday. Most everyone was asleep. Granny, Sara, and Arlene were up organizing breakfast. Lyle, Carew, and Red were heading to the barn to tend the livestock. The Apaches would be finishing their first night patrol by 6:20 a.m.

John announced the events of the night during breakfast. The news got the attention of all of them. They were now convinced that there were some evil people mixed in with the predominance of Christians who were constantly arriving at the farm, or somewhat marooned in Danaville and several nearby towns.

The rain abated around 9:00 a.m., and many of the housebound gladly went into the yard and walked around. A meeting was held in the living room by the clerics, with John, Summers, Stanton, Tobias, and Ackerman. Plans were made to pack and move the copper scroll to Israel. Transportation and security were the most important part of the discussion.

Tobias told them he had talked twice with the president's chief of staff, who would arrange for the Department of the Air Force at the Pentagon to coordinate all necessary logistics to carry out the mission. He added that it would take two or three days before such a move could be arranged.

The chief of staff suggested to him that a squad of Special Forces personnel act as an honor security guard for the scroll. Every moment of the mission would be conducted with the highest level of decorum this country can offer, as tribute to this historic religious event. Vice President Tyree, his Secret Service detail, and several aides would accompany the scroll to Israel, along with the four clerics from the farm.

An Air Force Pave Hawk helicopter, flying to the farm from Eglin Air Force Base near Fort Walton Beach, with six of the Special Forces squad, would pick up the scroll and four clerics and return to Eglin. Then, the clerics and the security personnel would board the vice president's plane and return to Andrews AFB. During an hour layover for fuel, the vice president and his people will board and everyone will be on their way.

"Seems to me you ought to be in Washington running things, Ralph," John said with a chuckle. "You sure you didn't leave something out?"

The eleven men all laughed. It helped to lighten the load a little.

They were thankful for Tobias's attention to detail. All agreed that Monday was acceptable for starting the scroll on its journey.

Tobias then told them that the president wanted to send special representatives to pay respects to the holy site, the scroll, and the farm on Sunday. They would come from the State Department, Defense, Treasury, and the attorney general's office. He added there would be twelve or fourteen in the group. They would land at Eglin and arrive at the farm by helicopter. Estimated time of arrival would be around 1:15 p.m., and they would stay for a minimum of two hours.

The information didn't really surprise any of them, they had expected some reaction from the White House, but the timing was a little close. It seemed that lately everything was that way. They took it in stride.

Metz, Griffin, and Butler took several reporters to see the scroll. These were news types that had arrived just prior to closing the farm to the media. John, Summers, and the clerics were making sure that all TV, newsprint, and a few radio people had access to everything on the farm. But the clerics were allowing only three or four at a time to visit the barn storeroom.

Jim Summers and Tom Gordon were near the door of the main barn. Summers was on his phone, talking with the pilot of the Bell 212L helicopter that was to pick up six major foreign news media representatives at Panama City Regional Airport. The editor was informed the Delta flight from Atlanta was a little late, but they would arrive at the farm by noon.

"These newsmen are comprised of one each from Rome and Paris, two from London, and one each from Tel Aviv and Jerusalem," Gordon said. "That will increase the total of news media here to the size of a small army," he quipped.

"That's true," Summers replied. "I think we should inform the media here at the farm that their numbers have to be reduced. There're just too many to deal with. I propose we call a meeting with the entire bunch and let them choose several pool reporters and one pool TV crew to stay. That would take care of more than half of them, making things much more manageable."

"I think you're right," Gordon said. "We have to work closely with the foreign press, especially the Israelis and their government.

They're going to be the key in helping to keep the lid on about what's going on regarding the treasure."

"We need to meet again with agents Magee and Nesson and Captain Stanton real soon and review the plan of dealing with the Middle East media specifically, and the larger region generally. Press relations are handled a little differently there, than they are here."

Gordon looked at his watch. "We'd better hustle; our foreign guests are due within an hour."

Both men walked toward the house. They spotted Stanton talking with John and Ackerman under one of the big oaks. They quickened their steps when they saw the NG commander turn and head toward the bivouac area.

"John, Captain Stanton, wait up," Summers called out.

Both men had started toward the house, but stopped and waited.

The four of them talked for a couple of minutes, then walked on to the house to find the two agents.

Magee was on the front porch, talking on his cell phone. He nodded to them and held up one finger, indicating he'd join them shortly. John led the other three to the end of the long porch to a row of high-backed rocking chairs and a swing. As they were getting comfortable, the agent joined them.

"I just talked to Washington and was briefed that four Mid-East types are traveling together in a car possibly headed east from Pensacola. Other than knowing that they stayed at a West Pensacola motel last night, we have no idea where to start looking. They checked out before sun up this morning, and the night manager didn't get a good look at their car. However, he thought they went east on I-10. The manager was suspicious and called the police, and some heads-up cop called the local FBI access number used by city and county law officers. Our man called Washington immediately."

"Any thoughts on who they may be?" Stanton asked.

"Not really. They could be anybody. But it's a little unusual for four men, perhaps all Arabs, in their twenties and thirties, with little or no luggage, to be on the road together and leaving a motel before dawn. One of them seemed to be the boss and handled check-in and checkout. He spoke English with a heavy accent, and paid cash from a large roll of fifties. They stayed in two adjoining rooms."

All of them on the front porch mentally chewed on Magee's report for a few moments.

"If they are headed here, it makes sense it would be by helicopter. That means they'd have to steal one," John said.

"Yes, we're sticking to that theory," Magee replied. "As you know, the FAA has alerted as many helicopter leasing and operating companies as possible. There are private ones here and there that may not have gotten the word. We'll have to keep our eyes open. Thank God for the Apaches."

Nelson came out and joined the porch group. He had been in the dining room, talking to Lyle, Teresa, and Arlene, getting background information on Enrique and those he had worked for.

Summers and Gordon reminded the agents and the others about the soon-to-arrive foreign press, and that it was extremely important to convince their foreign visitors that their cooperation was key to not divulging any details about how and when the scroll was due to arrive in Jerusalem, and more so, not a word to them about the treasure. After returning to their home, the two Israeli news representatives would be steered by their government's secret service, the Mossad, working with the FBI.

The two FBI agents and John and Stanton agreed with Summers and Gordon.

The two newsmen left the porch, headed to meeting the incoming helicopter at the designated landing area—a short distance beyond the main gate to the fields. It was a safe distance from the livestock.

It wasn't long before they saw a red-and-white helicopter approaching from the south. As Summers and Gordon opened the gate and walked toward the aircraft's target, it descended and landed. The door slid back and six men exited, and with the pilot assisting, started unloading their luggage.

Agents Magee and Nelson, along with John, followed their two news spokesmen to join in greeting their new visitors. The agents had told John that it would silently make a statement if two FBI agents were among those meeting the helicopter. John and Stanton had readily agreed.

After being welcomed and exchanging handshakes, the six guests were taken to the house and introduced to other family members and served lunch. A number of American media onlookers wondered why so much attention was being given to the six foreign newsmen.

Making accommodations for the foreigners wasn't easy, but it was done. Captain Ackermen donated two four-man tents and set them up under the oaks, near the parked cars. It wasn't first-class, but it was better than the other media people had in the Pasternaks' pasture. The foreigners didn't complain.

FRIDAY AFTERNOON PASSED without any further noteworthy activity. There seemed to be a temporary respite for the farm.

However, that night around ten forty-five, a group of twelve anti-God radicals of unknown origin made an attempt to penetrate the southeast corner of the perimeter fence. A four-man National Guard patrol caught them in the act, and the surprisingly well-armed radicals opened fire. It turned into a small war. After the last shot was fired, there were two radicals dead, and eight wounded. Two guardsmen were wounded—one badly, and the other with a minor wound to his foot.

The two unwounded radicals were made to lie down while the two able NG guards quickly checked their own and then called for emergency help. Corporal Lewis, the senior patrol member, was unaware that the intensity of the gunfire had been heard for over a mile away. Captain Ackerman and a platoon soon showed up in two trucks.

Some of the wounded radicals could be treated on the spot and were able to wait longer than others for medevac. There was no doubt that the two guardsmen would be on the first flight to the hospital.

The trauma team in Danaville was standing by. It would take three trips by the medevac chopper to bring in all of the wounded. The hospital staff was astonished at the number of patients they were about to receive. The badly wounded cultist who was brought in the night before would have company.

Lyle was talking to Carew in his small apartment in the big barn when they heard distant gunfire. They looked at each other with wide eyes and bolted through the door. Just as they got outside, the firing stopped, but both men knew it had come from the southeast fields—probably along the fence. Each of them said a silent prayer for the safety of all involved.

Most of the family were in bed, but those still outside, along with many members of the media, had heard the melee. All of the media scurried around, trying to get to the scene or going to the bivouac area and interviewing Captain Ackerman when he was available.

At breakfast Saturday morning, the conversation was all about the shootout. Everyone had thought the Thursday-night fight with the cultists was a one-time incident. Now, they knew it was not. The six foreign newsmen had been greatly affected by their first night at the farm. It was very evident to them that they were involved in something big.

All at the farm were hoping and praying the two nights of incidents would be the end of it.

That was not to be the case.

AROUND MIDMORNING, SUMMERS, Gordon, John, and Magee showed the six foreigners the holy site, and stood by as their visitors showed amazement and respect as they looked at the sealed casing head, knowing it was the entrance to God's special place. Nothing was said by their hosts as the six walked around and looked at the terrain. When one of them asked what happened to the circle on the ground they had seen in photos aired on TV, John told them it faded away the night the copper scroll was discovered. That just magnified their awe.

They were then taken to the small barn storeroom. When they walked in and the foreign newsmen saw the copper scroll under the floodlight, they were dumbfounded as they looked down on the Lord's work.

The special tour was held for the six men to make a point to them about the immeasurable importance of protecting the scroll—emphasized by the presence of the FBI. They reflected that the point had been made.

Rabbi Metz, Father Walsh, and Reverend Griffin were there to provide a few general facts to their foreign visitors. Metz concentrated on the two from Israel. They would be of primary importance to conducting tight security when exploration and recovery was begun in their nation.

They were invited to take photos. An agreement to use the live pool TV hookup was made later for their on-camera reports to their respective countries.

CHAPTER FORTY-TWO

AGENT MAGEE GOT a call at 8:55 Saturday night from Agent Krause, alerting him that a Bell 212L helicopter had been stolen at gunpoint from a Panama City Beach sightseeing service at approximately 8:25 by four men who were thought to be Arabs.

It would be learned later that the four had walked into the flight-service office and asked for a night tour of the beach and downtown Panama City. When the owner-pilot, who was alone, told them he did not fly after dark, he was pistol-whipped and knocked to the floor by two of them. One cocked his pistol, held it to the pilot's head, and had threatened to kill him. The leader grabbed the arm of his companion and shouted something at him in a foreign language. The key to the chopper was demanded, and the owner mumbled that it was in the top desk drawer.

The leader kicked the owner, and then another man taped his wrists and ankles with duct tape. The key was found, and just before they went through the sliding glass door to the large concrete pad, one of them ripped out the phone. The four olive-skinned men hurried out to the chopper. The owner watched them through a glass sliding door from his position on the office floor as they loaded a heavy duffle bag and several automatic weapons into the helicopter.

In their haste, they had badly bound the owner's wrists in front of his body rather than behind. He had worked his hands free by the time the chopper reached lift-off rotor speed and grabbed his cell phone from a small bag that had been overlooked by the four animals that took his pride and joy—his business— away from him. He punched in the speed dial to the FBI, which luckily, for some reason, he had put into his phone months ago.

The leader was evidently a seasoned pilot and had fully checked out in the Bell 212. He lifted the helicopter off smoothly into the night.

The FBI took the message and told the owner it would be forwarded at once to the proper people. He asked if he needed medical attention. The owner said no; he'd take himself to a nearby emergency clinic and get checked.

Magee knew the farm only had perhaps ten or twelve minutes before the terrorists arrived. It was then nine thirty. He quickly alerted the Apache crews and Captain Ackerman. Luckily, John and Tom Gordon were nearby and were asked to tell everyone to vacate the house and barn at once, gather under the large oaks, and spread out.

All at the farm was experiencing a bad case of butterflies in their stomachs.

The two Apaches, designated Alpha and Bravo, changed their flight pattern to concentrate on the north and south approaches.

Within eight minutes, the Alpha pilot let his crew on the ground know his radar was tracking an incoming craft at ten miles, moving 110 knots at two hundred feet altitude.

The four terrorists were in fact radical Muslim Arabs who had been in the United States for over a year, carrying out a few disguised train derailments, industrial and forest fires, and possible recruitment. Now, armed with firearms and explosives and whatever else, they were bent on hitting the holy site and either destroying or taking the copper scroll. It was an impossible mission from the start. They were doomed.

The terrorist pilot was aware of that.

Though a quarter moon provided a little light, the large group standing under and around the trees were tense. They couldn't see much, but could hear the two helicopters.

When the terrorists were three miles away and closing in, Bravo's instrument laser dot locked onto the oncoming chopper and a Hellfire rocket flashed toward its target. It met the terrorists with a huge fireball and clap of thunder when they were one and a half miles from the south perimeter fence. The Bell 212L helicopter fell to the ground in many burning pieces, scattered over a one-thousand-foot elongated pattern, into a shallow pond and a surrounding marsh. The explosion was like a clap of thunder as its sound reached everyone on the farm, even in downtown Danaville.

It was all over. The Apaches immediately started scanning for any other aircraft that could be trailing or coming from another direction. They flew over the crash site and the surrounding area to see if any buildings or other properties were hit by debris or fire. They reported an all clear.

Everyone at the farm under the trees were totally dumbfounded by what they had witnessed. Many of them had more of an understanding and appreciation why combat can be devastating. They were stunned at how quickly the interception by only one of the Apaches happened, and how efficient and devastating its action was. Agent Magee told them that the terrorist helicopter was also carrying explosives on it, which added to its total decimation.

John, Captain Stanton, Magee, Nelson, and all the others breathed a sigh of relief. They knew there would be no other assault on the farm now. The message was sent. It was totally evident to anyone that they could not succeed.

An inspection team made up of two FBI agents, Deputy Beck, and several NG soldiers were on their way to the scene in two Humvees.

The clerics and many others gathered on the back porch for a short prayer service of thanksgiving. They prayed that God would bless the more than two thousand souls, with their candles and signs, gathered at the perimeter fences along State 77 and County 26, as well as around the main gate. The great majority of the masses were Christians, a lesser number were Jews, and there were also several small groups of anti-Christian radicals.

It was near eleven thirty when things began to settle down, and by midnight, a majority of the extended family and guests were in bed or about to turn in. Six or eight others, along with John, Magee, Tobias, and Summers, were still talking about their visitors from Washington due the next day.

Tobias informed them that the visiting group would stay only two hours. A tour and briefing would have to be short. The press was going to want their turn also.

The discussion broke up a few minutes later, and everyone called it a night.

SUNDAY MORNING BROUGHT a clear, bright day that portended a warm afternoon. Various people at breakfast were showing the strain of the night before, plus the two nights before that, but as a whole, seemed in good spirits.

Sheriff Bernam arrived at the farm before the scheduled worship service at 10:30 a.m. He informed John and the other men that with the help of the additional state troopers and NG troops, there had been a clamp down on the altercations, breaking and entering, and stealing. The lawmen had arrested scores, both in Danaville and along the roads around the farm. They were being charged and locked up in the Mason County Agriculture Center's auction hall. It could be adequately and securely guarded.

He and Captain Stanton had agreed with Jim Summers's suggestion that a carefully structured information program of procedures that would regulate traffic and crowds be initiated at once. The program would inform people nationally and internationally that the farm would be off-limits until a few temporary measures could be taken to accommodate a controlled number of visitors. They would be allowed to visit the holy site for a maximum of two hours.

There would be specific rules regarding traffic on all roads within a ten-mile radius of the farm. Minimal parking and camping facilities with water and toilets were to be set up as soon as possible.

Summers told them that John had talked to Karl and Tisha Pasternak, and they were willing to allow fifteen acres of unused pasture to be used. This was adjacent to the heliport area. John had told Karl that the family would compensate him on an acceptable lease basis as soon as many other details were reviewed and acted upon. The Pasternaks agreed. It had been several years since Karl had sold his last cow. Taxes were due every year—he and his wife were glad John had called them.

The men felt better about the setting up of ways and means to manage the task ahead. There was a flicker of light at the end of the tunnel. The first one or two steps had been suggested, and all of them were agreeable with the program.

Later, after a spirit-lifting, soul-filling Sunday service held in three parts with Billy Durdin, Father Walsh, and Rabbi Getz each presenting his studied viewpoint on the everlasting power of God, everyone felt energized and thankful. Metz, with his warm smile, reminded them that Jesus had been a Jew and a rabbi. They all smiled back, knowing what he meant. It was obvious that they all loved God and each other.

Four VIPs and nine aides arrived from Washington via Eglin AFB at 1:35 p.m. in a large Sikorsky helicopter. It seemed the farm fields were being turned into a chopper base. There were now five parked aircraft. John had requested early on that they fly carefully planned patterns into and from the farm to prevent flying low and directly over the livestock.

John, Lyle, Magee, Stanton, Tobias, and Summers walked up as the chopper touched ground. Before moving closer to meet their guests, they waited until the large turning blades were pitched flat by the pilot, to decrease the downdraft and blowing debris.

The thirteen special representatives of President Burke exited the craft and were warmly greeted by John and the others. Names and handshakes were exchanged: Cliff Urbeck, White House Press Secretary; Randolph Bowen, undersecretary of state; Lt. Gen.

Carl Swain, Department of Defense; and George Hoover, assistant attorney general. It was apparent all of them had been briefed to some extent. They were certainly aware of John Kelly and Ralph Tobias. The various aides of the officials were also introduced.

John's apology regarding the long walk to the house was quickly put aside. Lieutenant General Swain commented that all of them could use the exercise.

After arriving at the house and being introduced to the family, they started their itinerary. On the way to a number of waiting cars that would transport the large entourage to the holy site, Urbeck wanted more details from John as to how everyone on the farm was holding up under the stress.

The senior Kelly smiled at the president's "eyes and ears," and told him that he and all of his family and guests felt privileged and spiritually euphoric to experience the implementation of God's plan.

Urbeck smiled and nodded his head, indicating he understood.

The visitors, like all the others beforehand, were totally awed to look upon the Lord's special place. John related the events of the drilling and exploration and recovery of the copper scroll. Though they had heard general details from the media during the past several days, John's facts were astonishing to them.

The last part of their tour was seeing the scroll. They were stunned to see it. Metz glanced quickly at the Washington officials. The lieutenant general, the undersecretary of state—all of them, no matter their past experience in national and international affairs—were speechless.

Before being shown to the house, the Washington group, once outside the barn, allowed ten eager members of the media a fifteen-minute interview. After that, it was lunch time.

Granny, Sara, Teresa, and Arlene served the special guests a light lunch and dessert. All of them were highly impressed with the farm, the house, and the people they met. They would never again see anything that could approach the power of what they had observed and felt at the Kelly farm.

The visit came to an end, and after many heartfelt goodbyes, the guests, escorted by John and many other family members, walked the one hundred yards or so to the helicopter and boarded.

John, Lyle, and Carew were walking and talking together as they headed toward the small barn storeroom to carefully measure the scroll jar and construct its crate. "I think the culmination of our work is at hand," Lyle said.

John and Carew agreed. In fact, many others at the farm felt the same.

"Without an unexpected setback, and after the scroll is safely in Israel," John added, "we start doing the rest of God's work here by changing the future of the farm and our lives. Further big changes will occur. There'll be no more farm crops and livestock. Our family will be overseeing one of the most important jobs in the world—in many respects, maybe 'the' most important for many more generations of Kellys," John looked at Lyle and smiled.

Lyle's heart jumped into his throat. He returned his dad's smile. "You can count on it."

"Amen," Carew said somewhat emphatically.

SUMMERS PHONED THE sheriff and arranged for a deputy to pick him up along with Tom Gordon of IPN and take them to the editor's office in town. They wanted to collaborate on writing a news release announcing the departure of the copper scroll to Israel for its placement in the Shrine of the Book, a section of Jerusalem's Israel Museum. The purpose of the scroll was highly confidential. It would never be mentioned by those at the farm. But there was no doubt its purpose would leak to the press at some point in time. They hoped it would be after the twenty-eight treasure locations were found and secured as the excavations were carried out.

A FEELING OF sadness permeated the farm on Monday morning. Not only was the copper scroll being taken away, but also four of the clerics were accompanying it on its long trip to

Israel. God's masterpiece would be greatly missed, along with Reverends Durdin and Griffin, Rabbi Metz, and Father Walsh. They and everyone at the farm had formed an everlasting bond.

All the clerics, except Reverend Butler, were sitting on the front porch with John, Sara, Lyle, Teresa, Granny, and Carew. Butler and his wife had been taken to their home by a deputy sheriff. He would return before his four brother clerics and the scroll departed.

"The work Carew did on the crate for the scroll is a masterpiece!" Durdin exclaimed. "It's solid, very secure, and designed for four men to carry."

"That's the way he does everything," John said. "When my adopted brother and I teamed up twenty-four years ago, he immediately showed that he was a 'can do' man."

Carew looked at Durdin and John with a broad grin. "Many thanks for braggin' on me, but if John and Lyle hadn't been there telling me what to do, I would still be going in circles."

The porch erupted in laughter as Carew continued to grin.

"Well, all of us here know that the work he, Lyle, Parker, and Red did in drilling into the Lord's special room and retrieving his blessed scroll was remarkable. We and the world are indeed indebted to them," Father Walsh said.

All of them chorused "amen."

It was late in the morning and the helicopter with the five-man Special Forces honor guard would arrive in approximately two and a half hours. The four clerics had contacted their families and packed for their trip, but wanted to have a last prayer service before departing the farm. It was scheduled for noon. Granny and the other ladies went to finish preparing the noon meal. It would be served after the honor guard had arrived.

The men talked for another few minutes and then went their separate ways, to meet again in thirty minutes with everyone on the back porch.

THE PRAYER SERVICE had a special meaning to everyone. They were saying goodbye, at least for a time, to four of their beloved clerics. As before, the porch barely accommodated the crowd. Reverend Butler and wife Ruth had returned. FBI agents Magee and Nelson were there, as were several media types. Sheriff Bernam, Chief Deputy Beck, and Marvin Gardner arrived just before the service started. This was a unique time. All on the porch were glad the copper scroll would soon be on its way to Israel, but they also had a conflicting sadness.

The departing clerics shared their personal feelings with them, each giving a touching prayer for the farm, the family, and God's work. The porch crowd was deeply moved—some silently crying.

The never-to-be-forgotten service came to an end, with Sara leading them all in a well-chosen hymn for the occasion, "Nearer My God to Thee."

CHAPTER FORTY-THREE

AT 1:00 P.M., the second Sikorsky helicopter in two days appeared in the southwestern sky, approaching the farm. Everyone went through the main gate to the fields and soon halted to watch it descend some one hundred yards away. They knew the day was significant—a major step toward fulfilling the Lord's plan.

The chopper soon landed, kicking up a lot of debris. As the huge rotor blades whirled to a stop, a five-man honor guard stepped sharply out of the craft. They were wearing dress army greens with white gloves and white scarves and berets. Each had on a web belt with a sidearm. Four soldiers would handle the scroll crate, and the accompanying master sergeant would direct them.

The waiting crowd, with John, Lyle, Ackerman, and the clerics leading the way, went to meet their new visitors.

The soldiers briskly stepped into two, two-man ranks, with the master sergeant abreast of the first rank. They then moved in measured steps toward their hosts. The air crew followed at some distance behind.

They all met about halfway between the chopper and the gate, with the five soldiers halting at attention in front of Captain Ackerman and John.

Master Sergeant Dorchus saluted Ackerman and reported that his honor guard was at the disposal of the captain and a Mr.

Kelly. The National Guard captain returned the salute and quietly told the sergeant to be at ease and dismiss his men in order to be greeted by the farm crowd. Within moments, the three-man Air Force crew walked up and waited several yards behind the soldiers.

John stuck out his hand to the sergeant and smiled. "I'm John Kelly. Welcome to you and your men, Sergeant, it's a real pleasure to have you here."

"Sir, we are honored to serve you and this mission. We've followed the news and were also briefed, and know the mission is the most important one we'll ever be assigned. You, your family, and all the clerics can rest assured that my four soldiers here and the remaining six that will join us at Eglin will make sure the scroll and the four accompanying clerics will be secure at all times."

It was evident to John and the others around him, that this six-foot tall, physically fit Special Forces master sergeant with a large cluster of ribbons on his chest meant what he said.

"You and your men and the air crew join us at the house for some lunch," John said. "The Apache air crews and their ground-support troops will be here shortly."

Captain Ackerman told the sergeant to pass the word to his men and the aircrew that they refrain from answering questions from the media.

Everyone wanted to talk with the military guests as they all walked together toward the house and shade. It was a warm day.

After lunch and good conversation, John, Lyle, Billy Durdin, and a few others showed their new friends around. Putting them into five cars, along with two more clerics, they were driven out to the holy site. John, Durdin, and Rabbi Metz explained the drilling into God's room and how Lyle recovered the copper scroll. All of the highly trained and experienced soldiers and airmen were totally awed into a period of silence as they stared at the casing head.

They also looked at Lyle with deep respect.

After returning to the house, the army Apache crews and their support personnel joined the crowd along with two NG lieutenants and four sergeants from their bivouac. It looked somewhat like a military invasion had taken place. But it was another high point for the extended farm family—a truly enjoyable and spiritual time for all.

The two hours had passed quickly. It was time for the honor guard to load the scroll onto the chopper for its trip to Eglin, along with the four clerics, to rendezvous with the vice president's plane—Air Force Two.

The Sikorsky's crew went out to preflight their craft.

The farm family crowd followed along as the Special Forces soldiers and the clerics went to the small barn storeroom. When the nine men entered the door, the crowd lined up side by side, several feet apart, all the way to the main access gate leading to the fields. Soon, the honor guard exited the barn, led by Master Sergeant Dorchus. They smartly carried the crate at a medium pace, with the four clerics trailing behind, passing the silent family members one by one, who then stepped in and followed.

When they arrived at the helicopter, the crowd stood silent and watched the four soldiers make precise short steps in cadence the last ten feet, called out by Dorchus, who stood at attention to one side of the large sliding door.

The crate, with its invaluable contents, was carefully lifted aboard and tied down to special lift rings in the center of the fuselage floor. After another round of hugs, handshakes, and goodbyes, the clerics boarded.

After the door was closed, and many waves later, everyone moved back as the large rotors started turning, gathering speed. Soon the craft lifted off. Everyone had to turn their heads; some of the women holding their hair and skirts because of the huge downdraft hitting the ground and spreading 360 degrees. No one minded.

They stood and watched the clerics, who had a gigantic job ahead of them, and the precious copper scroll become a speck in the distant southwest sky. Then, everyone headed to the house, already missing Durdin, Griffin, Metz, and Walsh, and to a much larger degree, the significant and unique work of God.

Doc McNally called John late Monday afternoon to tell him the National Guard patients were doing well. The wounded members of the two radical groups were in various condition, but the FBI had already arrested them. NG guards were standing watch. Some would be hospitalized longer than others, and would be moved to a federal holding center as soon as they could travel. Backgrounds on all of them were being prepared.

"Doc, how you doing? I know you and the other doctors and staff must be dragging."

There was a chuckle. "We could use a lull in the action. I think our situation is pretty well under control now. Just don't have any more shootouts up there—at least for a day or two."

"We—the FBI, the Defense Department, all of us—feel the extreme attacks are over. The only thing left—and it's important—are possible altercations caused by anti-God types and general troublemakers looking for some easy money. Thank the Lord that the great majority of the visitors are dedicated, reverent Christians, and some Jews."

Doc said he was needed and had to go. John again thanked him for setting up the triage care unit, and hung up.

After another long and full emotional day, the family was tired. Dinner was later than usual, but no one seemed to mind. Granny and her four helpers were weary, plus, figuratively speaking, they were scraping the bottom of the larder. Everyone was eating a little lighter.

Carew and Red had already suggested they make a run to Dothan the next day and pick up more food and ice. John said they first should sit down and discuss all their needs because some, if not most, of the farm crowd would start returning to their homes as soon as tomorrow, and that would mean less needed supplies.

John told everyone Sheriff Bernam felt that order had pretty well been reestablished in Danaville and the county due to more state troopers and National Guardsmen being available. Most all of the current troublemakers and lawbreakers had been arrested.

The roads were under better control and more passable, but traffic was still a little slow. The situation in downtown Danaville had improved markedly. Though the number of people had decreased, they were still numerous, but much less threatening. The great majority of visitors to the area now were religious and respectful. One big hurdle had been cleared. John and the others felt a little more assured.

The worldwide press release by Summers and Gordon, regarding the copper scroll being moved to Israel, was filed Tuesday morning at nine. Air Force Two, with the scroll and clerics, landed in Israel five hours earlier, giving the FBI and the Mossad plenty of time to secretly place the precious cargo in the Israel Museum, behind impregnable doors, and place a tight guard around the building.

The plane was met at an Israeli Air Force base by the prime minister, his aides, and other Israeli members of government, including the head of the Mossad. The U.S. vice president's arrival, along with the copper scroll and the renowned clerics, called for a greeting on the same level as that for a head of state. In fact, everyone thought of its importance as being the highest honor that could ever be given.

TUESDAY WAS A completely different day at the farm. The family had experienced a lot of aggression in the past few days, but persevered, and now the scroll had been safely delivered to Israel. Everyone felt a renewed spirit.

The roads were under better control and passable, but traveling on them was still a little slow. The crowds were somewhat smaller around the farm, but large enough to keep all lawmen and NG personnel busy.

Danaville's situation had improved markedly. The amount of traffic and people had lessened, and the overall situation had improved. The merchants were breathing a little easier, along with the town residents.

Parker told John the night before that he needed to move his rig back to Jackson County the next morning. Owens and Kent would move their trucks also. The three men had to fulfill contracts that had been made two weeks before.

"I really hate to leave, even for a few days," Parker said. "But although the events are continuing to unfold, I'm bound to bring water to people."

John had been impressed with this man from the first time he met him. The shared experience of the last week or so had closely bonded them.

"Your leaving is fully understood, Clayton. Once you finish your contract, I want you to consider joining us here. Your talents, work habits, and faith would be a great plus for God and for us."

"I will, Brother John. I certainly will."

The family gathered on the lawn, near the main driveway, and waved and called out their thanks and good wishes as the big blue rig slowly passed, with Parker and his wife waving back. The long flatbed truck and the large crane with Owens and Kent followed behind. The crowd wished them well also.

It was near 11:00 a.m. Lyle and Teresa had determined they'd better let their parents know that it was time to announce their wedding plans before some of the family departed for Danaville after lunch. Young Kelly and his bride-to-be wanted to tell everyone in person rather than by phone. However, they'd have to call Parker and his wife, knowing it was highly improbable the two could attend because of the job he was on. They would be missed.

"We thought Friday night would be as good a time as any," Teresa said to Arlene and Sara. "The sooner the better."

"Well, neither Arlene nor I are surprised. We've discussed it and have it pretty well planned, based on the conversation the four of us had two weeks ago."

Arlene reached over and took her daughter's hand. "Besides, dear, when Ralph Tobias obtained the marriage application forms from the county clerk's office and had you two to fill them out, that was a sign the wedding was imminent."

"Our license is in my dresser drawer. Sheriff Bernam brought it from the courthouse yesterday," Lyle said with a smile. He looked at Teresa and squeezed her hand and added, "Reverend

Butler will be available Friday night, even Thursday for the rehearsal."

"My, my, you two have been busy," Arlene said teasingly. "One would think you're eager to be husband and wife."

Sara pulled John aside before lunch and quietly told him the news. He looked at her with a smile.

"I'm not surprised in the least, and the timing is about as good as it will get for a while. A lot of work will be taking place here real soon. Friday is great." He chuckled. "I think you and I are ready for a daughter."

"Yes, we are, John. I'm very happy."

"I know you are, sweetheart." He bent over slightly and gave her a peck on the forehead.

Sara went to the kitchen to help the others finish preparing lunch. When she walked in, Granny and Pat looked up from preparing to fry some chicken. Both of them had a hint of a smile. "You look like the cat that ate the canary," Granny commented.

"Or the pheasant," Pat added.

Laughing, Sara replied, "Maybe the pheasant. It seems we're going to have a wedding Friday night."

Both of them quickly wiped flour off their hands and hugged Sara. Arlene came in, smiling broadly, and joined the hugging, saying, "It's true. It's true."

As usual, everyone was sitting in different locations in twos, threes, or fours, inside or outside, eating lunch. As they were finishing, Lyle and Teresa went to all of them and announced their coming wedding and personally invited each one.

Most had known the marriage would be soon, but were still surprised. All of the women were ecstatic and hugged the two. The men hugged Teresa, but only shook Lyle's hand, and that suited him.

LYLE'S GRANDMA AND grandpa Kessel, along with Ralph Tobias, his wife, and two sons, and Reverend Butler and his wife Ruth, plus Brandon Cook, were leaving for Danaville within the next hour or so. But they would return for the wedding.

FBI agents Magee and Nelson had left the night before. Magee told Stanton and John that he and two other agents were staying in Danaville. The other three would return to Atlanta.

Parker and his wife, plus Owens and Kent, having already departed, brought the total of those not staying at the farm from that night on to thirteen—almost half of the crowd that had been there for the seven or eight nights before. It was quite a relief in workload for Granny, Sara, and the others. They thanked the Lord.

John, Lyle, Carew, and Red welcomed the chance to take care of farm details that had somewhat gone lacking.

There was a lot of mail. Paul Daniels, Pat's husband, had been collecting it from a deputy that had been bringing it out each day since the past Friday, and sorting through it. Most of it was positive with spiritual, loving messages to the Lord and his holy site, the copper scroll, and the Kellys. There were some messages, however, that were negative, claiming the happening as a hoax, putting down God and all of those that followed him. A few were badly worded threats against everyone at the farm. These were turned over to the FBI.

John and Sara had decided that the spiritually supportive letters would be answered just as soon as possible. It might be weeks or longer, but they would be answered. Summers had suggested that a well-done form letter with different members of the family notating a personalized comment at the bottom would be practical.

The senior Kelly knew Summers was right—there was just too much mail, and none of them had the time to answer with personal letters. It frustrated him.

Late in the afternoon, John and Carew walked around, looking at the various vacated temporary quarters and made plans to dismantle them within several days.

Most of the news media had gone, but a six-man reporter pool selected by their peers would stay on for an undetermined period of time. Arrangements had been made for a chartered helicopter to pick up the six foreign news service representatives at ten o'clock the next morning and fly them to the Panama City regional airport. They needed to be on their home turf as soon as possible now that the scroll was in Israel.

Reverend Claussen wanted to leave as soon as possible for Nashville to make a personal report to the Southern Baptist Convention's front office. He decided to take a flight from Dothan, Alabama, at 6:00 p.m., via Atlantic Southeastern Airlines to Atlanta, then Delta to Nashville. Carew volunteered to drive him, with Reverend Butler riding along to discuss the convening of a committee consisting of high-level representatives from each protestant denomination, as well as the Catholic and Jewish religions.

The six clerics had agreed earlier at the farm that a temporary structure be built immediately. It would protect the holy site from rain and sun, and accommodate hundreds of visitors a day. A master plan would be drawn up in the meantime, and hopefully approved in three months. Construction would start immediately. County 26 would be widened, with entrance and exit roads put in place to access the site. It would feature a beautiful permanent structure. All of the surrounding farm fields would become landscaped parks with connecting roads, restroom accommodations, parking areas for cars, buses, and RVs, and a large heliport.

The key element to this gigantic project was setting up an ongoing funding plan that would finance all costs of building and maintaining the great tribute to God. The Kellys would retain their home and be well compensated for managing all construction and upkeep of the holy grounds. The six clerics had already agreed this should be done as soon as possible. The Kellys would be well-compensated. The four-generation family's sacrifice was enormous, but they were thrilled and thankful that the Lord chose their farm as a repository for his message, and the family to be his stewards.

Butler and Claussen discussed all of this and more during the hour-plus drive to the Dothan Airport. Carew found their conversation riveting. After seeing the Baptist minister off, the return trip home was quiet, but still he and Butler talked a little about things of smaller importance. Actually, both of them were tired.

CHAPTER FORTY-FOUR

ON WEDNESDAY, THE wedding was on everyone's mind. John, Sara, and Arlene were anticipating Friday evening. Their kids were getting married in two days, and the parents were anxiously waiting for the moment—so were Granny and Pat. The family and guests felt deeply about Lyle and Teresa. They all knew it was a match made in heaven. It had great significance.

Paul and Pat Daniels offered his father's beach home in Panama City to Lyle and Teresa for a two-day honeymoon. They were overjoyed; however, security was a must. Jack Stanton readily agreed with John that no chances could be taken. A four-man security team wearing casual clothes and driving two unmarked cars would provide transportation to and from the beach home, keeping an eye on the property from a discreet distance while there.

John received a call from Billy Durdin at 10:00 a.m. Durdin told him he was on a speakerphone, along with the other three clerics. They all said hello and hoped and prayed that all was well at the farm.

The senior Kelly felt a close brotherhood with all of the clerics, especially the four on the phone. "And a hello to all of you from all of us. Everything is going well. We miss you and are praying for you."

Durdin thanked him along with the other clerics. "We've already made several important contacts, and things are moving well," Billy said. "Details of what's going on will be sent to you via e-mail. It's important we keep our information secure. The Mossad is a great help. Rabbi Metz is doing a fine job with his government and the top antiquities expert at the Hebrew University. On another note, we have arranged funding for starting the first phase of the temporary work on the holy site. Also, a separate amount that will reimburse you and the family for the expenses incurred to date, plus an income amount agreeable to you, to be paid to you on a monthly or quarterly basis, whichever you prefer. This would start within a month, and be in excess of what the farm brought in prior to God's intervention."

John was quiet, trying to digest what he had just heard. He knew what the clerics had discussed with him several days ago, but he had not thought about any financial arrangement since then. He had been too busy. The offer was very generous.

"Billy, I really don't know what to say. I've never worked for a salary. Our income has always been an uneven thing—up one month or year, down the next. I averaged it all, and somewhat derived our monthly expenses."

"You leave the details to us," Billy said. "We'll work it out real soon. John, we've prayed mightily about this, and we all feel the Lord has spoken to us. We're only doing what he wants us to do. Remember, he picked the farm, you, and your family."

"Yes, we know that. The 'why' is becoming more evident every day."

"We'll be in contact about all of this within a few days. In the meantime, e-mail the total of the expenses you and the family have incurred since the beginning, plus your average income for the past year. Then add 50 percent to that. Use the address Rabbi Metz gave you."

John almost fell out of his chair. He was quiet, trying to think.

"You still there, John?" Billy asked.

"I don't know what to say. I hope all of you understand that I've got a lot of thinking and praying to do. In the meantime, I'll send you the information you want."

After a few words of encouragement from the clerics, John wished them well and hung up.

He sat at his desk for a few moments in silent prayer. He thanked God again for choosing him and his family to be his servants—to witness for him through their work as stewards for the holy site. With his mind working overtime on what the clerics had presented to him, he got up and went downstairs to find Sara and Lyle to tell them of the clerics' conversation with him.

ON THURSDAY AFTERNOON, Sara, Pat, and Arlene, along with Carew and Red, spent three hours cleaning the house and moving a few pieces of furniture. Even the piano was moved to another location to make more room for an aisle between twenty-eight or thirty folding chairs. When they set out the large baskets of flowers on Friday afternoon, a tall arch of roses would be placed in the wide entranceway of the dining room, where Reverend Butler and the bride and groom would stand for the ceremony. Sara would use only pink roses and white carnations, all complemented by ferns and other greenery. Ruth Butler volunteered to bring two six-foot-tall candelabras from the church.

Reverend Butler and Ruth arrived around six thirty for the rehearsal. John observed their warm, good mood. It appeared their minister wanted to get the two young folks married right away, but John mused, this was only a practice run. He teased Butler as they came into the house. "Wade, it seems to me you're anxious to perform the ceremony tonight," John said with a grin.

He chuckled, "Oh, we're as excited as can be. It'll be an honor to marry those two wonderful young people. I wish we didn't have another twenty-four hours." He pointed over his shoulder toward the front porch. "Those two candelabra are at the base of the steps. I don't do steps with heavy stuff."

John laughed as the three walked down the enormous hall toward the den and kitchen.

Lyle and Teresa were in the kitchen with Arlene and Granny. After John asked his son to please retrieve the candelabra, Lyle shook the reverend's hand and quickly hugged Ruth, then went to fetch the candelabra. Teresa hugged them both. Granny and Arlene were hugging the Butlers when Sara and Pat walked in. They got in on the act also.

"All of you stand right here for a moment while Ruth and I go back outside, and reenter. We both need another one of these greetings," the reverend said with a broad grin.

Normally, a retort like that would bring only smiles, but everybody in the room broke into loud laughter. It was a result of the time they found themselves in, and the happiness of knowing another very meaningful event was about to take place—John and Sara gaining a daughter, and Arlene, a son.

Lyle soon returned with a slight expectant look, and asked what all the laughter was about. When told, he commented that he had left at the wrong time. Sara said, with slight laughter in her voice, "No, you had your hugs, it was our turn." Everyone smiled, and at that, went toward the living room.

The rehearsal went well. Lyle and Teresa spent much of the time looking into each other's eyes. The ceremony would be simple and reasonably short. There would be a short aisle starting in the foyer for Teresa to walk down on the arm of her mother. Pat was thrilled to be her bridesmaid.

Carew would be best man, but tried to act "in control" about it all. John saw through his "brother" and smiled inside. He knew Lyle would have had no other as his best man.

Dinner was served around 7:00 p.m. Fourteen people enjoyed a very delicious sit-down dinner in the dining room. The reverend and Ruth left near 8:20, with their state-trooper escort; Pat and Paul Daniels departed soon after with theirs. It now took an average of fifteen minutes to make the three-plus miles drive to Danaville as compared to thirty or forty minutes four days ago. Things were improving—somewhat.

Arlene had privately given Lyle her fist wedding ring several days before. Her first husband, Teresa's biological father, had put it on her finger twenty-five years ago. She told Lyle that Teresa had always loved the ring, and though it had been in its box, stored away for a long time, Teresa would occasionally ask to see it.

Lyle was astonished at its understated beauty. A grouping of four small diamonds mounted on a silver base, shaped like a small ribbon bow. He thanked Arlene and hugged her. Time and circumstances had prevented him from giving Teresa an engagement ring. It made no difference to her, there had been many more important things going on.

Unknown to Lyle, his mother had purchased a wide gold band through Jim Summers from Laney's Jewelry in Danaville. When shown to Teresa, she put it in her palm and closed her fingers around it. They embraced for a moment.

SATURDAY AFTER BREAKFAST, John, Lyle, Carew, and Red brought out six sawhorses from the main barn, along with several four-by-eight-foot sections of heavy plywood, and took them to the nearest oak. Two long tables were set up underneath its huge limbs for the reception, later to be covered with tablecloths and various decorations.

On Friday, Red had strung a power line atop a number of seven-foot-tall two-by-fours from the smaller barn to the large lower overhanging limbs of an oak. There would be six hanging lights over the tables.

The folding chairs would be brought out immediately after the wedding.

That afternoon, the men went to the bean field. John wanted to check the holy site, as they had been doing since Parker, Owens, and Kent had moved their equipment. He and the others were humbled, and drew strength from the holy site. After praying for the Lord's blessing on the wedding, they all returned to the house to get ready for the special event.

It was 2:30 p.m. when Sara, Pat, and Arlene finished setting out the large baskets of mixed flowers, featuring carnations, and decorating the ceremonial arch with roses. They all were very pleased with the results. The foyer and living room were beautiful.

They went to the kitchen to help Granny hurriedly finish the food details, covering much of the finished dishes, setting them aside, and putting the other items in the large refrigerator. Then, all the ladies went off to "prepare" themselves. It was getting late.

People started arriving a little after 4:00 p.m. They drove their own cars, but the state troopers had prearranged for one patrol car to lead every two families or individuals to the farm. By 4:40, all of the guests from town had arrived, most all of them being those who had left the farm two days ago and returned to Danaville. Sheriff Bernam, his wife Nell, Deputy Beck, and FBI agents Magee and Nelson, plus Marvin Gardner and Jim Summers—all were exceptions. There was a total of fifteen returning guests. Adding to the eighteen that were still living at the farm, the total for the wedding and reception would be thirty-three.

Carew did a quick nose count and realized he was three folding chairs short. He brought in extra straight-backed chairs from the breakfast room. They barely fit, but the problem was solved.

Everyone was dressed up for the occasion. Even Bernam and Beck had on suits. All of them knew that it was more than just a wedding. It was an event never to be forgotten.

Most of them had taken a seat when Sara started playing "Amazing Grace." The others quickly sat down, and the room became quiet as they listened intently to a beloved favorite. After that, John got up and looked over the crowd.

"Sara, Arlene, Lyle, Teresa, and I deeply thank all of you for being here. If just one of you had failed to come, you'd be greatly missed. We ALL are family. The Kelly name doesn't define the extent of the family—it takes in all of us in this room. Your last name may be different, but that doesn't change a thing. God brought us all together in a very special way. He's our undeniable father. We are ALL family."

Everyone in the room nodded their total commitment.

"We're here to celebrate the marriage of two wonderful young people. Lyle and Teresa will soon become man and wife, extending the generation of Kellys to four. In good time, and with the Lord's blessing, they'll give us all a grandson, or to some of you, a nephew or cousin, and the beginning of the fifth generation of Kellys.

However, if God has other plans and wants us to have a granddaughter, we'd be teary-eyed happy."

John and Sara traded a loving look as he sat down beside her. She covered his hand with hers.

Pat moved over beside the piano, and Sara accompanied her as she sang, "I Believe." The crowd was spellbound with the song and her beautiful soprano voice.

When she finished, Reverend Butler took his place under the rose-covered arch. "It means so very much to me to perform this ceremony in this house. This is a special place and a special time for all of us. I feel the presence of the Lord, and I know each of you do too."

He looked over at Lyle and Carew, and they came up and stood to his left, facing the group. Pat stood to the reverend's right. Sara started the wedding march and everyone became expectant and started sneaking looks over their shoulder toward the foyer entrance to the room. Soon, Teresa and her mother turned from the hall into the back of the room and very slowly, step by step in time with the music, walked the twenty-five feet or so to the flowered arch—every eye in the room following them.

Teresa was radiant. She wore a pale blue suit, a white blouse with ruffled collar and cuffs, and pale blue pumps. Arlene's subtle peach-colored dress complemented her daughter's beauty.

All of the wedding party wore a single rose.

Lyle, in a dark blue suit, white button-down shirt, and a maroon striped tie, complementing his thick dark hair and well-proportioned build, waited with eyes locked on his bride-to-be.

Carew, wearing a medium blue blazer, white shirt, black tie, and black slacks, looked very distinguished. He felt very proud to be Lyle's best man. He was beaming.

Teresa stopped beside Lyle and took his left arm, and they looked intently at each other as they turned and faced Reverend Butler. Arlene took several steps back and sat down next to Granny.

Butler had a sense of the poet about him. He creatively administered the marriage rites with added phrases, mostly explaining each vow in terms of God's law. It was a very spiritual and inspiring ceremony. When the couple exchanged rings, Teresa was totally surprised and delighted as her mother's cherished ring was slipped onto her finger. Lyle was very proud of his gold band. He thought how astonishing it was that he was marrying his beloved Teresa. Moments later, the reverend pronounced them man and wife, and they kissed—perhaps a little longer than usual, but this marriage was different.

Everyone stood, and Pat sang "The Lord's Prayer"—the perfect prayer for all of them to take with them.

Instead of playing a postlude, Sara hurriedly went over to the newlyweds, along with John, Arlene, Granny, Pat, and all the rest. There was crying, laughing, hugging, smiling, and light back slapping. Many congratulations and best wishes were said. Finally, Lyle, holding Teresa's hand, told the happy crowd they would change clothes and finish packing, then meet them at the reception in thirty minutes or so. The crowded room was a little warm, so most of them headed for the back porch and yard. Granny Arlene and Pat soon went to the kitchen with some of the men to move the prepared food and the wedding cake to one of the tables under the trees. Several baskets of flowers would also be moved to the reception.

AT 6:40, THE "KELLY farm crowd," as Granny so aptly put it, was standing around talking, sipping iced tea or lemonade, and waiting for the bride and groom to join them. No one said a word about their being a little late. They knew the couple was packing slowly while doing a little hugging and cooing.

Someone had brought a large boom box that was producing soft background music. The mood was festive, and the Kelly farm crowd was happy and relaxed. Even with the great responsibility that God had put on the Kellys and their extended family, all of them were right where they wanted to be.

Two reporters, a still photographer, and a television cameraman with a producer had received permission the day before from John to cover the people and events around the wedding, but not the service itself. They were moving about, interviewing different people—especially John, Sara, and Arlene—and taking photos along with videos. Like everyone else, they wanted to talk to the bride and groom.

"Here they come," Sara announced. The crowd met them and formed a semicircle around the beaming new husband and wife, congratulating them and calling out various affectionate phrases with zeal. Lyle and Teresa had a slight puzzled look on their faces, when suddenly everyone started throwing rice from small bags that Pat had passed around earlier. The couple was surprised and moved quickly from side to side with their hands up, trying to evade the rice, especially protecting their hair. It was soon over, with the crowd and the newlyweds laughing uproariously.

Applause broke out. John, Sara, and Arlene were so proud and happy that they were about to burst with joy—so were the others.

Lyle and Teresa were dressed in casual clothes, ready for their trip to Panama City Beach after the reception dinner. When they joined their parents at one of the tables, Lyle seated Teresa and remained standing until it was a little quieter. Some began to applaud.

He held up his hands, signifying an embrace to the crowd, and to quiet them.

"Thank you, folks. Teresa and I are so full of your love. And we love you very, very much."

Teresa stood up and added, with a broad smile, "I'm so thrilled and honored to now be an official member of the Kelly family. I feel so much at home." There was more applause, with several verbal encouragements, as she and Lyle sat down together.

Reverend Butler thanked God for the gifts set out before them all—those seated at the table, the Kellys, Lyle and Teresa, and the food.

Everyone formed a line at both tables and served themselves.

After dinner, they all relaxed for a few minutes, conversing with those next to them or across the table, while the newlyweds, their parents, and Pat, Paul, Carew, Red, and his family had a short warm get-together.

There were gifts neatly stacked on a small table off to one side. Sara asked them all to gather around while Teresa and Lyle opened them. Lyle deferred to his bride. It was a woman's thing to open gifts, he quipped. John grinned and whispered to Sara that there was hope for the marriage—their son already knew his place. Sara rolled her eyes in mock disdain and gently nudged him on the shoulder.

Due to the circumstances during the past week and limited access to shopping, there were a number of envelopes with checks or cash and personal notes of good wishes—very acceptable to the young Kellys.

After the oohs and ahhs of gift opening, it was time to cut and serve the cake. It was large and beautiful. Granny had baked it, but Arlene had a talent for decorating and had done a superb job. It was tiered with four layers having a white icing base and covered with a few large sculpted red roses on each layer, topped with a large pastel pink satin bow. Many had their cameras and took pictures of the cake and the couple cutting it and Teresa and Lyle feeding each other. Needless to say, a couple of napkins were needed.

The dinner, with gift opening and cake cutting, took one and a half hours. It was 8:20 p.m. when people started getting up. Lyle and Teresa were ready to fetch their luggage and meet their escorts. Handshakes and hugs started again.

It was twilight. The western sky had deposited the sun behind the horizon, and darkness was at hand. The lights that Red had arranged on the limbs of the overhanging oak added a special touch.

Carew suddenly pointed to the eastern sky and said, "Look at that! It's a meteor!" It lasted only two or three seconds, but the wedding party began to see a few more. The blue white streaks of light seemed at first to be small or far off. But soon, that changed. There were more of them, and they appeared to be closer and more numerous.

The crowd was mesmerized as they stood and watched the growing spectacle.

"There are more meteors tonight than last week," Sara said to John in an excited whisper.

"I know, but it seems these are closer or brighter or both," he replied.

Lyle and Teresa were fascinated—each feeling there was more than just a meteorological significance to the display. John, Sara, Reverend Butler, and others felt the same way.

Suddenly, several brighter streaks flashed over the farm, then many more—all within four to six seconds.

Sheriff Bernam, Deputy Beck, and FBI agents Magee and Nelson thought the fantastic aerial display was not a coincidence. All of them had been convinced earlier of God's presence and power when they saw the bean field, the holy site, and the scroll.

The meteors became more intense—countless streaks of light over what appeared to be the center of the farm. John looked toward the east, where the sky was darkest, and he could see no meteors. A few small butterflies stirred in his stomach.

"What are you thinking, John?" Sara asked as she put her arm around his waist and looked up at him.

"I'm thinking the Lord is reminding us of his presence and his power. Also, I think the timing is a sign of his blessing for Lyle and Teresa—for all of us. It gives me even greater hope."

Sara pulled herself closer to him. "I feel that way too."

Seven meteors in an irregular but close pattern streaked directly overhead—the last one larger and brighter than the others. Its bright bluish silver tail was longer than that of the others.

After that, the sky was completely dark—not another meteor could be seen. Everyone stood there breathless and silent for several minutes.

"I think it's clear to all of us that we just received a message from God," John said. "I'm not quite sure what it was, but I don't think it would be unreasonable to think it covered two things: one, a blessing for us and our newlyweds, and two, a promise that he will be guiding us while we carry out his plan."

"Amen," Reverend Butler said.

They all walked slowly toward the house, thinking and talking about what they had just witnessed. It gave them resolve.

The Kelly gathering was on the front porch and steps to escort Lyle and Teresa to one of the troopers' two waiting unmarked cars. When the couple came out of the house, there were a lot of calls of good luck and a few humorous remarks, such as "Don't forget to come back" and so on. Another round of hugs, and they were off.

The four casually dressed troopers were pleasant and respectful of the newlyweds. They felt honored to provide security for them. John, Sara, and Arlene were pleased with the arrangement.

It was 9:30 p.m. Most of those returning to Danaville had departed. The rest of the crowd went inside or to the back porch. John and Sara walked the length of the front porch and sat in the swing. The night was pleasant. They could hear the crickets along with barely audible singing coming from quite a large number of people along the fence line of C26 and farther away on 77. Lights were flickering as many in the crowd held flashlights or candles. There was still some slow vehicle traffic, but not as much as before. The late hour had something to do with that.

"You know, Sara, with all we've been through in the past two-plus weeks, I feel like we are just starting our lives, and a great journey lies ahead."

"I feel the same way, sweetheart. I think your grandfather Frank would be so proud about what has happened to the original seeds he sowed seventy-five years ago."

"You're right. It's very evident to me that God has been with the Kellys from the start. We have a lot to do for the Lord, and I know the family is looking forward to all of us working together. We are truly blessed."

She snuggled up to him, with the swing slightly moving, while listening to the distant sounds of God's children.

EPILOGUE

J OHN KELLY WAS well aware that the coming months and years would be a huge challenge to him and his family—even Lyle's family, eventually.

Now that the world had learned the scroll had been moved to Israel, no one—other than the clerics, the Kelly family, and leaders of the Christian and Jewish religions—had any knowledge of the treasure it described. But the news media, governments, and various radical groups of some Middle Eastern religions, especially the Muslims, desperately wanted information as to what the scroll contained.

Within three weeks, all twenty-eight treasure sites, from one end of Israel to the other, had been secretly located and discreetly marked. In another three weeks, engineers and labor personnel and equipment, under the guise of doing archeological exploration, extracted the silver and gold from each location at night. The specially selected recovery teams were amazed that the ingots were exact in shape and weight, whether they were gold or silver. That made the recovery much easier to estimate weight and size for lifting, transport, and storing. Every piece gleamed under the lights, as if it had just been cast. The clerics knew that it had.

However, the first thing clerics Durdin, Walsh, Metz, and Griffin did after arriving in Israel was to arrange the temporary financial assistance package that Billy told John about earlier. Then, an explanation was sent to him via e-mail that suggested a very generous amount for John and his family to have for the future. Durdin added that the total figure would be reviewed each year and adjusted for unexpected family expenses and operation cost of the holy site and the surrounding grounds, the house, and all other farm property.

John was well satisfied with the financial-assistance package he received from the four clerics one week after the wedding. He could now start the temporary preparation of the holy site and a small section of the surrounding grounds for visitors until the master plan could be completed and the larger work initiated.

The work would start immediately, and according to Parker, who would oversee all the details, the first phase could be completed in two months. That would suffice for three to four months until the major work could start—a practically designed site, with beautiful functional grounds, to be completed within eight months.

Lyle and Teresa returned from Panama City with a glowing look, ready to take on their share of the family's task ahead. John shared with them the details of what the clerics and he had arranged to cover the costs of all construction work and reimburse the family for loss of the farm's production. He added that Durdin and Father Walsh had urged him to accept a 50 percent increase of their past averaged income. They reminded him that his responsibility would now be much larger. He and the family were now stewards of a place chosen by the Lord.

The newlyweds were very happy about the news. Lyle retrieved a few concerns from the depths of his mind, having stored them away prior to the wedding. He knew his dad had been worried about their lack of income. Now, that would no longer be a problem.

The situation with people and traffic outside the farm had improved, but there were still many problems. Foreign visitors were now showing up, having been uninformed about the lack of accommodations. Most of them had to find places to stay as far as 150-200 miles away and then charter a bus, if they could find one.

Most didn't mind their inconveniences—to be very close to the hallowed ground was enough. Some of them would take photos of the farm and the surroundings and pick up a small amount of dirt or pebbles as treasured mementos, but they all would be fulfilled with God's spirit by just being there.

THE WHITE HOUSE worked closely with Governor Ashton through Jack Stanton and Ralph Tobias to ensure that tight security remained at the farm for as long as needed. Regular army troops would relieve Captain Ackerman's NG unit very soon. State troopers would continue to monitor all highways and roads.

The FBI would continue to work with the Mossad and other friendly foreign security organizations to keep a close undercover watch on the vast treasure and its financial-management group. Their top priority was to ensure that all monies were dispensed according to the instructions given by the four clerics—Durdin, Walsh, Metz, and Griffin—representing the governing bodies of their respective religions. All security organizations were extremely aware that it was the most important assignment all of them ever had—and for the highest ranked commander in the universe.

It was apparent, three weeks after the miracle became known to the world, that radical and emotional extremism had somewhat subsided. Cities, highways, and airports were more manageable, although a lot of security was still required and would continue to be for the near future.

A worldwide press release was sent out by Jim Summers and IPN to inform everyone that a temporary preparation of the holy site was beginning and would be completed in approximately two months. A minimal number of visitors would be allowed until the permanent structure and grounds were completed within one year. The release went on to explain all pertinent details and requirements for visitation.

When the world saw and understood that the holy site was being prepared as fast as possible to accommodate large crowds, there would be more patience and fewer problems.

THE VAST TREASURE totaled more than $100 billion, $500-plus million—a sum beyond the first estimates, a sum that would make a tremendously positive impact in the application of God's plan. The first priority for managing and dispensing the treasure was to keep all costs at a break-even level. No profit to anyone or to any institution, with one exception, that being John Kelly and his family. The compensation paid to them was a fair, acceptable amount agreed to by both parties, and it followed the Lord's plan.

A LITTLE OVER three months had passed when on September 11, 2001, to become known as 9/11, a horrific murderous suicide attack by radical Muslims was carried out in New York City and Washington DC, and a failed but deadly attempt that ended in a Pennsylvania field. The shock to the United States, and to a lesser degree, most foreign countries, was incalculable.

One person being interviewed at the time by a television reporter summed up the experiences of the American people during the past four months: "God gave us an earthshaking, wonderful miracle in May, and Satan revealed a glimpse of hell this morning."

The Kellys and their extended family gathered at the farm on September 12 around 7:00 p.m. and held a prayer service for the victims, their families, and the nation. They knew it was the beginning of a different, difficult time for Western countries. After the attempt on the farm by the four radical Muslims in May, all of the family had a little more insight of the enemy that struck the day before. It was clear the large radical element of Islam was bent on destroying the works and people of the God that rules Christians and Jews.

THE TEMPORARY CONSTRUCTED shelter for the holy site and two hard-surfaced acres around it had been opened on July

12. A large stream of people was coming through each day. The army personnel that had replaced the National Guard troops stood watch, assisted the visitors, and kept them moving, with an allowed short stop at the site. Most of them prayed, and many read their Bible. A road that encircled the site had been graded and surfaced to accommodate the walk-through traffic.

TERESA GAVE BIRTH to identical twin boys on May 22, 2002, in the Danaville hospital, with Doc McNally presiding. Mother was tired, but extremely happy. She and her two young sons were doing very well. Lyle walked around with a big smile, almost speechless. John, Sara, and Arlene were joyous and teary eyed. Granny, Pat, Carew, and Red were beside themselves, especially Granny, who was now a great-grandmother.

Lyle and Teresa named the boys Matthew and Mark. The new parents prayed that God would help their sons live up to their biblical namesakes.

John was ecstatic, knowing he now had two grandsons to keep the Kelly generations going. He knew his papa Seth and grandpa Frank were happy. The Lord was very good to him and his family. He silently gave thanks for his ever-present grace and love.

IN TEN AND a half months, 90 percent of the three hundred acres had been converted to beautiful parks with young grass, shrubs and trees, roads, and parking, including space for house trailers and RVs. There were two large heliports. Support facilities, such as toilets and showers, would be available, especially for those wishing to camp for an allowable maximum of two nights. The clerical advisory board wanted to make the site as functional and beautiful as possible. People were coming from all over the world to see the origin of God's miracle and to worship him.

The protection and presentation of the holy site itself was the focal point of the architectural planners and the clerics. The structure was round in shape, with a moderately high-domed roof painted gold, eighty feet in diameter. It was open sided with twelve granite columns, sixteen inches in diameter and fourteen feet in height, floor to ceiling. The flooring was also red granite, right up to the casing entrance to the cave. The round casing had been weather coated and painted dark gray. It was sealed with a steel top, painted dark gray also. Eight four-foot-high stainless-steel stanchions with stainless-steel chains were set out six feet around the casing. There would always be full-time first-class security at the site.

TWO LARGE DEVELOPMENT companies moved into the Danaville area and built several hotels and restaurants. One organization erected a large strip-shopping mall just outside Danaville, on 77, to the chagrin of the downtown merchants. But there was nothing they could do.

John and the others knew that thousands of visitors per year would be coming to the holy site. Most of them would need a place to stay for one, two, or three nights. The hotels and other commercial developments would be continually monitored to prevent any price gouging. The county commissioners agreed to ensure a first-class community to compliment the special spiritual attraction at the Kelly farm. Souvenirs or mementos would be solely controlled by the Kellys and would be free of charge.

The only souvenir that had been agreed upon by the family was a small plastic 1 1/2 x 4-inch bottle full of bean-field dirt, with a white cap and a nice label, stating the contents and where it was from. John knew that "quick buck" artists would hound him and others starting soon. The family knew what had to be done, and County Attorney Tobias would handle it.

John sold all the livestock except for two milk cows and a dozen chickens; the small tractor, along with plows, harrows, discs, rakes, and planters; and various other farm tools were also sold.

He, Lyle, Carew, and Red were leaning against the fence behind the main barn one day, reminiscing about old times.

The senior Kelly looked at his son and adopted brothers, and grinned. "There was a time I thought I could never give up farm life. Now, with what we've been through and what we know and the mission given to us by the Lord, I'm a happy man." The others quickly agreed.

When most people throughout the world learned about the contents of God's copper scroll, its vast hidden treasure, and how it was being used, they were awed. It was extremely clear that he was indeed a loving, powerful God. They desperately wanted to have a worshipful, loving relationship with him.

ACKNOWLEDGMENTS

- To Dana Foerster, my dear sister-in-law, who was gracious in allowing me to use her name for Danaville, a fictitious town.

- To my farmer friends Ralph and Carolyn Carter, for planting idea seeds in my mind regarding farm life.

- To Wayne Nash, a longtime professional water-well driller and instructor, for his knowledge and suggestions.

- To Terry Belten, for his patience and expert input during our discussions about drill pipes, drill bits, and casings.

- To Harley Means, Florida Geological Survey, for supplying maps and other information regarding geology in the Danaville area (the Marianna Quadrangle).

- To the staff of the Washington County Extension Service of the University of Florida, for furnishing in-depth information about northwest Florida farm crops.

- To Brandon Bolinski, meteorologist at the National Weather Service, Tallahassee. Many thanks for details regarding Doppler radar and other weather-related information.

- To Debbie Karamullah, for patience in turning my manuscript into a well-prepared disc for my publisher.

- To Greg Haigh, an account representative, and the editing and production staff members at Xlibris Publishing.

- To Jim W. Foster, of the Texas Annual Conference of the United Methodist Church, for his thoughtful input.

BVG